THE ELEGANCE OF FIRST CLASS. . . .
THE RESPECTABILITY OF SECOND. . . .
THE HOMELINESS OF STEERAGE. . . .
AND THE SERVANTS WHO RUN IT ALL. . . .

There was a swell in the crowd. The last crew members were trying to get to their posts. From officers in smart uniforms on down to the barmen and bellhops, they all rushed past her. Constance had heard the crew on the *Paris* numbered nearly a thousand, and the passengers—from the top hats and monocles traveling in the elegant cabins at the top, to the tattered emigrants under the waterline—were twice as many. She stopped to take in the great ship looming ahead. Its length took up the entire pier and, with three brilliant red funnels towering above the highest decks, it dwarfed all the other boats in the harbor.

* * *

"Set among the grandeur and the heartbreak of the post–World War I era, *Crossing on the Paris* chronicles the intersection of three women's lives as they embark on a transatlantic voyage. With rich detail and elegant prose, Gynther creates a vivid canvas on which to explore the timeless and universal themes of love and friendship. The result is a resonant and memorable tale which historical fiction connoisseurs will surely savor."

—Pam Jenoff, international bestselling author of *The Kommandant's Girl*

Crossing on the *Paris*

DANA GYNTHER

G

Gallery Books

NEW YORK LONDON TORONTO SYDNEY NEW DELHI

G

Gallery Books
A Division of Simon & Schuster, Inc.
1230 Avenue of the Americas
New York, NY 10020

First Gallery Books trade paperback edition November 2012

GALLERY BOOKS and colophon are registered trademarks of Simon & Schuster, Inc.

For information about special discounts for bulk purchases, please contact Simon & Schuster Special Sales at 1-866-506-1949 or *business@simonandschuster.com.*

The Simon & Schuster Speakers Bureau can bring authors to your live event. For more information or to book an event, contact the Simon & Schuster Speakers Bureau at 1-866-248-3049 or visit our website at *www.simonspeakers.com.*

Designed by Davina Mock-Maniscalco

Manufactured in the United States of America

1 3 5 7 9 10 8 6 4 2

Library of Congress Cataloging-in-Publication Data is available.

ISBN 978-1-4516-7823-9
ISBN 978-1-4516-7825-3 (ebook)

In memory of my loving father,
Malcolm Donald Gynther

A Prologue in Three Conversations

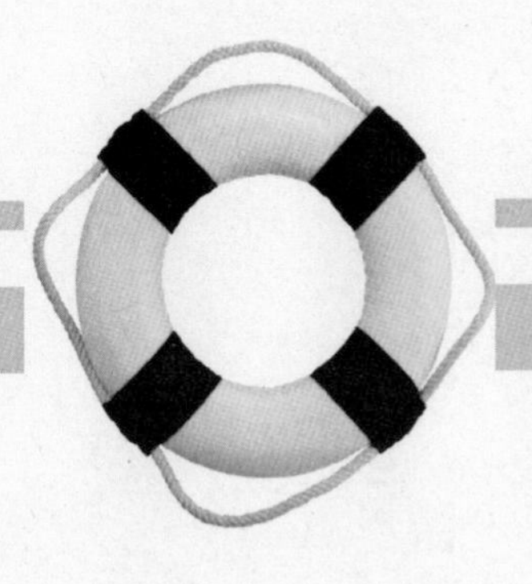

Constance Stone

"George?" Constance rapped lightly on the door to her husband's study, opening it as she knocked.

He peered over his reading glasses and smiled at his pretty wife. On his crowded desk lay a pile of papers; he was sharpening a red pencil.

"So, how are your parents today, dear?" George asked casually, as if she could answer with a cheerful "fine."

Constance frowned. Her visit that day had consisted of trying to coax her mother, wide-eyed and filthy, from behind the garden shed. Her mother grunted frantically when she grew near, then hurled a clump of dirt at her, hitting the side of her face.

"About the same, thank you," she replied curtly, nettled by his indifference. She ran her fingers through her hair—dislodging a bit of sand near her ear—then continued, her voice slow and hesitant. "Father's had a new idea, though. To make Mother well again."

George took off his reading glasses and sat back in his chair. "What's that?" he asked, expectant.

Was that skepticism in his voice? With her fingertips, she lightly grazed the top of her husband's collection of rocks and minerals—the smooth agates, glistening metallic pyrite, shards of quartz—as if stones could be read like Braille. She picked up a cluster of amethyst from the long shelf in front of his desk. Weighing it in her hand, she remembered that the Ancient Greeks thought this stone would protect them from drunkenness.

"Faith," she said. "He wants to bring Faith home."

"Faith!" George snorted. "Your father, the *psychologist,* thinks that will cure your mother? Lord knows, it might make her feel worse! Now, I agree that your sister should certainly not be in Paris on her own, living like some kind of gypsy. If she were my child, I'd have never allowed it! But I just don't see how her wanton daughter's reappearance is going to help."

Constance paused, putting the amethyst back in its place as George began packing his pipe. She glanced over at the armchair, hoping to sit down. As usual, it was filled with a tower of scrolled maps. She leaned on his desk, noticing, from that vantage point, that her husband's bald spot was widening rapidly.

"You're probably right, George." Constance let out a long sigh. "I don't know if Mother even realizes that Faith is gone. But Father wants her home."

"Well, good luck to him." He relit his pipe, then inquired through a puff of smoke, "Has he wired her yet?"

"He's tried. Several times, in fact." Constance picked up the nautilus fossil, her favorite piece in his collection. Stroking its spiral, she added, "But now he wants to try a more *radical* approach."

George's brow came crashing down against his eyes, forcing his lips out in an exaggerated pout. A caricature of confusion, he stared up at his wife.

"What's that supposed to mean?" he asked.

Constance stopped her pacing and stood before her husband.

"He wants me to go to Paris and get her," she said, trying to make it sound as if this request was on par with a trip to the market. "To put her on a steamer and bring her back to Worcester."

"You!"

His face burst open, falling to twice the length it had been moments before. When his jaw and eyes came back to their proper places, he began to chuckle.

Constance watched the spectacle of George's face, trying to recall what about it had attracted her when they'd married eight years earlier. Perhaps it had been his then-graying hair, which promised the inherent security of marrying an older man. Or the serious, academic way he puffed his pipe through his beard. In the beginning, she had also been grateful for his ability to fill awkward silences. Listening now to his bemused laughter, she couldn't remember why she had undervalued silence.

"Well, you know Father can't go," she said, looking down at the nautilus. "He can't leave Mother."

"But I can't go with you, dear. I'm in the middle of term. And I'm behind with my grading as it is," he said, waving his pipe around his desk to emphasize his point. "And, needless to say, you can't go on your own."

"Why not, George?" she asked softly.

He looked up at her in surprise.

"Why, for a dozen reasons! I'd be worried sick about you!" He shook his head. "Anything could happen. You could get lost out there on your own!"

"I think I can board a liner and take a train as well as any other. I don't see the mystery there."

"And while you are gallivanting off to Paris, what's to become of your own children?" George asked, eyeing her sternly, paternalistically. "Who is to take care of them?"

"The servants can manage," Constance sighed. "And this would be no pleasure cruise, believe me. Oh, George, it would only be a couple of weeks."

Finally, he stood up from his chair. Looking up at his wife, he felt, was putting him at a disadvantage.

"You sound like you are seriously considering this madness! Off on a fool's errand, in search of your shameless little sister—who you've never even gotten along with!"

Constance put the nautilus back on the shelf. Suddenly exhausted, she went over to the armchair and toppled the maps onto the rug. She let herself fall in, ignoring George's silent protest.

"The fool sending me on this errand is my father, George." She closed her eyes, stroking her brow. "You weren't there when he asked me to go." She could still see her father's reddened eyes staring into his empty palms, the faint smell of hard cider on his breath. "I couldn't . . . I can't say no. He's so miserable in that house, so desperate."

"Constance." George's voice nearly chipped as he looked down on his wife. "You are not going to Paris on your own."

She sighed, raised herself out of the armchair, and looked her husband in the eye.

"Yes, George. I am."

Vera Sinclair

Amandine shuffled through the parlor's open door, slightly out of breath from the trip up the stairs. Vera sat in a brocade chair, her thin legs covered in a throw, a black Scottish terrier lying at her feet. She was turning the pages of a large kidskin journal.

"Yes?" She looked up at her maid, amused by the girlish smile on her lined face.

"It's Mr. Charles, ma'am." Amandine beamed. "He's taking off his galoshes and overcoat in the hall. He'll be here directly."

As she quickly removed her reading glasses and the blanket ("Up you go, Bibi!" she whispered to the dog. "You know how a throw ages a woman!"), Vera peeked out the window. The rain was still pouring down. It had been one of the wettest, grayest Paris springs she could remember and her gauzy skin ached for sun.

"Hello, love!" Charles Wood entered the room with his customary panache. A dapper gentleman nearing sixty-five, he had a full head of white hair and bright blue eyes.

A smile spread across Vera's face in a ripple, until wrinkles flooded every corner.

"Charles!"

She put her book down and rose to embrace him. He awarded her a brief, stiff half-hug, then bent down to pet the dog. Vera frowned, remembering when, not too long ago, his body used to yield to hers and truly embrace her, despite his Britishness.

His gaze traveled to her journal, which he picked up and thumbed.

"Are you writing today?" he asked, smiling at a doodle in the margin.

"No, I was just skimming through an old entry. The one about the horse races."

"Ah yes." He chuckled as he set the book down. "Our great victory at Chantilly. What was the horse's name again? Naughty Tweed?"

"Nearly." Vera laughed. "It was Devil's Fool. But, come. Sit with me." She took his hand and led him to the sofa. "I haven't seen you for ages." Her eyes twinkled from their hollows; her grin was that of an adolescent. "That wouldn't mean that you have a new *friend*, would it, my dear?"

"Always prying, aren't you, love?" he said in mock exasperation, his eyes cast on the floor.

"You know me," she said with a sweep. "Say, let's have Cook prepare us something truly exquisite this evening. Do you fancy bouillabaisse? Or perhaps coq au vin?"

"Oh, Vera, I can't stay for dinner. I've got other plans." He shifted on the sofa, uncomfortable, still avoiding her gaze. "I just wanted to pop round to see how you are."

"Then *look* at me," she ordered.

He dragged his eyes up to hers, forcing himself to look; he was amazed at how much the illness had changed her face since his last visit, too long ago. He managed a weak smile, but was visibly relieved when Amandine walked into the room, stooped with the weight of the silver tea service.

"Let me help with that!" Charles jumped to his feet.

"You *can* eke out a few minutes for a cup of tea, I hope," Vera said drily, arching an eyebrow.

"Of course. That is, if some of Amandine's chocolate biscuits are on offer." He winked at the old servant, who gave him a look usually reserved for mischievous boys—that is, mischievous boys who are clever and good-looking.

Vera shot a glance at Charles while stirring her tea.

"I've been thinking lately," she began, then paused, awaiting his full attention. She looked out the window; the Jardin du Luxembourg was empty and unappetizing in the rain. When Charles finally responded ("Yes?"), she finished her sentence. "About returning to New York."

Charles raised his brow in mild surprise.

"Have you, then?" he asked.

"Yes." She nodded. "I think perhaps it's time. After thirty-odd years here in Paris, maybe it's time to go home."

"Permanently?" he asked.

"Well, at this age, what does that mean?"

He nodded silently and they both took a sip of tea.

Vera stole another glance at Charles, an easy feat considering he seemed to be studying the weave of her rug. What a pathetic reaction he'd had to her news! He should have shot out of his chair, burst out laughing, or thrown a biscuit at her! The *idea* that she should leave Paris!

"When might you go?" His voice was steady, unemotional.

"Soon," she said. "Summer? Perhaps earlier, if this bloody rain keeps up."

"Paris won't be the same without you, Vera."

He managed a swift glance up at her eyes, attempted another smile, then turned back to the floor.

"I need to run, darling," he murmured. Indeed, he looked ready to bolt, to flee. "Amandine, get my coat, please."

Amandine looked at Vera, who was sitting properly with her hands folded in her lap.

"*Au revoir,* Charles," she said. Now it was she who could not look up.

"I'll be in touch," he said, his hand glancing off her shoulder, the warmest touch he could muster.

After he left, she sat motionless. She could not believe it. Usually, Vera considered herself lucky with odds. Horses, backgammon, roulette. But, that day, she had wagered that her oldest, dearest friend would talk her out of leaving Paris. That he would argue that her place was there, near him; that returning to Manhattan was absurd, a terrible mistake. She would have agreed rather quickly, even if he had only reasoned that he selfishly wanted her by his side. She had gambled and lost.

The next morning, Vera Sinclair, still disappointed, wrote a handful of letters to America, to cousins and friends, then booked passage for June.

"Amandine," she announced at noon, "we are moving to New York."

Julie Vernet

Julie blinked repeatedly as she walked into the house; the poorly lit corridor seemed dark after the glare of the milky Le Havre sky. She listened for her mother but heard nothing. After a brief search, she found her propped in a kitchen chair, looking out the window at the ships docked at port.

"*Bonjour, maman,*" she whispered.

They had become a nearly silent family since the Great War, as if their losses had included their voices as well.

Mme. Vernet turned slightly toward her daughter, her only surviving child. As a form of greeting, she let out a small sigh.

"Is Papa here?" she asked.

Her mother shook her head. Julie supposed her father was out on one of his long walks by the shore. Or perhaps he'd gone to the bar for a solitary round of pastis. She debated a moment whether she should wait for him to share her news, but decided it didn't really matter. Her father had been even more absent than her mother these last three years.

"I've brought in the mail," Julie said, exposing a single envelope in her small hand. "There's a letter here from the Compagnie Générale Transatlantique. I've been given my first assignment."

Waiting for a reaction from her mother, Julie paused, nervously tapping the birthmark above her lip with the pad of a finger. Had she heard? She knelt down next to the chair to hold her mother's hands in hers. The fingers were splayed and wavy, twisted from arthritis. As Julie picked up her mother's hands, meaning to rub some warmth into them, she saw the photograph; her older brothers' portrait was snuggled among her skirts.

Julie looked down upon her brothers, dressed as soldiers, and called to them in her head: Jean-François, Émile, Didier.

"Pity there's not a photograph of Loïc in uniform," she murmured, then chanced a look at her mother's face. Her chin was shaking, her eyes tearing.

"I know, *maman*," Julie said softly. "I miss them too."

She sat at her mother's feet in silence. It was nearly impossible to remember now how their house had been before the war, cramped and noisy, filled with the cries and laughter of men. Mme. Vernet wiped her eyes with the cotton handkerchief that she kept tucked into the sleeve of her cardigan, always at the ready.

Julie finally summoned the courage to recall the day's post. She reached for the envelope and opened it again. She pulled out the letter there at the window, for her mother to see.

"It says I'm to ship out on June fifteenth, on a brand-new liner—the *Paris*." Julie considered a smile, but decided it would be inappropriate. "Of course, if you need me here, I could refuse or get my assignment postponed for a later ship. Maybe—"

Her mother squeezed her daughter's hand with her own useless one, then opened her mouth. Her voice came out like a rusty groan from lack of use.

"Go," it said.

DAY ONE

THE LAUNCH

JUNE 15, 1921

"I'd better be reporting for duty now," Julie said softly, though she did not move.

She glanced over at her parents, who had come to see her off. After a lifetime together, sharing heartfelt sorrows and homely meals, they had begun to resemble each other. Strikingly different when young, they now looked like kinfolk, with the same height and girth, the same stoop, the same wrinkles, the same frown.

Julie sighed, passing her small bag from one hand to the other, and looked around her. She reckoned every child from Le Havre was there on the dock that day waiting for the *Paris* to launch. She watched as they filled their eyes with the rich scene, and occasionally their hands: a fallen bun from one of the bakers' huge baskets; an overblown rose left after a florist had gathered his freshest wares; light strokes of dress silk from the Parisian ladies, so much taller than their own mothers.

Julie Vernet used to be one of those children. About once every year, a great ship was launched and the local kids loved being part of the festivities. They'd mimic the stuffy first-class travelers with their cigarette holders and walking canes, and the foreigners, speaking funny languages. Clowning around in front of the photographers, they'd goad them into taking their pictures. A few little imps inevitably tried to sneak onto the ship, with the idea of stowing away and making their fortunes in New York.

When she was ten or twelve, Julie enjoyed running around the dock, collecting all the longest, cleanest pieces of streamers she could find. She would tie them like ribbons in her hair or wrap them around her fingers and hands, making multicolored paper gloves.

The first launch Julie could remember, at age five or six, she saw with her oldest brother. Jean-François held her hand so she wouldn't be lost in the crowd, and when they got close to the bow, he crouched down to help her spell out the name of the vessel. L-A P-R-O-V-E-N-C-E. He explained to her that, like Le Havre, Provence was on the sea. But there, it was sunny and warm all year-round; the flowers, he added, smelled so sweet, the air was like perfume. Years later, when she was a teenager, Julie would still see that ship in the harbor from time to time and think fondly back on that launch. By then, Jean-François had been killed in the war. Who would have thought that an ocean liner, despite its monstrous size, could outlive a big brother?

"Mama, Papa." She looked at the small couple dressed in black. "I should be going now. I still need to put on my uniform."

It was her first trip away from home; little Julie Vernet had gotten a job with the French Line and was going off to sea.

"That's right," her mother said with a nod. "You don't want to be late."

With no more words, they gave each other four light kisses, kissing air, kissing ghosts. She put her bag over her shoulder and headed toward the steerage gangplank. Making her way through the crowd, Julie absently bent down to snatch up a long green streamer and quickly wrapped it around her hand, glad to see there were other crew members who still hadn't boarded. Weaving through passengers and locals, she was startled by a photographer's flash. Well, he wouldn't be taking a picture of her!

As she reached the ship, she saw a group of youngsters from her neighborhood, Saint François. Like tightrope walkers, they were fearlessly balancing on the fat mooring lines running from the ship to the dock, challenging one another to count the ship's countless portholes, bragging that their fathers had welded this bit or that. They looked up at Julie.

"*Au revoir,* Julie!" the children shouted, waving from shoulder to fingertip, jumping on the corded hemp. "*Bonne chance!*"

Now, with her parents behind her, she allowed herself a grin—"*Au revoir, mes enfants!* Good luck to you too!"—then leapt onto the ramp. As Julie crossed the gangplank, she already felt a bit lighter. She was leaving behind the gray world of her family home, the nonlife of Le Havre, ready to start anew. No more wordlessness, no more emptiness. The water, clapping against the hull of the ship, applauded her arrival.

Once aboard, she went out on the low-ceilinged third-class deck. Julie took advantage of her small frame to pass through the thick crowd, people packed around mooring machinery and cargo hatches. She made her way to the side of the ship and stationed herself on a narrow strip of unoccupied rail. She found her parents below; they had backed away from the crowd, as far from the ship as they could. She nervously began to wind the long streamer around her fingers; she'd been both thrilled and regretful about this day since she'd received her assignment in the mail almost a month ago.

Looking at her parents, she wondered whether, without her there, they would ever speak again.

In the center of the dock, amid cries and laughter, neighing and clanging, bursts of accordion and fiddle, Constance Stone shook her sister's hand formally, then gave Faith's French boyfriend a brief nod.

"Good-bye, then," she said stiffly, taking a step toward the ship. Unable to contain herself, however, she immediately turned back to her sister.

"You *know* you should be boarding with me," Constance said through her teeth, gesturing toward the enormous ship before them. "If you had any sense of duty whatsoever, any feeling of responsibility toward the family—"

"For years you've moaned about how lacking I am in notions of moral obligation," Faith interrupted with a sly smile, stressing the last two words sarcastically. "I suppose you were right."

Constance stood opposite her little sister, shaking her head in disdain. Faith, still baby-faced at twenty-three, was dressed in flowing, bohemian scarves and skirts, long beads, and a bejeweled turban. She looked ridiculous, a veritable circus performer. Both her hands were loosely wrapped around the arm of her beau, Michel. He was some eight years older, dressed in dark worker's clothes, though his boots were spattered in paint of every color.

"Indeed!" Constance sniffed, turning again.

"Bon voyage!" Michel, unable to follow their conversation, smiled sweetly.

"Adieu," Constance said to them both, then walked away with no further hesitation.

As she approached the ship, she heaved a sigh of relief. On the long train ride from Paris she had hardly said a word to Faith, much less Michel. After the tense atmosphere of the last few days, it was refreshing to be alone, to take respite from bitter words, curt replies, and silent glares.

She had gone to Paris at her father's bidding, to bring her sister home, with hopes that her reappearance would improve their mother's condition. Faith's refusal had made the entire expediton a waste of time. Constance thought of her own daughters, crying on the platform as her New York–bound train pulled out of the station in Worcester, and of her husband's utter vexation.

She had gone against her husband's wishes, and to what end? Faith had been unwilling to leave her new life in Paris. Whether her return would have helped their mother was beside the point.

Walking toward the ship, Constance saw a few newspaper men up ahead. Reporters were craning their necks looking for a good story while photographers took pictures; there was a cameraman there as well, capturing the event for a newsreel. Just in case she were caught on camera, she quickly adjusted the big loopy tie at her neck, smoothed her skirt, and, breathing deeply, wiped the last traces of scowl from her face.

She was wearing the same traveling suit she had purchased for the voyage east, to Europe, just a few weeks before. She'd felt so elegant when she'd tried it on: a long black skirt, a white silk blouse, a large red bow around the neck, all set off by an airy gray hat. But when George—by then resigned to the fact that she was traveling to Europe on her own, but still bitter—had seen it, he'd teased her.

"Oh, my dear!" he'd shouted. "How *clever* you are! You'll match the ship! Look, black, white, funnel red, topped with a puff of smoke!"

Constance, taken aback by her husband's nasty tone, not to mention his rare burst of imagination, had tried to find something else, but it was too late. Now, walking toward the *Paris,* she hoped no one else would make that connection, especially those newspapermen. She could just see the caption: "Provincial Woman Lost When Camouflaged by Liner!"

At that moment, a sandy-haired photographer appeared out of the crowd a few yards in front of her.

"*Souriez!*" he cried with an explicatory grin, as his flash went off.

The background of the photograph was not the liner itself (thank heaven for small blessings!) but the crowd behind. Looking around, Constance saw the sudden flash had also startled the two women nearest her: a petite, young woman with bright copper hair stopped a few paces in front, while to the side stood an impossibly thin elderly woman firmly wrapped in a long, plum-colored coat. They each paused a moment to blink, then continued toward the ship. Wondering where that photograph might land, she glanced over at the two women, who also appeared to be traveling on their own.

Suddenly, there was a swell in the crowd and she lost sight of them both. It seemed the last crew members were trying to get to their posts before the passengers boarded. From officers in smart uniforms on down to the barmen and bellhops, they all rushed past her. She'd heard the crew on the *Paris* numbered nearly a thousand, and the passengers—from the top hats and monocles traveling in the elegant cabins at the top, to the tattered emigrants under the waterline—were twice as many.

Before boarding, she stopped to take in the great ship looming ahead. Its length took up the entire pier and, with three brilliant red funnels towering above the highest decks, it dwarfed all the other boats in the harbor. Constance thought the liner must be as long as the Eiffel Tower was tall, but it was massive, solid. She supposed she ought to feel lucky to be a part of the *Paris* launch, its first tour of the famous French Line: Le Havre, Southampton, New York. Though, really, she was in no mood for celebrations.

She was jostled by a man on the fringe of the crowd. At the foot of the second-class ramp, impatient travelers were trying to get on, as those going up inevitably paused to take in the view. He turned to her, as if to scold her for stopping at such an inopportune place, but when he looked into her face—beautiful, by all accounts—his expression changed.

"*Excusez-moi, mademoiselle,*" he said, drawing closer to her with a leer.

Not unused to such smiles, Constance nodded crisply in return, then walked straight into the throng to access the second-class decks. After several minutes of being far too close to strangers than she would have liked—the feel of their outer garments, their limbs, their breath upon her—she made her way up the ramps and to the rails nearest her cabin.

Everyone on deck was crying out enthusiastically—Americans returning home or Europeans on holiday, young couples on a first voyage, affluent Jewish emigrants off to New York—all throwing colored streamers and waving their hats. She looked down onto the dock and easily spotted Faith and Michel below. How could you miss them?

Like all the other well-wishers on the dock, they were now smiling at her (what cheek!); with one arm wrapped around the other's waist, they were cheerfully waving up at the second tier. Constance waved back brusquely, but she soon tired of looking back at them. During her two-week visit, she had been a third wheel, a mere witness to their affection.

In their company, she constantly found herself comparing their giddy happiness to her relationship with George. Although she didn't understand their French conversations, she envied the frank admiration she saw in Michel's face when he looked at Faith, the undercurrent of passion in their voices. She knew that Faith found her relationship with George dull, flawed, unacceptable.

Tired of looking down on their self-satisfied faces—Faith clutching Michel and grinning—she was ready to leave the festive crowd on deck, find her accommodations, and get to sea. Nervous as she was about going home empty-handed, Constance was happy to be leaving France. Arranging her puffy gray hat as she came in off the deck, her smile cornered downward. Faith was, without a doubt, the most selfish person on earth.

Vera slowly let go of Charles's arm; it was time to board the vessel.

"What am I going to do without you?" she asked him sadly.

"Shall I stow away in that enormous coffer of yours?" he asked, his eyes shining brightly. With the realization that their time was limited, Charles had spent much more time with Vera these last weeks, although it still crushed him to see her decline. "An elephant could travel comfortably in there! A trunk in a trunk, you know."

Vera smiled at her friend. "How I shall miss you," she sighed.

"Oh, Vera. This isn't farewell! We'll see each other again."

"Of course." She nodded.

Charles bent down to kiss her cheek and they held each other, both reluctant to let go. Pressing her cheek against his, she was surprised to feel a tear slide past. She smiled into his watery eyes, brushing the tear away with her thumb.

"Call me sentimental," he whispered with a shrug. "I'll miss you too, love."

Charles took a step away from Vera to say good-bye to her maid, Amandine, then pat the dog's head.

"Good-bye, you three!" he said with a smile. "*Au revoir!*"

Walking toward the great ship, Vera could still feel the warmth of Charles's cheek upon her own. She reached up to touch it, to see if her hand could detect such heat, perhaps store it for later, but merely felt the chill of her own aged skin. Part of her still wanted him to call her back, to beg her not to leave, but their choices had been made.

She turned again to smile at him, to give him a slight wave, then began making her way across the dock, her black Scotty leading by just a foot, while Amandine lagged a few steps behind. As this small, single-file parade of three curved around the confusion of horse carts, motorcars, crates, and trunks, she noticed other tangles of people—families, crew members, emigrants, groups of tourists—also twisting like seaweed, eels, through every available space on the waterfront, as if drawn to the ocean liner by the tide. The smell at port, she noted with distaste, which was usually dominated by the salty freshness of the sea, today was overtaken by the pungent odor of humanity.

Vera was already exhausted. Finally approaching the *Paris,* the enormous steamer that would take her home to Manhattan, she paused, leaning sharply on her cane before beginning the long climb up the ramp. The scene around her was so hectic: the shouting and shoving, the bright sun, the glare. Wait, was that a camera flash? She blinked a time or two, then looked up to find a young blond photographer in front of her. Gesturing to the camera, he gave her a sheepish grin.

"It's for the steamer paper," he said in French. "Have a look at the launch article in tomorrow's edition. You might see yourself!"

She nodded at him politely. At this point in her life, seeing herself was the last thing she wanted to do. Vera watched him scuttle off, startling other people with his flash. Still trying to catch her breath, she listened to the voices around her; a clatter of superlative exclamations and eulogies all honored the ocean liner before them.

"Comme c'est beau!"

"C'est le transatlantique le plus grand de la France!"

"La salle de machines est magnifique!"

Vera, unmoved by the ship, was saddened to think how much she would miss hearing the French language. After having spent nearly half her life in Paris, she realized that from now on, she would have no call to use the beautiful language she loved and had strived to perfect. For whatever time she had left, she would be surrounded by English speakers.

Vera soon reached the first-class entrance, where, upon crossing the threshold, the machine's steel hull transformed itself into a modern-day palace. Vera tottered in, oblivious to the luxurious wood paneling and plush carpeting, the enormous bouquets of exotic flowers, the fawning smiles of the French Line service crew. She passed the grandiose stairway and took the lift to the top floor, where her cabin was located. Once on deck, she handed the leash to

Amandine and went over to the rail to bid Charles good-bye. It took her a minute or two to find him among the large crowd still below—mostly comprised of landborne friends and nautical admirers now that the boat was slowly filling—and waved.

Grasping the handrail, she looked upon her dear old friend, who returned her gaze from what appeared an exaggerated distance. An elderly man—a year or two older than she, although nowadays anyone would guess him to be far younger—he was stately looking and well dressed. With a melancholic smile, Vera noted that, however many years he might live on the Continent, something about him would always betray his nationality. What was it about him? The set of his jaw, his perfect posture? His full head of white hair? Were these things British?

Looking down at the handsome portrait he made—one hand tucked into a pocket, the other casually holding his cane—she could scarcely believe that she would not be seeing him again.

The party at the rail next to her shrieked with laughter as they popped their champagne and got caught in the spray. One of them lifted the bottle to his mouth to catch the gush of bubbles spilling out, dousing his theatrical traveling cloak to everyone's great amusement.

Ready to quit the decks, Vera lifted her palm to her friend for a final farewell. Before he turned to go, to take the train back to Paris, Charles tipped his hat to Vera and threw her a kiss. She watched him leave the dock, then, before retiring, allowed herself one last glimpse at France (though this port town was not *her* France), another mournful parting. Back in her cabin, she lay down. Vera had never liked forced gaiety and these big ocean-liner launching celebrations were the epitome of such nonsense.

Julie stood against the rails of the steerage deck and waved at her parents. She could see them at the farthest end of the dock. So small, in mourning dress, they looked like a pair of blackbirds at the edge of a field. She thought she saw her mother wave back; from this distance it was hard to tell.

She slid her fingers along the sturdy rail. All her life, Julie had seen spectacular ocean liners come in and out of port, right outside their kitchen windows. She watched them as they passed through their surprisingly short life cycles: their feted launches and fashionable youths, their less popular mature years, then their retirement, sometimes terribly scarred by fires or accidents only five or eight years after their maiden voyage. This, however, was the first time she'd ever boarded one.

Julie's family was from a small working-class neighborhood wedged in among wharfs. A crooked collection of wattle-and-daub houses with canals on all sides, it was a veritable island within the port. She grew up with water all around her, water and great ships. But, up to now, she had never been on anything larger than her father's fishing boat, a vessel so humble it was too small to accommodate all his sons at once. This ship, the *Paris,* was even bigger than her quarter, her native Saint François.

She almost looked out at her parents again, but quickly turned her gaze. They had come to see their last surviving child leave home and Julie couldn't bear to see them so somber and resigned. It was time to go below, to get ready for work, but she could not yet make herself leave the deck, to disappear and abandon her parents completely. Besides, she wanted to see from this new perspective how the great ship would maneuver out of the harbor and, little by little, leave Le Havre behind.

There were still a few sailors and uniformed workers enjoying the festivities, shouting and gesturing to the people onshore. Just then, two young crew members who looked like brothers (except one was almost a full head taller than the other) shouldered into a spot next to her on the rail and waved vigorously at a blond girl holding a pug tightly in her arms. She grinned at them, waving the dog's paw back. The shorter boy rolled his eyes, then looked straight down the sleek hull of the steamer, down to the water.

"I've never been this far off the ground," he said to his friend.

"You mean, this far off the water!" his friend replied, looking down himself.

Julie peeked too, her neck reaching out farther and farther, her gaze gliding down the side of the ship until it found the sea. It was surprisingly far. She unwound the streamer from her fingers and let it drop, holding her breath until it reached the dark water below. She quickly looked back up and glimpsed out toward her parents. Both waited patiently; they were experienced at this. She shook her head with a sigh, knowing herself a poor substitute for sons.

"Hey," said the short boy, still hanging over the rail, contemplating the water from that great height, "have you ever wondered where the extra water comes from when the tide rolls in?"

"Yeah," replied his friend, nodding in mock seriousness, "it's a mystery . . . like, where does the extra meat come from when your pecker gets hard?"

His friend jerked his head up with a look of surprise, making his tall companion burst into laughter, clapping him on the back. Julie had to look away to hide her smile. Sailors! Had the soldiers in the trenches also joked around and laughed like that?

Suddenly, a boater hat, perched carelessly on a man's head down on the bow, was taken up by the wind. As it flew by, Julie stretched out her hand and caught it so effortlessly that the boys next to her stopped laughing at once and stared at her, as if she too had just come out of the sky.

Julie was so small that people generally didn't notice her at all, but when they did, they usually stared. Her hair was a remarkable shade of copper and, in sunshine such as this, had the metallic sheen of a well-polished kettle. Her skin, pale and delicate, had the translucent gleam of a pearl, decorated by nearly imperceptible swirls of blue and pink. Her brother Loïc used to say she looked otherworldly, like an angel or a nymph, or like Pygmalion's statue at the very moment it came to life. But Julie was fully aware that what people were really staring at was the large birthmark that was wedged between her nose and her lip, perfectly outlining that tear-shaped groove in the middle.

She watched as the boys' gaze immediately found it, then bobbed back up to her eyes, embarrassed, yet unable to hide their distaste. This is how strangers had looked at her as long as she could remember; she was used to it.

"Great catch!" the shorter boy said, a few seconds too late.

She turned the hat around in her hands, shrugging off her skill. "I grew up with four brothers," she explained.

Already, the owner of the hat had made his way to where she was standing, brushing it off as if the air had made it dirty.

"Thank you so much!" he cried. Though he spoke to her in French, his deep voice had a musical accent.

He accepted his hat back with a small bow, then looked into her face. She noticed that his eyes did not dip down to her birthmark; they had not yet seemed to find it.

"I bought this hat just this morning. A ridiculous purchase for an engine man." He smiled and put out his hand. "I am Nikolai Grumov."

He was big and tall, reminding Julie of those strapping American soldiers she'd seen during the war who all looked as if they'd grown up on dairy farms, raised on milk and beef. Although he was probably just a few years older than she—maybe twenty-four?—his shaggy brown hair was beginning to recede. His tanned face, she saw, was lightly pocked. All in all, he had a ruggedness she found appealing. She shook his large, warm hand with a smile.

"Julie Vernet. Pleased to meet you," she said, stumbling slightly over her words. "I'm also working here on the ship."

"You must be in the service crew. We don't get pretty girls down in the engine room." Nikolai grinned.

Julie, unused to attention from men, blushed and looked down. Suddenly, a loud honk blasted out, the first warning that the ship would soon be leaving the harbor.

"That reminds me! I have to report for duty!" Julie said.

She picked up her bag and, as she pushed away from the rail, looked back at Nikolai.

"Maybe we'll run into each other again?" she suggested shyly.

"I sure hope so!" He winked, saluting with his boater.

She scooted past him and went inside, feeling his eyes on her still. Inside the door, she paused and smiled to herself. This voyage might be a new beginning indeed. Julie then realized she had forgotten to wave a last good-bye to her parents. She took a deep breath—it was too late now; she would feel silly going back out on deck with that boy still there—and promised herself to write to them as soon as she had some free time. She put her bag over her shoulder and headed toward the female workers' dormitory.

Even though the ocean liner was huge, she knew where to go and made her way for the lower level. During her training classes—her weeks spent at the Centre d'Apprentissage Hôtelier—she had nearly memorized the layout of the entire ship. She had not learned much more, however, as the women on board did the same jobs they did on land: laundry, cleaning, child care, or working in shops and salons. The English lessons, a mandatory course for people working the French Line, weren't so difficult for the people from Le Havre, which had been overrun with Allied soldiers during the war.

Julie went down various stairways, the air getting warmer and warmer, the drumming noise from the engines louder and louder, until she arrived at the tip of the bow. This area, which felt the ship's roll more than any other, was used for storage, equipment, and housing women workers.

She peeked into the female dormitory and saw a low-ceilinged room filled with bunk beds, lockers, and benches, all riveted to the checkerboard floor. Next to the dormitory, there was a dining room. Dim lightbulbs dangled over long tables and benches, from one slanted metal side to the other. A cheerless place for the female crew to spend their free time, eating, sewing, playing cards.

As she walked toward her bunk, a few heads popped up and murmured greetings, which were barely audible over the dull drone from the engines below. Most of the women, however, were busily tying aprons and arranging caps, trying to get to their stations without delay.

Julie smiled at the women she passed. At a glance, she could guess the jobs they'd been hired to do. The pretty girls, with stylish hairdos and delicate hands, obviously worked in the public eye, in the concessions, selling tobacco or flowers. Others, attractive still, but in a more practical way, were probably hairdressers or manicurists, or maybe maids or nannies for the second-class passengers who weren't traveling with their own. The big, strong women were most likely washerwomen; their faces looked watery and worn, as if they too had been left to soak.

Julie, considered too unsightly to work with the genteel passengers and too small to wash clothes, was put on maid service for the steerage class. Just as well. We are neighbors down here under the waterline, no need to go rushing about, all over the ship.

She sat on her bed and opened her bag, thankful she'd been assigned a lower bunk. She brought out an intricate piece of white lace with a stylized *V* in the center and put it gently on her pillow, smoothing it with her hands. It was from her mother, a lace maker, and dated back from when Julie was a little girl. She could still see her younger mother tatting at the window and hear the sounds of the bone bobbins—*click, click, clack*—as she wove, plaited, and looped the strands together. That was before she'd gotten the arthritis.

Almost everything—the collars, cuffs, coifs, the linens of all kinds—had been sold. Of course, that was the whole point!

Though her work was done for the wealthy families of Le Havre, her mother managed to save a few pieces for her children. This one she'd intended for the future bride of her eldest son. Then came the Great War.

Mme. Vernet lost her four sons, a boy each year, in chronological order. Jean François, the eldest, was killed immediately, in Lorraine, the very first week of the war. Émile fell at Ypres, then Didier at Verdun. They lost Loïc in 1918, right before the armistice. Although the war was won, the Vernet family had been defeated. Without a proper owner, this piece of lace was given, without ceremony, to her youngest, her daughter.

"You might as well have this, Julie," her mother had sighed, handing over the lacework, folded up in a tiny square. "Seeing as you're leaving home."

Julie stored her other things in her locker—toiletries, undergarments, a book stuffed with letters—then pulled out the brand-new black uniform, so starched it smelled scorched. She thought again of her parents, also in black, standing silently on the dock, not touching each other. This is how it had been since they'd lost Loïc, their final sacrifice to the war.

"Mademoiselle Vernet?"

Julie looked up to see the frowning face of a thin, lined woman of perhaps fifty. She looked from Julie to her clipboard and back again. They were alone in the dormitory; all the other women had reported for duty.

"Yes?" Julie gave her a hesitant smile, causing the woman's brow to furrow. She decided on a solemn look.

"Yes, *ma'am*. I am your superior here," she said, standing straighter. "Madame Tremblay, head of housekeeping."

"Sorry, ma'am."

"What are you still doing in here?" Mme. Tremblay tapped her foot impatiently. "Come now! Get your uniform on! You should already be in the steerage common room."

"Yes, of course. Ma'am," Julie added quickly, as the head housekeeper whisked out of the dormitory.

Angry with herself for having caused a bad first impression, she quickly buttoned her uniform, then began to put on her crisp white cap. Within seconds, Mme. Tremblay popped back into the dormitory.

"Get a mop out of the utility closet. There's some vomit here in the corridor," she said, her sharp chin pointing toward the right.

"Yes, ma'am," Julie murmured with a slight frown. Having been hired to work in steerage dining, she hadn't realized mopping vomit would be part of her job.

"The ship hasn't even *left* yet and someone's already thrown up!" Mme. Tremblay rolled her eyes, then disappeared again.

As she was tying her apron, Julie thought she could sympathize. The heavy, unsavory air smelled as if it had already been breathed in by others, by people with tooth decay or head colds.

Suddenly she heard a muffled cheer from the decks. The *Paris* was pulling away from the pier, leaving the harbor. She felt a sudden lurching, as if the tide were tugging at her center of gravity; as big as it was, she could feel the ship moving, especially from there at the bow, right above the engines. Even as an island girl, she was unprepared for this motion, this roll, and held fast to the metal bedpost. Already too warm, Julie began breathing hard.

Vera lay nearly motionless on the bed with her dog at her feet, her eyes closed, trying to ignore the racket from the deck. Suddenly, it was amplified to its highest possible pitch, with firecrackers, hoots of laughter, and some three or four cheers repeated manically:

Bon voyage! Vive la France! Vive l'Amérique!

She understood what this meant and tried to feel, through all the liner's layers, the gentle motion of a ship leaving port. Vera thought she could detect it—like once in Crete when she felt the smallest shimmer of an earthquake—and was relieved when, little by little, the excited crowd drifted away from the decks, looking for the next bit of adventure.

This was her tenth crossing, her tenth great transatlantic ship. Sitting up on the bed, she opened her eyes and looked around her room, her lodgings for the next five days. She raised her eyebrows in surprise at the sight of a telephone on the table, then sighed. This was not nearly as majestic as the *France* had been on her last crossing, eight years before. Inspired by the palace at Versailles, that elegant old steamer, with its gilt fireplaces, beautiful beveled mirrors, and carved dressers was a floating piece of art. This ship was much more modern; the lines were sleek, simple, and certainly not Vera's idea of sophistication. Another sign of the times. Or the fact that she was getting old.

She bent over and scratched her sleeping dog under her graying chin. They had gone through a similar evolution, she thought, the same aging process: passionate in their youth, haughty and irascible in middle age; now they were both prone to sighing and lethargy. A black Scottish terrier, she had started her life with the dignified name of Bête Noire. Charles thought it a pretentious name for such a little trollop, and she was soon demoted to Bibi.

She thought again of Charles, and how pleased she had been when he had insisted on taking the train to see her off in Le Havre. After all the years she had lived in Paris—thirty-one to be exact—Vera had scores of acquaintances, was a member of various circles, and had many loyal devotees. But Charles was the only person she would miss.

She'd met Charles Wood when she first arrived to Paris. A cousin with British in-laws had given her a letter of introduction and he'd invited her round for tea. Fashionable and attractive, they were both just over thirty, single, independent, and sparkling with joie de vivre. That same day, they went from having tea to dining out, then off to the cabarets for champagne and dancing. They spoke honestly about their lives—the very first time they met! She told him about her absent parents and poorly chosen husband; he told her about his aristocratic but emotionally crippled family. When he took her home at dawn, he whispered in her ear: "My dear Vera. I suppose you could call this love at first sight. Ah, if only you were a man!" provoking a fit of laughter that left them both with aching sides.

For decades, Left Bank society considered them a couple—at least on seating charts for dinner parties—and they were a highly sought pair. During the war, they had even lived together. Too old to serve Britain, Charles had served Vera, foraging good cuts of meat and coffee from his black market sources, keeping her in firewood, holding her close during zeppelin air raids over Paris, and always, always making her laugh with his dry, unpredictable wit.

After all her experience with the opposite sex—an absent father, a temporary husband, a dozen or so lovers—it was Charles who held uncontested claim to her heart, in spite of the fact that he wasn't attracted to women. It was not an unrequited love; it was mutual, rich and true. Of course, like Vera, Charles had his lovers. Sometimes he would disappear for weeks at a time, only to return with a devilish grin and occasionally, depending on whom he had been with, booty to share: an ancient bottle of Bordeaux; a crate of pomegranate; chocolate truffles, handmade in Bruges. Unlike Vera, who enjoyed discussing her male friends with him, examining their failings and virtues, Charles never spoke about his secret companions. Both of them understood, however, that lovers were transient. The solid, lasting relationship had always belonged to them. Vera thought of him standing on the dock, his last sweeping kiss, and bit her lip. What in the world was she going to do in New York?

Glancing around the room again, she saw her bags had been

delivered, neatly placed in the corner. The set of six trunks constructed a pyramid, with a triangular carpetbag forming the apex. Vera was sentimental about these old steamer trunks—over twenty-five years old by now—and would not consider replacing them. Her young secretary, Sylvie, oblivious to their charm, had periodically urged her to buy new ones, but Vera had long resisted. Their beige and brown sides were covered with stickers from journeys past—ports along the Mediterranean and the Scandinavian seas as well as those of the French Line: New York/Le Havre. Most of these stickers were now faded and half-torn, the newest ones already two years old.

In the past, she would have needed most of these trunks just for the social activities on board, where one would change clothes—for meals, strolls, dancing, games—at least five times a day. On this crossing, Vera had no intention of wasting such time on her toilette, but had needed the larger trunks to move some personal items from her Paris home. She did not ship anything back to New York, deciding to limit her packing to the space available in the weather-beaten trunks. These past few years, especially after the war, she had discovered that things—most things, anyway—were not so important after all.

Amandine, already half-asleep in the armchair, suddenly shifted, then licked her dry lips with closed eyes. What a pathetic little threesome we are, Vera thought, listening to Bibi's snores. Three old ladies, torpid and sluggish, feeble bears in a perpetual winter.

"Amandine," Vera called softly, rousing her at once. "Pass me the bag, please. Yes, the one with the books. Now, you may go and get yourself settled in. Your room is right next door, none of that running from first to second class on the *Paris*."

She smiled to herself, imagining slow Amandine at a full run.

"You're sure you don't need my assistance?" the old servant asked. "I could hang your dresses, unpack your shoes . . ."

"No, thank you. I'm not going to worry about clothes for now," Vera answered. "Just the *thought* bores me! Why don't you relax for a while? I'll let you know if I need anything."

Amandine went to the conjoining room, giving Bibi a pat on the way out.

Vera began unpacking the carpetbag. First, she took out a small portrait of herself, framed in dark mahogany. Vera gazed at it, remembering the day she'd had it done. She was in her late thirties then, and Charles had suggested—dared her, more like!—she sit for that dwarfish painter with the enormous lips. *Quelle aventure!* The two of them had climbed the steep hill to Montmartre in the rain to meet the grotesque little man, and they all ended up getting quite tight on anisette (or was it absinthe?!). He had produced, in just an hour or so, an oil pastel likeness of her.

That painter (what was his name again?) later became quite famous and then died young, much younger than she was now. He hadn't liked them, had sensed they were mocking him, and had overcharged her (at least he reckoned he had). And, at the time, Vera hadn't liked the drawing. He had exaggerated all her defects—her long nose, angular face, sharp chin—deriding her in return. But now, in the drawing, she saw the woman she used to be—attractive, proud, self-possessed, somewhat mischievous, even—and had a great affection for it.

She leaned the framed picture on the bureau in front of the mirror, then slid it to the side, taking in both images—the drawing and her reflection—at the same time: the woman in her prime alongside the woman in decline. Vera looked at the latter critically; this thinness had exaggerated her wrinkles, leaving her skin with nothing to do but to hang. She tilted her head back slightly and looked at her neck. "You have a lovely neck," her grandmother had told her once, the only compliment she had ever given her. Now it looked as if a group of tiny adventurers had scaled it and, from the hollow under the chin, had thrown a rope ladder down to their less vigorous companions. What might they do once they all reached the top? Paddle up the ear canal into her brain? She imagined minuscule Verne characters manned with ropes and pickaxes, in search of a center. It certainly felt that way more and more these days.

She took a last sentimental glance at her portrait, at her former self, then looked out the window, which, she noted with approval, was larger than the portholes she was used to. Although they were already surrounded by water, having left the coast behind, to her mind, they were not yet "at sea." They would still be stopping in Britain before truly beginning the crossing. Le Havre, Southampton . . . how provincial it sounds! Really, it should be called the Paris, London, New York Line, which would be every bit as accurate.

Vera continued unpacking. She pulled out her toiletry kit, opened it, and peered inside. She had half a mind to apply some Ferrol's Magic Skin Food ("for filling out wasted necks!") but knew it was pointless. With a slight snort, she stashed the toiletries away in the drawer and looked back inside her bag.

Here was the book Charles had given her for the voyage, a slim volume of poems by a Greek acquaintance of his. She noticed with a smile that he had taken the liberty of turning down a corner to mark a page. Ah, a poem not to be missed. Well, she would save it for the last day, then send Charles a wire saying she had just seen it. Or, perhaps she would use this telephone! Chuckling to herself, she tried to imagine what could possibly be so urgent that one would need to telephone from the middle of the sea.

Finally, Vera took out her journals, three heavy volumes, and lay them neatly on the small writing table. Then, from a pocket in the side of the bag, she brought out her fountain pen, placing it carefully on top of the pile. She had written every word with that pen; in fact, it was the pen itself that had given her the idea of writing her memoirs some seven years ago.

It had happened just a few months before the war. She was on the train returning from a dreary weekend at Deauville, the de rigueur holiday resort on Normandy's flat, gray coast, which had deviously slipped its way into the itineraries of the fashionable set. That particular weekend had been especially dull, as the horse races had been rained out.

They had settled into their first-class compartment for the six-hour journey back to Paris; a drowsy lot even then, Amandine was asleep on her shoulder, and Bibi on her lap. She herself was feeling very relaxed—an English nanny couldn't rock one to sleep any better than a French train—when, an hour into their journey, a distinguished-looking gentleman came into their compartment. He sat down on the empty seat in front of them, took off his hat, and smiled, bowing his head politely in her direction. He then rustled in his bag until he found a book, put on his glasses, and began to read.

Feigning sleep, she watched him through half-closed eyes. She could see from his clothes that he was not French and his skin was darker than those pale Europeans of the north. His hair was turning silver, there was a bit of white in his neatly trimmed beard, but over his deep brown eyes, his thick, perfectly arched eyebrows were still black.

Vera liked watching him read, his eyes flickering back and forth under his gold-rimmed glasses, his tapered fingers waiting expectantly for the next page. She glanced down at the cover of the book and read:

VALLE-INCLÁN
TEATRO

The name seemed so exotic, a pre-Columbian god. She thought the dark stranger must be in the world of theater: a playwright, a director, or perhaps an actor? She imagined him reading out loud to her (plays were meant to be performed, were they not?), his voice turning the Spanish prose into music, operetta.

She watched him take out a pipe, consider it, put it back in his bag, to find a notebook and pen. As he sat writing on crossed knee, Vera was suddenly aware of the warmth in the compartment, she who was always cold. She smiled to herself, allowing herself a rare moment of reverie: she was no longer traveling with her old servant and dog, but with this intriguing gentleman, and out the windows there were no gray-blue fields, but castle-topped hills in the sun.

Eyes closed (had she fallen asleep?), she suddenly heard him repacking his things, readying himself to leave. The train was pulling into Saint Germaine, she knew; they were almost to Paris. Vera decided against opening her eyes, only to see the disappointing tip of the Spaniard's hat accompanied by a polite smile. She preferred to imagine him bidding her farewell with a long, regretful gaze and hesitating at the door.

The whistle blew and the train begrudgingly recommenced, pulling its vast weight, slowly, rhythmically. Finally she opened her eyes to look at the empty hollow of the cushion where the man had been sitting. And, between the velvet cracks she could see the tip of a fountain pen. Holding Bibi carefully in one arm, she reached over for it, with a small laugh. A love offering, she said to herself.

Vera had many fine writing instruments: two desk sets, a collection of dip pens, a half dozen fountain pens from the best houses in Europe. But this one was truly exquisite. It had a mother-of-pearl cap, a rich brown resin barrel, and a silver clip. She fingered its lines, then slowly unscrewed the top. The nib was decorated with a stylized cross. Charles, who knew such things, told her later that it was the Cross of Santiago, the one Velázquez had painted on his own chest in his monumental canvas *Las Meninas.*

Perhaps the pen had been specially made for the Spanish traveler? At any rate, there was very little chance of seeing him again to return it. The best she could do was to write something worthy of it.

She decided to write—with this pen and only this pen—the only story she really knew: her own.

She contemplated at length the right way to approach her memoirs. Vera could not imagine beginning with "I was born" and following along with several years' worth of information that she herself could not remember. Instead of writing her story chronologically, she decided to write it alphabetically. She chose to describe emblematic moments, funny anecdotes, running themes, all categorized by letters, from *A* for Appendix (the tragicomedy of suffering from appendicitis while visiting her grandmother, who was then senile) to *Z* for Zeppelin (the terror of watching the deadly, silent balloons stalking Paris during the Great War).

She reveled in the choice making for each letter, some obvious selections, others more obscure. When two years had passed, she had finished writing her alphabet memoirs with her fetish pen, always in indigo ink. However, after she had finished that volume, she wanted to continue writing: tales that had not fit into the original twenty-six, had been forgotten, or those she had not been ready to tell. She then decided to write vignettes which involved a significant number, giving herself infinite possibilities. Of course, it was impossible (and did not appeal to her) to start from one and go on from there; rather, she chose important, symbolic numbers, in whatever order they occurred to her. She began with 1057, her parents' address on Fifth Avenue.

In these volumes, the margins, and sometimes a full page, were scattered with line drawings—comic sketches, portraits leaning toward caricature, illustrations for the text—also made with the pen, but occasionally shaded in later with pencils or pastels. Although Vera had never liked needlework, she loved drawing. In fact, when she'd first arrived in Paris, she attended the Académie Vitti, a private art school for women, but she soon tired of the routine of live models and weekly critiques. Preferring to work on her own, she visited the Louvre often and copied works in pencil or pen, simplifying

Greek or Egyptian sculptures into a few sharp lines. Writing and drawing came together to make up her journals, the disjointed story of her life.

Now, thumbing through her alphabet journal in a luxury cabin on an enormous ship, she thought again of the Spaniard from the train. Just yesterday she had absentmindedly looked for him, as she had for years in train stations. Passing through the Gare Saint Lazare with Charles, she wondered whether she could recognize him, whether he were still in France. Had he fought in the war, lost a limb, or was he even alive? He had taken on that mythic quality only truly attainable with total strangers. For years, Charles had teased her about him playfully, occasionally nudging her, pointing out unlikely candidates, asking her if perchance that was he? But her old friend had also been very encouraging of her writing, and had been, so far, her only reader.

She suddenly put the pen down.

"Damn it," Vera muttered, realizing that she had forgotten to tell Amandine to reserve her deck chair.

As she roused herself to knock on her maid's door, she frowned. She was becoming more and more forgetful.

Constance stood in line at the steward's desk, waiting her turn. She was behind a slow-moving, gray-haired woman; the graying dog at her feet had already lain down, preparing itself for a nap.

"*Oui, je voudrais une chaise longue de première classe pour Madame Vera Sinclair,*" she requested.

Constance, idly eavesdropping but understanding almost nothing, decided that "Sinclair" did not sound like a terribly French surname. As the old woman turned to leave, animating the dog with a gentle pull on the leash, she nodded to Constance.

"*Au revoir,*" she murmured as she shuffled off down the corridor.

Constance took her place at the desk.

"Yes, a deck chair, please, on the second-class deck," she articulated well, in case the steward's English was below par. "My name is Mrs. Stone, Mrs. Constance Stone. Please make sure it's on the port side. The *port,*" she repeated for emphasis.

As a novice traveler on the way to France, she hadn't known how important it was to order a chair on the sunny side of the ship. With the Atlantic breezes, it had been bitter cold on the shady side and she hadn't been able to enjoy the deck at all.

When an acceptable deck chair had been assigned to her, Constance made her way back to her room. Sitting on the bed, she took off her hat, unbuckled her boots, then looked around her cabin.

Ah, a new ocean liner on its maiden voyage . . . It was not the celebration that appealed to her, but this cleanliness. To be the first person to ever use this room, the first person to lie on this bed. The faucet and washbasin, the inviting armchair with its bright upholstery: it was all so pristine! She breathed in the honey-laden smell of beeswax given off by the wood paneling, then rubbed her face along the bedspread. This newness was an especially welcome change after spending a fortnight in a Paris hotel. Supposedly a high-quality establishment, it had been musty and damp, with worn sheets and a medieval toilet down the hall. In such a sickly environment, it was a miracle she hadn't caught pneumonia.

She picked up her purse and brought out two studio photographs printed on thick card stock. The first showed her three young daughters—ages two, four, and six—holding hands and smiling at the camera, large bows in their thick hair. Constance smiled back at them, longing to kiss them, to let her lips linger on their smooth, round cheeks. She wondered how they were, whether they had managed to grow or change in just a few short weeks. The other photograph was of her husband, George, standing in a formal pose, eyeing the camera suspiciously. He had given it to her before they'd married. In it, he was as stiff and serious as he was now, though he looked much younger; he was not yet wearing glasses, his hair was still dark. Now, what was left of it was gray, and his beard was that of a neatly trimmed Father Christmas.

She stood both photographs up on her dresser, her eyes trailing from one to the other. What would she and George have to talk about in twenty years' time, when their girls were gone, married, and raising families of their own? She couldn't bear a middle age filled with pained silences and unnatural politeness; she'd had a lifetime's worth during childhood. Constance flicked her husband's picture over with her finger, letting it fall facedown.

She propped open her new steamer trunk, specially purchased for this trip, and opened its drawers, checking that everything was there, intact. She picked up the fine lace shawl she'd bought for herself in Paris, brought it gently to her cheek, then put it back. She examined the gifts for her girls—porcelain dolls decked out in the finest French fashions—and made sure they were not cracked or chipped. She saw that the present she'd gotten her parents—a bottle of Veuve Clicquot—was also unbroken. Wrapping it back in its tissue paper, Constance chided herself: when would her parents have the occasion to celebrate with fine champagne? She stored it next to the dolls, then closed the trunk, aware that she hadn't bought anything for George. Nothing she'd seen on her trip had seemed a fitting token of affection or reconciliation or even an appropriate souvenir. Perhaps that was because she'd just as soon he forgot her trip entirely.

Leaving her trunk in the corner, she plopped down in the little armchair, stretched, and glanced out the porthole. Funny, how quickly one becomes used to traveling. On her eastbound voyage, her first Atlantic crossing, she had been nervous and, unaccustomed to being alone, was unable to settle down. She supposed that was why she had spent so much time with Gladys Pelham, the fellow traveler assigned to share her cabin.

Gladys, a terribly shy old maid of about forty-five, and her friends, an uneven number of matrons, widows, and spinsters from

St. Louis, were keen to take Constance under their wing. Those gregarious ladies were intrigued why a young woman should be traveling all alone.

Constance found herself telling them quite a bit of her story, in fact, more than she had told any of her friends back in Worcester. It was almost a giddy experience to speak freely, here alone, where no one knew her family. She was able to talk undisturbed, without her father quickly quieting her with a disapproving huff or her husband interrupting her, to take on her story as his own. Back home, she was viewed as quiet, responsible, and perhaps a bit too formal (though hopefully not dull like George!), but on the ship, with these women's rapt attention, she was able to say what she pleased and paint herself to her own liking: selfless, devoted, worldly even.

She explained to the ladies that her father was sending her to Paris to retrieve her younger sister, Faith, who had run away from their aunt while touring Europe the previous year. Constance told them that her sister had been living with a painter and modeling—nude! Now their mother had become gravely ill ("Who wouldn't, with such a daughter?") and her father felt she was the only one capable of convincing Faith to leave that sordid life behind and come back home. And she had left her dear husband and three darling daughters behind to do this small service for her loving parents.

Constance was aware that this select version of the events made her family seem almost normal. She had, of course, left out all of the unpleasant details, including the fact that she was the last person her sister would listen to. Bitter rivals since childhood, Constance thought Faith an insufferable brat and knew that her sister considered her a prude. She had also failed to mention that her mother would probably not care whether her daughter returned to Worcester or not.

High-strung and prone to fits of hysteria, her mother, Lydia Browne, had once been their father's patient. Gerald Watson had met her as a case study and, although he was old enough to know better, he had fallen in love with her fragile beauty and vulnerability. Although it caused quite a scandal within the psychology department at Clark University, his colleagues utterly disapproving, they were married after a short, intense courtship. Constance was born within the year, then Faith, some five years later. Their mother, despite her engulfing dependence on Gerald, was never able to divide her affections to include her children. Lydia neglected them both completely, leaving her girls to servants, aunts, and grandmothers. Their only clear childhood memories of their mother consisted in long, cold silences, frightening bouts of laughter or tears, wide-eyed shaking, and, once or twice, their father restoring her senses with a slap. Constance supposed that their mother's abandonment could have brought the sisters together, made them close, but it had had quite the opposite effect.

At any rate, on the crossing over, Constance's company was widely in demand. When she and the other ladies weren't discussing her "mission," as they called it, they indulged in the ship's many pleasures: shuffleboard games and table tennis, high tea and hands of cribbage. Constance parted ways with them in Southampton—Gladys and her friends were traveling to London—with hugs and tears, and promises to write.

This time around, however, she couldn't stand the idea of socializing. She had even paid the supplement for a private room, ignoring the steward's disapproving look as she was given one of the cabins typically reserved for bachelors. Not only had her mission failed, but she felt like a failure herself. When Constance thought of the poignant conversations (nothing more than gossip, really) she'd had with those ladies from Missouri (who were all rather drab, in retrospect), she felt like a fraud, not to mention boring.

Boring and conventional. After this trip, Constance, who knew herself to be beautiful, had never felt so old and dull. She remembered overhearing Faith laughing at her wedding, saying that if "a rolling stone gathers no moss, what will happen to a Constant

Stone? It'll be covered in thick green bracken before the year's out! A right bog it'll be!" Constance frowned at the memory. She had been married now for eight years, and Faith's prediction had come true.

Not that she would trade her staid life for what her sister had chosen. "Fée," as she now called herself (Constance had assumed it was French for "faith" and couldn't believe it when she found out her sister was going by the name of "fairy") was living in truly appalling conditions: no hot water, no indoor plumbing, no maids or help. Living on the fourth floor of an old building, they had to walk up steep steps, nearly always with bags and parcels, to reach the small, moldy flat, where the best room—the large one with French windows—was given over to Michel's studio.

Although it was small and their possessions were few, the place was not only dirty but in complete disarray. There were piles of books and papers on the floor, two divans covered in rumpled blankets and dirty clothes, footstools, broken lamps, tabletops jammed full of colored glass, small tools, beads, bottles of wine, coffee cups, and pipe tobacco.

Among this squalor, Faith, Michel, and their friends and acquaintances—a steady stream was constantly coming and going, stopping for a minute then staying for hours, with someone inevitably producing some strange bauble they would all gawk over—were bewilderingly content. And so busy!

During the day Faith worked on intricate pieces of enamel jewelry (where had she learned to do that?), odd pieces that Constance would have never worn but recognized as strikingly original, beautiful even. Faith always wore her own work—brooches, hatpins, earrings, pendants—and had even managed to sell some. Then in the afternoon, she'd run over to Montparnasse to model for various artists, who paid her as well as they could. It was not for her looks that they all wanted her to pose, she'd told her sister simply, but because she kept so still (unbelievable, Constance thought, unbelievable). At night, they were always off with friends, drinking and singing in cafés, tasting an invention someone had just cooked, or enthusiastically talking about their ideas and opinions, well into the night.

Constance found it all completely exhausting.

Squinting at the sunlight piercing through the porthole, she felt a dull throbbing behind her eyes. She considered a nap but got to her feet, suddenly restless. She could hear people in the hallway—children's shouts and running footsteps, fragments of foreign conversation—and, in the quiet of her single room, she was pestered by the old-house creaking of the modern ship. Constance quickly rebuckled her boots, grabbed her purse, and left.

Strolling down the cabin-lined corridor, she noticed in passing that some passengers had already put shoes out to be shined for dinner. She hadn't even thought about it! What she'd wear, whom she'd be dining with, what strange French sauces and jellies she might be served . . . She emerged from the hallway toward the stern, near a cluster of small shops.

She lingered at their narrow windows. The tobacconist was showing an older gentleman an extraordinary variety of cigars; the florist was arranging evening corsages for dinner. She passed a drugstore with French perfumes in the window, a souvenir shop boasting tinted postcards and toy steamers, then stopped in front of the stationer's. In the window, there was a display of watercolor sets.

When she and her sister were young, Constance was always considered the one with creative talent. Not only had she written fairy stories and nature poems as a girl, but she'd also enjoyed a certain reputation as an artist among the family. In the summer of '10, when Constance and Faith had been sent to Aunt Pearl's house in Boston, it was she herself who had been praised for her work painting china pieces. Her aunt and cousins had marveled at Constance's steady hand and her ability to copy the pattern to perfection, again and again. Faith, on the other hand, had made such a mess of it, she wasn't allowed to touch the paints for the rest of the summer.

She opened the door, tinkling its small bell, and marched inside the stationer's shop. The attractive woman behind the counter offered her a fetching smile.

"Good morning, madame. How may I help you?"

"Yes, I'd like a watercolor set and a sketchbook, please," said Constance.

"Ah, *aquarelle*! You are a painter?" The shop assistant's eyes widened in admiration as she reached for various paint boxes to show Constance.

"No, no." She shook her head modestly. "Just a dabbler."

Thinking twelve tubes of paint sufficient, Constance selected the smallest box, then chose a thin pad with twenty leaves of thick paper.

"I think this will do nicely." Constance smiled as she paid for her purchase. "I'm planning on designing patterns for porcelain dishes," she added, pleased with herself. If Faith could make pretty things, by all means, she could too.

"It must be wonderful to have time to do such things." The shop assistant sighed as she wrapped up the paint set and paper in thin paper.

Constance wondered whether she was being mocked. Was painting china frivolous, then? A boring pastime for matronly sorts?

"I hope you enjoy your paints!" She handed Constance her purchase, renewing her smile. "And the voyage! *Au revoir!*"

Constance gave her a quick nod and left the shop. She clutched her purchase to her chest and went out on deck; it was crowded with determined promenaders and the sun, glaring off the sea, was exaggeratedly bright. She closed her eyes and pressed a hand to her brow, hoping she wasn't getting a migraine. Completely out of headache powders (she'd needed her entire supply while visiting Faith), she decided to go to the infirmary.

A walk through dark, empty corridors felt soothing compared to strolling on deck. After several wrong turns—the repetition in the décor undid any reference points—she found the doctor's office. Entering the waiting room, she saw, sitting on the chair just opposite the door, the gray-haired maid and the old Scotty from the steward's desk. Next to them sat the withered lady with the smart plum-colored coat she'd noticed on the dock. Elegantly dressed but frail and worn, she looked like the ailing dowager of a defunct royal family. Perhaps this was Mme. Sinclair?

Vera Sinclair was waiting in the antechamber of the infirmary with her small entourage when a lovely woman came through the door, her perfect hourglass figure nearly obscured by last year's fashions. She watched as this young person, having detected her stooped form, at once straightened her back and pulled herself up to her full height, marking the difference between youth and age. An inefficient strategy for keeping Time at bay, Vera mused.

The new arrival sat down on the edge of the chair next to Vera, her posture stiff, and lay her purse and parcel neatly in her lap. They nodded politely to each other.

"Good afternoon," they murmured simultaneously; Amandine and Bibi said nothing.

At that moment, the doctor came out of his office. He wore a white coat over his nautical uniform; his hair was neatly combed, his mustache dapper. He was an attractive man nearing middle age; still slim and youthful-looking, his face was decorated by delicate crow's-feet and graying temples. He smiled at the group of women waiting for him in the antechamber; his eyes lingered in appreciation on the younger one before he waved the older one in.

Vera observed that swift exchange—the doctor's keen approval, the woman's artless blush. She herself had never been impressed by beauty of that sort. Her experience had proved that such a perfect outer covering usually contained a rather vapid interior.

She hoisted herself up and followed the doctor into the infirmary. Once inside, the surgeon closed the door.

"Good afternoon, Doctor. I am Madame Vera Sinclair. My physician in Paris, Dr. Edgar Romains, asked me to contact you." Her French was formal and correct, but betrayed the accent inevitable to those who become expatriates after reaching adulthood, far too late to distinguish sounds with a child's ear.

"I am the doctor Serge Chabron," he said with a bow. "Oh, and Madame Sinclair," he added carelessly, "you can speak English with me if you prefer, if it is easier for you."

A few years back she would have been insulted, found him impertinent. Now she couldn't be bothered.

"Quite," she said, shifting to her mother tongue. "I suppose it is easier."

He took her wrist to feel her pulse, staring at his watch. Vera's eyes moved tiredly around the white, windowless room, pausing on glass cabinets filled with little boxes and unpleasant-looking instruments. She detected the lingering smell of ether in the air. She had known men who breathed ether for pleasure, relishing the oblivion it provided. It was usually a question of loving the wrong person: one too young, already taken, or of the wrong sex.

"Are you feeling ill, madame?" he asked politely, although the question seemed almost rhetorical. Anyone could see her condition was serious.

"I am dying," she said with a sad smile. "And I'm going home, back to New York. Rather like an old elephant, I suppose."

"Dying?" he repeated, taken aback by her directness. "Is this what your doctor in Paris says? What are your symptoms? What is wrong?"

"I believe Dr. Romains's diagnosis is cancer in the breasts. It seems conclusive enough. As for symptoms . . ." She sighed. "Well, at this point everything seems a symptom. When I get back to New York, I plan to call on an old friend, a physician, who has treated such things. But I realize there's not much hope."

"Ah, madame, there is always hope!" His voice was so sincere, so encouraging, it made her sad.

"Well, like I said, my Parisian doctor, always the worrier, thought I should see you once the ship was under way. And now, onboard, I am hoping to enjoy the sun and sea air. What a dire, gray spring we've had in Paris!"

"Indeed, I wish you a pleasant voyage." He smiled. "Sunny skies, salt air, deep sleep, wonderful food . . . A crossing can be so revitalizing. You'll arrive feeling ten years younger!"

"Wouldn't that be lovely! I haven't seen my cousins in years. The little vanity I have left couldn't bear for them to see me looking so weak and thin." Vera held out her hand. "But I will go now. I should like to rest a little before dressing for dinner."

"Of course, Madame Sinclair." He took her hand and pressed it warmly. "And if you need anything during the voyage, anything at all, let me know."

Vera was amused to see the doctor quickly checking himself in the silvered-glass wall mirror before opening the door. As he was ushering her out of his office, already offering the young woman in the antechamber a welcoming smile, a small girl in a dark uniform and white cap popped into the infirmary.

"*Monsieur le docteur?*" she asked, nearly out of breath.

Vera was struck by her appearance; her pale oval face, lovely on its own, was marred by a large brown birthmark. The old woman was instantly reminded of collecting eggs on her uncle's Connecticut farm when she was a child, her delight turning to disgust when she picked up what seemed to be a perfect white egg only to find a brown clump of chicken droppings on its underside. She looked briefly at the attractive woman, who had already risen from her seat for her turn with the doctor, then over at the girl. Letting her cane slide through her hand to regain the floor, she slowly turned to Amandine, who was standing with Bibi, ready to help Vera back to her room.

Julie Vernet had rushed up to fetch the doctor on Mme. Tremblay's direct orders. When she opened the infirmary door, ready to deliver her message, she saw the doctor busily escorting an elderly woman out of the office. He was handing her over to her maid, while a younger woman stood hesitantly to the side.

Julie was intrigued by the older woman, who carried an air of wealth and grandeur. Although her bony fingers, covered in rings, clasped her cane as if holding a scepter, she was gaunt, bent, and clearly unwell. Julie could see that had this woman been a third-class passenger, she wouldn't have passed the health inspection. She'd seen the exams given at the port hotel, doctors and nurses checking for lice, scabies, and contagious diseases, weeding out those ticket holders too weak or too ill to travel. It was plain, even to her, that had this frail, old woman been poor, she would not have been allowed to board the *Paris.*

The other woman, on the contrary, was young and healthy, beautiful even, with shell-pink skin and loads of thick hair half-hidden under a huge hat. Tall, buxom, without a flaw. Life must be easier for women like that, thought Julie.

As the elderly trio slowly made their way out of the office, the ringed woman paused, leaning on her cane; she browsed Julie's face, then nodded pleasantly. Julie bowed slightly, surprised. Unless they were needed—arms for doing chores, legs for running errands—the servant class was usually invisible to the rich. When the door had closed behind them, Julie turned to the younger woman, who was clearly waiting to see the doctor.

"Only a moment, madame," she said, her hand raised in apology. She then addressed the doctor, speaking quickly in French.

"Sir, Madame Tremblay sent me up here to tell you that dozens of passengers in steerage are suffering from *mal de mer.* It's stuffy down there and the ship's roll is so unpleasant. . . . They're nauseous, just miserable! If you could come down when you have time, we'd really appreciate it."

Julie did not mention that she felt terrible herself, a condition that had not been improved by mopping up vomit.

"Usually I have a nurse or two on board to see to such things, but it seems on this crossing I'm on my own. I hope this will all be worked out in New York. I don't know what the deuce has happened here!" He shook his head and sighed. "Of course I'll come. I'll just see to this lady here, then I'll be down there directly."

"*Merci, monsieur,*" Julie said to the doctor, who gave her a fatherly nod, then bobbed a quick curtsy at the pretty woman. "And thank *you,* madame."

She left the infirmary and quickly went back to steerage, afraid Mme. Tremblay would think she was dawdling.

Alone in the office, Dr. Chabron reached out for Constance's elbow and escorted her into the inner chamber.

"Now then, come into my office. Tell me what's troubling you."

Constance, pleased to finally have the doctor's full attention, was grateful to hear his fluent English and was charmed by his slight accent. In Paris, she couldn't communicate with most of Faith's friends and, not wanting to appear dour or disapproving (which oftentimes she was), she'd sat there smiling. She felt like a simpleton, smiling without understanding, and knew that, on occasion, they were talking about her, mocking her. She was relieved to find she would not be reduced to pantomime with this man.

"Hello, Doctor," Constance began shyly, then suddenly felt silly.

"Well, you see, sometimes, I get terrible headaches. When I was on deck earlier, I felt one coming on. And I don't have any powders with me. I was just afraid—" She stopped short, surprised by the fact she was on the verge of tears. "Heavens! I don't know what's wrong with me!"

"There, there," he said, his voice comforting and warm. "These long voyages tend to make people nervous, though I think you'll find it quite pleasurable once you get used to it." He handed her a clean handkerchief with a smile. "Now, tell me, what's your name?"

She paused, dabbing her eyes. She had the sudden impulse to give him her maiden name, but after a moment's hesitation replied dully, "Constance Stone," omitting the "Mrs." and feeling foolish. "And you, sir, what's your name?"

"I am the ship's doctor, Serge Chabron," he replied, then shook his head as she tried to return his handkerchief. "No, please keep it. The voyage isn't over yet!" He smiled again, then got to his feet and began rattling around in a metal drawer. "Headaches, you say?"

Constance watched him flick through a row of small white boxes, embarrassed at the realization the pain was now completely gone.

"Here," he said, and handed her two thin boxes. "Some aspirin for the headaches, as well as some sleeping powders. If you can't relax tonight, take one envelope with water before going to bed. Now, please allow me to walk you back to your cabin. I'm afraid I need to see to some passengers down in steerage."

Dr. Chabron locked the door to the infirmary, offered Constance his arm, then set a leisurely pace down to the second-class cabins.

"Tell me, then, are you from New York?" he inquired.

"No, I live in Massachusetts. I went to Paris to escort my sister home. She's been living there a year now."

"Ah, your sister lives in Paris? A beautiful place, don't you agree?"

"Yes, of course," she said, though there was a lack of enthusiasm in her voice. Having felt so out of place there, she had been nearly immune to its charms. "Are you from Paris as well?"

"No, I'm from Rennes. But, to tell you the truth, after fifteen years working aboard ships, I feel more at home when I'm at sea. I even spent the war on an ocean liner, when the *France* was turned into a hospital ship. An odd sight it was," he recalled, creasing his brow, "men covered in bandages—some terribly burnt or missing limbs—sitting on elegant settees, surrounded by luxury." As Constance murmured in commiseration, he quickly turned back to her, as if suddenly remembering to be charming. "Perhaps," he said, resuming his jovial tone, "my land is simply the sea."

Walking down the corridor, with its flowered carpet and teardrop crystal lamps, Constance couldn't picture it filled with wounded soldiers.

When they reached the deck, Dr. Chabron pulled out a cigarette case. He offered one to Constance, which she declined, then lit one for himself. Pausing at the rails, he blew a smoke ring, then turned back to Constance.

"Do you travel often, miss?"

"Not at all! In fact, I've spent almost my whole life in the same town," Constance said. "And your life here at sea . . . I can't imagine! Never waking up in the same place, always raising the anchor and moving on to a different port."

"It can be exciting"—Dr. Chabron smiled—"or quite dull. It depends on the weather, the crew, the passengers . . . But I always have several good novels in my cabin, just in case. *They* can always provide me with good company."

"I have three or four in my bag as well," she said with a smile. "What kind of books do you like best?"

"I read all kinds of things," he said, opening the door to the cabins to let her pass through, "but at the moment, I'm reading a collection of Sherlock Holmes stories."

"Really?" she cried, her smile widening into a grin. "Sherlock Holmes! Oh, I love detective stories!"

"You don't say?" He laughed. "Murder, drugs, beggars, poisons . . . Not the sort of thing all ladies go for."

"Oh, come now," she said, joining his laughter. "Who can resist a good mystery? Especially when, at the end, it can all be logically explained."

"My, my," he said, shaking his head in mock amazement. "A woman who likes grimy detective tales *and* logic!"

They had arrived at her cabin and she stopped.

"Thank you for escorting me back to my room," she said, putting out her hand to give his a light shake. "It's been a pleasure."

"The pleasure has been all mine." Dr. Chabron took her hand with a slight bow. "I always enjoy meeting fellow admirers of Mr. Holmes. Well, perhaps I will have the occasion of seeing you and your sister later on during the voyage, Miss Stone?"

She opened her mouth to correct his mistake, to inform him that she was, in fact, a missus. But, instead, she decided to let it go. After two weeks as Faith's frightfully dull, older, married sister, she wanted a few days all to herself, to be young again. To not be Mrs. anything.

"Oh," she replied simply, "my sister didn't care to join me."

"Well," he drawled with a keen smile, "it is she who will miss what promises to be an excellent crossing. Now then"—his voice resumed its courteous, professional tone—"perhaps you should get some rest. And, please, if you have any more headaches, or problems of any kind, come back to see me. I'm afraid, Miss Stone, I must now take my leave and see how they're faring down in steerage. *Au revoir!*"

Constance stood outside her door, watching Dr. Chabron make his way down the hall. What a pleasant man! Gazing at his tall frame and quick step, she thought it frustrating—unfair even—that a woman's history could be told in a single word: missus. A man's honorifics—Doctor, Captain, or even Mister—revealed absolutely nothing about his private life. But really, what did it matter if the ship's doctor called her Miss or Missus? Surely it was just a compliment, a small commentary on her youthful appearance.

She unlocked her room and, back inside, pulled a mystery novel out of her bag with a smile.

On the fringe of a large group of unhappy third-class travelers, Julie listened hopefully to the doctor in the common area. He greeted the roomful of patients with a hearty voice, welcoming them on board.

"I understand you are feeling seasick," Dr. Chabron continued. "Well, that's normal for a first voyage and I'm sure you will all get your sea legs soon."

There was a general groan of incredulity, followed by expectant silence.

"Now, my advice to you is to lie on your beds and close your eyes. This will restore your sense of balance and calm your nerves." He looked around the room at the seasick voyagers, his eyes traveling from face to face. "Alternatively," he suggested, "you could spend time on deck. Remember, it's the center of the ship where you feel the ship's roll the least. And keep your eyes on the horizon. It has a curative effect that is most beneficial."

"But, Doctor, sir, is there no medication we can take?" inquired an older man in the front, nearly begging. "Something to put our stomachs to rights?"

"No, I'm afraid not." Dr. Chabron shook his head with an empathetic frown. "Your body must get used to the motion. But don't fret; I'm sure you'll all feel fine soon."

Dr. Chabron wished his patients good luck, then quickly left them below to return to the patients on the top decks. With audible sighs, the green-faced passengers dutifully began drifting off to their cabins, surrendering themselves to their bunks, or climbing the stairs to the mooring deck, in search of fresh air and the horizon line.

Discouraged, Julie remained motionless on the side of the room. The doctor's recommendation of resting or going up on deck was unavailable to her. Like the other women working in the steerage dining room that evening, she was expected to begin serving dinner—in various shifts, to over eight hundred passengers—in an hour.

Julie suddenly heard brisk footsteps coming from the dormitory and Simone Durat, a girl about her age, entered the room. She was from Harfleur, a town about ten kilometers from Le Havre, and they had attended the same training course. Her hair was thin and mousy, her skin blemished, and her smile was drawn tight to hide missing teeth. Accordingly, she had been assigned to work in steerage.

Relieved to see someone she recognized, Julie offered her a shy wave. As plain as Simone was, she was talkative and outgoing and, during the course, she was usually found holding court in the center of a group of girls.

"Hello there," Simone said, joining Julie at the wall. "Aren't you from Le Havre? Didn't we do our training together?"

"That's right. I'm Julie Vernet," she said, returning Simone's four kisses. "You're Simone, aren't you? Is this your first assignment too?"

"Yes! Don't you love it? Though, I must admit, I was disappointed when they told me I'd be working down here. I wanted to hobnob with the rich and famous in first class!" Her lips stretched into a closemouthed grin. "And you? What do you think?"

"Well, to tell you the truth, I'm having a hard time so far," Julie answered. "I've never been on a ship before and I feel just awful. I keep having to rush off to the toilets, but I'm trying to hide it from Madame Tremblay. What a nightmare! And pretty soon we'll be serving dinner—garlic soup and rabbit? God, I hope the passengers can keep it down!"

"You're not kidding! I've cleaned up enough throw-up for one day," she said, rolling her eyes, then remembered Julie too was unwell. "Oh, I'm sorry to hear you're feeling bad."

"And you? What's your secret?" Julie asked, slightly hopeful.

"No secret. I guess it never even occurred to me that my life here wouldn't be perfect," she said with a shrug, then glanced down at her watch. "Already half past four? It's time to start setting up the dining room."

Julie groaned as they set off down the metal corridor. There, they ran into four other girls heading toward the steerage kitchens and they fell into step. Simone, who had already met them, began talking enthusiastically to everyone at once.

"Have you been in the kitchens yet?" Simone asked, her eyes wide with excitement. "Have you ever seen so much food in your life? And the portions served up—even here in third class! When I think of all the rationing during the war . . . The seagulls following this ship eat better than we did!"

The other girls nodded and laughed; Julie tried to smile despite her nausea. She had overheard the purser and cooks discussing the astonishing quantities of food needed for the five-day voyage: twenty-five tons of beef, ten tons of fish, five tons of bacon and ham, eighty thousand eggs . . . The higher up on the ship, the more food the passengers consumed. Since the launch that morning, she herself had only been able to eat some dry toast. How people were tempted into gluttony aboard a moving vessel was beyond her.

The girls gathered the white tablecloths from the linen closet, covered the long tables, then sat down to begin their premeal task of folding napkins. Julie listened to the chatter around her—Simone leading discussions on the amenities in first class, the wonders of New York, the best-looking crew members—and, although she said very little, she was happy to be a part of the group. Wishing she felt better, Julie picked up a napkin and twisted it into kinks and knots: an echo of her insides.

Vera could see the soft cliffs of the Isle of Wight out her cabin window; the ship was cruising toward the Solent and the port town of Southampton. There they would dock for an hour, collect passengers and mail, then set out for America in earnest. She put on her coat and grabbed her cane.

"Bibi," she murmured, attaching the leash to the dog's collar, "let's go out and take a last look at old Albion."

On deck Vera looped the leash around the rail, though the dog had already made herself comfortable at her feet, and reached into her pockets for her gloves. It was decidedly chilly out now. Looking at the hills and sea ledges of the British island—was that village over there Bembridge or Ryde?—she couldn't help but think of Charles.

The last time she'd been on an ocean liner, he'd been with her; off on an American adventure, they'd crossed the Atlantic on the *France.* Side by side, they had watched the channel isle go by, perhaps at this very point on the deck. He told her about the childhood holidays he and his family had spent on the Isle of Wight after Queen Victoria had made it so fashionable. That evening, nearly a decade ago, as they passed the quaint villages tucked into bays, they'd discussed the possibility of renting a cottage there one summer. Vera sighed. So many things left undone.

The ship was now maneuvering toward the mainland, up to port. She chuckled to herself, remembering the silly jokes they'd made about the Southampton rivers: the Test and the Itchen. How she wished Charles were with her now!

Vera pulled up her collar with a frown, wondering how it had come to this. This entire decision of returning to America had been hastily made one rainy Parisian afternoon, while playing a game of chance. Really, she had only wanted to shake Charles up a bit, to remind him that she would not be around forever. She'd felt his absence keenly this past year and wanted their friendship to retrieve its former glory, for him to revel in her company like he had before the cancer.

Just as Vera had known those who fed off the unwell—people who enjoyed wielding power over the weak or those who relished the protagonism of the sickbed martyr—Charles was on the opposite end of this spectrum. He abhorred illness. He couldn't bear Vera's sunken face, her thin frame; he grieved to see her constant fatigue, her forgetfulness. When they were together these days, he could no longer pretend they were still in their prime. She had become a grim reminder of mortality—his own as well.

Although she couldn't stand the way he'd been looking at her (or, rather, how he avoided meeting her eye) since she'd become ill, she'd missed his provocative conversation, his generous laugh. Vera had not been alone this last year; every day friends had visited and she'd been invited to dozens of soirées. But those relationships could not compare to the camaraderie she'd always had with Charles.

Looking out on the lights of Southampton, Vera shook her head softly. Why in the world was she on this boat? She couldn't imagine enjoying her slack family ties and the brittle society of Manhattan. Paris was her real home. Was she really just trying to teach Charles a lesson? How strangely one behaves in the face of Death!

Night had fallen abruptly and it was time to dress for dinner. She made a little clicking noise to rouse Bibi, then slowly made her way back to her cabin, thinking herself a perfect fool.

On her eastern voyage across the Atlantic, Constance had discovered that in the absence of social obligations or family duties, errands or chores, one was forced into a state of utter leisure. Besides relaxing on deck chairs, reading, dancing, and sports, on an ocean liner, adults found themselves playing parlor games and participating in silly contests. Without a doubt, however, the key events on board were meals: luncheons, teas, cocktails, snacks, and dinners. The French Line was renowned for its delicious food, and passengers, not to be outdone by the wonders on their plates, dressed up to eat, donning lace, velvet, flowers, and jewels.

Since she was traveling alone, Constance had not reserved a table for the voyage but had left her evening diversion, her dining companions, to chance. In her lavender satin, she slowly entered the large room, which was already filled with people. Feeling self-conscious, she was ushered to a table toward the back; not the most prestigious place on the seating chart, she noted. Only one seat was empty; everyone else had arrived.

She smiled around the table, which was made up mostly of men, and introduced herself. In turn, she met the others: two business partners from Holland with excellent English but unpronounceable names; a British military officer, Captain Fielding, a quarter of his face still pink and shiny from its reconstruction; and the Thomases, a married couple from Philadelphia.

Mrs. Thomas, though probably only a half dozen years older than Constance, had already resigned herself to middle age; stout and serious, even here in the dining room of a luxury steamer, she was wearing a brown woolen suit. Constance smiled at Mrs. Thomas, her only female companion at the table, but received a rather cold nod in return. She was obviously not delighted to be sharing this group of male diners with such a young and attractive woman, particularly one who was traveling alone. Although she was a graying matron, Mrs. Thomas still maintained the quiet pout of a spoiled child.

"Well, Mrs. Stone, what brings *you* on board the *Paris*?" asked Captain Fielding. Obviously, before she'd arrived, this question and its complaisant answers had already made their way around the table.

"I've been visiting relatives in France," she replied, not wanting to attract any attention. "I'm returning home."

"France, you say?" repeated Captain Fielding. "How did you like eating frogs? And snails?" He made a face.

"I'm afraid I didn't try them," she answered, smiling politely.

"Did you just stay in France?" asked Mrs. Thomas, her brows knit in an exaggerated gesture of surprise. "You went all the way to Europe, but didn't travel farther afield?"

"No, I was mostly in Paris."

"What a shame to cross the Atlantic and not visit Venice!" Mr. Thomas exclaimed.

"Although it is my hometown, I can objectively say that Amsterdam is every bit as charming," said one of the Dutchmen. "I daresay we have even more bridges and canals."

"Hang the cities! The most beautiful place in Europe is the Alps," argued Captain Fielding.

A debate ensued of all the best places to go on the Continent, and Constance had visited none of them. Again, she sat in silence with a gracious smile on her face, as she had been doing for the previous two weeks.

She had been prepared for questions about her trip alone, her family, her life, and this time around, she was determined not to discuss any of it. She had invented a tale about visiting an aunt, her Parisian husband, and their houseful of children, her fictitious cousins. She was even considering the idea of passing herself off as a widow. But these dining companions were not curious about her in the least. Constance felt greatly relieved and mildly snubbed.

"They might call this fine dining," said Mr. Thomas with a chuckle, when the fish course arrived, "but back home we cut off the head and tail before bringing it to the table!"

Constance was surprised at his willingness to expose his provincial background. She preferred her fish filleted as well, but would have never voiced this aloud.

"Do you gentlemen fish in Europe?" Mr. Thomas inquired, absently straightening his hairpiece.

The men went on to have a lively discussion of that sport, including a lengthy conjecture about the types of rods and reels one would need to fish directly off an ocean liner and exactly how long the line would have to be.

"I'd say a hundred yards long . . . at least!" Captain Fielding guessed. "It would be like trying to fish off a ten-story building. And if you caught anything worth saving, what a struggle it would be to haul it up!"

Since, again, she knew nothing about the subject at hand, she let her eyes wander around the large paneled room. A father in tweed was lecturing his adolescent son, who was pointedly ignoring him; a velveteen mother was wiping purée off her toddler's chin. Constance wondered what the ambience would be like in first class. Surrounded by beauty, would the conversation be better crafted as well? And steerage? Would the working-class chatter be raucous and risqué? She imagined that in either case, dinnertime would have to be more interesting than it was at the table where she sat.

The slow passage through British coastal waters and the stopover at Southampton had calmed the nerves and settled the stomachs of most of the steerage residents. Spirits were high at dinner—voices raised with frequent outbreaks of laughter—and nearly all the plates were so carefully swabbed with bread, the maids wondered whether they'd been used at all. Julie was feeling better, less nauseated and more energetic, and wasn't too disappointed when Mme. Tremblay informed them that they'd be serving an extra dinner shift that evening to the Brits and Irishmen who'd boarded at Southampton.

Many of the new arrivals to steerage, as well as the ones who had boarded at Le Havre that morning, were planning on emigrating to the United States. There had been rumors in the press about the American government hardening its immigration laws, and passages were quickly being booked before any such reforms could take effect. Julie went down the long table, refilling the newcomers' glasses and bread baskets (how hungry they all were!) and listening to their excited banter.

"New York here we come!" toasted a group of young Irishmen with the house red.

"To fast cars and faster women!" cried one lad, who hadn't bothered to take off his wooly cap for dinner.

"My uncle Ned tells me there's a lot of construction work on skyscrapers," said a pale, freckled-faced boy. "That's what I'm going to do."

"What?" exclaimed a redhead. "Prancing around up there on those steel beams? One hundred, two hundred meters off the ground? Imagine if you fell!"

"Well, you'd have time to say three Hail Marys and an Our Father on the way down!" laughed the boy in the cap.

"I'm going to try and get work on the waterfront," said the redhead. "Doing the same job we did back in Liverpool, but earning double—that's the important thing!"

"When we're *not* working is the important thing!" said the boy in the cap. "In New York, there's jazz clubs and boxing, horse races, and—"

"*And* no drink!" said the redhead with a frown.

"Oh, Uncle Ned says you can find drink!" said the pale boy. "In fact, he says you can find whatever you want!"

"Hey, miss!" the redhead called to Julie. "More wine over here!"

As Julie poured another round, she thought about New York.

Almost all the passengers in steerage were impatient to get there, to begin their new lives. Looking forward to seeing its stylish skyline from the ship, she hoped the crew would be given a few days to explore, before turning around and crossing the Atlantic again.

When the last of the Southampton arrivals finally left the dining area and drifted out into the common room, the mooring deck, or their cabins—four bunks to a room—the steerage help cleared the tables, then wiped them down. When the dining room was clean, Julie's first day had come to an end.

She went to the dormitory and took off her uniform. Julie brought it to her face and sniffed; her clothes had taken on the smell of stale sweat, hearty foods, ammonia, vomit, and the stench of the passengers themselves. Well, that about summarized her new job.

Putting on her bathrobe, she looked around the room. Although the women who worked in the upper classes—the hatcheck girls, nannies, cigarette girls, and so on—would still be up for hours, most of the steerage workers and laundresses were already in bed.

After moving her mother's lacework, carefully placing it under the pillow, Julie crawled into her bunk, feeling the engine's vibration. Over its drone, she could just hear the sounds of the women around her, the breathing and snores, the shifting and nestling, the odd murmur. Simone, in the bunk above hers, was making no noise at all, sleeping in absolute silence. Julie closed her eyes and tried to cool her neck with her clammy hands. The queasiness had returned when the *Paris* had regained the high seas; she was eager to recover her balance, to feel absolutely normal.

Suddenly, she was startled by something moving at the foot of her bed. She looked down, straining to see in the dim light, and discovered the shine of two little eyes: a mouse. There had been plenty of mice around her parents' house on the waterfront and, against her mother's wishes, she'd even tried to domesticate a few. She'd line up bits of stale bread for them to eat, trying to coax them into a box, to make them into pets. Julie smiled at this one, wiggling her fingers to see whether it would come to her.

Watching it sitting on its haunches, moving its delicate hands, she was reminded of one of the letters her brother Loïc had sent from the front outside of Reims where he was stationed for nearly six months. He was the only one of her four brothers who had regularly written from the trenches and Julie was always fascinated to read about his life there: the inexplicable coziness of the dugout; the daisies, poppies, and cornflowers that grew wild in No Man's Land; what falling asleep in wet boots does to one's feet.

Loïc once wrote about how, after weeks of rain, the trenches became so slippery that frogs and field mice fell in and couldn't get out. Hundreds of them were trapped in those deep muddy ditches and, at night, the men couldn't help walking on them, crushing them in their heavy boots. Julie felt her nose twitch and her throat contract—the early warning signs of tears—and slowly breathed out, refusing to cry her first night in the women's dormitory.

"Are you trapped in here, little one?" she asked the mouse in an unsteady whisper. It jumped off the bunk, zigzagged across the floor, and scurried away.

Julie thought that she too would get up and take a walk. Despite the number of tedious chores she'd performed throughout the day, she wasn't tired. All day she had longed to be on deck, in the sun, breathing fresh air. She leaned onto her elbow and looked toward Mme. Tremblay's bunk on the other side of the room. A slight form lay unmoving under a mass of blankets. Silently, Julie got out of her bed and, in the narrow floor space between the bunks, put on her civilian dress and jacket. She carried her shoes out of the dormitory, slid them on in the corridor, then began the climb upward. During the ascent, the air cooled and the noise of the engines became fainter.

On deck, she looked for the exact middle of the ship, where it was reputed to move the least. She crept silently past couples kissing in the shadows and a few moonstruck strollers, and edged over to the rail. Wrapped in night air, she stood looking out, the ships' lights behind her. She caught faint strands from the orchestra playing in the first-class ballroom, and the musical hum, with its warbles and trills, of the impeccably dressed dancers and late-night diners, those passengers who undoubtedly found it difficult to remember they were at sea.

After only a minute or two—her face cocked to the sky, eyes shut, relishing the cool breeze—she felt better. Her mouth was no longer producing so much saliva, the tingling behind her ears had stopped. Slowly, she opened her eyes and looked up at the stars. From where she stood, in the middle of the ship, in the middle of the sea, they were infinite. From her kitchen windows in Le Havre, this ship had seemed vast beyond measure, but here, nestled between the enormity of the black ocean and the night sky, it was small, vulnerable even.

Looking up at the Milky Way, she thought again of Loïc. Her older brothers, Jean François, Émile, and Didier, had been between eight and twelve years older than them. After they'd become working men, those three had sometimes seemed more like boarders than brothers, always coming and going, usually present at meals, occasionally playful but often tired, aloof, uninterested in children's antics. Loïc, on the other hand, was almost her twin. As they were separated by only thirteen months, their parents and brothers had always referred to them collectively as "*les petits.*" Almost never called by their names, or individually for that matter, they were scolded, given orders, and embraced as one.

When her three older brothers enlisted in the Armée de Terre in 1914, they had their portrait made in their new uniforms, a photograph that later became thin from caresses and mottled with tears. Standing together with Émile, the tallest, in the center, they all sported standard-issue mustaches and new kepis, jauntily perched on their heads. Although the photograph was sepia colored, Julie could still see the bright crimson trousers emerging from tailored blue coats. Having only before seen them wearing grimy coveralls for working or cheap suits for going out, she thought her brothers had never looked so handsome, so distinguished.

Hanging out the windows of the train, each one off to his own regiment, they brandished their lances and grinned with excitement as the crowd shouted, "To Berlin!" The townsfolk already looked at them as heroes. On the platform, their parents beamed with pride.

Julie lost a part of herself each time a big brother died at the front. At the fishmonger's or the bakery, she would find herself reliving her precious childhood memories—the storytelling, the horsey rides, the amateur magic tricks—and silently begin to cry, ignoring the shopkeepers' pitying looks. While Julie dissolved into grief, her parents, so absorbed in their own, distanced themselves from their youngest, retreating further with each official letter they received. Julie became nearly invisible to them as they turned quiet and cold, the hollowed shells of their prewar selves. Then Loïc, when he turned seventeen, announced that he was going to war as well.

"Hallo! Julie Vernet!"

Julie swung around, alarmed, wondering who could be calling her, who knew her name. Would she be reprimanded for being out on deck at night? Was she allowed to wear normal clothes on board? A big man walked out of the shadows and, as he walked toward her, she recognized him as the Russian she'd met before the ship quit port, the man whose hat she'd caught.

"It's Nikolai, isn't it?" she said, laughing in relief. "You scared me for a minute. I thought I might be in trouble for being up on decks."

"Don't worry about trouble with me around," he said with a wink.

He stood next to her and looked up at the stars, bright in the chill of a cloudless sky. Beside him, she felt like a small child. Alongside her tiny hands, his massive fingers tapped carelessly on the rails, a ragtime piano. Above his wrist she saw a blue tattoo of four or five intercrossed lines. She tried to make it out; was it a secret symbol, a tool, an upside-down cross? She had the fleeting notion that it must have had something to do with the war, that here was another former soldier who had fought and lived.

Often, Julie found herself resenting men who had survived the war. She knew it was irrational, but she couldn't help but wonder why they had been spared while her brothers had not. Tonight, however, she was grateful that the friendly man at her side was a survivor. Immediately feeling silly, she looked away from Nikolai's wrist and up to the sky.

"Ah, I love coming up on deck at night. It's so calm and beautiful." Nikolai turned to her. Although he wasn't touching her, he was so close, she could feel his body heat in the cool night air. "And I'm so glad you're out. I was hoping I'd run into you again."

"Oh, well, here I am," she said, looking down with a shy smile. She paused a moment, struggling to find something to say. "Tell me, then, how was it down in the engine room today?"

"Hot!" He laughed. "And noisy! And you, how was your first day on duty?"

"Not too good, I'm afraid," she sighed. "I've been seasick all day."

She regretted it as soon as she'd said it. What an unappealing image! She certainly didn't want him to picture her green-faced and hovering over the toilet. Thankfully, however, he looked genuinely concerned.

"Oh no," he uttered. "I'm sorry to hear that. Is this your first time out?"

"Yes, the *Paris* and I are both on our maiden voyage." She smiled, daring to look him in the eyes. He smiled down at her from his great height, then leaned his elbows on the rails so that their arms touched.

"Listen, I have some ginger tea in my kit that I make when the seas get rough," he said, lowering his voice and making their conversation intimate. "It really helps. I'd be happy to give you some."

"Thank you," she said. "That would be lovely! I've been hoping for a miracle cure."

"You must not be used to the sea at all. Where are you from? Alsace? Auvergne?"

"Far from it! In fact, you were in my hometown this morning. I'm from Le Havre. And you?" she asked, sneaking her fingers up to comb her hair. "Where are you from, Nikolai?"

"St. Petersburg. Petrograd, they call it now. But my family left after the revolution in 1917. We eventually made it to Paris."

"It must have been very difficult, leaving Russia during the war," Julie said quietly.

They stood in silence for a few moments, looking out on the water, his arm still radiating warmth next to hers. Julie couldn't help but wonder what he was thinking. Did he find her attractive? Did her birthmark not bother him? She was rather glad he was standing to her left.

"Ah, you can hear the music," Nikolai said, propelling her from her thoughts; indeed, the orchestra was playing a waltz in the ballroom. "In Russia, there was always music. We're always singing . . . in the poorhouse, in prisons, even at war!" He smiled sadly, then turned to look into her eyes. "You have a musical beauty, you know," he said in a low voice. "You are so small, so delicate, yet you have captivated me, like a little tune that won't stop playing in my mind."

No one had ever paid Julie such a compliment. She wondered whether he was joking (or had he been drinking?), but he seemed perfectly sincere. She had never had a suitor before and didn't know what to say, how to act.

"You must have many admirers in Le Havre," Nikolai added, then reached out and put his hand on hers, folding both her hands in his one.

"N-n-no," she stuttered, feeling the color rise to her cheeks. "I wouldn't say that."

His warmth made her body sway in toward him. Nervous and embarrassed, she looked down and caught a glimpse of the blue tattoo. He bent down and whispered in her ear.

"May I kiss you, Julie?" His voice was soft, nearly liquid. "Please?"

She could feel him breathing in her hair and knew this was all going too fast.

"I have to leave," she mumbled, untangling her hands from his. "The head housekeeper will be looking for me. She'll be angry. Really, I must go."

"Oh, come on, Julie," he coaxed, catching a strand of her hair. "Stay a little longer."

"Good night, Nikolai!"

She had already started walking down the deck. She was afraid he might follow her—part of her wanted him to—but he stayed at the rails.

"See you tomorrow, my little Julie!" he called with a confident smile.

Her heart pounding, she began to walk faster and faster—as if she could escape her own excitement—until she was running. She flew along the corridors and spun down flights of stairs. She ran back to steerage, like a little mouse scampering back to its hole.

Outside the dormitory, she stood panting, trying to catch her breath. She slipped off her shoes, still wondering at what had happened. Nikolai wanted to kiss her! She thought of his ruggedly handsome face smiling at her, his lyrical voice whispering compliments, and stood for a moment in the corridor, fingering her birthmark in disbelief. Finally, Julie ducked back into the room, now nearly full of sleeping women, and silently changed back into her pajamas. Under the momentarily cool sheet, she shivered, remembering the warmth of his skin and imagining the feel of his lips. Recalling his last words—that he would see her tomorrow!—Julie stared up at Simone's dark bunk and grinned.

DAY TWO

The early-morning air was chilly, but Vera was glad to be in the sun. She was cocooned in her deck chair, snug inside the red steamer rug with Bibi curled up on her feet. Most first-class passengers preferred the nights on board the ship: playing long hands of bezique or euchre, roosting in wingback chairs sharing secrets with strangers, dancing the tango with one while exchanging glances with another . . . But Vera—too impatient, too tired, too old for such things—now opted for mornings.

In fact, even dressing for dinner and sitting to table with five or six unknown companions held no intrigue for her anymore. And she, who had always had a great taste for fine French wines and haute cuisine, could not work up much of an appetite, even for the sumptuous meals served in a French ocean liner's first-class dining room: velvety lobster bisque with just a hint of cognac, prime sirloin cooked rare, peach melba topped with fresh raspberry sauce and vanilla ice cream . . . The infinite courses and choices were now more of a chore than a pleasure. Last night Vera had picked at her food, barely aware of the conversation of her dining companions, which faded into the distant buzzing of the engines. She'd realized, quite suddenly, how ancient and dull she must have appeared to them and, after dessert, quickly excused herself to lie down.

However, just as she could no longer truly enjoy eating, the delights of sleep now escaped her as well. In the past, Vera had frequently lingered in bed, lolling in quilts and eiderdown until almost lunchtime. But these days, her slumber was as light and as brief as her appetite. In the last few years she had lost all her Epicurean skills, forced into the austerity of a nun.

She picked up her carpetbag from next to the deck chair and pulled out her most recent journal, one of those written numerically. She nestled it on top of the warm blanket, then took out her fountain pen, toying with the idea of adding a new entry. After watching the Isle of Wight drift by yesterday evening, she'd been mulling over all the different transatlantic voyages she'd made in her life: from the first time she'd crossed, on a rickety paddleboat at the age of fifteen, off on her grand tour of Europe, to her honeymoon with Warren, to her permanent move to France, right on up to this last, uneventful voyage on the *Paris.* Today, she was contemplating adding the number 10 to her memoirs: Ten Crossings.

She posed her pen on a fresh page and wrote "X Crossings," opting for the Roman numeral. Delighted with the boldness of the *X*, she began to elaborate on it, transforming the title into a treasure map. She drew a small schooner on the side from which a looping trail led, dot by dot, to the dramatic *X* in the center. "Crossings," she mused, was an evocative word in itself.

The title completed, she stared at the page, shaking her head in frustration. She could no longer control her hand; it was now so unsteady that straight lines had been rendered impossible. This looked, indeed, like the work of an unschooled, half-drunk pirate. How very *authentic*, then. Aging was such a loathsome business.

She let out a large sigh, then put down her pen. No, she would not write anything today. In fact, she'd been unable to add anything new to her journals for the last couple of years. Whenever she picked up one of the leather-bound books—which was more and more often—she found herself rereading the old entries instead. At times, she saw herself as a character of fiction, a heroine whose harrowing plights could move her to tears or whose youthful antics could make her laugh; at others, she felt like a time traveler, nostalgically reliving her experiences. Occasionally, she could even cajole herself into being surprised by their endings. She had ceased to be the writer of these memoirs, and instead had become their most avid reader.

Vera began thumbing through the journal, trying to decide which entry to read, when she suddenly remembered the gift Charles had given her. She put the journal aside and fished out the book of poems from the carpetbag. Upon opening it, she saw a dedication, written in his firm, architectonic hand: "To my love of this life. Until we meet on the other side. Yours, Charles." She stared down at those words, tears welling in her eyes. He was obviously not referring to oceans here. So, Charles had finally been able to acknowledge the fact she was dying. Somehow, that made it even more real. Vera wiped her eyes with her dry hands, pondering a new life without him.

With a deep breath, she shut her eyes, imagining a typical day in Paris, her life before boarding the *Paris*. She imagined waking in her high-ceilinged apartment, then taking Bibi on a morning stroll through the Jardin du Luxembourg. They would pass the Guignol puppet theater, where a group of children were laughing at the French Punch, up to his old tricks. On the way to meet Charles at an outdoor café, she would buy a baguette, bite off the tip, then send the crumbs flying toward a flock of fat pigeons. He would be waiting for her, impatient as always, and quickly stand as she approached, nearly upsetting the off-balance table. She could see every detail. She could almost smell the bread.

Vera closed the book sadly, incapable of reading poetry. Reaching down to pet Bibi's side, to stroke her ears, she again deemed this voyage rash, ill planned. To forget the present, she chose to immerse herself in better times; she gathered up the journal again, leafing through the pages to get off this ship. Vera would be arm in arm with Charles once more.

TURNING 50

A week before I was to turn fifty, one late breakfast, whilst spreading a thick layer of butter on a thin slice of bread, I suddenly decided what to do to mark the occasion: I would treat myself to one of Paul Poiret's marvelous gowns. Charles would want to accompany me of course. He always enjoyed an outing to the design houses of the Faubourg Saint-Honoré, elegant palaces of haute couture where fashionable women were fitted and draped (and, on occasion, seduced by young dandies as well). But I also thought it wise to invite my friend Mme. Pauline Ravignan, who was known for her exquisite taste. Charles, I knew, could have very well convinced me to buy harem pantaloons or a hobble skirt.

On the day, we three took a cab to the shop, where M. Poiret, donned in striped trousers and a canary yellow jacket, paid us the honor of greeting us at the door. This Man of the Cloth welcomed us graciously, leading us past statues and flower arrangements to an all-white sitting room where we would be shown various models.

Here, women came out in a brilliant array of colors (no lilac or pink chez Poiret!) in his day-wear collection of svelte tunics and kimono coats, in evening gowns inspired by the Arabian Nights, and in long robes with loose folds, like the Greek statues in the Louvre. We were the captivated audience of a fabulous parade, a walking ballet, the Beaux Arts Ball! So sensual and exciting it was.

With Pauline's help, I chose an extraordinary red gown covered in black and silver beadwork. As we were making plans to come back for alterations, I mentioned to Paul Poiret that his ball gown was my birthday present to myself. He was delighted to hear that it was my birthday and, clapping his hands like a boy, exclaimed that I should celebrate by having my fortune told.

"Oh, please, monsieur!" I raised my eyebrows in disbelief. "Don't tell me you keep a palm reader here on staff?"

"Not here, but yes, I know a man who is a true visionary. I ask his advice on all things!" He stroked his pointed beard with a ringed hand, looking like a magician himself. "Would you like to take a trip up to Montmartre and meet him? I think you will find it amusing even if you don't believe what he tells you."

Charles stepped in with a sly grin to accept this invitation, affirming that, indeed, we would not miss it!

After Poiret had swaddled my and Pauline's heads in linen scarves and put on driving gloves and goggles, the four of us climbed into his open automobile, a bright red Cottereau Phaeton with gold accessories, and took off toward the Butte. As we drove under the affable May sun, he told us more about the man we were about to meet.

"He's a poet by the name of Max Jacob," he said, shouting over the roar of the engine. "Lives in dastardly conditions up on the hill with all of his artist friends, but he's a mystic all right. What insight the man has given me over the years!"

Montmartre never seemed like part of Paris to me, but rather a quaint village in the country. We breezed past the windmills and wooden houses, bumped along the unpaved streets dotted with gas lamps, till M. Poiret finally stopped the shiny crimson automobile. Truly, Captain Nemo's submarine would have been no more conspicuous on that lane! He led us through a courtyard to a small Shed, squeezed betwixt two buildings of a more reputable size. The rich designer was pleased with our open-mouthed surprise as he dramatically whispered that—voilà!—we had arrived to the home of the mystic.

He tapped on the door with his walking stick. A pale man, wearing a monocle and a well-tailored, though rather tattered, frock coat, ushered us into his home with an elaborate sweep of his top hat, exposing a bald head. Refraining from looking us in the eye, he politely requested we wait in the corner a few minutes as he was currently occupied with another client.

We certainly needed this time to adjust our eyes and noses to this novel ambience, this dizzying gloom. In marked contrast to the delightful spring morning outdoors, the air inside was heavy with a swirling combination of tobacco, incense, ether, and oil. The oil was from the lamp, the only light in the one-room shed. I looked around his poorly lit chamber and saw it was only fitted with the most basic furniture: a mattress, a table, two chairs, and a trunk. On the largest wall, pictures were drawn in chalk; I could make out the signs of the zodiac, a religious icon, and various verses, poem scraps. This hovel reminded me of the set for Puccini's La Bohème, *though perhaps the lowly garret onstage at the Opéra de Paris was more sumptuous.*

The occupant of these lodgings was at the table, talking to an old woman in low tones while carefully inspecting the bottom of her morning coffee cup. Finally, she nodded somberly, pulled a small sack of potatoes out of her bag as payment, and walked out the door, her Destiny foretold. He then bowed lowly to M. Poiret, inquiring what services we needed of him that day.

"Madame Vera Sinclair, please meet the poet Max Jacob, my spiritual adviser." When we had shaken hands, M. Poiret continued, "It's her birthday, Max! An excellent time to review life, to ponder fate, don't you think?"

"Please sit down, madame," he said. "Your birthday, is it? Then, you are Taurus, a feminine sign, ruled by Venus. As the bull, you are a strong, willful creature."

"You might even say stubborn!" Charles joked, but catching Poiret's reproachful look, he held his tongue after that.

"Would you like me to read your palm?" he asked. Since I had not brought my breakfast china with me, I thought this would be the easiest course of action. I nodded. Somehow the atmosphere there—the oil lamp and incense, the chalked Christ figure—did not encourage spoken words.

"Give me your dominant hand," he said. I put my right hand on the table. Very gently, he stroked it, studying the fingers, knuckles, thumb. "An air hand," he mumbled. Then, as if he were examining a rare map, he began twisting it, turning it, peering at the mounts, lagoons, points, and lines: life, heart, head, and fate.

"I see great intellect, great vitality." Mr. Jacob pulled the oil lamp closer to my palm. "Yes, the heart and head lines join. This could mean you are practical, sensible in questions of love."

I glanced at Charles, who was smiling down at me. Was Our love sensible? No clairvoyant worth his salt could possibly be referring to my husband—a mere escape vehicle—or the Gaggle of silly lovers from my past.

He evidently found something interesting at that point, and needed to confirm it with my other hand. He gently took hold of my left, explaining that this hand showed my inheritance, what I had brought with me into this world. Mr. Jacob sat a moment in silence, studying both hands, comparing the two.

"I see you are in the process of acquiring the character of one of your ancestors. It's not a matter of possession, of course," he added, with a fleeting smile, "nor any type of Eastern rebirth. But, I clearly see, with age, you are becoming your own Grandmother."

Pauline Ravignan burst out laughing, merrily crying out "Oh, she's not that old!" as Paul Poiret patted Max Jacob on the back in amusement, thinking it quite a good (though naughty) birthday joke for a woman of a Certain Age. As for me, I felt myself going pale and quickly curled up my cold, exposed hand, sheltering my palm from any more scrutiny.

"Thank you, Monsieur Jacob. This has been an illumination," I choked out, as I rose to leave. Charles gave him a few francs, taking my arm as we walked out the door. Surely Pauline and M. Poiret thought I had been offended by this reference to aging, but I think the poet understood. I knew he was not having fun at my expense, but making an accurate, terrifying prediction: indeed, I was slowly turning into the woman who raised me.

When Charles and I got home, he held me while I cried, remembering Her. If not having to raise one's children is the privilege of the upper classes, my parents were like English aristocrats in that sense, leaving me to nannies, servants, and the watchful eye of my Grandmother Sinclair.

Perhaps this is unfair. I suppose I was orphaned by politics, my father's three terms in the Senate encompassing my entire childhood. My parents spent most of that time in Washington—especially during the War Between the States, when the support of Republican Senators was necessary—

but they also took leisurely holidays from the tedium of government, always enjoying their season in Newport. Truly, I was solely under my grandmother's care.

She was a widow from youth, and it was hard to imagine her ever having a mate, being in love. Though stylish and attractive, she was lacking in all human warmth. Incapable of Affection, she had long since adopted Truthfulness as her creed, all notions of tact or sensitivity abandoned. It was she who had insisted on my name, Vera, veritas: *truth.*

Camilla Wright Sinclair. When I came to Paris, I reclaimed my nom de jeune fille, *Sinclair. Having had no children, no reason to keep an extraneous surname (I was no Harris!), I had taken back the name of my senatorial father, my formidable grandmother, My name. And now, at fifty, the age she was when I was small, it seemed I was taking on her characteristics. Like my Sinclair Elder, I too was becoming tactless, condescending, bitter, contrary.*

I looked up at Charles through tears and dared whisper, "Is it true?"

He looked into my face with exaggerated vexation. "Now, Vera, are you seriously suggesting that my kindred spirit, my accomplice in this life, is a shrew? A wicked old hag?" He looked at me sternly before adding, "What, then, does that say about Me?"

I snorted a great, weepy laugh, soiling his jacket in the process, and wrapped him up in my arms. He pulled away, brought out his handkerchief, and, while wiping himself off, said, "All right, then! By my watch, it's still your birthday. And it's still oyster season! Get your coat, love!"

Vera's eyes were moist with tears. Fingering the pages, lined with quick fashion sketches, esoteric doodles, and a fast though remarkably accurate portrait of her grandmother, she thought back on that day. She was convinced that it was Charles who had prevented the poet's prediction from coming true; he had saved her from the fate of becoming an embittered old woman. After thirty years together, what did it matter that he had not been able to watch her die? Truly, it was meaningless. She put down the book with a sigh.

Well, she thought, at least her end would not be like her grandmother's. Camilla Sinclair had had such vinegary blood that it kept her body alive longer than it did her soul. She was left, in her final years, without memory or knowledge. Vera would be spared such a fate. Death does have its silver linings.

Vera's attention was suddenly drawn back to the present by the deck steward, smiling down on her, carrying the midmorning ritual of bouillon and saltine crackers.

"Are you ready for a bite, ma'am?" he asked cheerfully.

"Yes, of course," she answered. "You wouldn't happen to have any raw oysters on that tray, would you?"

"No, madame," he said, unsurprised. "However, I'm sure that I could get you some, if you'd like." He added a servile bow.

"No, that's all right." She smiled. "Bouillon will be fine."

About that time, a young woman sporting a fashionable bob haircut sank down into the next deck chair.

"What a cute little dog!" she exclaimed, reaching over to pet the old Scotty with a manicured hand.

"Good morning," Vera said, somewhat taken aback by the woman's forwardness. "I'm Mrs. Sinclair and this is Bibi."

"What a pleasure to meet you! Both of you! I'm Miss Cornelia Rice. Of the Buffalo Rices." The woman turned her attention back to the dog. "You're a precious little thing, now aren't you?"

"Yes, a pleasure," Vera said, raising her eyebrows a fraction as she looked back out to sea. She brought the cup of bouillon to her lips, blowing it gently.

Cornelia, she thought, was the name of her childhood maid.

She had come up north on the Underground Railroad and Vera's grandmother, who admired bravery wherever she could find it, had taken her on. Vera had written a lengthy account in her journal about Miss Cornelia, a remarkable woman, strong, dark, and silent with pain. This pale, young Cornelia could not compare.

When one is old, thought Vera, finishing her soup, everything reminds one of something already heard, said, or done. King Solomon must have been around her age when he declared there was no new thing under the sun. Yes, her age—about five hundred. Cornelia, Rice, Buffalo. A few years back, she would have stored those words and pulled them out again when needed. Now they just fell to the floor, forgotten; her memory had no use for such things.

Vera looked down at Bibi, shifting slightly in a dream state, and then dozed off herself.

Constance awoke with a start. It was almost twelve and she was still in bed. Those sleeping powders were certainly potent, she thought with a stretch. There was an insistent knock at the door—Was this the second one? Had the first one woken her?—which made her jump out of bed.

"Yes, yes, I'll be right there!"

She put on her robe and, after checking herself in the mirror, Constance opened the door to find a bellhop, who looked no more than twelve, peeking out through the top of a fruit basket.

"Miss Constance Stone?" he asked. "This is for you."

He handed over the heavy gift with a sigh of relief and quickly made his exit.

She looked through the apples, bananas, and oranges until she found a card: "To your health!" it said. "Serge Chabron." A smile spread across her face; was he this attentive with all of his patients?

Indeed, she had found the ship's surgeon charming: both his kind, professional manner at the infirmary as well as his playful banter as he escorted her back to her cabin.

He was very European, but polite, gentle even; so unlike Faith's quirky acquaintances in Paris with their dirty hands and coarse manners. And a world apart from her George! She frowned, remembering her husband, who was always the one to talk, never to listen. She picked an apple out of the basket and gave it a large bite. She should stop by the infirmary later to thank him. Perhaps she could even confide in him—this foreign physician so far removed from her hometown—about the nervous condition that ran on her mother's side of the family. Maybe he'd have some sound advice on the matter.

As she ate the apple, Constance turned her gaze toward the photograph of her daughters, which was propped on the dresser next to her powders. "Good morning, little ones," she murmured to them. "Elizabeth, Mary, Susan," she greeted each of them in turn.

Constance had deliberately chosen simple, pretty names for her girls. Names that had no meanings, no destinies to fulfill. She imagined them on this lovely June day, playing in the garden and mussing their pinafores with wildflower fingers. They would be so very engaged—exploring under a stone, stalking ladybirds, their pace determined despite short legs. She smiled at her girls, then reached out for the photograph of George. She changed her mind, however, and left it on the dresser top, prone. Every time she thought about going back to Worcester she began feeling empty again. Empty, and a bit sick. Not knowing what words to use, she hadn't even wired yet to tell them she was coming home.

When she finished the apple, she felt a sudden impatience to be outside, to take advantage of the beautiful day, to see who might be on deck. She nonetheless chose her clothes carefully and applied a touch of carmine to her lips. After packing a small tote with a book, one of the doctor's bananas, and a mousseline scarf in case of wind, she donned a broad-brimmed hat to shade her face from the sun. At the door she hesitated, then went back to her trunk and shuffled through the jewelry in the top drawer until she found the ring Faith had given her.

One of her own creations, it was a large rectangle made of colorful enamel squares, an inch-long stained glass window. It was meant as a peace offering; Faith had presented it to her sister on her last day in Paris, while reiterating that she would not be returning to Massachusetts. At the time, Constance had thought she would never wear it; so big and gaudy, it wasn't her taste at all. But today, she felt like being someone new. She tried it on several fingers before leaving it on her ring finger, obscuring the thin gold wedding band. She held her hand out and admired it, then picked up her tote bag and left.

Once outside, Constance found her lounge chair and made herself comfortable. With a rug carelessly thrown over crossed legs, she opened her book: a new novel, *The Mysterious Affair at Styles.* It was the first detective story she'd ever read that was written by a woman. Thinking back on her brief conversation with Dr. Chabron, she wondered what he might make of that.

Although she was fascinated by the crimes themselves—the sordid underbelly of life—mystery novels really appealed to her because she found them comforting. No matter how confusing or chaotic the story was, everything was ultimately explained, tied into a neat bow. All of the tiny, seemingly unimportant details were found to have great significance and, like she'd told the doctor, it all came together at the end. Another one of the reasons she'd loved mysteries since childhood—and this she failed to mention to him—was because her maiden name was Watson. This had given her a great affinity for Sherlock Holmes's kind doctor friend.

After reading the first few paragraphs of the very British adventures of the curious little detective, Hercule Poirot, she became distracted, lost in her own thoughts. Had she not been on a quest to bring back an errant sister, had she been traveling for her own sake, she would have gone to England instead of France. Constance had always been attracted to English culture, from Wilkie Collins's moonstone, to Jane Austen's Mr. Darcy, to Pip's sudden fortune in *Great Expectations.* It all seemed so proper, so civilized, so much more her "cup of tea." It peeved her to think that she had crossed the ocean to no purpose—and had not even visited London!

Almost wishing she'd gotten off the night before in Southampton, she looked out toward the water, their constant progress toward America, toward home. When they'd made the stopover in England, she found herself wondering yet again what had become of her first beau, Nigel Williams.

A young Englishman from the unlikely sounding village of Leighton Buzzard, Nigel had come to Clark University to study psychology. Her father, Dr. Gerald Watson, became his major professor, helping him with his research on mood disorders. Constance found Nigel, who was altogether too thin, nonetheless appealing; she was immediately captivated by his charming accent and manners, his soulful gray eyes, his spruce appearance. He was a frequent visitor to the Watson home, at first to borrow books from his professor, then to join the family for meals, and finally, as Constance's official suitor.

They would sit on the porch for hours, in all kinds of weather, holding hands and whispering earnestly. Now she could scarcely remember what they talked about, but she could never forget how she felt: the surprising newness every time he said her name, the cozy daydreams of a common future, the warm tingling when he kissed her on the lips. The wonders of first love.

He had courted her for seven months and, had he stayed in America, Constance felt sure her parents would have deemed him a suitable match. But due to a family emergency he had been obliged to return to England. Although she was quite sure that her father would never have allowed her to live abroad, Nigel had not even asked. There were no harebrained schemes about meeting in London, no desperate entreaties to elope. When she went to the station to see him off, she already felt jilted; despite his kisses and tears, she knew they would never see each other again. That night, heartbroken, she sobbed her face into distortion—hideously red and swollen—then finally fell asleep.

Shortly after Nigel's departure, her father, with the intention of cheering his daughter up, had asked Constance to serve punch at an afternoon gathering for new professors. There, she met George Stone, a geography professor thirteen years her senior. When he came round the following day to pay a call, Faith delivered the news: "There's a fossil in the parlor to see you." A month later she found herself, with surprising swiftness and far too much formality, engaged to marry him. They had now been together eight years.

"Dorothy! Eli! Oscar! Winifred!"

The shrill sound of a woman's voice stirred Constance from her thoughts. She turned her head toward the names being called and saw a stampede of towheaded children, their heavy shoes pounding down the teak deck, their bedraggled parents straggling behind. They stopped suddenly and swarmed over the deck chairs right next to her. The youngest was about the age of her oldest and the other three wavered around ten.

"Good morning." Constance nodded to the mother.

"Hello, there!" she answered as her husband fell into a chair. "We're the Andersons."

Constance felt the pang of this group introduction, keenly aware of her singularity next to them, "the Andersons," a veritable clan. Should she introduce herself then by saying, "I am the Stone"?

"Pleased to meet you all," she said simply.

Watching these children, she realized how much she missed her own. How delightful it would be to share this ocean voyage with her three young girls! She envisioned them there by her side, with little Susan toddling along the deck and the older two girls climbing up on the rails, scanning the seas for whales. And George? What would he be doing? She could imagine him engaged in endless conversations with her tedious dining companions, Mr. Thomas and Captain Fielding, discussing those topics that bored her so much: motorcars, hunting and fishing, their unequivocal admiration of Theodore Roosevelt . . . She thought their serious, masculine talk would suit him just fine.

"I want to play deck tennis!" cried one towheaded Anderson.

"No! Shuffleboard!" whined another.

"You goose! Ping-Pong is much more fun!" insisted a third, rounding out his argument by sticking out his tongue.

Their mother skillfully hushed them, then proposed a logical order of deck games. Before letting them fly off, she inquired whether they were hungry or thirsty, or needed the bathroom.

"And Dorothy! Don't take off your sweater!" she called.

Constance looked at the little girl and smiled to find she was wearing gray patent leather shoes, Mary Jane silver slippers. When she was little she'd read the Oz books, desperately wishing for a cyclone to take her to a new world, to a new family with grown-ups who wanted nothing more than to take her by the hand and go off on an adventure. Adults who, although filled with straw or made of tin, were never dark and despondent, but fun-loving and kind. As a child, she had written stories about happy families: a pretty girl with adoring parents and loads of big brothers, living together on a beautiful farm. As an adult, she had tried her best to be a good mother, to shower her daughters with love, equally, all three.

"Dorothy!" the mother cried again, pulling herself up and giving Constance an apologetic look before disappearing into the game area.

Constance smiled to herself at the thought of how alike all mothers were: the same worries, complaints, challenges. Then, again, remembered her own.

Tossing her head—a firm refusal to think of her mother—she

pulled the banana out of her bag and, as she began to peel it, noticed the ship photographer and his assistant making their way down the deck. They were taking portraits of families and traveling companions, as well as those fast friends met on board. Taking small bites off her banana, she watched the groups posing at the rail. The assistant handed each assortment of people a ring-shaped life buoy with PARIS written on it and they made a formation around it, smiling.

She watched a young couple (honeymooners, obviously) pose for the camera, his arms close around her, their smiles glowing and natural. She'd seen them earlier, snuggling in the same deck chair, furrowing their brows over that new craze, the crossword puzzle, and chewing on the same pencil. Their kisses still tingled, Constance thought, their daydreams were still cozy.

A large family got up for their picture next. The assistant handed the life buoy to the youngest child, who peeked through it with a grin. Constance watched in amusement as the mother sang out, "Say cheese!" and, instantly, the children's spontaneous smiles became pained and artificial: a tortured grimace, a wide-eyed snarl.

The photographers then came to her chair.

"A souvenir for the folks back home, ma'am?" asked the photographer, taking off his straw hat, his smile half-hidden by a large mustache.

"No, thank you." She shook her head. It seemed a sad sight to pose for the camera all by herself, banana in hand.

"Oh, come on, ma'am! You're already as pretty as a picture!" he said with a wink, as his assistant stood next to him, waving the life buoy enticingly. "Are you sure?"

"Quite," she said, picking up her book and staring into it until they moved on.

Peeking up to watch them take their next photo—a couple of Texans, judging from their hats and boots—Constance wondered, if she were with Faith, would they have had their photograph made?

She couldn't imagine her sister smiling at her side on the *Paris* deck. If she were there, heading home, she would have looked like the grim victim, the condemned man. She then pictured her own family photo at the rails, the sea twinkling in the background. She would be next to George, holding little Susan, while Mary and Elizabeth stood in front, holding the buoy together. She snapped the shutter with her eyelids, seeing their familiar smiles. Would George be smiling too? She tried to envision him, but could only dredge up the image of the stern, formal photograph lying on the dresser in her cabin.

With a glance down at her detective story, she imagined her husband going missing, and the gentlemen from Scotland Yard asking for his "distinguishing characteristics." Try as she may, she could think of none. In fact, she feared, if George changed his coat and shaved his beard, she might not recognize him on the street!

The photographers now gone, Constance stretched out her legs. With her book still in her hand, a finger marking her place, she walked up to the rail to the sound of shuffleboard pucks swishing along the teak floorboards—*clack!*—the odd shout, eruptions of laughter. It was a fine day and it seemed every person on board was outside, enjoying the sunshine.

Absently looking down at the decks below, she suddenly noticed Dr. Chabron—without his white robe, but neat in a uniform—talking with a couple of crewmen. She was pleasantly surprised to find him there, away from the infirmary, and contemplated going down and thanking him for the fruit basket. Debating whether that would be considered too forward, she reached up to fix her hat and found she was still holding her detective story.

Watching him chatting in the sun, gesturing with a cigarette, Constance thought perhaps he would make a good character for a mystery novel: a dashing French doctor traveling the world on an elegant ocean liner. But what would be the intrigue behind his story? Would his wife suddenly vanish? No, not a wife. Would he be wrongly accused of an accidental poisoning? Or perhaps be a victim of blackmail? As Constance was working out a good story line, Dr. Chabron turned, tipped his hat to a group of young women, and walked out of view. Smiling, she entitled her nonexistent story "The Singular Affair of the Ship Surgeon."

Lingering at the rails, Constance considered going to see him at the infirmary, but after a few minutes' deliberation, she decided to wait. Although she would enjoy his company, he was probably too busy to chat and she was, she had to admit, feeling fine.

She sat back down and opened her book again, but after reading a page or two, she discovered that the dialogue of Hercule Poirot—peppered with bits of French—was clearly being spoken with the doctor's voice. In her mind, she could hear his slight accent, its musical tone. She was laughing at herself when Mrs. Anderson, back from the game area and trying to relax, called to her.

"Excuse me? Miss?"

Constance looked over to find her holding out the ocean liner's daily newspaper, *L'Atlantique.* It was opened to a page of photographs under the headline "The *Paris* Launch!"

"I believe this is you!" She smiled.

Mrs. Anderson handed the paper to Constance. When she found her photograph there, she grimaced. It was a highly unflattering shot. Her face showed serious surprise—her eyes wide, her mouth in a straight line—and her hat, George's "puff of smoke," looked far too big. After scrutinizing her own image with an inaudible groan, her eyes finally wandered to the other two women in the picture.

Next to her, she found the young crew member she'd seen at the doctor's office. At the infirmary, her hair had been covered in a cap, but the birthmark (which looked here like a blotch of printer's ink) was undeniably hers. The perspective was thrown by the difference in their sizes; although the girl had been several feet in front of her, in the photo it looked as if they were walking in stride, nearly hand in hand. She studied the girl's face; it looked nervous but determined. Constance thought her brave to be going off to sea at such a young age.

The other side of the picture was underdeveloped, the woman there fading into white. Was it the elderly woman, stooped and sickly, who had also been at the doctor's? It was too faint to say for sure, but the clothes were similar; she thought she recognized her purple coat, here a charcoal gray. That, and the skinny frame. Her eyes focused again on her own image, then she quickly folded the paper and handed it back to Mrs. Anderson.

"Thank you for pointing that out," she said pleasantly, then closed her eyes, facing the sun.

She hoped Dr. Chabron would not have the time to bother with the newspaper today.

Serving stew to third-class diners, Julie noticed how, in the twenty-four hours the passengers had been on board, they had already become members of stable groups, strangers drawn together by common languages and cultures. She handed out bowls to clusters of English speakers, Russians and Slavs, and those passengers from southern Europe who made themselves understood in a pan-Latin patois. The Germans and Austrians were joined not only by language but by the fact that, together, they had lost the Great War. Although three years had passed since the Armistice, they kept to themselves, feeling ostracized and avoiding conflict with the Allied diners.

Julie went down each table, carefully ladling generous portions out of a tureen, timing her movements to the roll of the ship. ("How slow you are!" bristled Mme. Tremblay. "The others are hungry too!") As she served bowls down one long table, she listened to a group of Mediterranean passengers bickering. As they eagerly reached out for their lunches, they debated whose national dishes were the best. Spaniards raised voices about their rices, Italians about their pastas, the Portuguese their codfish recipes. The French passengers sat back, looking on in amusement, confident in the knowledge that the greatest European cuisine was clearly their own.

Though they were quieted by the full bowls in front of them, Julie was saddened by these bursts of national pride. She knew these passengers were abandoning their homelands, forced to look beyond their borders for better circumstances. Julie realized that the ship was a No Man's Land, a gap between two worlds: their former lives and the next. What, then, did that mean for the people who *worked* on board? Were they forever in limbo, without country or home, tied to thankless tasks on a never-stopping ship?

Julie made her way up the aisles, now refilling glasses, and remembered how she and her friends had envisioned these ships from land. The transatlantic liners had always seemed the very image of beauty, luxury, wealth, and power. But here under the waterline, it was nothing of the sort. Far from glamorous and exciting, it was drudgery; Julie, who had always shunned the idea of working in domestic service, was doing the exact same chores. Here, she was a maid, but one who worked in an enormous tumbling machine that rendered her breathing shallow and her bowels functionless. And instead of serving stew to a bourgeois family, she was serving it up to eight hundred people!

Julie sighed and, looking up, was surprised to see Nikolai grinning at her from the corridor just outside the dining room. Her mouth fell open, then managed to grin back. She tried not to blush (impossible!) and quickly looked around to see whether anyone had noticed. She could hardly believe that they were all still chewing calmly, unaware that a man had come looking for her. She looked over at Mme. Tremblay's thin frame standing guard near the kitchen doors, then at Simone, smiling with her mouth closed at a passenger's pleasantry. Wheeling back around, she was relieved to find him still there. With the exaggerated face of a question mark, Nikolai pointed at her, then at his watch. Looking at her own, she saw she should be finished in an hour. After she'd made the sign for one, he pointed toward the door with a quizzical shrug, trying to make plans to meet.

Julie was nodding with a smile, when suddenly she felt Mme. Tremblay beside her. She quickly snapped her attention back to her work, forcing herself to look serious.

"Please don't stop, Julie," she said loudly. "The passengers to your right have empty glasses as well."

"Yes, ma'am," she uttered, moving on to the next passenger.

Lunch dragged after that with passengers fiddling with fruit peels and asking for second cups of coffee. Finally the last table was cleared and the dining room cleaned in preparation for the next meal. Before venturing out into the corridor, Julie took off her cap and ran her fingers through her silky hair. With a peek into the mirror over the riveted sideboard, she smiled at herself—trying to imagine what he saw—then groaned slightly. What did he see?

Cautiously, she peered out into the hallway. He was there, leaning against the metal wall and whistling softly.

"Hi there, Juliette!" he called, interrupting his tune. "Are you on break now?"

"Finally," she said, joining him at the wall and catching a faint petrol odor coming from his jacket. "But, we serve so many shifts, that once the last passengers are finished with lunch, the first ones are ready to start dinner."

"Well, do you have time for a little walk?"

"Of course!" she said quickly, letting him take her hand. "I'd love it!" she breathed. "Let's go outside. It'd be nice to get some fresh air."

"How are you feeling, then?" he asked, leading her out the door to the mooring deck.

"Better, I guess." She shrugged. Although she hadn't thrown up since the day before, she still had bouts of dizziness and breathlessness that made her wary of food.

"I've brought you the tea, Julie," he said, producing a paper bag. "I hope it helps."

"Oh, thank you for remembering, Nikolai," she said, taking the package and glancing up at his face as they surfaced out into the sun. "You're so sweet. Are you sure you won't need it? We may have rough seas yet."

"Ah, don't worry about this old sea dog," he growled playfully, escorting her to an empty spot at the rails.

"All right, then," Julie said, leaning on the rail next to him, their arms already touching. "I'll give it a try. There's just something about the air down there . . ." She wrinkled her nose. "How is it in the engine room?"

"Better than it used to be. You know, when I started working on steamers, they all had coal engines. There'd be a whole army of us—black-faced and sweating rivers—stoking those engines day and night. We called ourselves the Devil's Crew. It was like working in the pits of Hell." Nikolai smiled nostalgically.

"Aren't we running on coal?" Julie asked. "With those funnels blowing smoke up there, I just took it for granted."

She remembered her brothers, who all worked at the port, talking excitedly about ship engines. Perhaps Nikolai was also fascinated by such things? Standing next to him, listening to his magnetic voice and feeling his body heat, she was relieved to be producing words of any kind.

"Oh no." He shook his head. "Not on the *Paris*. This ship has a brand-new oil-fired turbine engine. No coal, no boilers pumping steam. The engine room is filled with huge cylinders and complicated little devices."

"Well, even in steerage we can hear it," Julie said. "It must be really loud down there."

"You can't hear anything! You can barely hear yourself think! But this!" he said, gesturing with his arm toward the blue water, then bringing it back to hang around her shoulder. "This is worth coming to sea!" He squeezed her closer with a smile. "A beautiful day with a beautiful girl! Say, shall I buy you some pastries to go with the tea?"

"No, thanks," she said with a pause. She didn't want to admit that she had been living off saltines and soda water since she'd boarded. And now, with Nikolai's arm around her, she couldn't even imagine eating crackers. "I had a late lunch."

"Then, shall we take a walk around the deck?"

She looked up at his face, from his pleasant smile on up to his eyes. She was taken aback to see how cold they looked. Narrow and hard. Maybe it was the glare of the sun?

"Actually, I think I should be getting back to steerage. None of my fellow workers are out here," she said, looking around, suddenly nervous. "It makes me wonder if there's something I ought to be doing. I still haven't gotten the hang of this job." She looked a bit sheepish, then added shyly, "And you? If you're going back down to the engine room, maybe you could walk me to the women's dormitory?"

"I'd love to. Really, it's the only thing I can imagine that could tempt me back into that hole," he said with a laugh.

He put his arm around her waist, making her stiffen. It seemed such an intimate place, there in the very middle of her body. Was this proper? The only time a boy had ever touched her there—years ago and oh, so lightly!—they'd been dancing. After a few steps, however, the difference in their sizes made it impossible for him to keep his hand in place and he moved it up to her shoulder. This too she found awkward; she wasn't used to walking in tandem. They began an ungainly descent to the ship's depths.

As they were reaching Julie's floor, he jumped to the landing, leaving her three steps above, now at his eye level. With a hand on each rail, as if to bar her way, he leaned over until their foreheads were almost touching.

"Will you meet me on deck again tonight, little Julie?" he cooed softly. "Perhaps you'd allow me a dance? We could waltz outside the ballroom."

She suddenly felt dizzy again; this time, she knew, it had nothing to do with stale air. With his face so close to hers, she could see his pupils enlarge, feel the warmth of his breath, but could only stammer out a few unintelligible syllables.

"Until tonight, then," he whispered.

He touched her brow with his own, then drew back an inch to look at her. He scanned her face, moaning in approval—*mmmmmm*—then planted a kiss, forceful but brief, on her mouth. She gasped, staring at him with wide eyes, but did not move.

He pulled away with a smile. He began sauntering back down to the engine room, then called back up to her: "Enjoy your tea!"

She looked at the paper bag hanging limply in her hand; she'd completely forgotten about it.

"Thanks," she called down to his head top, dreamily waving good-bye with the bag.

She darted into the empty dormitory and threw herself on the bed, more aware than before of the dull vibration coming from the machines below. With a shiver, she licked her lips, wondering whether Nikolai had left a trace there. Lifting her hand to examine her birthmark, to determine whether it had somehow grown smaller, she discovered, again, the paper bag. Smiling uncontrollably, she opened it.

Inside she found a small bag of ginger tea and a note. With trembling hands and a deep breath, she unfolded the paper. Although the spelling was faulty, the handwriting was surprisingly lavish, with flowery strokes and elaborate capitals; a profusion of nonsensical accent marks decorated the words, sprinkled on like dried herbs.

Dearest Julie,

I want you to have this bag of tea, with hopes that it will prove to be a miracle for you, as you have for me. When you caught my hat that day, it was a sign. There is a connection between us and I know you feel it too.

Yours,
Nikolai

A love letter? Julie blinked a time or two. She could barely believe this was happening to her. A *man*—a big, strong, good-looking *man*—was attracted to her! For the first time in her life, she had an admirer.

Her hands warm and clammy, she opened the bag of tea and breathed in its aroma. The smell was intoxicating. The spices recalled the heat that radiated from Nikolai—his hands, his voice, his lips. This engineman was his own furnace, she giggled to herself. Her insides felt liquid; she sniffed the tea again with her eyes closed.

The dormitory door wrenched open and two washerwomen came in, complaining loudly about claret stains and ready for a nap. Julie curled the tea bag shut, then took her old book out of the locker: a worn copy of Jules Verne's *Michael Strogoff,* which had long served as a stronghold for her brothers' letters. Almost light-headed, she reread the lines again before carefully stowing this new letter between its pages. Then she headed toward the kitchen, eager to try Nikolai's miracle.

Julie had taken to Pascal, the head cook in steerage, when they'd first met the day before. He was a portly man, three times her age, with a big nose and just a ring of hair from ear to ear ("It keeps the chef's hat on!"). He was one of those rough old sailors who liked to think himself foul tempered, when in fact he was a warmhearted softie. Maybe Jean-François or Didier would have grown up to be a man such as this?

He took a moment out from roasting beef bones for stock to make Julie a cup of tea.

"Ginger, eh?" he said, sniffing the tea. "Not feeling well, are we? And with the seas like glass. *Pauvre petite.*"

He handed her the cup, giving her head a light pat, then went back to his preparations for the evening meal.

Julie went into the women's dining hall, juggling the hot cup, the bag, and the book. She had thought to read a few passages of the old novel while drinking her tea, but she couldn't concentrate. She pulled out Nikolai's note and reread it again and again. Tracing its loops and curls with her thumb, she focused on the words: "miracle," "connection," "Yours." With a long sigh, she glanced at the other women in the room, mending hosiery or playing cards, to make sure they weren't stealing glances at her, curious about the letter in her hand. No, they were completely oblivious to the small girl holding a common piece of paper. She took a sip of tea—his tea—safe in the knowledge that she was neither floating nor aglow.

Suddenly, Simone plopped down next to her on the bench, her eyes shining with excitement. "You'll never guess what's happened!"

"What?" Julie asked with a jolt, nearly spilling her tea. For a split second, she thought Simone might give her some news about her Russian admirer.

"Mary Pickford and Douglas Fairbanks boarded the *Paris* in Southampton!" Simone squealed. "They're right here! In first class!"

Julie, although amused by Simone's botched logic that first class was "right here," was impressed nonetheless.

"No kidding!" Julie said with a whistle. "Wait, don't tell me you've seen them!"

"No, but Louise did. She picked up their washing a few minutes ago." Simone sighed happily. "Hey, wouldn't that be wonderful if we got to meet them? Let's go up to first class tonight and peek into the dining room!" Simone clapped her hands. "Or maybe they'll be on deck, dancing in the moonlight—just like in the pictures!"

"That would be fun," Julie admitted. "I was already thinking about going up on deck tonight."

Julie thought for a moment, then, with no one else to confide in, decided to show Simone Nikolai's note. She pulled it out of her book, then hesitated, holding it in her hand.

"Simone, can you keep a secret?" she asked.

"Sure!" she said, staring at the folded paper. "What is it?"

Julie handed it to her, then, to hide her blush, stuck her nose into the cup and breathed in the last remnants of ginger. She watched Simone's eyes slowly read the note.

"Wow!" she said, looking at Julie in wonder. "Who is he?"

"He's a Russian engineman. I met him as we left port yesterday," Julie explained. "We've seen each other out on deck once or twice. He asked me to meet him up there tonight."

"You lucky dog!" she exclaimed. "You made a catch on our very first day out!"

"A catch?" Julie stammered.

"Yeah! During the training course I heard that for every hundred men working on board, there are just two women. I thought that, for the first time in my life, the odds would be in my favor!" Her smile stretched so widely across her face, she looked a bit like a frog. "And these sailors are strong and able-bodied!" she continued. "Not like the men who came back to Harfleur after the war, missing this or that."

Julie stiffened. She took the note back and tucked it away into her book.

"Very romantic, Julie," Simone said with the air of an expert. "Say, I wonder if he has a friend?"

"A friend?" Julie repeated, regretting having mentioned Nikolai to her at all.

"Well, we can ask him when we go up on deck tonight," Simone said, the evening plan already clear in her mind.

"About tonight," Julie stumbled slowly. She didn't want Simone up there, embarrassing her by saying the wrong things. "I'm worried about Madame Tremblay. I don't think she'd be too happy if she found us missing."

"You don't think we'd lose our jobs if we got caught?" Simone whispered, looking from side to side.

"I don't know," Julie said. "Let's think about it, all right?"

"Sure." Simone nodded. "But I would really love to catch a glimpse of Douglas Fairbanks! *And* meet your new boyfriend!"

Julie turned red and looked away. She noticed that other women in the lounge were gathering their things—decks of cards, knitting needles, sewing kits—and looked up at the clock. Though it was only half-past four, it was time for them to return to work; the mouths in steerage were fed earlier than those above decks. Julie picked up her well-worn book.

"We'd better get going," she mumbled.

"What've you got there?" Simone asked.

"It's a book by Jules Verne," Julie said, grateful for the change in subject. "I've read almost all his books, but this one here is more of a souvenir." Julie looked at the faded cover fondly. "My brothers loved his stories. In fact, that's why they named me Julie. When my mother was expecting me, my three older brothers each read this book. They decided, since our family name is Vernet, that they wanted a little brother named Jules. Well, they got me instead."

"Lucky you! I only have sisters . . . five sisters!" Simone replied, rolling her eyes.

"Yes," Julie said softly, holding the novel against her chest. Peeking back down at the cover, she smiled; the hero, brave Michael Strogoff, was also Russian.

Vera woke up on the deck chair, wrapped tightly inside a nest of warm blankets. She opened her eyes briefly, surprised to see it was already twilight. She noticed Bibi was gone, and her journal was back inside the carpetbag. Amandine had, no doubt, decided to tidy up and take the dog for a stroll without rousing her. Since her sleep had become so precious and rare, Vera was generally cross when it was interrupted. Or perhaps, Vera mused, Amandine had thought she'd passed away and did not relish touching a corpse?

She was looking up into the evening sky with its sprinkling of early-rising stars, taking pleasure in not moving, when a shooting star fleeted past. She shivered in delight; seldom, at this stage, did Vera still feel life's little moments of magic. She thought back to April 1910 when, for nearly a week, Halley's Comet had hung over Paris like a gas lamp. To get a better look, she and Charles had taken off their shoes and climbed out on the roof. It was chilly on their bare feet, but how nimble she'd been out there, holding her skirts, without ever imagining she could fall. Was that only eleven years ago? Aging did not take place gradually, she sighed, but in sudden leaps, horrible jerks.

Halley's Comet . . . Vera was reminded of that quote by Mark Twain, who was born as the comet passed and rightfully predicted that he would die when it returned. "The Almighty has said, no doubt, 'Now here are these two unaccountable freaks; they came in together, they must go out together.'" Twain was one of the few great Americans in her opinion, only rivaled in humor and ingenuity by Benjamin Franklin.

Near her own end, she pondered his. It was well known that Twain's last years were ripe with cynicism and disappointment; but, how had he felt when he knew his life was coming to a close? Did he fear the comet's approach? Or long for its passing? Did he feel remorse at leaving this beautiful world so full of imperfection, or was he glad to let go, to leave humanity to rot? She thought of herself these last few months, reading and rereading her memoirs, reliving her past. Did Mark Twain also find himself studying the stories of his youth, eagerly perusing his *Life on the Mississippi*, his *Innocents Abroad*?

Mark Twain. She sat thinking of his mischievous eyes and white tousled hair, his intense gaze and Wild West mustache. Yes, she thought, even as an older man, he was attractive. And, judging by his quick, cantankerous wit, he was undoubtedly an excellent lover as well. Her lips curled into a slow grin, the first visible movement she'd made since waking (if nearby, Amandine would fear rigor mortis was twisting her face into a hideous death mask), then, Vera finally began to shift her limbs, rolling her shoulders and stretching her legs. Now *that* was a sure sign of old age, she decided, when you can see the allure of your contemporaries, those the young would view as sexless grandfathers with loose skin and looser teeth; when you look for Mark Twain's portrait in your mind and find a desirable bed partner.

Chuckling to herself, wondering whether she too were an "unaccountable freak," Vera reached into her carpetbag and pulled out her alphabet book. She opened it in the middle, then let the pages settle themselves. She smiled upon a large letter *H*. A brief, lighthearted entry, it fit the moment perfectly. There was just enough light left to read a short piece such as this; though, truth be told, she knew most of the words by heart.

Handsome

One day, in my eleventh year, when at an Awkward stage of growth, my lips and nose both occupying more than their rightful share of my face, I was sitting in the window seat, my embroidery forgotten, watching the horses and buggies on the street. Was it the light from the window that drew her toward me? All of a sudden, Grandmother took my chin in her hard, cold hand (Less Human than marble, it was more like metal; nay, Lady Liberty's hands must be warmer) and peered at my face, moving it from side to side.

"You will never be pretty, my dear," she declared, shaking

her head. "With luck—and I say, With Luck—you will be rather handsome."

She gave me a serious look, then recovered her chair, put her pince-nez in place, and went back to her book.

Tears filled my eyes. I was devastated by this prophecy (what was a woman worth but her appearance?) made by one of the great beauties of her generation, my grandmother, Camilla Wright Sinclair. I sat in the afternoon light, wondering what it could possibly mean.

I learned in the years that followed, as I quickly developed into one, what exactly a Handsome Woman was. They are not ugly, of course, nor plain, nor excessively manly. But unlike their soft, rounded sisters, with pouty lips and precious eyes, these women tend to have a fine jaw, a noble brow, and eyes that, rather than beautiful, are oft described as Intelligent. These facial characteristics are usually accompanied by a straight back and a long, swift stride. Therefore, unlike Beauties, decorative objects whose task it is to adorn a room, to provide visual delight to others, the Handsome Woman, unable to evoke approval and appreciation by her appearance alone, is free to contribute and develop in other ways.

Many women claim to admire these looks and a few odd men, mainly those referred to as Men of Character, are irresistibly drawn to them, spellbound. Such men have the sensation of being a Discoverer, the first to spot beauty in a wasteland. And thus, he feels the explorer's pride in there planting his flag. Intrepid, he cares not that few others would envy that particular territory.

I myself have met my share of this rare breed of man. The first time, I was fourteen. Standing with friends at the Autumn Ball, a tall, slender boy approached me. After a few minutes of artless small talk, he stopped, gape-mouthed, and earnestly stammered out the clumsiest compliment I have ever received:

"Hang it! I don't care that my friends don't think you're pretty. I think you're Beautiful!"

Indeed, this is the fate of these Men of Character, to want a prize that so few value. In one's youth, that is. But then, one finds that the handsome woman ages so much better than her pretty sisters. Compare the loveliness of dried leaves to the pathetic unsightliness of the dead flower, bloated and ill smelling.

Perhaps Grandmother's prophecy, so damning, so malignant, was truly an unintentional blessing. A Fairy Godmother's Gift.

Handsome indeed, she thought with a smile. In her prime she had certainly had her successes with the opposite sex. In fact, she had written a journal entry a few years back entitled "Thirteen Lovers," detailing her exploits with all the men—an archaeologist, a wealthy banker, a photographer, a handful of writers, and so on—she'd been with after giving up on marriage. Who knows? Perhaps she would have even been able to captivate Mark Twain.

The sky was considerably darker now, high time to retire from the decks. She looked around and saw that the deck steward had already stored away all the other rugs and deck chairs. He was leaning against the rail, smoking a cigarette, undoubtedly waiting for her to return to her cabin so he could finish his evening task.

She reached for her cane, tucked away under her chair, and pulled herself up. Vera stretched again, picked up her bag, then walked to the rails. Looking out on the ocean, a lovely shade of dark green at this time of the evening, she noticed that, on the deck below, people in second class were already dressed and filing into their dining room in twos and fours. Odd, she thought. I'm still not hungry.

Constance decided to wear her nicest outfit for dinner, the new gown she had bought in Paris: a pink sleeveless silk with a champagne-colored sash. Uncomfortable exposing her bare arms, she pulled out the lace shawl—pleased to find an occasion to wear it—to put around her shoulders. She was satisfied with the effect. Faith's ring did not exactly go with this outfit, but she left it on anyway; it made her feel younger, more chic.

Not wanting to make a grand entrance on her own, she skirted around the edge of the dining room, past mirrors and potted palms, alongside the bar and the wine steward's station. Passing other second-class diners, she glanced around, idly wondering where the doctor ate—with the crew, with first class, alone in the infirmary, in his rooms?

"Good evening, everyone," she greeted her fellow diners when she finally arrived.

Already engaged in conversation, the men at her table only granted Constance brief nods and slight smiles as she sat down.

"Good evening, Mrs. Stone," Mrs. Thomas whispered, not wanting to interrupt them.

The waiter soon appeared, in a short white jacket and bow tie, managing to look extremely busy yet unruffled. He gave them three or four choices for their first course, none of which Constance understood, then poised his pencil on his pad and waited with an air of faux patience while the guests made up their minds.

"I'll have the crème vichyssoise," Captain Fielding said so decisively that the other, less traveled guests opted for the same. The waiter made a careful note before taking off in great haste.

The wine steward then sidled up to the table, offering them a chilled bottle of white wine. After everyone had been served, Mr. Thomas raised his glass to give a toast.

"Here's to the end of Prohibition!" he cried, tossing the wine back in one gulp.

Constance's hand was on the stem of her glass, expecting a conventional toast regarding health, good cheer, or friendship. Taken aback, she felt uncomfortable lifting her glass; wouldn't that imply she was rather too fond of drinking? Unlike many women she knew—those who had heartily campaigned for the Eighteenth Amendment—she was not a teetotaler. George had always liked brandy with his cigars and, before the ban on alcohol passed the year before, she had occasionally joined him with a dash of sherry. She peeked over at Mrs. Thomas, who was smiling quietly but not joining in on the toast, and followed suit. However, the European men at the table were delighted and lifted their glasses high.

"I don't understand this Prohibition," said one of the Dutchmen with a lick of his lips. "The idea that *drink* could be illegal is preposterous, unthinkable!"

"Certainly!" seconded the other. "If this notion came up in our parliament, we would defend our port and pints of stout to the last!"

"Here, here!" cried the men.

"You know"—Mr. Thomas grinned, wiping his mouth with his napkin—"I saw Carrie Nation once, in a bar in Kansas City. First she greeted the bartender: 'Good morning, Destroyer of Men's Souls.'" He said this in a high, mimicking voice. "And then she brought out her hatchet and went to work, breaking all the whiskey bottles in the place!"

"What? Who is this?" asked one of the Dutchmen.

"She was a crazy woman," he said. "Called herself 'Jesus's bulldog'! She claimed liquor was the root of all evil, that it made people do all sorts of sinful things. She'd go into saloons and smash up all the bottles she could, then she'd take a break to play hymns on the piano. It was Carrie Nation who waged the war against alcohol. And she won, the old cow."

While they were discussing Prohibition, another bottle of wine was ordered and their soup course served. Constance took a spoonful of the creamy vichyssoise and was vexed to find it cold. Before complaining, she waited for Captain Fielding's reaction. She was disappointed to find he liked it.

"Carrie Nation," repeated one of the Dutchmen with disdain. "I am surprised to hear that a woman could be so powerful. I don't just mean her barging into a man's place of business and threatening his livelihood, but you say she actually changed a national law!"

"Well, I suppose that's what happens when women get the right to vote." Captain Fielding shook his head sadly.

"I don't know why they call it women's suffrage"—Mr. Thomas winked—"when it's us men who suffer!"

The four men at the table all chuckled and raised their glasses. Although Constance was used to George dominating conversations at home, she found this group of men far more vulgar and even less inclusive. These gentlemen did not seem to even remember there were ladies at the table! Annoyed with them all, Constance was looking away from her fellow diners with a huff when she noticed the doctor making his way toward their table. Although she was glad to see him—his pleasant nature would be a welcome change from this lot—she felt her cheeks turning red. As he approached the table, his eyes flitted to hers, gleaming, before coming to land on those of the Englishman.

"Captain Fielding!" he said, greeting the officer with a warm handshake. "I saw your name on the passenger list and I wanted to come round and give you my best!"

"Ladies and gentlemen," said the captain, "I'd like to introduce Dr. Chabron. Thanks to him, I'm still alive."

"Oh, you would have lived"—the doctor smiled—"though you may not have been so good-looking!"

"Are you part of the *Paris* crew, sir?" asked Mr. Thomas.

"Yes, I'm the physician here on board." As he shook hands around the table, Constance felt her heart pounding. When he took her hand, his smile widened. "And I've already had the pleasure of meeting Miss Stone."

Out of the corner of her eye, she saw Mrs. Thomas's thick eyebrows collide; "*Miss?*" the matron murmured in a long hiss. Constance was relieved that this went unnoticed by everyone else, as the men were all insisting that Dr. Chabron join them at the table.

"I hate to interrupt . . ." he began, to the general dissension of the party.

"We were just discussing the political ec-cen-tricities of recent years," said Mr. Thomas, emphasizing that word with a comical grimace.

"Yes, Prohibition in America and the spreading plague of women's suffrage," Captain Fielding said, rolling his eyes. "Do women have the vote in France?"

"Not yet." The doctor smiled.

"The French have always been an enlightened bunch!" the Englishman sighed. "Women got the vote in Britain a couple of years back, although, I'm glad to say, not without restrictions. Our lady voters must be over thirty and either householders or university graduates. I mean, you can't expect charwomen and milkmaids to choose your prime ministers, can you?"

"Good thinking!" Mr. Thomas said with a shake of his head. "In the States, they've given the vote to them all!"

"We have two American women here at the table," said Dr. Chabron, nodding at Constance and Mrs. Thomas. "Pray, ladies, what do you think of all this?"

All eyes fell on the startled women; they had not expected to be included in the discussion and were not prepared to voice their opinions. Indeed, it had been so long since Constance had uttered a word, she thought her jaw would need oiling before she spoke again. She took a breath.

"Well . . ." She and Mrs. Thomas began at the same time. Constance blushed, then deferred to her elder. "After you," she said courteously.

"I agree with my husband," Mrs. Thomas said, smiling at her mate. "We women shouldn't bother ourselves with politics! Our job is to make a comfortable home for our families, not to take to the streets, campaigning, protesting, or picketing."

"Well said, my dear!" Mr. Thomas beamed. "And you, young lady. I daresay you're of the same mind?"

Constance looked into the expectant faces of the people at the table, her fellow diners and the doctor, and imagined the presence of her father and George there as well. She had heard arguments similar to Mrs. Thomas's for years: "a woman's place" and all that. But that wasn't really the question.

"It would be difficult for you gentlemen to imagine," she began slowly, "what it's like to go through life making almost none of the decisions that affect you most intimately. Men wonder at the helplessness of women—our dependence, our inabilities—when, actually, this situation is imposed upon us."

She took a breath and looked at their muddled faces.

"Silly girl," said Mr. Thomas, "that is no invention of man! It is the feminine condition!"

"Sir, it is not our *condition* to be left out when decisions are taken, when choices are made," Constance said defiantly. "We women can think for ourselves, you know. We don't need fathers and husbands always telling us what we can and cannot do, be it schooling or marriage, work or travel . . . I think it's fabulous that women have finally earned the right to vote," she said, suddenly adopting a firm position on the matter. "In fact, I plan on registering as soon as I get home!"

She quickly stood up from the table. "Now if you will excuse me . . ."

Flushed, Constance stormed away from the table. Her heart

was pounding; unused to confrontation, she was embarrassed and invigorated at the same time. She went out on deck and held the rails tightly. Thinking of Mr. Thomas's wide-eyed surprise (his toupee had nearly popped off!), she couldn't help but laugh. She was startled when Dr. Chabron's laughter suddenly joined hers.

"You were brilliant in there, Miss Stone," he said, now beside her at the rails. "Your Professor Moriarty was soundly defeated."

"I don't know what came over me!" Constance laughed. "Moriarty, you say? Well, I don't know if I'd call that man my archenemy. Though, I must say, he *is* rather smug."

Constance chuckled again, looking out on the sea and savoring the moment. It was a warm evening for the Atlantic and the light from a three-quarter moon played on the waves. She then realized that she had barely had anything for dinner—just a few spoonfuls of cold soup (!)—and gladly remembered the fruit in her cabin.

"Oh, Dr. Chabron," she began, then wondered whether she was being too formal. Should she have called him Serge, like he'd signed on the little card? Or was that presumptuous? She coughed slightly. "I wanted to thank you for the fruit basket. It was so thoughtful of you."

"It must have made you feel better," the doctor replied. "I noticed you didn't need to come by sick bay today."

"I'm sorry. I should have come by to tell you how much I appreciated it," she said with a pretty, apologetic wrinkle. "But, the truth is, after taking the sleeping powders last night, I slept till noon! I woke up this morning feeling wonderful, then spent the whole afternoon lounging on a deck chair and reading a mystery novel. It's just come out—and guess what! It was penned by a woman!"

"You don't say!" He smiled back at her.

They were standing side by side, so close that she could smell his scent: hints of tobacco, peppermint, and cologne. She breathed it in with a tingly shiver. Were they being too intimate?

"You must be chilly," he said, edging a bit closer to her.

"Yes, I should be returning to my cabin," she said reluctantly.

"Please, allow me to walk you back, Miss Stone," he said, threading her arm through his.

They slowly walked down the deck, toward the second-class cabins, passing groups of friends laughing over highballs. There were also several couples out—Constance recognized the crossword honeymooners kissing next to a lifeboat—which made her wonder whether she and the doctor also looked like a romantic couple on a moonlit stroll.

"So," he said, smiling, "will you really register to vote when you get back home?"

"You know," she said, "I think I will."

"I have every belief in a woman's capabilities," he said. "We couldn't have gotten through the war without our nurses. They were fast, clever, just invaluable!"

"Yes, during the war there were many women back home who took on men's jobs," Constance began, trying to think of a moment in her life when she herself had been invaluable. "I had my own victory garden. And did some volunteering," she added feebly, then blushed. How paltry it sounded next to war nurses!

"The war wasn't won by soldiers alone," he said earnestly.

"What a generous thought, Dr. Chabron," she said, pausing to give him a smile.

"Please, call me Serge," he said, gently pressing her arm. "And may I call you Constance?"

"Yes, of course." She liked the way he pronounced it; with a French accent, it didn't sound frumpy or serious. She was disappointed to find they'd already arrived at her door.

"Constance," he said, "I'd like for you to dine with me tomorrow night. You see, I am to join the captain's table in first class. I think you'll find the company there more to your satisfaction than your usual dining companions."

"That would be lovely!" she said.

What a delight it would be to dine with Serge, who seemed genuinely curious about her ideas and opinions. Such a stark contrast to those rude men at her table who had been ignoring her for the past two days. In fact, he seemed more interested in her thoughts than George ever had.

"If you have time, why don't you pop round to the infirmary in the morning and show me that new detective novel?" he said. "I *am* curious to see a woman's take on crime."

"Of course," she replied, flattered that he'd found her earlier remark of interest.

"Oh, and the earlier the better. As the day goes by, passengers discover the most ingenious ways of injuring themselves."

She laughed, shaking his hand lightly as she went inside her cabin.

"Good night," she called, then, turning around for a parting glance, added, "*Bonne nuit*!"

She went into her room and rummaged through the fruit bowl, but found she wasn't hungry anymore. As she undressed, the evening's events replayed in her mind. With a little laugh, she tried to remember her exact retort about women and decision making. "We don't need fathers and husbands telling us what we can and cannot do," she'd declared. If George had been there, he'd have been every bit as surprised as Mr. Thomas.

Reaching into her trunk for her dressing gown, she thought about what to wear to dine with the ship's captain. Her lavender satin, the pink silk . . . nothing seemed elegant enough. The first-class dining room was reported to be majestic, and the meals there far more exquisite than the ones served in second class. How thoughtful Serge had been to invite her!

How very glad she was to have made such an affable friend on this voyage, a man who not only was attractive and polite, but with whom she shared common interests. She thought of his accent, his charming manners, his smile, and for some reason was reminded of

Nigel, her first love. She breathed out a long sigh, filled with regret and disappointment. Nearing thirty, a wife and mother, her chances for romance were long past.

Constance tucked her little girls' photograph in for the night, then got into bed. She picked up her detective novel and read a few pages, wondering if, indeed, Serge would like it too.

"Julie!" Simone called from the kitchens as the help was filing out of the dining room. The long dinner shift was over in steerage and the workers were going back to their dormitories.

"Hey, Julie!" Simone caught up to her, panting slightly. "I was just talking to Roger, you know, the sous chef. He said that Pascal and the other cooks are playing cards this evening." Simone lowered her voice, nearly skipping with excitement. "And guess what? Old Tremblay always joins them!" She shot Julie a mischievous smile. "So, there's nothing to keep us from going to the top decks! What do you say?"

"Well . . . ." Julie strung this word out while she was thinking. Simone's grin was so enthusiastic, it was on the verge of bursting open. Julie nodded with a sigh. It seemed she had no choice but to take her on her rendezvous with Nikolai. "If you're sure that Madame Tremblay will be busy, I guess so."

"Great!" Simone said. "Let's get ready!"

Back in the dormitory, they decided to leave their uniforms on; in case someone asked, they could say they were out delivering a message. They took off their caps, however, and let their hair down. They brushed it out ("Ah, Julie, what I'd do to have hair like yours!"), then Simone pulled a small, worn makeup bag out of her kit.

"My sister Marguerite gave me her old powders," she said.

Simone took out a compact, some rouge, and a sticky nub of rose-colored lipstick. She looked into the compact's small mirror, then vigorously rubbed the remnants of pressed powder with the puff. She dabbed it on the patches of spots on her forehead, cheeks, then her nose. She then applied the rouge and the lipstick.

"How do I look?" She smiled.

"Just fine!" Julie smiled back. Really, with makeup, Simone merely looked more colorful.

"And now you!" She approached Julie with a studious expression. "With that pale skin, you really need some rouge. This one is called 'fresh peach.'"

Her brow knotted in concentration as she dusted Julie's cheeks with a few masterly strokes. Simone picked up the lipstick, then paused over the large birthmark above Julie's lip.

"Uh . . . I think your lips are fine as they are," she said diplomatically.

"This is silly," Julie said, touching her birthmark lightly with her finger. "In the moonlight up on deck, you can't really make out colors anyway. Everything is gray."

Looking back in the compact's small mirror, Simone brushed some more rouge on her own cheeks.

"You never know!" she said.

Julie took a quick look around the dormitory. Two or three women were already putting on nightgowns, slippers, and hairnets, others were chatting and relaxing on their bunks. Louise, the washerwoman who slept in the next row, was leafing through the ship's newspaper. She suddenly called out to Julie.

"Hey, you! You got your picture in the paper!"

Simone was hunched over the paper, squealing, before Julie even approached the bed.

"Look, Julie! It *is* you!" she said with a grin.

Julie picked up the paper and looked at it suspiciously. Very few pictures of her existed and none that she liked. When she was twelve, her parents took her to a portrait studio and the photographer insisted on her posing in profile. The photograph was quite flattering—her elegant brow, straight nose, her hair nestled into a bun at the nape of her neck—but it was not her. Without her birthmark, that face was a lie. Here, not only was her blemish plain (and so dark!) but her face looked cross, and what on earth was that on her hand? The streamer, she sighed. It was her—for better or for worse.

She then glanced at the other women in the photo: one was wearing a serious expression and a big hat, and the other was ghostly white and overly thin. Inspecting the photo more closely, she was surprised to find the two women who had been in the doctor's office the day before. The sickly old lady with her rings, dog, and maid, and the woman awaiting the doctor who, despite being beautiful, seemed so self-conscious.

"Look at this," Julie said, passing the paper back to Simone. "I've met these two ladies. We were all at the infirmary yesterday at the same time. How strange that, just a few hours before, we'd all been walking together on the dock!"

"Right." Simone nodded sarcastically. "You three . . . and about five thousand other people! Come on! Let's go!"

Simone tried to hand *L'Atlantique* back to the laundress, but she was now engaged in the rather pointless task of painting her nails.

"No, you keep it, honey," she said.

Julie looked at the women in the photograph again, wondering how *their* voyage had been so far, traveling in luxury on the upper decks. She carefully tore it out and put it inside her Jules Verne book of keepsakes. They left the room quietly, throwing the rest of the newspaper away on their way out, then began the trek up the stairs. Finally, on the last steps, they felt cool air on their faces and saw a patch of evening sky; Julie began breathing properly again, despite the climb.

Just as Simone and Julie were about to surface on the top deck, they heard a couple talking right outside the stairwell. The man's voice was a long slur, the woman's laughter a cackle. The couple was dancing around, obviously in their cups, giggling and falling onto the rails. The girls could detect bits of English.

"Americans," Simone mouthed to Julie, with a little snort.

They waited a moment below the deck for the couple to move on. With a sigh, Julie tried to remember the last time she'd danced, celebrated, or laughed long and hard. Was it the Fête Nationale in 1914? It seemed another life, and she another girl. Perhaps tonight she would be that girl again.

"Well," said Simone, when they were alone again, "I think it's safe to say that *wasn't* Douglas Fairbanks and Mary Pickford!"

They came out onto the decks and looked around. Couples were tucked into small spaces: between lifeboats, at the rails, on the benches riveted into corners, around the deck-chair storage bins. No one even glanced at the two young women from steerage.

"What do you want to do first? Should we go peek into the ballroom?" Simone asked.

"Oh, Simone, do you really think we'll be able to mix in with the first-class passengers? Like this?" She curtsied, holding out the hems of the unflattering black uniform.

"I guess you're right," Simone said. "But look! The moon's out. Let's go to the rails and listen to the music. Maybe *they'll* come to *us*."

The sound of a string quartet floated out of the dining room. After a few minutes, Julie felt a tap on her shoulder.

"May I have this dance, mademoiselle?" Nikolai asked with a smile.

Vera walked into the dining room and was led to her table by the maître d'hôtel. She was glad for his assistance, as she would have never found it on her own. She sat down and saw that, although everyone was there, two additional places were set at their ample table.

A waiter in a black tie and a thin mustache came by to take their orders. Without looking at the menu, Vera said, "*Oui, un croûte au pot pour moi, s'il vous plaît,*" then greeted the others at table.

"Good evening, everyone. I trust you've all enjoyed a pleasant day." Vera placed her napkin into her lap, feeling she had already made her contribution to the conversation for that meal.

Her dining companions returned to the discussion they'd been having before her arrival. Americans returning home after traveling in the Old World, they were all agreeing on the superiority of their own country.

"Europe . . . quaint, I'd call it. But so dilapidated! Their capitals are nothing but peeling paint and broken plaster!"

"Well, there *was* the war!" conceded one.

"Even so! Compare, if you will, the Brooklyn Bridge and New York's skyscrapers to the dusty—"

Vera sighed at the predictable dullness of their reflections and let her eyes wander around the room.

She noticed that the captain's table was receiving an uncommon amount of attention. Vera looked to the center of the room and saw that famous Hollywood couple (who were they again?) seated regally at the captain's side. Amused, she watched as pompous poseurs around the dining room strained themselves to watch them through their monocles and behind their fans. Indeed, Vera mused, this celebrated couple was the embodiment of American culture (in all its superlative glory!): melodramatic film stars who acted without their voices.

Suddenly, a young couple was standing behind the two empty seats at the table.

"Excuse our tardiness," said the man, bowing slightly before seating his wife, and then himself. "We boarded last night in Southampton and we've spent a tiring day tracking down a lost trunk." He smiled around the table. "Now, allow me to introduce myself. I am Mr. Josef Richter and this is my wife, Emma."

Vera nodded at the couple. There was something familiar about this young man: his high forehead and Roman nose, his straight bearing and graceful gestures. Pity she hadn't caught his surname. She tried to be attentive as the others at her table introduced themselves to this handsome pair; she'd long since forgotten who they were. Finally, the circle came around to her.

"And I am Mrs. Vera Sinclair," she said politely.

The young man dropped his napkin and stared at her.

"And, where are you from, Mrs. Sinclair?" he asked pointedly, his voice strained.

"I'm originally from New York, but I lived in Paris for ages," she said, surprised at his curiosity as well as his tone. She would have continued, adding something lighthearted or witty—about homelands or aging—but his expression did not encourage it.

"I believe you knew my father, Mr. Laszlo Richter, from Budapest?" he asked, eyebrows arched.

Ah, thought Vera, this is why I thought I'd seen him before! He looks so like his father! Of course she remembered Laszlo. One of her "Thirteen Lovers" from times past, he had left a mark. In fact, after him, it was a long time before she had another.

They'd met the summer of '99 at the Grand Hotel Bad Ragaz in Switzerland. Vera and her friend Mathilde had gone there to spend a rejuvenating month taking baths in the thermal waters; Laszlo, she understood later, was being treated for melancholia. With thick, dark hair and a perfect profile, he was an extremely attractive forty-odd—even more so than his son was now—and she enjoyed the challenge of making him smile. Vera and Laszlo began spending their days together: taking long strolls through the beautiful Alpine grounds, dining, dancing; the following week, they began sharing a bed.

One morning, toward the end of the month, she woke up in Laszlo's arms to find him crying. "Oh, Vera," he sobbed, "I don't want to let you go." After confessing to being married, he began making promises to leave his family—a wife and son—and come to Paris to be with her. Although during their brief time together, she had reveled in his company (and had even admitted to herself that, for once, one of her affairs seemed to have true potential), she wouldn't allow it—not with a child involved. As a young girl, Vera had suffered her own parents' absence; as a new wife, she'd discovered her inability to bear children. No, she would not destroy a family, one boy's childhood. She asked Laszlo to give her time to think, then began packing her bags.

Without saying good-bye, Vera left Bad Ragaz, entrusting Mathilde to deliver a farewell note. On the train home, she stared blindly out the window, angry with him for keeping the truth to himself but, even more, grieving for their stillborn relationship. For months afterward, at least once a week, she received thick letters from Budapest and dutifully sent them all back, unopened. She was relieved when, the following spring, they'd abruptly stopped coming. She never heard from him again.

"Yes, I remember him!" Vera smiled at the coincidence, wondering whether she was looking now at the same boy his father had mentioned over two decades before, in her bed at a posh Swiss spa. "Such an elegant man. A banker, I believe. How is he now?" she asked pleasantly.

"My father has been dead many years, madame. Didn't you know?"

The young Richter's voice remained steady and sober, but Vera could tell he was on the verge of losing his temper. His wife, Emma, was staring at her in wonder, her mouth ajar, but her eyes riveted.

"When I was a boy, he killed himself." He paused, clearing his throat but keeping a sharp eye on Vera. "After he was gone, my mother went through his papers and read his letters. There were hundreds of pages addressed to one Madame Vera Sinclair, rue Danton, Paris." He nearly spit out the name and address; he'd been carrying them in his mouth for years. "She told me my father died of a broken heart."

"Darling!" his wife whispered, dragging her eyes away from Vera, grasping his arm. "Please! Now's not the time . . ."

With tenderness, she tried to get her husband's attention, but his gaze remained fixed on Vera. Their fellow diners stared at Vera and Josef Richter in silence, their eyes darting from one face to the other. An older gentleman took a quick gulp of wine, considered intervening, then closed his mouth, dumbfounded. Although their conversation had not been loud or even ill-mannered, a visible change in the table's countenance had taken place; this attracted the attention of people at neighboring tables, who began murmuring unanswered questions.

Vera's fallen face paled as she tried to take in Richter's words. Laszlo had killed himself? She clasped her eyes shut with a groan. What had those letters contained? Aching to flee, to be alone, she made herself return his gaze; she looked into the eyes of Laszlo's son.

"I can't tell you how sorry I am, Mr. Richter," she said, her voice reedy and odd from the strain of not crying. What could she say to this miserable young man that would ease his pain? She considered a few kind words about his father, but thought that would be in bad taste. Instead, she tried atoning. "I've made many mistakes over the years," she continued, sliding her long strand of pearls through her hand. "Done reckless things that have undoubtedly hurt other people. I hope one day you will be able to forgive me."

She rose from the table.

"Again, you have my greatest sympathies," Vera added, her voice now flat and tired. He finally looked away, suddenly impatient for her to be gone.

She excused herself from the others at the table and left, trying to hold herself straight, to right her posture. In all Vera's years, despite her many antics and exploits, she had never been cast out in society and intended to carry it off with dignity. She felt the heat from the silent stares at the table behind her, and as she made her way through the room, she met questioning gazes from all the diners she passed.

No matter, she thought, as she smiled politely into those curious faces. Surely they would think a withering old woman incapable of causing scandal. It had all happened so quickly—the first course had not yet arrived—that anyone would assume that the poor dear was merely going to retrieve her dentures, her ear trumpet, or some other necessary apparatus lying forgotten in the cabin. She made it to the corridor before her face cracked.

Her eyes filling with tears, she leaned heavily on her cane and began the slow procession back to her quarters. Vera thought back on her long conversations with Laszlo. She remembered her shock when he told her about his own father, who had corrected his behavior with a horsewhip; her commiseration that last day when he told her about his wretched marriage, forced upon him by family ambitions. Though he was an unhappy man long before she met him, she supposed she was to blame for his suicide. Vera was guilty of exposing him to joy.

She passed through the arcade leading back to the first-class cabins. There, she caught a glimpse of a young couple dancing on the deck. Their sizes were so dramatically different that they looked like an illustration from a children's book, an amusing exaggeration depicting Big and Small. As the waltzing couple swung near, she recognized the girl. She was the member of the service crew she'd seen in the infirmary, the one with the face of a dirtied egg. Their eyes met for a moment and, despite her own sorrow, Vera couldn't help but smile at her. She looked so happy.

"Young lovers," she sighed to herself, then shivered.

Did love ever end well? She had the sudden urge to warn the girl, to try to protect her from the clutches of a man's affection. As she passed the couple, Vera glanced back and shook her head. What advice could she presume to offer?

She was exhausted when she arrived at her cabin; from the physical exertion of walking down corridors, from not having eaten, but mostly from trying to keep composed. Vera sank down on the bed, letting her cane fall to the floor, and threw her face into her hands. She was still trying to absorb what she'd heard. All these years she'd assumed that Laszlo's letters had stopped coming because he'd finally come to terms with the idea that they couldn't be together. Now, she realized he never had.

After a few minutes, Amandine knocked softly and entered.

"You're already back?" she asked, concerned. "Are you unwell?"

"I don't know," Vera answered truthfully.

"Would you like me to brush your hair?" When faced with the unknown, Amandine offered practical solutions. "Do you need help with your bedclothes?"

"You go on to bed," Vera said. "Don't worry about me."

Amandine silently hung Vera's cloak and poured her a glass of water. Before going back to her quarters, she filched the copy of *L'Atlantique* from the table. Earlier that evening, she'd noticed Miss Vera on the fringe of a poor-quality photograph. Skinny and white, she looked like a skeleton. It was the last thing she needed to see at the moment.

Once alone, Vera scanned the room for something to make her feel better. She looked at her journals on the table next to her bed but couldn't open them. Not tonight. She felt ashamed of the entry detailing her conquests, her Thirteen (unlucky!) Lovers. She then spied the telephone on the writing table. Upon its discovery after the launch, she'd found it ridiculous. Now it seemed a miracle.

She crossed the room and picked it up. After a few seconds' delay, she gave the number to the operator. The cranky mechanical ring sounded again and again; she was about to hang up when she heard him.

"*Allô*?" he said through the static.

"Oh, Charles!" she cried. The relief, the joy of hearing his voice made her throat tighten.

"Vera?" he asked in wonder. "But, where are you? Didn't you board the *Paris*?"

"My cabin has a telephone, if you can believe that," she answered.

"What *is* the world coming to?" Despite the shaky connection, she could hear the smile in his voice. "Tell me, then. How is the voyage so far?"

"Oh, Charles, I feel like hell," she said, trying not to cry. "Bloody, bloody hell."

"Well, I see some kind sailor has been giving you elocution lessons," he began.

"I'm serious!" she cut him off.

The buzz on the line seemed louder as he hesitated.

"It's not . . . your . . . condition, is it?" he managed.

"No, it's not my body. That would be easy! I'm afraid it's my conscience," she said, her voice dropping.

"It's about time!" He laughed, obviously relieved not to have to discuss her illness.

"Oh Charles, stop joking." She had to raise her voice to talk over the static. "Listen, do you remember some twenty years ago, I met a Hungarian man at Bad Ragaz? The one who used to send me all those letters?"

"Yes, in fact I do," replied Charles, serious now. "You never opened a single one. You just jotted on them '*Retournez s.v.p.*' and back to the post they went. At the time I thought you suffered from an appalling lack of curiosity."

"Well, due to an unfortunate twist of fate, his son was sitting next to me at dinner tonight."

Charles said something in response, but Vera couldn't make out his words.

"Will you speak up, dear? I can't hear you over all this crackling," she was saying when the line went dead. Vera stared into the receiver for a moment, considered calling him back again, then hung up. She kicked off her shoes and lay down on the bed, curling herself into a ball, missing Charles and feeling more alone than she had since childhood. Vera began to cry, hard painful sobs that burned her throat. She wept for Laszlo, yes, but she also wept for herself.

Shivering with cold, Julie sat on the metal bench, nervously watching Nikolai dance with Simone. During their last waltz, he'd said he felt sorry for her, just standing there, looking on. Julie would have found him gallant and thoughtful if they didn't seem to be having so much fun; ever since the song started, they'd been chatting and laughing like old friends. She was sure that Simone had clever things to say and undoubtedly had not once mentioned ship engines or seasickness. How did she do it? Simone seemed so at home in a man's arms. In comparison, Julie was anxious, stiff, dull.

When the song finally came to an end, Nikolai and Simone walked back to the bench wearing satisfied smiles.

"Well, I'm going to leave you two lovebirds alone," Simone called out to Julie's horror. "Don't be too late getting back to the dormitory!" She winked, then waved. "Great meeting you, Nikolai! See you around!"

As they watched her sashay back to the stairwell, he shook his head with a grin.

"Your friend's a real hoot!"

"Yes," Julie begrudgingly agreed.

Nikolai nested himself on the narrow bench and pulled Julie onto his lap.

"You, on the other hand," he said, whispering into her hair, "are something much more special."

He quickly rubbed the warmth back into her arms, then wrapped her in a long embrace. Closing her eyes, she thawed with a little moan. He *was* interested in her. Perhaps Simone was the kind of girl boys liked being friends with, but nothing more?

Nikolai cupped her face in his massive hands, then reached down to kiss her. His lips played on hers, grazing, pecking, nibbling, until he gently toyed hers open and kissed her passionately. Julie felt her pounding heart fall into her stomach; light-headed and trembling, she was glad she was sitting down. When he pulled back to look at her, she reached her hand up to his face, timidly exploring his chin, his lips, then slid her fingers through his shaggy hair.

He was bending down to kiss her again when a half dozen first-class tourists began filing out on deck. Dinners finished, cigarettes in hand, they had come out to enjoy the moon before going up to the ballroom. Passing alongside the bench, one of the women was startled by the couple in the shadows.

"Oh my!" she said, clutching her breast and raising her lorgnette to see them better, as if this were a comical scene from an operetta where she herself discovers two lusty servants.

Nikolai and Julie jumped up; he grabbed her hand and began to run. Dodging strollers and air vents, they bolted down the deck hand in hand until they reached the bow. Panting, they stood for a moment grinning at each other, trying to catch their breath. Nikolai then grasped her waist and began waltzing around in circles.

"Odin, dva, tri—odin, dva, tri—odin, dva, tri . . ."

He counted in Russian as he spun her faster and faster, until they both fell back onto the rails, laughing. He put his arm around her and, facing the water and the moon, they were hushed by the dark and the silence.

"Oh, Nikolai, you must miss Russia very much," Julie said softly, suddenly realizing that she too had left her homeland.

"Yes, I do," he said, nodding slowly. "But I miss a Russia that doesn't exist now. It's changed since the revolution, you know. We Russians are emotional, sentimental, spiritual people. That's why my father took me to get this tattoo." He showed her the dark intersected lines on his arm. "It's the orthodox cross. He wanted me to remember the real Russia, not what it is now. Those Bolsheviks are cold, godless machines." He breathed heavily, squeezing Julie closer. "Now, it seems everything's changed."

"I understand what you mean." Julie nodded. "France has also changed since the war."

"Eh, the war!" Nikolai spat.

She looked up at his face, wondering what he meant.

"Did you fight?" she asked.

"For about two weeks!" He barked out a bitter laugh. "Then I got out. What idiots those men were, rotting in the trenches!"

"Idiots!" she cried. "Those were brave men who fought and died. And you? What were you? A deserter? A coward?"

"Hey, hey! Calm down!" He grabbed her shoulders and stared into her face. "I am no coward! If I'd been alive when Napoleon invaded Russia, I would have fought—and proudly! But this war was madness! Just nonsense!" Nikolai sneered. "None of those poor dupes in the mud knew why they were down there, just waiting to die."

"My brothers were those poor dupes!" she shouted, furious now. "And, yes, they died! But they would have never left their comrades in the trenches and deserted. How could you!"

She whisked around and ran. She heard him calling her name, but she quickly darted into the first door she saw. Her feet sank on the deep-pile carpet. Skittering down the corridor, she slid her hand along the mahogany paneling, grazed the damask curtains. Perfume hung in the air. Still shaking with indignation, she slowed down to admire the beautiful place she'd wandered into. With a snort, she realized it was merely a hallway, a lowly passage from one magnificent place to another. How different life was up here!

When she finally found a stairwell, she made a rapid descent down to more familiar quarters: metal walls, rope railings, linoleum floors. Back in steerage, she snuck back into the dormitory as quietly as possible. Julie peered over at Mme. Tremblay's bunk, searching her narrow bulge in the covers. She wasn't there. Was that good or bad? She was relieved to see Simone was asleep; she certainly didn't feel like talking to her about Nikolai. Silently taking off her dress, she smelled him there, a light scent of petrol sweat. Strangely, she did not find it unpleasant.

She got into bed, where, on the pillow, lay her book, a Christmas gift her brothers had received before she was born. When her eyes had adjusted to the dim light, she studied the cover: there was Michael Strogoff, the czar's courier, on horseback, ducking rebel fire, speeding bravely ahead. *That* Russian was no deserter. To calm herself down, Julie began flipping through the pages.

Running her fingers over the cheap pulp, wrinkled and soiled from wear, she thought of her brothers. She found dark smudges that looked like fingerprints, grease from their oil-stained hands. On one page she found a long, thin stain, as if someone had once used a blade of grass for a bookmark. Which one of them might have done that? And here, had a gnat been killed between these pages? Leafing through this book, she felt connected to all four of her brothers at once; she felt their presence.

From its splayed pages, she began pulling out letters, dozens of thin letters from Loïc, the rare postcard from Didier and Émile. *Idiots.* She thought of her brothers, uniformed, mustached, and smiling. *Poor dupes.* They hadn't felt that way about the war, had they? Surely they had found meaning in what they were doing, *waiting to die*? Did they know what they were fighting for? Or had they too thought it nonsense, madness?

Among this precious correspondence, she picked out a yellowed envelope: the last letter Loïc had sent her. She opened it carefully;

like all the others, the creases of the thin pages were fragile from all the times she'd folded and unfolded it. From the random spots of ink and the scrawled handwriting, Julie had always imagined Loïc writing this letter on his knees while squatting in the trenches.

31 October 1918

Dear Julie,

As you can see from the date above, tomorrow is All Saints' Day. Do you remember going to the cemetery when we were children? How serious we were as we lay flowers on our grandparents' graves? Tomorrow will you go and honor our brothers as well? Here, between the fighting and the Spanish flu, we would need a train to carry the flowers to remember all our dead.

It is cold and rainy in the trenches, but we mole men are used to mud and worms. At the moment, with an army blanket over my shoulders and some bitter coffee to take off the chill, I'm listening to my fellow soldiers talk of going home. You see, there have been rumors of peace here lately. After the fierce attacks of spring and summer, they say the Germans are coming to the end of their resources. But here in my underground home, it's hard to imagine a normal life. And, sadly, many of the things I used to enjoy somehow seem pointless to me now.

I often think of Jean-François, Émile, and Didier—"les grands"*—and wonder if they too were cold and miserable. Did they dream about Maman's oyster fritters and tripe like I do? Did they relish each cigarette and look forward to the odd shot of pastis? Did they love their comrades? And their officers? Were they gallant men, worthy of ordering troops to their death? I do hope so.*

If all this talk of an armistice is true, then I should be seeing you shortly.

Your big brother who loves you,
Loïc

Julie had already written the response, a lighthearted missive about life in Le Havre, when they got the official letter with the military seal. It was November 11.

"No!" her mother screamed. "Not Loïc! Not my baby!"

The postman had delivered it around nine; the church bells began ringing at noon. The streets overran with people, sporting impromptu tricolor ribbons and breaking out dusty bottles of liqueurs and wine to toast on the streets. Groups erupted into "La Marseillaise" but only a few could sing more than a few lines without crying, tears of pride, joy, and relief streaming down their cheeks. Saint François was celebrating, but Julie and her parents remained at home, indignant at the unfairness of fate. The armistice would not bring Loïc home.

Julie took the last letter she'd written him and carefully folded it into a paper boat. She walked outside to the canal that ran behind their house and placed the boat in the water. She'd watched it float, bobbing up and down, until it got heavy, waterlogged, and sank. Then, finally, she burst into tears. The church bells were clanging merrily, but for her, it was a death toll.

She refolded his last letter, returned it to its frail envelope, and tucked it back inside the book. She closed her eyes and imagined her brother's face. Unlike their older brothers, all three ruddy and stocky, Loïc had looked more like Julie. They shared the same pallor, copper hair, agate eyes. She imagined them walking along the waterfront, skimming stones on a summer day, the sun gleaming off Loïc's hair, a mirror of her own. In her mind, she saw her parents smile again, like they used to before the war.

Julie was stowing the letters and cards, one by one, when she came across the letter from Nikolai. She opened the thick, clean paper and reread the words. *There is a connection between us . . .* Impossible! A man who had left his comrades in the trenches to later insult their memory? How could she have been so excited about such a man? She didn't even know him. Julie angrily flicked the stiff paper with her finger. She was tempted to rip it to pieces, to wad it into a ball and throw it across the room. Instead, however, she stored it alongside the letters from her loved ones. She then closed the book and tried to sleep, willing herself to dream of Loïc, of all her brothers. To hear their voices and laughter again, to see them move.

DAY THREE

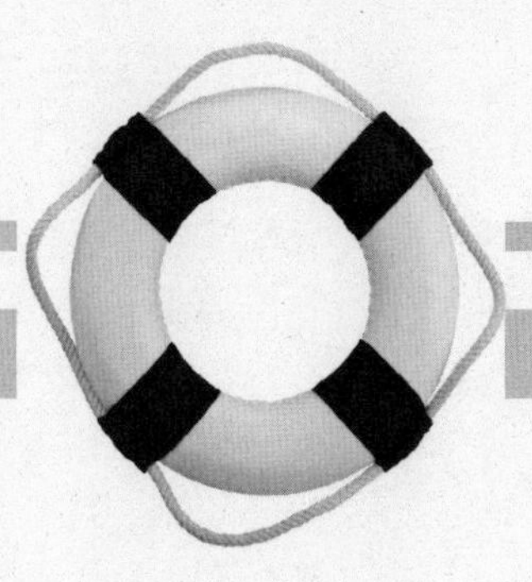

Constance's eyes flew open in the dark. Terrified and confused, she groped for George's sleeping body, only to bang her hand against a bed rail. Where was she? She fumbled for the light and was finally able to pull the chain of a small lamp she couldn't remember ever seeing before. Panting hard, her heart pounding, she scanned the tiny, wood-paneled room with the slow realization that she was (implausibly!) in an ocean liner cabin. She sat up and breathed out. She could still see the last, fleeting images from the nightmare that had woken her.

In the dream, Constance had obviously done something horrible. Her mother, grimly dressed as a pilgrim, was furious. A black chicken in her hand, she stopped plucking to point at her daughter, who was only the size of a child. "How could you, Constance! How could you!" Feathers flew around her as she cried out, loudly accusing her daughter of some unknown abomination. Constance breathed out again. What a relief to find it was only a dream, that no crime had been committed.

As she closed her eyes, the image of her mother was still clear in her mind. Although it was disturbing to see her looking so angry, it was a refreshing change to see her talking (shouting, even) and wearing different clothes. An unlikely outfit, perhaps—a black dress, an apron and bonnet, like Constance herself had once worn in a Thanksgiving play at elementary school—but it was clean and pressed. In the real world, Lydia had not spoken, washed, or changed her clothes in months. She had been haunting the family home in her nightgown—now a filthy gray rag covered in stains—her long hair loose and stringy, her body reeking of sweat and urine. A furtive, ghostly creature, she startled her husband, Gerald, in the kitchen at night, or in the back garden at dawn.

These last six months, Constance had been visiting her parents every day. With patience and care, she'd tried to soothe her mother, to encourage her to bathe, to talk; sometimes she treated her like a small child, at others she used reason. But Lydia rarely acknowledged her, and when she did, it was to put a safe distance between them. Constance had never captured her mother's imagination, had never interested her in the least. It almost seemed as if her attempts offended Lydia, the *thought* that her neurosis could be cured by the inane chatter of a daughter nearing middle age.

It was her father's despair that had led to this round-trip Atlantic voyage, his naïve idea that seeing her younger daughter might help (as if Faith's self-absorbed conversation was any more therapeutic!), though truly, no one—not even Gerald himself—believed it. Now, without Faith or hope, Lydia would be committed to an institution.

Constance shuddered under her warm blankets, dreading her return home. Near tears but unable to cry, her throat grew constricted and dry. She got up and poured herself a glass of water, her nervous hands spilling half of it on the floor. Swallowing the water in uncomfortable sips, she glanced at her travel clock; it was four in the morning. She eyed the sleeping powders on the bureau. Not wanting to risk sleeping late—she didn't want to miss seeing the doctor in the morning—she shook just a tad into her water, swirled it around, and gulped it down.

With a fidgety sigh, she climbed back under the covers of the compact bed, wondering what she might have done in the dream to make her mother so angry. Perhaps, she mused, it was future fury, reserved for the day they took her to the mental hospital. Really, though, Constance didn't believe in dreams. Meaningless little vignettes, absurd cabaret acts, this was how the mind entertained itself at night.

She turned off the light and, in the dark, felt her throat, still tight, for lumps. Was this just nerves? Or could she be coming down with something? Making an effort to control her breathing—inhaling deep, exhaling long—she slowly began to relax.

When she was younger, Constance had taken a great interest in her health. As a child, she always enjoyed a visit to the doctor's: the sterile smell of the office; the serious instruments; the caring, attentive faces of the doctors and nurses; their cautious explorations to determine what was wrong. As a young adult, convinced that a sound body led to a sound mind—and anxious not to repeat her mother's mental history—she underwent a variety of cures. Before her daughters were born, she had experimented with innovative, modern treatments—from vegetarianism to sexual abstinence, to enemas and Fletcherizing—and had routinely spent a few weeks a year in sanatoriums. Faith had always had a mocking attitude about Constance's devotion to her physical well-being, calling it a "pathetic hobby." But her sister—with her cigarettes, wine, and endless cups of coffee—was certainly not one to talk about health.

Feeling her brow with a cool hand, she thought that perhaps Dr. Chabron, if he wasn't too busy, could have a look at her when she brought him the mystery novel. She hadn't had a physical examination for ages—when Elizabeth was born six years ago, she had begun focusing all her attentions on her little ones—but after a fortnight in Paris with its mold and Old World dust, she thought she could use one. The ship's surgeon seemed an excellent professional (didn't Captain Fielding credit him with saving his life?) and was certainly kind and mannerly. Yes, in his hands, she was sure she would be well cared for.

No longer tense—the powders seemed to be taking effect—she nestled down into the blankets, determined to sleep, to dream, but not of her mother. As she began to doze, she was imagining the aseptic whiteness of the doctor's infirmary, the sheet of the cot pulled stiff. Dr. Chabron's eyes brimmed with worry over her, as his clean hands gently inspected her neck, then clasped her wrist to check her pulse. "I don't know what to make of your case," he was saying, his voice grave, yet passionate. "I'm going to have to examine you thoroughly . . ."

It was a little after dawn when Vera woke up, vaguely rested from a brief, dreamless sleep. From the window, a hazy white light filled the room; a thick cloud of fog hung in the outside air. She liked the idea that just some overzealous precipitation was able to make an ocean liner—a floating island decked with city lights—invisible. It was like waking up to discover she had become a ghost overnight.

Vera crawled down to the foot of the bed, waking Bibi in the process, then snatched her cashmere shawl from the top drawer of the trunk. Charles had given it to her for her sixtieth birthday, claiming it was just the thing for venerable old ladies. However, Vera's secretary, Sylvie, had joked that, so soft and sky blue, it would make a perfect baby blanket for a tiny boy. "That's what we need, my love!" Charles had cried enthusiastically. "A baby!"

Her smile instantly turned to a frown as she peered over at the telephone. Perhaps she should call him again, explain in detail what had happened at dinner last night? They could discuss what she could do to alleviate this strange heaviness inside her, or devise ways of making Laszlo's son understand. No, she couldn't bear to hear the static, the audible reminder of the distance now between them. She looked toward the window, thankful for the fog; she did not want to see their swift progress across the Atlantic, toward America.

She wrapped the shawl around her shoulders and snuggled back under the covers, wondering how to spend her day. The third day, the midpoint of the journey, always carried with it an air of ennui. Even for novice travelers, by day three there was little on the ship left to be discovered; they had already met their fellow passengers, explored all the decks and rooms, inspected the engines, and made attempts at various games. It was on the middle day afloat that people on board began growing restless, seeking entertainment in other forms—usually cocktails.

Vera thought back on her other, more lively voyages—fox-trotting for hours with a dapper gentleman from New Orleans, playing badminton with Charles until their shuttlecock flew into the sea, getting tight with that master fencer—then suddenly remembered how she and Laszlo, during their one-month affair, had also discussed crossing the Atlantic together. It was just the beginning of a plan, the germ of an idea: New York, Boston, Niagara Falls.

She looked out into the fog again. Perhaps she should not have been so noble. Would young Richter be a happier man today if his father had merely left his mother for another woman? Would it have worked out between them? If Vera had stayed with Laszlo, would he be here with her now?

By taking his life at the age of forty-two, she thought crossly, he had certainly limited his possibilities. Braiding her long, white hair, she wondered how he had chosen to do it. Though Vera knew she had no right to know, to be privy to the details, it had always been important for her to envision a death to believe in its finality. In her mind's eye, she had seen her parents swept away by the flood; her former husband thrown from the horse; her grandmother wasted away to mere skin and confusion. And Laszlo?

Pondering all the ways one might commit suicide and keeping his character in mind—his private nature, his discretion—Vera finally settled on hanging. Its simplicity, lack of undue gore, and muffled silence made it a likely candidate. How had he felt as he climbed onto the chair? Trembling? In despair? Or . . . victorious?

There was a light knock and Amandine poked her head through the door.

"Good morning," she said. "I thought I heard you moving around. Would you like me to help you get dressed?"

"Good morning, dear." Vera forced a smile. "With this fog, I don't think I'll be going out. Perhaps I'll spend the day in my dressing gown."

She saw no reason to don awkward-fitting clothes to stay in the cabin. Remembering her once inviting body, she now hated the sight of it—the skinny limbs, bulging varicose veins, pickled breasts, ribs ripe for counting—and avoided it as much as she could.

"And your meals, ma'am?" Amandine asked.

The wrinkles on her brow deepened as she called to mind the scene at dinner: young Richter's accusatory tone, the shocked stares from their fellow diners. Of course, those trifles could not compare to the revelation of why Laszlo's letters had stopped coming.

"I'll take them here today," she said.

"Shall I order breakfast, then?" Amandine asked.

"Just a pot of tea for now, thanks," she answered, ignoring Amandine's tentative look of concern.

"Come, Bibi," she called. "Let's go order some tea."

With a pointed lack of excitement, the old dog trudged over to the door and waited patiently for Amandine to secure the leash.

When they were gone, Vera bravely picked up her journal, leafing through various entries until she came to "Thirteen Lovers." Although she knew what words it contained, her heart was pounding. She scanned the first few pages, skimming the bit about when she and Pierre Landeau, a photographer from Marseilles, were first alone together:

I studied his face and was surprised to find that his lips fit together like jigsaw puzzle pieces; the subtle arches were perfectly matched, the weighty pout expertly joined. I then understood why he had neither mustache nor beard: beyond those Lips his face needed no further decoration. My eyes were then distracted by a jagged row of lower teeth. I longed to run my tongue slowly across them, to see if they might cut me.

Vera gave her former self an indulgent smile. Although she recognized her handwriting, sometimes she found the words themselves rather foreign. She flipped forward a half dozen pages, then paused again. Here was the rupture with Roderick Markson, the Scottish journalist she'd been with for some six months.

The relationship had come to its irretrievable end and had its proper burial, and like the Executor of a will, I made a complete inventory of everything that was left: a wee anthology of letters, an artful poem (Had it truly been composed for me? Or for one of my predecessors?), a dozen dazzling smiles, a small collection of well-wrought romantic compliments, and seven thin bracelets, mere gypsy-bands, which made a silvery ripple when worn together. I thought hard what to do with this Estate. There was no one to inherit such mediocre treasure, no one to purchase the used memories of a lost romance. The paper, I burned. The bracelets, one by one, I cast into the Seine, imagining their dire Repugnance as they began to attract ugly, whiskered fish-admirers. The other, less tangible items I had to make disappear like the magician at the circus.

Vera looked affectionately at the amusing illustration she'd made of a hideous, lascivious monkfish eyeing a slim bracelet with open desire. Then, with a slight moan, she turned the page to Bad Ragaz. Only three pages were dedicated to Laszlo Richter.

The very first evening, after taking a cursory glance at the guests, I remarked to Mathilde on the Anomaly of the handsomest man in the room dining alone in a corner. He was somberly staring into his consommé as if to read his future. I immediately got up from the table—not bothering to deliver a message via waiter—and asked him if he would care to join us. He looked at me in astonishment.

Closing her eyes, a tear sliding down her cheek, she could see his face perfectly, his quizzical stare slowly turning into a smile as he got up and followed her. He was shy and the ladies had to prod him into telling them—in uneven French, until they discovered his English was impeccable—about his life in Budapest. Even on that first encounter, he had chosen not to mention his family. Was his attraction firm from the start? He ate prawns that night; his long fingers with their pearly-white nails peeled them expertly with a knife and fork. She'd laughed and said, "From *birth,* we Americans are incapable of such table manners!"

She opened her eyes and shut the journal. Really, it was unnecessary to reread the entry—the long strolls, his gentle lovemaking, his urgent begging, the lonely train ride home. She remembered it all perfectly.

Vera suddenly noticed how warm it felt in the room. Shedding her shawl, she felt her forehead. The withered skin was scorching. Was it fever or Laszlo's memory? She couldn't decide which she preferred.

Julie was lying in bed, drenched in sweat. Panting heavily, she couldn't get enough air; would she drown down there under the waterline? She stared up at Simone's bunk with the horrifying sensation that it was going to come crashing down on her.

She'd had that nightmare again, the same one she'd been having ever since she lost Loïc. In the dream, she is by herself when three men come silently into her parents' house. She can't see their faces, but their bodies, half-covered in filthy rags, are hideously scarred by large, deep pox and raised, red splotches. They quickly begin filling their sacks; the speed of their long, thin fingers is supernatural. "Please, please," Julie cries out, begging the thieves, "just let me keep what my mother gave me! These few things here, they are valuable only to me." She grabs the lace as a voice from upstairs screams, "No!" Those fast, slinky fingers snatch it from her hands. They disappear into the night, leaving Julie alone again in an empty house.

Even the first time she'd dreamt it, she woke up knowing, understanding. The valuables her mother had given her were not the piecework but her brothers. She had not been allowed to keep them and Death made quick work of taking them away. Her breathing almost normal now, Nikolai's thoughtless jeers came to mind. She dug her nails into her palms, angry still.

Looking around the room—under the bare-bulb lights, women were pulling up stockings and twirling their hair into buns—Julie realized she'd slept late. She quickly got up, then, dizzy, steadied herself on the bedpost. She closed her eyes, inhaling, exhaling, then began to pull on a fresh uniform. Such a simple cut—a plain shift with big buttons and cotton drawers underneath—was easy to put on swiftly.

Although she still had no appetite, Julie went into the lounge for a quick cup of tea before serving breakfast to the passengers. She found a place at the end of a bench, sat down, and, gently blowing the steam off her cup, listened to the other women talk.

"I sold Douglas Fairbanks a dozen roses yesterday," boasted a pretty blonde. "He's a gentleman," she said with a knowing nod. "*Very* polite."

"I know!" exclaimed a tall, graceful woman down the bench. "He came in and bought Cuban cigars too!"

"Didn't you just love him in *The Mark of Zorro*?" Simone asked, receiving many dreamy sighs in response. "And *His Majesty, the American*?" she added. "He was so charming!"

"I saw Mary Pickford yesterday on deck," added another. "Her hair is as beautiful in real life as it is in the pictures!"

"Yes, but do you think it's a permanent wave? Or is it natural?" asked one of the hairdressers, considering the matter worthy of serious debate.

"Hmph!" One of the nannies gave a loud snort. "Those American actors cannot compare to our Sarah Bernhardt! Even now, with only one leg, she could run circles around those hams!"

Suddenly, Mme. Tremblay entered the room, clapping her hands. "It's seven already! Let's go, ladies! Time to get working!"

The women glanced up and sighed at the clock, then went off in different directions. Simone sidled up to Julie as they were leaving the lounge.

"Tell me, then!" she whispered with a grin. "How was your moonlit rendezvous? You two looked every bit like Fairbanks and Pickford, dancing up there on deck!"

"Well," Julie started, looking around anxiously, trying to decide what to say. "Getting to know him a bit better . . . I guess he's not the man I thought he was."

"Really?" Simone's expression squirmed about, trying to mask its own glee while looking disappointed for Julie. "He seemed so serious about you! When we were dancing, that's all he could talk about!"

"Is that right?" Julie raised her eyebrows, surprised to find herself feeling resentful. "I'm sure you two had other things to talk about besides me."

"We *did* have a laugh!" Simone smiled innocently. "What a shame it didn't work out between you!"

"I didn't say that!" Julie declared, suddenly jealous. "We just had an argument. Oh, it was nothing really."

"I see." Simone shrugged. "Well, keep me posted!"

Julie tried not to pout as they entered the dining room. Had things not worked out between them? Was her romance already over, just as it was getting started? Mechanically, she began setting the tables—walking up and down the narrow room, arranging the long rows of cups and saucers, spoons and plates—but her thoughts kept going back to those kisses. With an ill-tempered huff, she went into the kitchen to collect the sugar bowls and honey.

"Good morning," Julie greeted the chef.

Pascal looked up to smile but gave her a concerned grimace instead.

"You're still looking pale, Juliette," he said.

"I didn't sleep very well," she replied with a shrug.

Pascal thought for a moment, then said, "Listen. Why don't you do me a little favor? I'd like for you to go up to the main kitchens and get me some lemons. I think on such a gray day, lemons would be nice for the tea, no?" He handed her a little net bag. "Eight or ten lemons, then. Say they're for Pascal."

"My pleasure," she said with a weak smile, happy to go up to the first-class galley and get a break from steerage (and Simone).

"And Julie," he said softly, "take your time. While you're up there, get some fresh air. Hey—why don't you fetch some of *that* for old Pascal!"

She was heading down the empty corridor when a hand suddenly grabbed her arm, pinching the skin. Terrified, she turned around and saw Mme. Tremblay. Her lips were a straight line, her eyebrows a V.

"Where do you think you're going?" She did not let her go but grasped her arm firmly, as if Julie were a prisoner trying to escape. With her other hand, the head housekeeper looked at her watch. "Aren't you supposed to be in the dining room?"

"Pascal sent me up for some lemons, ma'am," Julie stammered, exhibiting the net bag as proof.

Mme. Tremblay dropped her arm but continued staring at her with her head cocked. Finally, she tucked a strand of hair back into Julie's cap.

"I'm going to need you tonight in hatcheck," she said slowly. "Marie-Claire was injured last night—stuck herself in the eye with a coat hanger, if you can believe that!" She scowled. "I hope you won't be so clumsy!"

"No, ma'am." Julie shook her head quickly, then added, "I have experience with hangers," feeling stupid even as she said it.

"I'll find a first-class uniform for you to wear," she said, looking her up and down, "though it'll have to be a child's size! Oh, and you'll wear your hair down."

"Yes, ma'am." Julie curtseyed with a grin.

"Marie-Claire should be fine by tomorrow," Mme. Tremblay said sternly, wary of Julie's excitement. "It's just for tonight."

As Julie climbed the steps up to first class, she imagined the evening ahead. As she assured all of the elegant passengers that she would take the very best care of their hats and coats, they would insist on tipping her generously. Then, when Douglas Fairbanks came by, he would give her a wink as he strolled into the dining room, a

Cuban cigar in his mouth and Miss Pickford on his arm, carrying dozens of roses.

When she emerged from the stairwell, her smile disappeared into the fog. In Le Havre, they had their share of mist and brume, but Julie had never seen it as heavy as this. The deck was empty, silent, even eerie. Looking around, she supposed the passengers were all seeking refuge from the damp in their drawing rooms and libraries. Vaguely disappointed, she doubted that any of the engine crew would be tempted above either. With a long sigh, she slowly began to make her way down the ship, using the rail as a guide in the white wintry landscape. When the low, two-note cry of the ship's foghorn blew out, she stopped to listen. The back of her neck prickled as Julie watched the fog's cloudy fingers moving around her—she could only see for a yard or two in any direction—and wondered, suddenly, whether this was what poison gas looked like. Were these smoky white tendrils like the ones that had slowly moved through the trenches?

She imagined the boys' terrified faces as they fumbled with their gas masks. Loïc had written to her about his fear of gas and how poorly the masks were designed. How, even during a drill, they would find they couldn't breathe in those monster masks with their big blank eyes and elephant trunks, and tear them off in a panic.

All of his letters—her last link to him—were so vivid that she'd been able to imagine the scenes perfectly; reading them, she could almost see his expressive gestures and hear his voice, a deeper version of her own.

"'*Your big brother who loves you,*'" Julie murmured, quoting his letters' closing line. Of course, he had only begun calling himself her "big" brother after all of the others were dead. "*Loïc.*"

Julie supposed that Loïc had inherited his descriptive skills from their father, who, although illiterate, used to be a magnificent storyteller. It was he who had insisted that his sons go to school—at least to the age of twelve—and was proud to buy his children the occasional book at Christmastime.

When it was Loïc's turn to begin school, he insisted Julie go as well, threatening to play truant if she were not allowed. Their parents finally agreed, especially since her mother was no longer able to teach her the tatting trade. Of all the family, it was Loïc who did best at his studies, though in the end Julie stayed in school longest, until the war broke out.

Loïc worked at the port like the other men in his family, until he decided to play soldier at seventeen. It was then he confided in Julie that what he really wanted to do was become a writer.

The night before he left for active duty, they were sitting together at the waterfront, watching the lighted ships. Their parents, far from feeling the ardent pride they'd displayed in 1914, were in the house, upset and angry. After a few minutes of silence, the water slapping the quays, Loïc reached into his pocket and brought out an article from a local newspaper. In no mood to read, Julie merely skimmed it—a poignant piece on how Le Havre, with all the international forces and military personnel stationed there, had changed during the war—until she got to the bottom, where her eyes were stalled by the initials *L. V.*

"Is this you?" she asked quietly. She was so impressed she couldn't speak above a whisper.

He nodded with a shy smile.

"Julie, I want to write about the war," he explained. "Not just articles, but a soldier's story. How can I, if I don't go? If I stay here at home like a little boy?"

And indeed, Julie could see the care Loïc took in the letters he wrote from the front; they were the obvious drafts of the book he was writing in his head. During training, they'd been rather innocent, filled with courageous words like duty, country, camaraderie. After he became a mole man in the trenches, his tone intensified as his experiences degenerated. It seemed that he wrote about events to rid himself of them, to pack them away for later use. Loïc did not treat the matter with girlish kid gloves for his little sister, but with a hardened stomach and an eye for detail. Sometimes, brambles of barbed wire, disemboweling horses, black, frostbitten toes, or gushing head wounds entered into Julie's dreams, as if she had seen these things herself.

"*Idiots,*" she muttered sadly. "*Poor dupes.*" Nikolai couldn't really believe that; he was just a blusterer, making excuses for himself. With a shiver, Julie relived the compliments, the dancing, the warm kisses in the cool night air, his eyes shining with desire. Despite his crude words, she still hoped that she would see him again, that their story was not over yet.

She pushed herself off from the rail and stepped through the first door she saw. When she finally entered the large upper-deck kitchen, steamy and bright, its homey chaos cheered her up at once.

A dozen men in chef's hats and long aprons were busy at work, peering into ovens and large copper pots, ladles and utensils dangling above them like Christmas ornaments. She took a deep breath, savoring the different smells that would come together to make up the à la carte luncheon menu: subtle, buttery fish stocks, roasting lamb and beef, caramelized carrots, fresh bread. She spied the pastry chef in the corner, putting the final touches on an assortment of cakes and puddings, each dripping with fruit, nuts, cream, or chocolate. Julie licked her lips. In the dark kitchen under the waterline, where fried onions were always the base for the family-style meals, she was never tempted by hunger.

Julie spotted a cook—the robust grandfather type—pausing to wipe his hands on a towel and cornered him with her bag.

"Lemons, eh?" he shouted. "Next he'll be wanting a champagne cocktail!"

After he'd filled the net with his finest lemons, he handed it to Julie.

"These are for old Pascal. And this, mademoiselle," he said, giving her a wink and a chocolate éclair, "is for you."

Constance sat on the edge of her bed, wondering when she should venture down to the infirmary. Serge had said "the earlier the better," but she didn't know exactly what time "early" was. She had noticed during her stay in Paris that the French seemed to have a different notion of time than Americans, often arriving late, dining late, staying late, sleeping late. She was restless in her room, but she didn't want to get to his office before *he* did.

Despite the powders, her sleep had been light and, at six, she was already up. She'd taken a long bath, applied talcum and perfume, then twined her hair up in a lilting bun like women were wearing in Paris. After eating a few pears, she'd tried on various outfits, unsure of what to wear: the long, loose dress with a tied waist was rejected when she remembered Faith saying it looked like a bathrobe; the soft blouse with the tiny pearl buttons was also ruled out. If Dr. Chabron had time to give her a physical (half remembering her dream, she blushed deeply), she didn't want to fumble around with seed pearls. Constance finally chose the sport suit with the straight plaid skirt, which was neither too formal nor too whimsical. Not only did it seem an appropriate choice for a call on a doctor, but the fit was so perfect, she nearly always received compliments when she wore it. She smiled at her reflection in the mirror.

In an attempt at patience, she'd then brought out her watercolors to practice some china patterns. Inspired by the fruit basket, she began painting a circular design, alternating apples and bananas, then using greenery and blue ribbons to round it out. But after fifteen minutes, she found it difficult to concentrate on the delicate strokes and she stopped with a sigh.

She looked at her watch—eight o'clock. Surely, not even a Frenchman could think her visit premature. She went to the washbasin and held the paintbrush under the tap until the water ran clear.

Constance picked up the detective novel and left the cabin. She quickly walked down the dark corridor, then out onto the deck, into the fog. She wrinkled her brow, her hand fluttering up to her neck to steady her silk scarf, caught by a gust of wind. Eager to see him, she realized how lonely she'd been—and not just in Paris, where Faith and her friends had nearly ignored her for two weeks, but in Worcester too.

The infirmary door was still locked when she arrived. She hesitated a moment, then knocked. Dr. Chabron opened the door and greeted her with a broad smile.

"I was hoping that would be you, Constance." His eyes twinkled as he offered her his hand. "Please, come in."

"Hello again," she began shyly, reaching out for his hand. She was about to take it when she heard someone approaching from behind. Startled, feeling almost guilty, she turned and saw a small woman in a black uniform carrying a bulging sack of lemons with one hand and licking a finger of the other. It was the girl she'd run into right here in the infirmary on the first day, the one from the photograph. Such a pretty little thing—a pity about that birthmark.

"Good morning," Constance said.

Wiping her hand on her apron, then shifting the sack, the girl smiled back at her. "Good morning!" she called, then nodded to them both. She was clearly in a rush to get to wherever it was that she was going. "Sir, ma'am," she added in passing.

After she'd disappeared down the corridor, Constance gave Serge her hand and let him lead her into the infirmary.

Once inside, she noticed that the doctor's mustache was freshly trimmed, his nails immaculate, and he smelled of cologne. She smiled at him, thinking that, perhaps, he too had taken care getting ready that morning. He guided her into the inner office, his arm draped loosely around her shoulders, and offered her a chair. He propped himself on a stool.

"I've brought you the detective novel," she said, taking the book out of her bag and passing it over to him.

"My word," he said, looking down at the cover with arched eyebrows. It showed a man in profile, walking with a candle, as two sinister-looking women looked on. "What's it about?"

"The proprietress of a large country manor is poisoned," she said, her eyes flashing mysteriously in fun. "And a number of houseguests are suspected of murdering her—including members of her own family."

"Not the bloodsucking stepsons and brother-in-laws!" he said, pretending shock.

"Quite so!" She laughed. "But, luckily we have a clever Belgian detective on the trail."

"What a relief!" he said, wiping his brow, then added, "Truly, it sounds like good fun. I'll pick it up in New York, if I have time."

"If I finish this in the next day or so, you can just have my copy," she offered.

"That's very kind of you," he said, his eyes gazing into hers with undisguised tenderness.

"Doctor . . . Serge"—Constance blushed slightly—"could I bother you for some medical advice?"

"What is it?" he asked, immediately concerned. "Have you had more headaches?"

"No," she said slowly. "There's a . . . nervous condition that runs in my family. Last night I had a bad dream—it was nothing really—but I woke up with my heart pounding so hard that it frightened me a bit. Well, I realized that I hadn't had a physical examination in years and thought that—if you had a spare moment—perhaps it would be a good idea."

"Of course, I'd be delighted to help you in any way I can. Here, why don't you sit up here on the cot?" He placed his stethoscope around his neck. "Now then, a nervous condition, you say? I doubt there's any cause for alarm, but let me listen to your heartbeat."

Constance sat down, her feet dangling from the cot like a child's. She removed her scarf and waited, passive and silent. He leaned his head in toward her, listening as she breathed, in and out, in and out. Constance could smell his hair, feel the warmth from his body. She felt the pads of his fingers around the base of the stethoscope, moving around her chest, searching for her heart. Having him so near her, she found her pulse quickening again. She drew a quick breath, then bit her lip slightly, wondering whether her heart would betray any secrets to him. What would he learn about her, having listened to it so carefully?

"Your heart sounds normal," Dr. Chabron said. "Strong, in fact. But let me take your blood pressure. Could you push up your sleeve, please?"

Constance mastered her embarrassment and slowly pushed her thin crêpe sleeve almost to her shoulder. She looked away as his hands delicately wrapped a black cuff around her upper arm, and then began pumping it full of air. It became tighter and tighter, until it felt like a violent hand were grabbing her. Using the stethoscope again, he listened to the sound of her blood coursing through her, the cool instrument moving softly around the tender baby-skin of her inner arm. Slowly, rhythmically, he deflated the pressure, until finally, he released the air from the cuff. She swallowed hard then, licking her lips, wondered whether her face was flushed. She could barely look at the doctor now.

"Everything sounds good, Constance. Now then, ehem . . ." His voice took on a clinical tone. "Could you lie down, please?"

Without a word, she swung her legs around and reclined back on the cot. With his brow furrowed in a serious expression, he began to knead her abdomen, feeling for the organs below. A tickling warmth rose from her belly, and she closed her eyes, hoping he would perform more tests, elaborate ones. Remaining ever so still, she tried to breathe quietly, extremely sensitive to his touch.

There was a knock at the examination room door; someone was in the antechamber. Constance quickly sat up, dizzy and disoriented. Dr. Chabron turned toward the door, pausing to collect himself, to arrange his hair. After a second knock, he opened it to find that rickety French maid drawn by the tired old Scotty. Constance remembered this pair; they both belonged to the wealthy old woman she'd seen the first day.

Constance wrapped her scarf around her neck and waited patiently on the cot while Dr. Chabron tended to the woman. He spoke with her swiftly in French, and Constance noticed that his voice sounded different when he spoke his native tongue, deeper and more expressive; he even used more hand gestures. She tried to make out some of the conversation and caught the word *américaine*. And didn't *fièvre* mean fever?

The doctor asked the maid a few questions, then said something to induce the old servant—surely, she was long past the age of domestic service!—to wait in the antechamber. He turned back to Constance.

"You're as healthy as you are beautiful," he proclaimed. "Really, you have nothing to worry about."

"Thank you," she said softly, watching him putting the stethoscope and a few other instruments in his bag. He took her hand and helped her down from the cot.

"I'm afraid I must go now. There's an emergency with an elderly passenger in first class."

Disappointed their time together had been interrupted, she peevishly wondered whether her appointment would have been prolonged if the ailing old person had been in third class. He bent his head toward hers and smiled.

"I'll collect you for dinner at seven," he said in a whisper. "I'm really looking forward to sharing the evening with you."

"Me too," she whispered back. The two short words came out like puffs of smoke; her insides were still simmering.

They all walked out of the infirmary, then Serge gave Constance a little wave as he left her behind in the hall to accompany the slow-moving pair to the elevator. After they'd gone, Constance let out a long sigh. How different her life might have been had she met Serge Chabron early on.

With a toss of her head, she decided to continue her treatment at the beauty parlor. White coats, piles of clean towels, the chemical odors of peroxide and permanents, little bottles and pomades: it was similar to a doctor's office, she thought, if the personnel wasn't too chatty. She wanted to do something different with her hair, something new, more daring. After all, she would be dining at the captain's table!

"Miss Vera." Amandine knocked lightly on the door, then walked into the first-class cabin. "The doctor is here," she announced, before retiring to her own room.

Vera was sitting in an armchair, wrapped in her shawl, looking at the doctor with a slight smile bordering on mischievous.

"Bonjour, jeune homme."

This was one of the privileges of the elderly that Vera enjoyed exercising: referring to anyone, no matter what his station, as "young man." At any rate, she had forgotten his name.

"Good morning, Madame Sinclair," the doctor replied amiably. "How are you feeling?"

"I fear that Amandine, ever since she heard of the gravity of my condition, is overly worried. Perhaps she's afraid of coming in one morning and finding herself face-to-face with a dead body? I think she was rash in calling you today. It is merely an elevated temperature."

He placed his palm on her forehead. "You do feel warm," he said as he opened his bag. He put a thermometer in her mouth, checked her pulse, then prepared a cool compress at the sink.

"Let me see," he murmured, reading the thermometer. "Thirty-eight. I believe that is 101 degrees Fahrenheit. A moderate fever. Nothing to worry about, I shouldn't think."

"I'm sure it's just cabin fever." Vera smiled. "With this fog, I haven't been out all day."

"And, I think you should probably stay in," he said as he applied the compress. "Have your maid change these when they get warm. And don't forget to ingest fluids. Plenty of fluids."

She looked into the doctor's handsome face, the strong jawline, the hazel eyes, and found something of Laszlo there.

"Doctor," she asked suddenly, "have you ever known a case where a person has died—literally died—of a broken heart?"

He looked at Vera's curious expression and knew she wasn't joking.

"I have heard about people who, once they've failed at love, have lost the will to live," he answered gently. "I haven't treated those cases personally; my experience lies mainly with war wounds and seasickness. And truly, I don't know if one would go to see a doctor for such a condition." He paused a moment, turned the compress over to its cool side, then asked, "Is there some reason you ask?"

"An old friend of mine died thus," she answered sadly. "I just heard about it yesterday."

"I'm terribly sorry," he said. "Did you receive a wire?"

"No." She blinked the tears from her eyes. "It happened over twenty years ago. I've just met his son here on board."

Her voice trailed off, then stopped. By her tight-lipped, pensive expression, Dr. Chabron could see their interview had come to an end.

"Now, get some rest," he said. He picked up his bag and turned at the door. "Tomorrow morning I'll come to your cabin and check on you, if that doesn't interfere with your plans."

He smiled at her and bowed, then was out the door. When he had left, Amandine came back into the room with her yarn and knitting needles and sat down in the small armchair next to Vera's.

"Yes, you were right," Vera answered her questioning eyes. "I do have a fever."

She turned away from her maid's concern and looked out the window. Everything seemed quieter in that white haze, as if cotton wool were smothering the sounds. Amandine's needles clicked softly, followed by a silent pause at the end of each row. Vera stared into the blankness, caressing her pearls, lost in thought.

"I was inside a cloud once, you know," Vera said abruptly. Amandine stopped her knitting midrow. "Back in 1903, when this century was new and full of promise, poor thing. Charles and I went down near Fontainebleau for a ride in a hot-air balloon with Franck."

"Franck, ma'am?"

"Yes, Franck Lamont. A handsome young man, we met him at one of the Baroness d'Oettingen's marvelous soirées. He was bragging to us foreigners that the French had come up with all the most diverting inventions: the motion picture, the bicycle, the gyroscope, the hot-air balloon . . . He told us he was a balloon pilot—I didn't know such things existed—and he asked us to join him, up in the clouds."

"Ah!" Amandine murmured on cue.

"Charles and I took the train and Franck met us at the station in his motorcar—what a passion the lad had for machines! We had a picnic first and when Franck went into the woods for a private moment, Charles began teasing me about the young man. He said that he'd been stealing glances at me, that it was obvious he was enamored with me. Even though I was old enough to be his mother!" Vera's lips curled into a devious smile.

"Then he took us to the balloon itself. It had a purple and yellow harlequin pattern, like an enormous Easter egg! We climbed in, the gas fire raging above our heads, and, with a quick jerk, we were up! How wonderful it was! Everything looked so different from above. The fields were like a patchwork quilt, and the roads like ropes, twisting through the trees. The buildings were mere boxes and parcels.

"The gusts of air lifted us precariously. We were in a wicker basket, you know. No iron or steel—just a basket! Like a modern-day Moses taken out of the Nile and into the sky!" She opened her hands in a grandiose gesture, then sighed with momentary satisfaction. "Then with a laugh, Franck navigated us into a cloud. A thick, puffy summertime cloud. And when we were enveloped in the mist, it was not my hand he searched for! It was Charles's!" Vera chuckled to herself. "So, it was not a proper Oedipus complex after all!"

Amandine nodded politely through her look of bewilderment, the usual result of these misdirected conversations, when Amandine became the recipient of Vera's private thoughts turned oral discourse.

"It sounds lovely," Amandine said, getting up. "I'm going to order something to eat now. Is there anything you'd like?"

"The doctor said something about fluids, but bring whatever you want, Amandine," she said. "Take Bibi out, will you? She would probably enjoy a little stroll. Thank you."

When Amandine had left, Vera opened the window and put her arm out into the fog to touch the wet haze. Her cloud felt a bit like that, she thought, closing the window again.

After that afternoon, Charles had disappeared with Franck for a few weeks, to be sure. As for Vera, she loved the notion of being airborne, encompassed by clouds, and had always wanted to take to the skies again. But, between the opera season, travels, horse races, and balls (and later, of course, the war), she hadn't, and now it was too late. Ah, if she were Daedalus's daughter, she would fly right off this ship—leap from the funnel!—and head back to Paris. She wouldn't soar to the sun like Icarus but would fly straight and true. As it was, she sighed, this was the closest she'd ever be to a cloud again.

Odd, she thought, she never wrote about that experience in her journals. How many things never got written! And the things that *were* written . . .

Her brow furrowed, thinking again of Laszlo Richter. Vera had treated their affair in a lighthearted way in an entry that described relationships with twelve other men. If the people she had written about had given their versions of the events, what different tales they'd have told! Each one would have emphasized moments she neglected, omitted parts she deemed essential, and altered the story past all recognition. Even Charles, after reading Vera's accounts, often claimed that their joint adventures had happened in a completely different way.

Poor Laszlo. Brokenhearted, he took his life, unwilling to accept he'd lost her. In her journal, he only commanded a few pages. She wondered for a moment what had become of the other twelve.

The consequences of each incident written in her journals could then fill many more tomes in turn. Consequences . . . What was that line from Kipling? Charles used to like to quote the Buddhist monk from *Kim* a few years back, making light of anything she did. Oh yes:

> *"Thou hast loosed an Act upon the world and as a stone thrown into a pool so spread the consequences thou canst tell how far."*

He would put on an accent and a learned expression, strike a scholar's pose (which to his mind meant holding up his index finger), and always make her laugh. But now, those words rang of truth. Indeed it seemed everything one did—be it cruel, kind, or even indifferent—had a rippling effect.

"A *Kipling* effect," Vera said aloud, playing the part of Charles.

Vera put her arm out the window again, trying to feel the fog with her fingertips, to nip off a piece. She left the window open and picked up the most recent journal, turning to the blank pages toward the end. With no intention of writing, she took out her pen and went to the very last page. She drew, with a shaky hand, a large hot-air balloon in the center of the page, surrounded by cherubs and doves. She put herself standing inside the balloon's basket, wearing her pearls and a beatific expression. Underneath she wrote with a flourish:

THE ASCENSION

She looked at the illustration, puckering her lips critically. Indeed, she thought, the next time she took to the air would be when her spirit left her body. There would be no trips in flying machines, nor summers on the Isle of Wight. And it was not just a question of the new experiences she would never have, but, even worse, of all of the simple things she would never do again. Like strolling though the Louvre or having a dress made. Or riding a horse, dancing, making love . . . Her eyes were filling with tears—God, to be in a man's arms once more!—when there was a rapid tap on the door.

Bibi came in first, made her way to Vera, considered jumping onto her lap, then collapsed at her feet. Amandine was followed by a waiter, carrying an enormous tray filled with liquids to tempt her mistress: asparagus cream soup, tomato juice, milk, chicken broth, tea . . . When Vera saw the champagne, she let out a chuckle, wiping her eyes and shaking her head. Although she didn't fancy drinking any, she was pleased to see it there. The tall glass sparkling, the bubbles rising, she was reminded of days past. Champagne Days.

"Amandine," she sighed, "you are a jewel."

Julie was crossing through the stuffy common room, which the foggy day had filled to capacity; a dozen languages were being spoken there as people idly chatted, smoked, played cards. And, as always, someone was singing. She paused a moment to listen to the beautiful, homespun music. Was that Italian or Spanish?

This was, Julie thought, the sole advantage steerage could boast over the upper classes. Above, string quartets, paid musicians in black-tie uniforms, performed instrumental arrangements to demanding, though distracted, audiences. Down below, it was the passengers who sang, from the young to the elderly, at times solo and on occasion forming veritable choirs. Although some soulful voices were best unaccompanied, usually a musician was encouraged to play along: guitars, harmonicas, fiddles, or regional instruments Julie had never seen before descending to the *Paris*'s third-class lounge. She usually didn't understand the words of the folk songs (the Gaelic or Greek, the Hebrew or Russian), but she knew their meaning. Voices in steerage sang of home and nostalgia, war and loss, happiness and hope. She doubted seriously that the musicians earning their monthly wage in the ballroom were capable of expressing such emotion.

The singing behind her, she went by the women's dining hall and peeked in. Simone was talking with the pretty girls from the concessions as they leafed through *L'Atlantique*. They were probably looking for articles about Douglas Fairbanks and Mary Pickford and re-creating all the details of their fleeting glimpses and minute dialogues with the Hollywood couple. She was relieved not to have to spend her break with Simone, who would want to discuss how Julie had botched her relationship with Nikolai. Instead, she went to the dormitory to lie down, to close her eyes and rest while she had the chance.

When she got to her bunk, Julie was surprised to find an envelope on top of her mother's lacework. In the center of the paper, her name was formally written in a careful, gushing hand. She gasped: Nikolai! She glanced around the room—women were napping, filing their nails, writing postcards home—until she caught the eye of Louise, who was watching her with a sly smile from the top of the next bunk.

"A big guy came by today while you were still serving breakfast. He asked me to put that on your pillow." The plump washerwoman cocked her eyebrow. "He's a charmer, that one. I can see why you're interested in him."

"Um, thanks," Julie mumbled with a blush.

She moved into the shadow of Simone's bunk, to block Louise's view; she wanted to read the letter unobserved. Picking up the envelope, she was surprised by a rattle, a bulky weight. She tore open the top and inside, coiled at the bottom, found a necklace. Julie slowly pulled at the gold chain until, at the end, a pendant was revealed. Holding it up to eye level, she gazed at it in the air, letting it hang like a hypnotist's pendulum. It was a religious medallion, beautifully worked in gold and silver. On it the Virgin Mary's eyes looked modestly down, a large crown planted on her head.

She weighed it in her hand, astounded by such a gift. It felt like real gold. When she flipped it over, she was surprised to see Nikolai's tattoo: the Russian cross, with its two additional bars, a small one at the top, a slanted one toward the bottom.

She cradled the necklace in her skirt, then reached for the letter. With an affectionate smile at his extravagant handwriting, she read:

My Little Julie,

Please forgive my insensitive words. If I had known your brothers were lost in the war, I would have never discussed it with you. I felt such a fool when you ran away from me last night—just as we were having such a marvelous time!

I still want to see you, to be with you. In this envelope, you will find a necklace. The pendant is of Mary, the Melter of Hard Hearts. I hope she can melt yours and that all can be forgiven.

Please wear it tonight and come meet me up on deck. I'll be waiting for you.

A kiss,
Nikolai

Her heart was thumping, her insides wriggling. With a silly grin, she reached up to touch her cheek—it must be bright red! She stroked her birthmark while reading the letter again, then a third time. After a moment, when her heart had calmed to a mere flutter, she trusted her voice to ask Louise when the envelope had been delivered.

"I don't know," she said with a shrug. "Maybe an hour ago? Two? Hey—what was inside it?"

"Just a little trinket," Julie said nonchalantly, slipping the necklace over her head and securing it under her dress. Made for a man, it was long on her, falling between her breasts. She liked the feel of it against her skin.

She looked down at her watch; there was still a good half hour before they had to prepare for the lunch shift. Dare she take a quick trip down to the engine room? She could thank Nikolai for the necklace and they could plan their evening rendezvous. Hatcheck duty ran much later than steerage dining; she wouldn't want to miss him and have him wonder whether she was still angry.

Murmuring a quick good-bye to Louise—who was still staring in her direction, hoping for more details—she hopped off the bed, out of the dormitory, then shot through the common room. The people in there were cheering on a Spanish dancer, swishing her skirts and stomping on the floor, but Julie barely noticed her. She beelined for the stairwell, her hand hovering over the hidden pendant.

Having always been prompted to go up from steerage, she had never ventured down. On her way downstairs, she was eager yet bashful about seeing Nikolai. Indeed, since she had received his letter, all of her anger and disappointment had instantly melted away.

When she reached the engine-room floor, she inhaled sharply. Even without the open fire of coal engines, the humid heat was suffocating. The walls were wet and the floor was spotted with puddles of seawater, reminding Julie that, on the other side of that steel hull, the ocean heaved.

She saw a small batch of men, making repairs, checking dials. Although she knew it was they who were powering the ship, she was somewhat surprised by what little resemblance they bore to the weather-beaten sailors she'd seen all her life around Le Havre. These men were pale and waxy, as if they had never seen the sun but had been raised right here, under the waterline.

Julie approached a man wearing a welding mask and tapped his shoulder to ask directions. The wailing machines were so loud and vast, she thought perhaps they occupied various layers of the ship.

"Excuse me." She had to shout to be heard over the machinery. "Is this the engine room?"

He took off his mask, peering at her in surprise. Julie knew she was a strange guest down there; the girls who worked on board did not usually spend their break time with the engines. He gave Julie a brief leer, which visibly changed to disinterest when he spotted her birthmark.

"Yes, milady." He swept his free hand as if introducing her to the machines. "These are the engines. Now, what brings you down here? Thinking of leaving service to join the engine crew?"

"I'm looking for an engineer," Julie called out in a clear voice. "A Russian, by the name of Nikolai."

"Grumov? An engineer?" He sneered slightly, unimpressed by her choice of acquaintance. "He's a greaser, that's all. And that would be fine, you know, if you could find him when the parts need greasing. But he's always disappearing, he is."

"Oh," Julie uttered, taken aback by the welder's low opinion of her new beau. "So, you don't know where he is?"

"Your guess is as good as mine. Who knows? He could be up dancing the polka in the ballroom for all I know. You can look around if you'd like. Take a look, but don't touch anything."

He put his mask back on and lit his torch, waving her off with the flame.

As she walked from one hot, moist room to another, peeking in dark corners and around control panels, Julie tried to think of something witty to say once she found Nikolai. The surprise of his letter had prompted this spontaneous trip below, but now she was nervous. She didn't want to bungle a reconciliation with clumsy words.

During her rounds, she encountered at least a dozen men with the same uniform and dimensions as Nikolai. Even though the engine room was populated with an extraordinary number of tall, broad-shouldered men, she discounted them all with a swift glance. No one there had his careless slouch, his confident gait, his hair, the color of nutmeg.

Finally, she gave up; it was time to go back to work anyway. In a sweat, her head pounding, she started up the stairs to steerage. Rounding the first landing, she came face-to-face with Nikolai.

"Julie!" he cried. He picked her up, swung her around, then dropped her lightly on her feet, keeping hold of her hands. "I've just been up in steerage looking for you."

"That's funny," she replied, her pink face shining with delight. "I was down in the engine room, looking for *you.*"

"You got my note, then?" he asked, drawing nearer.

"Yes, I did," she answered, fishing the necklace from out of her dress collar to show him. "It's beautiful. I don't know how to thank you."

"But, do you forgive me?" he asked, stooping down and taking the medallion in his hand. He tugged it lightly to pull her in, until their faces almost touched.

"Yes," she whispered, wanting to be kissed.

"Then you'll meet me tonight?" he asked, his breath tickling her ear.

"Yes, but I'll be in hatcheck until after midnight." She grazed his recently shaven cheek, smelling his soap and skin. "Is that too late?"

"Are you kidding?" he answered. "I'll be waiting."

His lips finally swooped down upon hers. As he kissed her, he lifted her in his arms and stood up straight. In his embrace, Julie felt weightless, made solely of the bubbles that were spreading from her lower belly out to the rest of her body.

"Oh!" she said suddenly, breaking off his kiss and reclaiming her arm to look at her watch. "I have to get back to work!"

Before putting her down, Nikolai carried Julie up to the next landing.

"I'll see you tonight, then." He winked. "That is, if you don't get lured away by some gent claiming a bowler."

"No chance," she said with a laugh, running up the stairs to steerage. "Till tonight!"

Compared to the engine rooms, the stale air and constant noise in third class were positively refreshing. But, again, Julie didn't notice a thing.

"Do you think I should cut it?" Constance asked the hairdresser, holding out a long lock of thick, honey-colored hair. "One of those new styles? A bob?" she added doubtfully.

"Oh, your hair is so pretty, it'd be a shame to just cut it off," said the beautician. The relief in Constance's face was visible. "Mary Pickford was in here yesterday afternoon. *She* still wears hers long, and yours is every bit as lovely! I'll just give it a trim. When that's done, perhaps we should try a Marcel wave."

Constance sat back, contented, watching the hairdresser at work. How exciting that she was on the same ship as Mary Pickford! What if she met her tonight in first class? That might even impress Faith! She closed her eyes for a moment, imagining her sister's look of surprise, her envy. When she opened them, she saw in the mirror that Mrs. Thomas was entering the beauty salon. The squat woman in sensible shoes spied Constance at once and came right over.

"Good morning!" Mrs. Thomas said to Constance's reflection. "It's nice to meet outside of the dining room for a change. Tell me now, was it Miss or Mrs. Stone? I didn't quite catch it."

"You can call me Constance," she said, forcing a smile at the other face in her mirror.

"Oh, we are to become good friends, are we?" Her response was sugarcoated. "I'm Mildred."

She took the chair next to her and a beautician began combing through her thinning hair with a doubtful frown. After giving directions for a dye and cut, Mildred Thomas turned again to Constance.

"That was a spirited discussion at dinner last night," Mrs. Thomas said. "Very interesting, indeed. I was surprised, however, when Captain Fielding's doctor friend excused himself to go after you. I suppose he thought you might need looking after," she said, with a studied look of concern.

"I was fine," Constance said, almost amused at the notion that her opinions about universal suffrage should warrant a doctor's attention. "Dr. Chabron was kind enough to escort me to my cabin."

"How charming!" she said. "Is he a friend of yours?"

"A very recent one. We've just met here on board," Constance replied, then diverted her attention to the hairdresser. "Are you cutting it a bit too short?"

"So, did you two enjoy some dancing last night after dinner?" Mildred persisted. "Cocktails and cards?"

Constance threw a baffled look toward Mrs. Thomas. She didn't understand her keen interest in her acquaintance with the doctor. Indeed, what would she say if she knew he had invited her to dine that night at the captain's table?

"No, Mildred," she said, suppressing the urge to call her dowdy companion "ma'am." "He escorted me to my cabin, where I spent the rest of the evening reading. How about you? Did you and Mr. Thomas dance the night away?"

"No, my husband and I don't go in for carousing," she said with a prim, self-satisfied expression that didn't quite go with her current appearance. The beautician was applying a gruel-colored glop onto her wet hair, which made her head look unnaturally small. "Now then, where did you say you were from?"

"I don't believe I did." Constance refrained from adding that her conversation had never been solicited at the dining table. Thrown by the inordinate curiosity on Mrs. Thomas's face, she opted for generalities. "I'm from Massachusetts."

"Boston, I presume? How nice!" she said, without waiting for confirmation. "Unfortunately, we don't know any New Englanders. We live in Philadelphia, the City of Brotherly Love. My husband is with the Biddle Motor Car Company. You've probably heard of it?"

Constance did have a vague recollection of the men discussing automobiles at one meal or another, but she hadn't been paying much attention.

She nodded and Mrs. Thomas rambled on about her husband's line of work. It was clear that, given a willing audience, this hitherto silent matron could talk as loud and as long as her husband. As Mrs. Thomas digressed, the sound of her voice faded into the hum of the salon and Constance enjoyed the privacy of her own thoughts. She couldn't help but replay the scene in the infirmary over in her mind. Serge's cologne, his voice, his touch. Gazing into the mirror, she watched the stylist, who was now at work with the curling tongs, transforming Constance's straight hair into fashionable, watery waves. Would Serge like her new look?

"Constance, dear," Mildred repeated, "I asked you what your husband did for a living."

"Oh, I'm sorry. I hadn't heard," she said with a cough, uncomfortable that her girlish fancies were interrupted by the reality of a husband. She stifled the urge to invent a different life—it seemed terribly unfair to George to suddenly become a widow—and answered. "He's a college professor. He teaches geography."

"Oh! I should have guessed!" Mildred exclaimed, triumphant. "Boston *is* known for its universities!"

With Constance's marital status now settled, Mrs. Thomas felt free to launch into a long anecdote about a distant cousin of hers who taught at Purdue. Constance had been on the brink of adding a few words about their children when Mrs. Thomas's talk had burst back in, and now—abandoning the pretense of listening entirely—she thought about them at her leisure. In just a few days, she would be able to hold them in her lap—together, all three!—and tell them about her adventures in France. What amusing tales could she tell them? Well—she smiled to herself—she would decidedly *not* mention that Auntie Faith's live-in lover had made roast bunny rabbit for dinner one night.

A manicurist came over to the styling chairs, offering a clipping, a buff, and the tiniest hint of pink enamel. Constance consented, Mildred declined. The manicurist alit on a stool next to her chair and began her work, gently holding Constance's hand to file her narrow nails. Mrs. Thomas, whose dye would have to set for another half hour, took her needlework out of her bag.

"What are you working on?" Constance asked politely.

Mildred held up a sampler with colorful numbers and letters embroidered into the fabric. In the center, she was stitching a large Christmas tree covered with candles, beads, and baubles.

"I know it may seem odd to work on a Christmas sampler in June, but I'm making twelve of them—all different!—for our church bazaar come December. My work is so very appreciated . . ."

Mrs. Thomas continued talking, but Constance had long stopped listening. She sat staring at that festive tree, trying to work out whether, after last year, their holidays could ever be the same again.

She and George had brought the children round to visit her parents on Christmas Eve. The girls were so excited. Elizabeth and Mary had helped bake gingerbread men for everyone and even prepared a few carols to sing. Dressed in ribbons and bows, the three little girls led the way into the parlor; Elizabeth proudly carried the tray stacked with cookies while Mary held a toddling Susan by the hand. Thrilled by the season, they entered the room grinning and singing: "We wish you a merry Christmas! We wish you a merry Christmas . . ."

Next to the unlit tree, their grandmother was crouched in front of the fireplace, barefoot. In her white nightgown, her long, graying hair loose, she was gazing intently into the fire, poking it with a thin branch. She didn't acknowledge their presence, as if she hadn't heard their entrance nor the girls' pealing song. Elizabeth stopped and called out.

"Gran!" She laughed. Could her grandmother—always rather quirky—be playing a game, pretending not to know they'd arrived, only to feign utter delight when she finally turned around? "We're here! It's Christmas!"

Lydia still didn't react. Constance brushed past her daughters, making her way to the fireplace in a few quick strides, as a smiling Gerald came on the scene. He had been locked away in his study as usual, but was lured out by the girls' cheerful song. His face paled as he saw his wife huddled there in her nightdress and he too rushed past the children.

"Mother?" Constance asked, reaching out to tap her shoulder. "Lydia?" exclaimed Gerald, right behind her.

Wild-eyed, she looked up at them, her pretty mouth twisted into a confused snarl. Brandishing the stick with its fiery-red tip, she scooted away on her backside, until she was safe behind the armchair. Once there, she held the branch close, then began to sear her forearm with the ember.

"I burn therefore I am," she muttered sharply. "If I can burn, then I exist."

Constance and her father stood in paralyzed shock, watching the welts rise on her arm as they caught a faint odor of charred skin and burnt hair. Gathering his wits, Gerald finally charged his wife, pushing the armchair aside and disarming her, throwing the maple branch into the fire. With one arm, he tightly held Lydia, who began uttering a long, ghostly moan, and with the other batted Constance away.

Panicking, she looked over at George and her children. The girls were sobbing, holding on to their father's pants legs, gingerbread men broken at their feet. Constance rushed over to her daughters, hugged them close, then whisked them all out of the room.

"What the hell was that?" George whispered in a huff, as if he himself had suffered a personal affront. "Good God!"

"Take the little ones home," Constance said, ignoring his blustering comments and trying to keep her voice calm. "I'll be there as soon as possible. I can't leave them like this. I'm going to call Dr. Matthews."

"It's Christmas, for heaven's sake, Constance!" he cried, still vexed.

"There's nothing I can do about that," she said plainly, then kneeled down to talk to the girls. "Don't worry about Gran," she breathed in a soothing voice, stroking their damp, puffy faces with her silk handkerchief. "She's sick and she needs a doctor. Now, you go on home to wait for Santa Claus. I'll be there directly."

George took the girls home, and Constance stayed, as she always did, to help her parents. The family doctor finally came round that evening. Lydia was still in her nightgown next to the fireplace, now cold. Dr. Matthews helped get her in bed—Lydia would listen to *him*—and gave her a sedative.

Christmas Eve . . . That was the beginning of this long episode, her worst ever. Had six months already passed since that night? For her mother—who hadn't spoken since—had any time passed at all? In her mind, did she still exist?

"The other *hand,* ma'am," the manicurist said, obviously not for the first time.

"Oh, right, sorry." The corners of Constance's mouth briefly rose into a makeshift smile as she exchanged one hand for the other.

"Aren't you the absentminded one today!" Mildred teased her in time with her stitches. "My, my!" She poked the needle in twice more.

Christmas, thought Constance, looking at the sampler's tree. This year, how would the girls react to the decorations, the carols, the sweets? Mildred peeked over at Constance, who was staring again at her work. Pleased, she held it up for admiration once more.

After another fifteen minutes, Constance was ready to go. Her hair was cut and styled and her nails shiny and trim. However, instead of feeling pampered and revitalized, she was utterly drained.

"Don't you look lovely!" Mildred Thomas said. "One might think you were getting all gussied up for someone special!"

She wrinkled her nose with a smirk. Constance gave her an uncomfortable little nod. This woman made her nervous. Perhaps it was a good thing that Mrs. Thomas was working under the erroneous notion that she was from Boston. Not only would she not relish a visit from the Thomases, but Worcester was a small town. Mildred seemed rather suspicious of her friendship with Serge. Constance wouldn't like to imagine her meeting one of her neighbors and saying . . . what exactly?

Constance was walking out as a beautician led Mrs. Thomas to the sink for her rinse.

"Good-bye, dear." Mildred waved. "See you at luncheon!"

"Good-bye," Constance said shortly, slipping through the salon door.

Once in the corridor, she took a deep breath. What a relief to be free of the close confines of the salon. The strong smell of the dyes—not to mention the noxious company of Mrs. Thomas—was making her dizzy. While sitting at her side, Constance had already decided to have lunch ordered to her room. But what she really needed now was some aspirin. She wanted to be able to enjoy herself tonight without any nagging pains hindering her mood.

Indeed, she mused, perhaps this evening would provide a sensational anecdote to tell her girls. How their very own mother rubbed elbows with the rich and famous—Mary Pickford herself!—while eating Crêpes Suzette with the captain under the domed cupola of the first-class dining room.

She unlocked the door to her cabin and, tossing her purse on the table, fell onto the bed. George might wonder, of course, why she'd been included in such a soirée. Though, truly, there was nothing wrong with a friendship between a man and a woman, even if there *was* a bit of an attraction between them. She lay back on her bed, recalling Serge's clean, warm hands exploring her torso that morning; with a deep sigh, she closed her eyes, her fingers flitting up to lightly stroke it herself. Suddenly, she remembered her fancy Marcel waves and sat up with a jerk.

Vera heard a knock at the door, which both woke Amandine from her nap in the other armchair and caused Bibi to produce a half-hearted bark.

"Amandine, would you mind answering that?" Vera asked tiredly. "Perhaps it's the doctor, checking to see if I'm still alive."

The maid opened the door to find a stylish woman in her late twenties, accompanied by a small boy of about five, in a green sweater and short pants, and what appeared to be his nanny.

"May I come in?" she asked. "I'd like to see Mrs. Sinclair."

Amandine looked over at Vera, who nodded, pulling her shawl around her more tightly. The young woman instructed the servant and child to wait outside, on deck, but before the door was shut, Vera caught the boy's eye; it was big and brown and was studying her shamelessly.

Amandine excused herself and retired to her own room, leaving the two women alone.

"Good afternoon, Mrs. Sinclair," she said. "I'm Emma Richter, Josef's wife."

"Yes, I remember you. Good afternoon," Vera said, while pointing to the recently vacated armchair next to her. "Please, sit down."

Emma tentatively sat on the edge of the chair.

"I couldn't help but notice that you didn't come into the dining room for today's luncheon. I wanted you to know that my husband and I have been reassigned to another table and you can feel free to join your companions at meals. Really, I shouldn't like to think we've ruined the crossing for you." There was a hint of confusion on her face. "This has all been so extraordinary . . ."

"I fear it is I who have ruined the crossing for you," said Vera. "I hope your husband is not too upset. And, please, don't worry about the dining arrangements. I am taking meals in my rooms now, for a variety of reasons."

"Are you ill, madame?" Emma asked, then immediately regretted it. She knew it was too personal a question to ask a stranger, especially a stranger who had such a violent effect on her husband.

Vera nodded and shrugged. "It is a part of growing old, I suppose."

"I would also like to apologize for my husband's outburst yesterday," she began, then hesitated. She knew Josef would be furious if he found out she was here, but she'd wanted to meet this woman for herself. "It was the shock, you understand."

"He had every right," Vera began, then faltered, stifling a sob and struggling to remain calm. She took a few deep breaths, then looked into Emma's face. There was no judgment there, no hostility. If anything, her deep brown eyes looked receptive. She decided to explain herself. "When I first met Laszlo, your husband's father, he was so serious, so despondent. All I wanted was to see him smile." She threw up her hands. "Isn't that ironic? That in the end I caused him so much pain?"

"You didn't know he was married, did you?" Emma asked softly.

"No," Vera said, shaking her head with a sigh. "I was falling in love with him when he finally managed to tell me that he had a wife and son. I left that same day. And his letters . . ."

"You never read them," Emma finished, looking at Vera's puzzled face with compassion. "But, I have."

"What?" Vera uttered, too stunned to say more.

"A few summers ago, Josef and I were staying at his family's country home in Solymár. I promptly sprained my ankle getting off a horse and was confined to my bed for the rest of the holidays. By the second day, I was bored stiff. I began poking around the bedroom, in search of some amusement, and I came across the letters." Emma offered up her open palms apologetically. "I'd heard about them, of course, and frankly, I was astounded that they hadn't been destroyed. They were in a drawer in the wardrobe—forty or fifty of them—tied together with a faded red ribbon."

"Tell me, then." Vera's voice trembled, her eyes welled with tears. "What did they say?"

"It was an outpouring of love, affection, apology, angst," Emma spoke with reverence. "Like nothing I'd ever read before."

Vera had lowered her face and covered it with one hand, listening with her eyes closed. Emma contemplated the elderly woman, her gnarled fingers, her wispy white hair. She seemed so harmless, so vulnerable. Was this really the woman who had driven Josef's father to suicide, destroying his family in the process? Vera finally released her head and looked back up at Emma.

"I didn't read them"—Vera spoke slowly, articulating carefully—"because I was weak and knew I'd be tempted. I just wanted to do what was right."

"I confess," Emma added, "as I was poring over them that summer—a brief pastime Josef was never aware of—I became curious about the woman who had inspired such passion."

"That woman," Vera whispered, wiping her eyes with her handkerchief, then balling it into her hand, "is long gone."

"You know, the letters did make me understand Josef's bitterness. He was only seven or eight when he lost his father, and his only memories are those of a stern, taciturn man. Silence reigned at their house, at dinner, in the drawing room," Emma paused for a moment, feeling a stab of guilt for discussing her husband with his rival. "I think he was hurt by the number of words—the veritable tomes—his father dedicated to you. But then, he never read them. He said just looking at the envelopes turned his stomach."

Emma stole a glance at Vera, afraid she might have hurt her; she was staring at the crumpled handkerchief in her hand. Emma reached out and touched Vera's arm.

"Perhaps," she added, searching Vera's eyes with her own, "he would be more empathetic if he had."

"I wish there was something I could do," Vera said. She rubbed her hands together, trying to warm herself. During this conversation, the heat from the fever had become an icy chill.

"I'm afraid there's nothing to be done, Mrs. Sinclair," Emma said, rising to leave. "And now I should be on my way."

Vera got to her feet and gave Emma's hand a warm shake.

"Oh, Mrs. Richter," she said suddenly. "When you rang, was that your son there at the door?"

Emma Richter smiled. "Yes, that was young Max."

"Would you mind terribly," Vera paused and bit her lip. "Would you mind if I made his acquaintance? Very discreetly. In the lounge, perhaps? I would so like to meet Laszlo's grandson."

Emma looked at the frail woman before her, wobbly, shriveled, pale. What was the harm?

"I have no objections to that, Mrs. Sinclair. He'll be with his nanny all evening. You could probably find them in the drawing room."

"Thank you," Vera said, "and thank you so much for coming to see me."

"Farewell, Mrs. Vera Sinclair," Emma Richter said as she walked out the door.

Vera breathed deeply, looking at the closed door of the quiet room. She dabbed her eyes again, then got back in bed, under the covers. She needed some rest. Later that day, she would meet the grandson of the last man she nearly let herself love. As she was falling into a feverish sleep, the smile on her face was unmistakable.

After having lunch in her room, Constance played with china patterns. Her headache was thankfully gone and, growing nervous about her dinner date, she was passing the time with her paints. Tired of her own design, she tried to remember the floral one she'd copied out so many times that summer at Aunt Pearl's. She successfully reproduced the rosebuds and swirling tendrils but couldn't quite manage the rest. Looking at her watch, she saw it was nearly four o'clock: teatime in the drawing room. With the decision to fortify herself with a strong cup of tea, she put the watercolors away and happily left the cabin. For the last hour or so, it had been shrinking smaller and smaller.

Since the deck was too foggy for all but the heartiest passengers, the drawing room was nearly full. As Constance looked for a place to sit down, she passed passengers napping, reading, playing dominos and chess. She noticed the young honeymooners she'd seen on deck. Instead of doing a crossword, at the moment they were busily feeding each other messy bites of mille-feuille pastries. Reminded of Faith and Michel, Constance looked away, deeming it too private an act to be done in a packed lounge.

Making her way through the room, she thought back on her honeymoon with George. They had spent an awkward two weeks holed up in a cottage on Martha's Vineyard, the pouring rain making outings or strolls impossible. There was no giggling or chocolaty feedings, no nude drawings or champagne silliness. And the bungling at night . . . Shaking *that* thought away, she reminded herself instead of the lovely piece of cross-stitch—a stylized *S* for Stone—she'd been able to produce on the island that fortnight, due to the uncooperative weather.

In the far corner, she finally found a vacant chair (a big striped armchair she would have liked in her own sitting room) next to an animated octet from London. They were about to begin a game of their own invention. Listening to their banter, their charming accents, Constance was again reminded of Nigel Williams. What was he doing now? Was he married? And *his* honeymoon?

"Excuse me, miss?" one of the British women suddenly said to Constance with a little wave to get her attention. "Would you mind helping us with our game?"

"Of course, I'd be delighted," Constance said, eager for some lighthearted diversion after a morning with Mrs. Thomas and a lonely lunch.

They had each brought a book, presumably to read, but as the barometer fell, they had become too skittish for literature, craving talk and amusement instead. They had all written down the last line from each of their books, then gathered the folded papers together and put their books out on the table.

"We're going to try to guess which last lines go with what books. But, we all know each other's handwriting, which would give away the answers." She gave Constance a friendly look. "Could you read out the sentences?"

"Yes, that sounds like fun," Constance replied.

Beforehand, however, after the waiter had come round offering tea and pastries to the passengers, they introduced themselves, sweetened their tea, and took a look at the books at hand. There was a wide assortment, from best-selling authors like Sinclair Lewis, Zane Grey, and Edith Wharton, to old favorites like Thomas Hardy and Charles Dickens, to unlikely choices such as Herman Melville.

"Robert, how can you read *Moby-Dick* while at sea? With its mad captain and vicious whale, a sinking ship with a sole survivor . . . Doesn't it all make you nervous?"

"Look around you, my man! The *Pequod* would fit into the ballroom of the *Paris*! There isn't a creature in the seven seas that could challenge an ocean liner!" He raised his teacup in appreciation. "Compare us with those poor blokes, eating their sea biscuits and boiling their blubber! No, I find it all quite comforting, I must say!"

When they were ready to begin, having looked at the books and taken a few tidy nips of cake, Constance joined in shyly.

"All right now, the first quote is: 'As soon as they had strength they arose, joined hands again, and went on.'"

A long, lively discussion ensued, where rational ideas mixed with the absurd. Some utterly implausible possibilities were tried, to link this hopeful ending with some of the well-known tragic characters at hand.

"Let's see. That may very well be the last line of *A Tale of Two Cities*. I don't remember exactly how it ends, but perhaps—I do say *perhaps*—after the Englishman is guillotined, his head joins back to his body. Then when he gets his strength, his hands join as well—for effect, you know—and then, well, all the body parts, they just go on."

This last was said with a sweeping gesture as the group dissolved into fits of laughter.

"That's *Frankenstein,* you twit!"

After many attempts were made to find the correct answer, the general hilarity was heightened still when the book was revealed to be *Tess of the d'Urbervilles*.

"What!" one cried. "Thomas Hardy! Mister Gloomy himself came up with that bit of good cheer?"

The last lines of the other books were contemplated and more cups of tea poured. Constance, who always tended to listen more than talk, never quite felt included in the group, the way the person who calls the numbers in Bingo does not play. Nevertheless, she enjoyed their company and passed an entertaining afternoon, forgetting all about Christmas samplers, frustrating china patterns, and unsatisfactory honeymoons.

As she walked back to her cabin, Constance lamented the fact that these good people, so delightfully clever and so very *English,* had not been seated with her in the dining room. How entertaining the crossing might have been! The positive side of her table assignment, however, was Dr. Chabron's appearance at last night's dinner. Thanks to his association with Captain Fielding, tonight she wouldn't have to see *any* of her tablemates!

A smile simmering on her lips, she glanced down at Faith's enameled ring ornamenting her manicured hand. It was a strange sight there on her ring finger, which usually revealed her wedding band. Her smile faded. Should she mention to Serge that she was married? She hadn't thought it important; an eight-year marriage was hardly pressing news. Perhaps he would laugh at such a naïve revelation (would she sound conceited, as if she assumed he was attracted to her?) or announce that, of course, he himself was married as well. They were only friends, for heaven's sake.

Back in her cabin, she opened her trunk, nervous again, and pulled out a half dozen dresses and scarves. She didn't have much time; Serge was to be there in just over an hour. She caught her reflection in the mirror and examined her new hairdo. She nodded to herself, yes, it was very becoming: stylish, yet feminine. Looking back at the pile of clothes on her bed, she suddenly decided on the long blue dress. After all, it was the one that went best with Faith's ring.

"There's nothing to it," Marie-Claire told Julie's back as she tied the strings of the decorative apron. "They give you their hats and coats, you put them on numbered shelves and hangers, then you give them a token with the number on it. When they come back after dinner, you find the number and give them back their things. It's easy!"

The two girls were facing each other again. The help in first class wore tiny lace caps perched on their heads and Marie-Claire, lips locked in concentration, was pinning one onto Julie. While she was securing it down with a bobby pin, Julie stole a glance at her bloodshot eye: half the white of her left eye was vermilion. She supposed it was with this same morbid fascination that people peeked at her birthmark.

"Hey, look at you!" Simone had just come into the dormitory and stopped in front of them, hands on her hips. She stared at Julie—tidied up in the fitted black uniform of the upper decks—with her mouth wide open. "What are you wearing that for?"

"She's substituting for me tonight," Marie-Claire said, pointing to her red eye, the temporary defect of a pretty girl. "Madame Tremblay doesn't want me scaring those sensitive souls up in first class. As if anyone ever really looks at the hatcheck girl anyway."

"That's not fair! Why'd she choose you?" Simone asked Julie, her voice angry, accusatory. "Everyone knows that *I* want to work up there! That's my dream!"

"I don't know. I ran into her this morning and she told me to do it. It's just for one night." Julie fought the instinct to apologize. "Really, Simone, it's not that important."

"Easy for you to say!" she cried, raising her voice and throwing out her arms. "When *you* get to go up there and meet Douglas Fairbanks! *I'm* the one who's seen all of his pictures!"

Her reddened face collapsed into a furious scowl. With her sleeve, Simone wiped hot tears from her eyes, then stormed out of the dormitory. Undoubtedly, Julie thought, to tell all the other steerage maids what a rat she was. Her shoulders drooped as she looked down, grazing the apron's stiff lace with her fingertips.

"Just to let you know," Marie-Claire said quietly, sidling up next to her, "although I saw those Hollywood stars walk by yesterday, they didn't check anything with me. *She* kept her fur stole on during dinner. Maybe she uses it as a napkin?"

Julie's head popped up at the blasphemous comment; Marie-Claire was giving her a sly grin.

"And *he* wasn't even wearing a hat. Perhaps," she said innocently, "with all the hair oil, it just slipped right off."

Julie snorted with laughter and gave Marie-Claire's hand a thankful squeeze.

"Don't worry about Simone," she added with a wink as she went back to her bunk. "I'm sure she'll get over it."

Julie nodded, but she wasn't sure. Although Simone was the person she'd spent the most time with since she'd boarded the *Paris*, they didn't have much in common. In fact, Julie didn't even know whether she could trust her. She'd probably told the other girls about her evening up on deck with Nikolai. Julie gave the medallion under her dress a light stroke, relieved that Simone had no idea that she was meeting him again tonight.

Mme. Tremblay marched into the dormitory with her usual straight step.

"You're ready, then, Mademoiselle Vernet?" she asked. She had Julie turn around to see the fit of the uniform, then nodded once.

"That will do for one night. Now, has Marie-Claire explained your responsibilities?"

"Yes, ma'am," Julie answered.

"Then you should be on your way," she answered, looking at her watch. "Some of the parvenu up in first still dine early, as if they'd never left the farm. The Americans, mostly." She rolled her eyes. "Now, I hope that the evening passes uneventfully. I don't want to hear any complaints about you."

She gave Julie a stern look, then left the dormitory at a quick trot.

"Good luck!" Marie-Claire called as Julie turned to go. "Beware the hangers!"

Giggling again, Julie waved at Marie-Claire and headed for the stairs, wishing they'd be working hatcheck together. At each level the air became fresher and the décor steadily improved, until she finally reached first class. She had been on their poop decks, had marveled at their kitchens and corridors, but had yet to visit their truly spectacular rooms.

Julie wiped her damp palms on her apron as she nervously tiptoed down the hallway toward the dining room. She admired the walls as she passed through; nooks were filled with classical sculptures and tropical flower arrangements, bursting out of glass vases. She soon found herself in an extravagant double archway at the top of an elegant, sweeping staircase. A glass dome—more delicate than any stained glass window she'd seen in Le Havre, more intricate than a peacock's tail—ballooned overhead. Julie quickly hid behind a pillar.

Did Marie-Claire walk to work this way? Surely the help was not supposed to make a grand entrance into first class! She imagined herself on Nikolai's arm, gracefully floating down the stairs, her hand lightly brushing the long curve of the banister, her head cocked at a flattering angle. How ridiculous they would look swooshing down the staircase in their dark, boring uniforms and flat-soled shoes. And her in this tiny lace cap!

She scanned the area for another way down, but after a glance at her watch (she couldn't be late), Julie plunged down the staircase with her eyes on the floor. Keeping her head trained on the carpet, she followed its geometric pattern to the hatcheck room.

She slid behind the counter and turned on the light. A glorified closet, this was a practical space, one she understood. She took a deep breath as she looked around the racks, shelves, and cupboards. There were a few items there from the night before—a brown fedora, a wool overcoat—forgotten in haste, or after one drink too many.

"Ehem."

She heard a discreet cough by the counter. Her first customer!

"Yes, sir, may I help you?" Julie asked with a smile.

With a phlegmatic expression of one who is doing something so obvious it need not be explained, he wordlessly handed her a brushed velvet top hat with a silk band. She nodded politely and turned to store it on the shelf. As she was returning to the counter, she heard his wife whisper, "I hope she hasn't soiled it with her dirty hands!"

She handed the man his token.

"Have a wonderful evening"—she bowed slightly to each of them—"monsieur, madame," but they had already left.

Julie looked down at her well-scrubbed hands, examining her palms and nails. Why had that woman said that? With a sigh, Julie thought that perhaps working up in first would not be so pleasant. Her evening had just started, but she was already looking forward to the shift's end and her rendezvous with Nikolai.

"Ehem," she heard from across the counter.

Another expressionless gentleman was standing before her, stretching a hat out for her to take. The woman on his arm looked bored in her fur stole. Taking his hat with a servile nod, she smiled to herself, thinking perhaps this lady used *her* fur as a napkin too.

Vera arose from her nap in the early evening, slightly more energetic, and shuffled over to the desk. Since she wasn't using it for writing, her largest trunk was stored underneath. She hadn't planned on opening it until she was settled in New York; there was nothing practical inside, nothing she really needed. Now she put the key in the lock and opened the lid, looking for a keepsake that could possibly amuse a small boy.

Beginning with the smallest one, Vera pulled open the trunk drawers and peered inside them. The first was filled with jewelry she hadn't worn in years, strands of jet, large brooches, hatpins. She opened the next, which contained an assortment of tins. Here was one full of embroidered handkerchiefs, each with its own story, and another, stuffed to the brim with photographs and daguerreotypes. She opened the latter. At the top were all the portraits dating back to her relationship with Pierre, the photographer. He had taken so many pictures of her the year they were together that her face at age thirty-four was disproportionately represented. She quickly shuffled through the box: snapshots of her friends in Paris, formal poses of her parents, grandmother, and cousins in New York. A magnificent one of Charles in golfing breeches, leaning on the putter and smoking a pipe. Might there be one of Laszlo? No, it must have been discarded years ago.

Underneath these two tins she found a box containing combs from when her hair was rich and full. She poked through them, the tortoiseshell, silver, and horn, then picked up a Spanish mantilla comb, twice as large as her hand, and stuck it in her hair. She looked in the mirror and chuckled at herself. The dramatic comb towered precariously over her white head, slanting to the left; her eyes shone with fever. That might amuse a child, she thought, or make him gasp in fear.

Vera put away the combs and opened another drawer. Among

the lace, she found a Chinese opium pipe. She picked it up, fingering the floral cloisonné design, and smiled at the memory of her and Charles's brief foray into the Parisian underbelly in the late nineties. She drew on it, marveling that she could still detect—after all those years!—its distinct incense flavor. No, she thought, putting it away, that was *not* a good toy for a child either.

She opened the bottom drawer, the largest one. Under her lyre (ah, what a siren she'd made!) and wrapped in crêpe paper, she found the two marionettes who had kept her company during her childhood. On a rare visit home, her parents had presented her with the knight and his lady, bought on a trip to Italy. Through trial and error, Vera taught herself to be a talented puppeteer and lived out dozens of adventures in that lonely house on Fifth Avenue. She picked up the knight. He still had his hat, his sword, his leather boots; the paint on his face still plainly showed his mustache, goatee, and rosy cheeks. He was in impeccable condition. His lady was also lovely, boasting a blue velvet dress, braids of real hair, and a thin silver crown. She looked at their faces with a sad smile. These puppets had potential—the boy would certainly be interested in them—but they were not very subtle.

Then, next to her grandmother's white Bible, Vera saw it. The silly mechanical bank—a painted, cast-iron girl and dog—she'd found at the flea market after the war. When a coin was placed on the girl's hand, the mechanism began: her jointed arm swung around and fed the coin to the dog, who wagged his tail. She had always loved the absurdity of it (a dog eating coins!) and heaved it out of the trunk with a gleeful smile. This old iron bank had always fascinated Charles's nieces and nephews and it was sure to delight Master Richter as well. Yes, this was it.

Vera slowly got to her feet, finally ready to dress for the day. She knocked on Amandine's door, then pulled a skirt out of the closet. She gathered together a blouse, jacket, and stockings; she was deciding on a pair of low heels when her maid walked in.

"Are you going out, ma'am?" Amandine asked, clouds of worry and surprise in her dark eyes.

"I just want to take a little jaunt to the drawing room," she answered. "Could you help me get dressed, please?"

"Of course," Amandine murmured, arranging loose cloth and fastening buckles. "You still feel warm, you know. If you needed anything, I'd be happy to order—"

"I fancy a change of scenery," Vera said, glancing around the paneled walls of her cabin. "I've also been told that Laszlo Richter's grandson, Max, is in there now. I'd like to meet the boy."

Amandine nodded silently, brushing Vera's hair. She twirled it back in a plump bun and pinned a chic felt hat on top. Finished with her toilette, Vera stood up—but much too quickly. Dizzy, she fell back down in the chair.

"You are quite sure you want to go out?" Amandine said in a whisper.

"Yes, of course," Vera said, reaching for her cane and pulling herself up by degrees. "Oh, Amandine, would you mind carrying that mechanical bank to the drawing room for me? I thought it might interest Master Richter."

The two women entered the lounge, which was nearly empty as most everyone in first class was now dressing for dinner. Vera spied the couple in a corner; the boy looked even smaller inside an overstuffed armchair, his feet nowhere near the floor. He didn't see them, as his face was hidden behind a large picture book, but his nanny, who was tiredly mending stockings, looked up.

They found armchairs at a watchful distance from the boy and his nurse. Amandine sat the bank on the coffee table while Vera brought out her coin purse. She put a centime on the girl's hand, which caused a slow, deliberate *whir-r-r,* then *clank!* The figures moved and the coin disappeared.

The small boy peeked around his book, curious to see what had made the noise. Vera pretended not to see him but fed the machine another coin with a trembling hand. After two more, she had the boy standing right next to her with his nurse behind him.

"May I try, ma'am?" he asked eagerly. "May I give the girl the next coin?"

"Of course, young man," Vera said, her eyes bright. "Here you are."

Vera gave him a handful of coins, then sat back to watch his delighted face as the girl and dog repeated their moves, again and again. She scrutinized his features, looking for bits of Laszlo. With a touch of sorrow, she recognized the full bottom lip, the shape of his eyes, his slim hands. Although she could see some of her former lover in the little boy, it was difficult to imagine Laszlo, an old soul at forty-two, as a child.

"What is your name, young man?" Vera asked, when he had exhausted the supply of centimes.

"Maximilian Laszlo Richter," he said, articulating precisely. "Or Max."

"Maximilian Laszlo," she said slowly, drawing it out. Although she wasn't surprised by the boy's middle name, hearing him say it had given her a chill. "What a lovely name."

"They're my grandfathers' names. But they're dead," he added with a slight shrug.

"Oh," she said, taken aback. Vera wondered what this child knew about his dead grandfather. Sadly, it seemed, Josef had not seen the best side of his father. "Well, how do you do?" She took his small hand in hers and gave it a formal shake, making him giggle.

"How do you do?" Max replied, a bit bashful. He looked down, at the iron bank. "Where did you get it? I want one too!"

"I bought it at a big flea market in Paris," Vera said, giving the bank girl's head a tap. "You know, they don't sell fleas there, but funny old things. This bank was on a table between a broken cuckoo clock and a bowl painted with blue windmills. I think I made the best purchase, don't you?"

"Oh, yes!" he said.

He looked up at her with curiosity. Did he recognize her as the woman his mother had visited earlier, the sick old lady still in her dressing gown in the late afternoon?

"What's *your* name?" he asked.

"Well, Master Max," Vera hesitated. She could not tell the boy her real name, as she did not want to risk his father's anger. "You can call me . . . Miss Camilla."

It just popped out. She stared at the boy, dumbfounded. Without thinking, Vera had given him the name of her grandmother. Of her own volition, she had finally made the fortune-teller's prediction come true. And wasn't he, the mystic, that poet, also called Max? Life is a carousel, she thought, spinning around in great circles.

"Miss Camilla," Vera repeated with a smile. "It's a flower, you know."

When seven o'clock chimed, Dr. Chabron appeared at Constance's door, dressed for dinner and carrying an orchid corsage.

"You are stunning, Constance," he declared as he took in every detail, from her Marcel waves to her blond satin pumps. She found him very handsome as well; he looked every bit as comfortable in his white-tie dinner jacket as he did in his white coat. "Let me help you with these."

"They're lovely, Serge," she managed, rather timid now that their casual acquaintanceship had moved on to a dinner engagement.

He bent over to fasten the corsage onto the folds of blue silk at her shoulder. Her whole body tingled as he stood next to her, so close she could feel his breath. When the orchids were in place, he lingered by her side, letting his hand graze the length of her arm. Trembling, she stepped back.

"I think I'll need my shawl," she breathed.

Wrapped loosely in lace, she took Serge's arm and they strolled together toward the dining room, their conversation safe and impersonal. From second class, they had to go up two flights in order to make their entrance down the grand stairway.

"Oh, Serge," Constance whispered from the top, peeking around at the billowing Art Nouveau designs covering the walls, arches, and dome. "It's magnificent."

"Yes, it is," he agreed, smiling at her delight.

Constance relished the descent, one hand twined around Serge's arm, the other daintily grasping her skirts. She felt like royalty, a fairy-tale princess. She imagined a plump valet in white livery announcing her name to the milling crowd below, causing dozens of admiring faces to turn to her expectantly. But, she thought, her brilliant smile faltering slightly, what name would he call out? Mrs. George Stone? Who exactly was that?

They continued down the corridor, discussing the magical interiors of first-class *Paris.* They were passing the elegant smoking room—a manly, conservative space with great wingback chairs—when Constance saw two elderly women heading toward them. It was the feverish American and her teetering maid, the same ones who had interrupted her appointment in the infirmary that morning. It seemed like every time she was with Serge, those two made an appearance. She watched their approach. For the life of her, she couldn't imagine *ever* being that old. She was correcting her posture when the doctor stopped in front of them and bowed.

"Ah, Mrs. Sinclair! You must be feeling better! Are you heading to the dining room? Shall I escort you?"

Constance looked over at him in surprise and saw him scanning the old woman's outfit. It was certainly fine for tea, but was far too casual for the first-class dining room.

"Please, do not add senility to my list of maladies, dear doctor!" Vera chided him playfully, gesturing toward her clothes. "No, I'm too tired for formal dining. I've been engaged this last half hour in the most invigorating conversation, and now I'm off to my rooms to order dinner."

Constance noticed that the maid was carrying an old curio, a mechanical bank, which made her wonder what mischief those two white-haired ladies had been up to.

"I'll come by your cabin tomorrow during my morning rounds, as promised," the doctor said, with a slight bow. "*Bon appétit*!"

"I hope you both enjoy a lovely evening!" Vera smiled, nodding graciously at Constance.

"Thank you," she replied softly, suddenly self-conscious, aware of how intimate she and Serge looked, standing arm in arm.

As the old woman and her maid took their leave, Constance heard Mrs. Sinclair mutter, "We've seen that pretty young woman before, haven't we? It's like a word you've recently learned—afterward, it seems to pop up everywhere! In the crossword, on the editorial page, at tea . . ."

As the elderly woman's voice faded away, Constance smiled weakly at the doctor. Did being compared to new vocabulary make her sound dull?

Before arriving at the dining room, they passed a series of discreet, useful spaces: the powder rooms, telephones, the cloakroom. At this last, she noticed an impatient line; half-past seven was a fashionable hour to dine. As they strolled past, Constance caught a glimpse of the girl behind the counter, a lace ruff pinned to her copper-colored hair. The other woman from the launch photograph! She was constantly crossing paths with those two. At the moment, the small girl was nodding soberly at a man who was shaking his finger in her face, warning her not to lose his wife's mink. Poor kid! She didn't seem to be enjoying her evening in first class.

After a few more steps, Serge ushered Constance through a large archway, past towering palms, and into the dining room. A double staircase led down to the main floor with a lookout landing at the top. They stood together, taking in the view.

"Ohh," she sighed, squeezing his arm as she looked around the room.

It was like an opera house, with an immense glass ceiling and, on each side, porticos and pillars holding a mezzanine. Each table was splendidly set with fine porcelain and fresh flowers; in the corner, airs of Chopin came from the grand piano. Lights and mirrors illuminated the room, which was humming with conversation and muted laughter.

They swept down the stairs, then made their way to the captain's table in the center of the room. Constance glimpsed around, hoping to spot the famous actors, but they were nowhere to be seen. No matter, she thought, as she and Serge breezed past tables of well-dressed patrons sipping whiskey sours and brandy alexanders. Even without Hollywood stars, this evening was full of promise.

When they arrived at their table, the other three guests were already seated: Mr. and Mrs. Pickens, an oil tycoon and his wife recently of Manhattan (formerly of Tulsa), and a famous war aviator, a Belgian ace called Lieutenant Fernand Jacquet. The commodore of the ship, Captain Yves Duval, a uniformed man with graying hair and handsome eyes, was addressing the sommelier when they arrived. After choosing the wines, he stood and greeted them both.

"Ah, I would like to present the ship's doctor, the invaluable Dr. Serge Chabron." Serge nodded to all seated, then the captain continued with a smile, "And this must be the young lady from Massachusetts."

"Yes, allow me to introduce Miss Constance Stone," the doctor said. The men rose and Constance dipped her head at each person at the table, blushing slightly at the erroneous title.

They took their seats and picked up the colorful menus on the plates: aspic de foie gras, Cullis of grouse, Carmelite velouté, Soufflé

Rothschild . . . Constance thought she would let Serge choose for her; he would know the best options. She had never tried any of the dishes before and didn't relish any more cold soup. The Pickenses deliberated aloud, raising skeptical eyebrows; French cuisine, although highly revered, seemed to be short on beefsteak and fried potatoes.

"The Pickenses have been telling me about the fascinating world of Oklahoma," Captain Duval told them. "I should truly like to go there, though it is very far from the sea. Tell me, Miss Stone, about your home. I believe Massachusetts is on the Atlantic seaboard?"

"Yes, and it certainly has a long coastline," she began, "but my family is from the interior, a town called Worcester."

"And what does one do in the interior?" he asked with a smile.

Avoiding the subject of George, she chose to talk about her father instead. "Well, sir, my father is a professor of psychology at Clark University."

"Psychology!" Serge chuckled. "Don't tell me he's a dream doctor!"

"A doctor of the mind," the aviator, a serious man, corrected him. "Like the Austrian, Dr. Sigmund Freud. I've read one of his books. A very interesting man."

"Actually, I've met Dr. Freud," Constance said modestly, enjoying the looks of surprise around the table before she continued. "The president of Clark, an eccentric fellow named Stanley Hall, invited him to Worcester to give a lecture series. Luckily, he and his protégé, Dr. Jung, lectured in German, and so they weren't able to scandalize the community *too* much."

"Did you go to the lectures, Miss Stone?" asked Lieutenant Jacquet.

"No, I was quite young at the time. But, my father had them round for tea one Sunday afternoon and I can boast that I lost a game of chess to Dr. Jung. Dr. Freud wasn't feeling too well, I'm afraid. He said American food didn't agree with him. He complained that our customs of drinking ice water and eating heavy meals were wreaking havoc on his digestive system. Though I can't imagine American cooking being any richer than German."

"Here, here!" said Mr. Pickens, raising his glass.

"You know," Constance continued, "my sister and I were too little to really understand the adults' conversation that day, but I was so intrigued by those foreign scholars, with their strong accents and odd ideas. My sister couldn't be bothered to 'waste the day with those old men in the parlor.' She spent the whole afternoon up in a tree reading *Treasure Island*!"

"She must not have your curiosity, your sense of adventure!" replied Serge. "Do you know, she didn't want to join her sister on this crossing either?"

"No? That *is* a shame. But, you must agree"—the captain smiled—"the girl has a fine taste in books!"

The conversation turned to Lieutenant Jacquet's war adventures, exciting tales of aerial victories. He'd even flown the Belgian king Albert I—the first head of state bold enough to take to the air—over the front lines! But Constance was only half-listening. She was still savoring her triumph over Faith. Although she had always been the pretty sister, until tonight, no one had ever considered her the interesting one, the adventurer. Thinking back on Faith's intellectual and artistic friends in Paris, she was sure they had to be great admirers of the psychoanalysts. They too would have been impressed by her acquaintance with them, as fleeting as it was.

Her thoughts were suddenly interrupted by Mrs. Pickens, speaking to her in low tones from across the table as the men continued to talk of flying machines.

"Dear, what a beautiful ring you're wearing!" she said with interest. "Wherever did you get it?"

Constance extended her hand to the older woman so she could better view the large, unusual piece.

"Thank you. It is colorful, isn't it? I got it in Paris. It's made of enamel," she paused, then added, "and handcrafted, of course."

"What a lucky find!"

"Yes, wasn't it?" She smiled at Mrs. Pickens, then turned back to the men. She would not let her sister win this hand.

She looked over at Serge. Would he also have been attracted to Faith? Her exuberance, her reckless charm? Although she was not nearly as good-looking as her older sister (and was really rather plain), Faith had had her share of steadfast admirers. In fact, it seemed she always had some man staring at her in fascination, choosing her to play lawn tennis or to be his partner at bridge. If Serge Chabron had met Faith instead, would she now be sitting at the captain's table?

The doctor caught Constance's eye and gave her a covert wink. His smile, slightly seductive, showed unmasked appreciation for the woman before him. As she held his gaze across the table, her heart racing, all the other people in the dining room faded away.

"I say, Dr. Chabron," repeated the lieutenant.

"Sorry," he asked with a slight jump, "wh-what was that?"

She smiled at his startled stumbling, confident that Faith, though fashionably thin and never lacking in amusing anecdotes, would not have interested him. Not in the least.

They all enjoyed a delicious, utterly French dinner. Serge had guessed her tastes exactly (would George have been able to do that?) and ordered her magnificent dishes that were neither daunting nor mysterious. After finishing the waiters' final offerings—sherry and port accompanied by bonbons and petit fours—the table broke up for the evening. The captain and the aviator made their way to the smoking room, reminiscing about the war and speaking French with great gestures, while the Pickenses, still early risers even after a full year residing in New York City, retired to their rooms. Serge and Constance were left alone. He moved to the chair next to hers, then under the table reached for her hand. She gasped lightly as his fingers interlocked with hers.

"Thank you so much for accompanying me tonight," he said. "Life on board a ship can be quite lonely. What a treat it has been to have your company."

Constance blushed deeply but gave his hidden hand a light caress. "It's been my pleasure," she murmured.

"Would you like to dance?" he asked.

"Of course," she answered. It would be a shame not to take full advantage of her special evening in first class. He rose and took her hand, leading her to the stairway.

"Usually, one can dance on the terrace under the stars, but tonight, with this fog, you couldn't even see the moon! We shall have to make do with the ballroom." He gave her a sidelong glance.

"I'd love to see it!" Constance followed him up the stairs, glowing with excitement.

On their way out of the dining area, Constance peeked over at the hatcheck counter to see whether the birthmarked girl was still there. Four or five men were crowded around her, all in a hurry, all wanting immediate attention. She looked harried and exhausted. Honestly, who could be in such a rush on a luxury liner? What pressing engagements could one possibly have?

After a quick stop in the powder room (her waves were holding beautifully!), the couple went up to the ballroom. A lit fountain gurgled on one side of the room and a twenty-piece orchestra played a waltz at the other. There were a few couples decorating the dance floor, but it wasn't crowded yet. Serge bowed at the waist, took her hand, then led her out. She leaned gracefully back as she'd been taught to do, her blue silk swirling around his legs as they swept around the room.

"Tell me, then." He smiled, holding her a bit closer. "How have you been enjoying the crossing so far?"

"Nothing can compare to tonight's dinner," she exclaimed. "The beautiful rooms, the incredible food . . . and the captain and the others were so interesting and friendly."

"Ah, do I get lumped together with these 'others,' then?" he asked, with a quizzical expression bordering on comical. "Those friendly, interesting sorts. I suppose I shouldn't aspire to more."

Constance began stuttering a weak protest ("What? No. That is . . .") when Serge twirled her quickly around. Back in his arms, she laughed.

"Serge, you couldn't be lumped in with anyone." She shook her head. "You are absolutely one of a kind."

He pulled her even nearer, relaxing his arms and slowing the pace. Constance became sensitive to their closeness: the warmth of his hand, the texture of his jacket, the smell of tobacco. It was intoxicating.

A young crew member suddenly signaled for the doctor's attention and the spell was broken.

"Excuse me, sir," he stammered. "I hate to intrude, but there's been an accident in the galley and a saucier has been badly burned. His hand mostly, and his arm as well. Could you come down and see to him?"

"Of course. I'll join you in a few minutes." The doctor looked annoyed. "First, allow me to escort my guest back to her cabin. In the meantime, have them apply some ice to the burn."

He held out his arm to Constance.

"I'm terribly sorry," he said with a frustrated sigh. "Duty calls. Again."

"I understand," she said. "You're in high demand on this ship."

She was about to add something about not expecting to have him *all* to herself, but stopped. Although she was disappointed that their evening—so extraordinary, exquisite, romantic—had been cut short, perhaps it was for the best. Where could it go from here?

In no apparent hurry, they began the descent back to second

class, strolling down corridors whose carpets and decorations became plainer as they passed through.

"I'm glad you enjoyed the dinner tonight, Constance," he said, "and I wish we could do the same thing again tomorrow, but the captain will be dining with a different set of guests. It's his duty to entertain all the dignitaries on board, you know," Serge explained as they walked along, arm in arm. "I believe he dined with Miss Pickford and Mr. Fairbanks—that charming couple from the pictures—their first day on the ship."

"Did he?" she asked, marveling that, on the *Paris,* she and Mary Pickford had dined with the same man at the same table.

"I must admit, it makes me feel guilty," he said, pursing his lips. "After spoiling you with an evening in first class, I hate to think of you spending your last night on board with those bullheaded tablemates of yours."

"Oh, please don't apologize for showing me a wonderful time!" she said with a smile. "Really, tomorrow's dinner isn't important. In fact, I may just have dinner in my room."

"What?" Serge cried. "You won't want to do that! It's the farewell gala!"

Constance shrugged, remembering the mildly pleasant gala of her eastern crossing. With Gladys Pelham and her friends, she had donned a mask and danced a few rounds. The highlight of the evening was an amateur talent show; lively passengers got on a makeshift stage and put on skits, told funny stories, and sang—all with varying degrees of success. She shuddered, imagining spending an evening like that with the Thomases.

Now at her door, he turned to face her, taking her hand.

"I thought, if you wanted, tomorrow you and I could dine privately in my quarters. Surely my company would be preferable to dining alone in your cabin or with your regular table companions."

Constance looked down. Even she understood where a tête-à-tête dinner could lead.

"The last night on board is very special, Constance," he continued persuasively. "After supper we could go to the first-class gala in the Grand Salon. I shouldn't doubt that the Hollywood couple will be there as well. Who knows, perhaps they'll even be inspired to perform!"

Constance hesitated, looking down at her hands, holding his. With a sigh, she reasoned that, as the gala followed the dinner, they would only be alone for an hour or so. It was not then so compromising, so terribly risqué. After all, he was a gentleman. And they were merely friends.

"That sounds delightful, Serge." She smiled.

"Capital!" he exclaimed in a low whisper, gazing into her eyes.

He leaned into her, his hands drifting up to her shoulders. As his lips slowly grazed her cheek, Constance closed her eyes. She was beginning to purr when she caught the smell of port in his mustache and stiffened with a jolt. Suddenly, she remembered all the smells she'd detected in George's whiskers over the years: gravy, soup, bourbon, cigars. She took a step back and began fumbling with her key.

"Serge," she stuttered, "you've forgotten the poor saucier!" Then, smiling at him, she added, "He needs you, even more than I."

"Until tomorrow, then." He gave her hand a parting squeeze.

She went into her room and sat on the bed. She could still feel Serge's hand on her waist as they danced around the ballroom, his warm lips traveling toward her own, the exploration he'd made of her torso in the infirmary. With him, her whole body felt alive. George had never made her feel this way.

With a small moan, Constance took off her shoes. Softly stroking her silk-stockinged feet, she wondered what it would be like to be married to Serge. Would those times in bed, when she put up with George's grappling and grunting, would those moments be more pleasant, more exciting? Would she enjoy it?

She took off the corsage and admired the orchids. They were so unusual: thick and fleshy, but delicate too. She brought them to her nose and breathed in, hoping for a smell that could define the evening. Disappointed, she found they hardly had any scent at all.

The kitchens had long been closed when Julie finally turned out the light in the hatcheck closet. A few tired waiters passed her ("*Bonne nuit!*"), their mustaches twitching as they drifted out of the dining room. She looked up and down the hallway, wondering where Nikolai could be; she'd assumed he'd be waiting. She ducked into the powder room, thankful to have a moment to freshen up.

After relieving herself (she hadn't had a single break all night), she examined her face in the mirror. Her usual pallor had taken on a grayish tint; dark circles sprawled under her eyes. She took the frilly lace off her head, stuffed it into her pocket, and splashed her face. Once dry, she frowned at her reflection, pinching her cheeks, then smoothing her hair. Julie looked at her watch. Half-past one. No wonder she looked like this.

Before leaving the lavatory, she pulled the necklace out from her dress and, in the mirror, looked down at Mary's face. The Melter of Hard Hearts. Perhaps it was a good thing they'd had words last night; now she knew how much he cared about her.

When she came out, Nikolai was standing with his back to her, staring at the empty hatcheck room. Buzzing with excitement, she reached out and touched his arm. He whirled around.

"There you are!" he cried, picking her up to kiss her firmly on the mouth. "I was worried you'd already left!"

"Now why would I do that?" she said, beaming back at him.

He was neater than she'd ever seen him, recently showered, his engineman's uniform slightly less rumpled, his hair combed. He leaned against the hatcheck counter and drew her close.

"Don't you look pretty," he said, pinching her chin. "I've been thinking about you ever since we met in the stairs."

"I've been thinking about you too." She smiled. "Sorry it's gotten so late."

"So, how was it up here in first class? Did anyone check a boater as admirable as mine?" He winked.

"You mean as airborne as yours." She laughed shyly. "No, no boaters tonight. All the hats and coats were dark and serious. And, according to their owners, extremely delicate and very likely to disappear—right from under my nose."

"Did they give you a hard time, Juliette?" he asked. "Or did they try to flirt with my girl?"

"Not at all!" She blushed. "In fact, most of them were terribly grouchy. And I thought the people on the upper decks would be so refined!"

"Money has nothing to do with class," Nikolai pronounced.

"It's true, the passengers down in steerage are much friendlier; we chat with them and sometimes have a laugh. Up here, they were just worried my hands weren't clean enough to touch their precious things."

"I wonder what they'd make of mine." With a grin, Nikolai held up his hands, the lines permanently stained with engine grease. "Hey, don't give those snobs another thought. Tonight is for us!" He took Julie's arm and began to lead her down the empty corridor. "Now, what do you want to do?"

For the workers on board, there was not much in the way of entertainment. When they were on break, they were not allowed in the passenger areas of the ship; in their own quarters, they only had same-sex dining halls that became makeshift lounges between meals. In third class, the help occasionally mingled with the passengers: clapping their hands to the impromptu music or dancing a reel. However, whenever this came to Mme. Tremblay's attention, the offender was seriously reprimanded.

"Shall we take a walk around the deck?" Julie suggested weakly. She hated to offer up such a boring idea—always the same!—but she knew no other.

"Whatever you want, *mon amour.*"

Before stepping outside, he stopped next to an enormous bouquet of birds-of-paradise. Half-hidden in the hallway, he pulled her beside him and gave her a long kiss. She went limp, a rag doll in his arms. When they finally emerged from the corridor, the cold, damp air made Julie gasp. In the cozy cloakroom, she hadn't realized how chilly it'd become. She crossed her arms over the thin uniform as they walked out to the rail. The fog had lifted, allowing them to see the choppy waters below.

"It's stirring up down there," Nikolai said, looking over the side.

"You think we're in for a storm?" Julie asked. She'd seen the consequences of heavy weather back home—broken masts, cracked hulls, missing sailors—and had a healthy respect for it. Her brow crinkled with worry.

"Let's just say that, come morning, you may be needing that ginger tea." He smiled and put his arm around her. "Hey, you're trembling. Let's go in. It's cold out here."

As there was nowhere else to go, they began heading down the stairs.

"You want me to show you around the engine room? At least it's nice and clammy down there." He grinned down at Julie. "It'll warm you up awful fast."

"Why not?" she said cheerfully, though she didn't relish the idea. When she'd been down there earlier, the depth and the heat had made her feel queasy again, recalling her nauseating first day aboard.

He took her hand and, at each stair landing, gave her a kiss. In the well-lit stairwell of the upper decks, he touched her lips briefly. Toward the bottom, where it was emptier and darker, he held her longer, pressing himself against her. She arrived to steerage breathless.

"Let me look around here a moment," she whispered. "I'd like to see if any of the service crew is still up. I don't know what time Madame Tremblay expects me back."

Nikolai waited in the stairwell and Julie crept down the third-class hallway. She could hear sounds of conversation coming from the common room; although she didn't understand the language, a group of men seemed to be playing dice. She debated peeping into the dormitory to see whether the head housekeeper was asleep. But, what if she wasn't? Julie wanted to spend more time with Nikolai. Turning back to the stairs, she decided to risk getting in trouble.

As promised, the engine room was hot and humid. Julie, already somewhat dizzy, had to walk with care; the pitch of the ship was much more pronounced than it'd been before. Nikolai led her through, waving at a couple of sniggering colleagues as they walked by.

"I don't know what you saw when you came down before," he shouted over the racket of the motors.

She looked around at the huge engines, cylinders, generators; she wasn't interested in any of it. Her uniform was sticking to her and she was beginning to feel faint. After stepping into a puddle and soaking a foot, she squeezed his hand.

"Nikolai," she called up to him, cupping her hands around her mouth. "Is there anywhere we could sit down?"

As he nodded, a slow smile spread across his face.

When the ship was being equipped for its maiden voyage, one mattress too many had been delivered to the male dormitory. A few quick-witted enginemen had snuck off with it, storing it in a dark corner behind the auxiliary engine, propping it up on four crates. In the three days out to sea, it had already proven invaluable: for catching a few winks on duty, sleeping off hangovers, or as a table for a furtive card game. To Nikolai's knowledge, none of the men had brought a woman there. Not yet, that is.

He brought Julie round the corner and gestured toward the bed. She gave him an uneasy look and he shrugged.

"There's no lounge down here, Julie," he shouted. "Not many places to sit."

Although the mattress and linens had been brand-new only a few days before, they were already showing signs of wear. The men obviously slept here with their boots on. She straightened the sheets nervously, whisking a smudge with her hand. Julie had never before sat on a bed with a man who was not her brother. With a chuckle, he plopped down, then sat her on his lap. Although it was a relief to be off her feet, her heart raced; she folded her hands together modestly and looked down. Nikolai picked up the necklace.

"It makes me happy to see you wearing my pendant, Julie," he said. In the corner behind the engine, the noise was particularly loud. He spoke in a near yell, but she mainly understood by gestures. He let go of the Virgin medallion to weigh her breast in his hand. "I'd like to see what it looks like against your skin."

Her mouth dropped open; wide-eyed, she saw he was already unbuttoning her uniform. With his other hand, he pulled up her chin, then distracted her with a long, slow kiss. Moaning slightly, she closed her eyes and fell into his embrace.

The front of her uniform undone, he found a camisole. After a light caress, he called into her ear, "Let me see what you look like." He gestured for her to take it off.

Julie was shaking. Was this what girls did with their sweethearts? Having no experience with men, she'd assumed only married couples did such things. However, as she wanted to please him, she pulled her arms out of the uniform sleeves and lifted off the camisole. As children, when she and Loïc had gone to the shore, they had always waded in their drawers. However, at twenty-one, she knew exposing her breasts was improper. The necklace slid down the line of her cleavage, shiny gold.

He stroked her skin lightly, marveling at its smooth paleness, and grazed her peaked nipples. With a smile, he gently pushed her breasts together, hiding the necklace underneath.

"You are so lovely!" he gushed, gazing into her eyes. "Absolutely beautiful!" Then, rubbing his stubbled face against her neck, he stroked her hair, his lips nipping at her ear. In a low growl he added, "I want you!"

A glowing warmth was spreading through her body—no one had *ever* called her beautiful—and she liked the idea of being wanted. But, what exactly did that mean?

Nikolai laid her on the mattress and hovered over her. She felt his heat on her, his bulky weight. His lips were on hers again, kissing her greedily. She moaned again, but this time, it was not excitement; her head was spinning, she needed air. She was relieved when the kisses stopped. Her eyes still closed, she tried to control her breathing, to not throw up.

Now his mouth was exploring her breasts, licking and sucking, as he gripped them hard in his hands. She squirmed on the mattress; this was all going much too fast! She poked him on the arm.

"No, Nikolai!" she cried. "Stop! I've never . . ."

He smothered her words with a messy kiss, straddling her with his legs. Immobilized, she struggled below him, cramped and awkward, beating his massive chest. His meaty tongue was gagging her, rendering her both sick and mute; nearly retching, she tried to make him look at her, to understand that she wanted him to stop. If anything, her panic excited him. His hands were everywhere at once: pinning her arms, grasping her hair, ransacking her torso, grabbing her buttocks. Then one of them, the size of a bear's paw, reached between her legs; its rough fingers prodded around for openings.

His kisses stopped again as he tackled his trousers, unfastening them with one hand. She couldn't see his face, only his half-buttoned shirtfront exposing another hairy, blue tattoo. Julie shouted into his chest.

"No, no, no!" she yelled, her words almost lost in the engine din. "No!"

He yanked down her drawers and, holding her tightly with both arms, thrust himself inside her.

"Nikolai!" she cried, then bit her lip. It felt like she'd been ripped apart.

He pumped her, up and down, to the pitch of the ship, to the rhythm of the bellowing engine. Gritting her teeth, she clasped her eyes tightly, too spent to fight any longer. He rammed himself inside her, again and again, until he cried out in what seemed like agony. He quivered, splattered her stomach with warm jelly, then slackened his hold on her in near collapse. Breathing heavily, Nikolai pulled her up onto his broad, blue chest and held her gently.

"Ah, Julie! My girl!" he cried, pouring sweat and panting. He bent down and licked her birthmark; he wiped his sperm off her belly with the soiled sheet. "That was fantastic!"

She rose up to look him in the face, her elbow digging into his ribs. He was beaming at her with affection. Between her legs was sticky and sore; she was bruised and bleeding. What had happened? Had he not heard her cries, not felt her blows? She stared into his eyes in astonishment; he gave her a peck on the tip of her nose. He seemed completely unaware he had hurt her. Should she try to explain? What could she say?

"Do you want to sleep here tonight?" he asked loudly, cuddling her with half-closed eyes. He seemed ready to take a nap after all his exertions.

Her whole body ached, her groin pounded; she was unbearably hot and so, so sick. Julie rolled off him, leaned over the edge of the cot, and vomited out a long, thin trail of black bile. When that was spent, dry heaves shook her upper body, tears squeaking through the lids. Finally finished, she rested on the vacant strip of bed, her arms wrapped protectively around her naked breasts. Why had she taken off her camisole? Had he understood that to mean that she wanted it? Had she somehow given him permission to tear into her? She stared at the wall, almost numb.

"I guess I'd better get you back," he shouted into her back, nudging her with balled-up clothes. "You don't look so good."

Half-hiding herself, she got dressed: the loathsome camisole, then the first-class uniform, now crushed and torn. Her wadded drawers were treading in the dirty seawater on the floor; she did not retrieve them. Creakily, she stood, then nearly fell; not only was she weak and unwell, but the ship was rocking much more than before. He jumped up next to her.

"Let me help you!"

With his arm around her shoulders, without speaking, they sloshed back through the engine room. She moved slowly, painfully, leaning on him to limp up the stairs. Steerage was silent. When they were outside the dormitory door, Nikolai finally opened his mouth. Julie stared at it, wondering what it might say.

"I'll come by to see you in the morning, *ma chérie,*" he promised in a low whisper, respectful of the newfound quiet. He lightly kissed her cheek as she reached for the doorknob. When she was halfway through the door, he called out softly. "Hey, Julie . . . tonight was special. I love you, you know?"

She saw him wink with a smile as the door closed behind her. There in the dark, she was surrounded by the sounds of a hundred sleeping women. Was that Simone's bunk squeaking lightly? Julie sat down on her clean bed and took off the uniform. It reeked of Nikolai: his sweat, his hands, his hair. She checked the pocket; the lacy cap was lost. She desperately wanted to go to the bathroom, to wash herself, to clean her teeth, but she didn't dare make any more noise. Shaking, fearing trouble, she pulled her nightdress over her head and lay down. Hesitantly, she reached down between her legs; it was tender and raw.

Trying not to cry, she put her head on the pillow, feeling the Virgin dangle between her breasts. Julie curled up tightly, hugging herself in disbelief. It had all happened so fast. She thought of her catechism classes: the nun drilling the girls about purity and honor, repeating that Mother Mary had never been touched by a man. She reached up for the medallion—the proof of his love—and rubbed it in the dark like a good-luck charm.

Nikolai had been so sweet for most of the evening; his compliments and pet names, his protectiveness, his fiery kisses . . . his innocent smile when it was over. His desire for her had made him weak. But why had he been so rough? Was that passion? It felt like she'd taken a beating.

Swallowing hard, she remembered Chantal, a neighbor in Saint François who had given birth to a fatherless baby. Everyone had called her such terrible things! Julie lay in her bunk completely still, hearing those names—tart, slut, pig, whore—virtuously spit out with violence. Then, with decision, Julie concentrated on Nikolai's last words.

"He loves me," she whispered to herself.

DAY FOUR

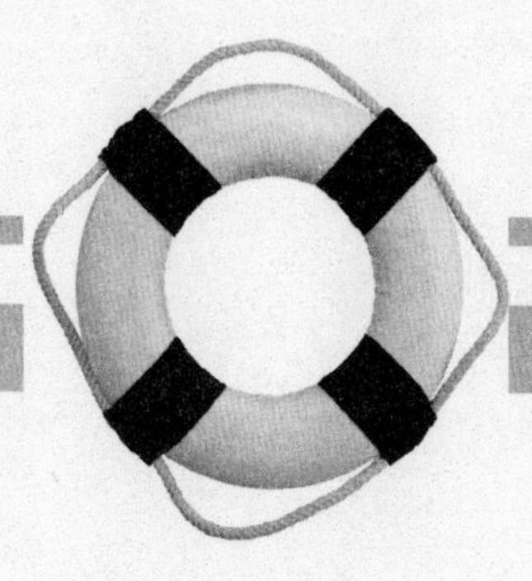

Vera lay on her bed, imagining that the roll of the ship were a flying trapeze. The view from her window was black—it couldn't be more than five o'clock—but the seas were clearly raging. From this perspective—a first-class suite on the uppermost deck—it was almost pleasant. What a contrast to her first hearty sea adventures, when the waves came crashing over the rails, soaking your skin and nearly flinging you off the boat. Snug in bed, Bibi at her side, she was smiling, assured there was no real danger, when she heard a crash.

She bolted up and groped for the lamp, then peered around the room for the source of the noise. Relieved to find the window intact, she was nonetheless disgruntled to see her portrait lying facedown on the floor.

A chill on her skin and an ache in her bones, she slowly eased herself out of bed, navigating the tilting floor. She grasped the picture with both hands, then swiftly returned to the warmth of the blankets.

Vera held the drawing in front of her, this portrait dating back to her prime. In it, her long hair was loosely gathered under a broad-brim hat, a hint of veil covering her face. A youthful thirty-seven, she playfully eyes the artist from the side, a cocky smile captured.

The glass was cracked on the face of her former likeness, giving it some of her current wrinkles. Could this bring bad luck, like breaking a mirror? But no, this image was so old, she had already lived through its seven years of misfortune: the war, her disease, a diversity of unpleasantness.

Vera was studying the drawing, the self-assured lines, the surprising color choices (she'd always relished that touch of sea green in her hair), when she realized that this was roughly what she'd looked like when she met Laszlo Richter. This was the face he had fallen in love with. What had he admired about her? It probably had more to do with her spirit than her looks. Again she thought back on their first dinner together; describing the most elemental details of his life in Budapest—his high-level post at an international bank, his old-fashioned house with a view of the Danube, his hounds and horses—his wife had not been included. Had this face bewitched him?

She reached for her journals and pen on the nightstand. She turned to an empty page in the back (with a weak smile for the soaring balloon) and tried to draw Laszlo's face. The visit the day before with young Max—who boasted some of his grandfather's features in miniature—had helped jog her memory. After making a moderately successful outline of his middle-aged face, she proceeded to age it. She let his jaw sag, she lined his brow, thinned out his hair. Would his ears have grown long and hairy? His eyebrows uncontrollably bushy? Would he have lost his teeth? She continued adding the pitfalls of old age to the drawing, until finally it resembled a ghoul. She chuckled sadly at the sketch, thinking that, indeed, they would have made a good match, here at the end.

Vera screwed the top back on her pen and laid it on the nightstand, next to the old bank. Last night, listening to Max's bubbly laughter as he fed the dog coins, she had already decided to give it to him. She would send Emma Richter a note. Perhaps she wouldn't mind bringing the boy round for tea?

Vera closed the book on the caricature and began to browse the alphabet memoirs, the first book she'd written. She flipped through the pages until she came to *L*, convinced that, although Laszlo had made an accidental, detached father, he would have doted on his charming grandson.

Love

I have been told that love, the most celebrated of sentiments, is generally experienced—first and foremost—within one's Family: parents and siblings and, on rare occasions, one's more far-fetched relations, such as grandparents, aunties, or cousins. These ties of childhood are then succeeded by the newfound family of one's Maturity: a spouse and offspring. However, my rather singular and solitary case did not offer me many opportunities to learn about Domestic Love. Indeed, perhaps my knowledge in this matter is rather too scarce to compose these lines.

Despite the fact my parents were eminent members of the community and had a reputation for their sociability, I barely knew them. For my education and amusement, my grandmother, the matriarch of the family and my personal guardian, provided me with a series of governesses. For the most part, these young ladies merely inspired indifference in me. A rare few I condescended to despise. One, I loved.

Miss Daphne was a refined young lady from Savannah. Although Sherman's March to the Sea had left her family impoverished, when the war ended, they sent their only daughter North, in search of a future. My grandmother engaged her and she became my companion during my seventh year. She was not sparing with affection and kindness like the other adults I had known, and I flourished under her attentions. Unfortunately, Daphne also taught me the frail and fleeting nature of love. After only ten months had passed, she left her position, leaving me brokenhearted and alone.

Vera's first taste of love had come not from a family member but an outsider, a girl with a lolling stride and a peculiar accent. How stricken she was when, after an academic year, Daphne had abandoned her to marry. After her first experience with love (so long overdue), Vera already learned to be wary of it.

Skimming down the sequence of thwarted sentimental endeavors, she came to her husband. Odd to find him here, she sighed, in a chapter about love.

I first saw Warren Harris at a club social. Telling a tall tale, whiskey in hand, he had the undivided attention of at least a dozen people. A brawny man down from the wilds of Canada, he was in New York visiting relations. In that tired, staid drawing room, he radiated excitement. I observed him. His pleasing face displayed the lines of experience; I estimated his age at Thirty-five. His carriage was self-possessed, his expression wry. His amusing anecdote, too loudly narrated for polite society, concerned frozen rivers and beaver traps. His finger bore no ring. I was immediately attracted to him, recognizing him at once as an extremely promising vehicle to carry me away from the confines of my Grandmother's house. I had just turned eighteen.

Marrying Warren Harris provided Vera with a legitimate means of escape. The marriage itself, which lasted a full five years, had many moments of reckless diversion, but none resembling the deep tenderness purported to be found in love. When it became clear that Vera could not have children, the festivities came to a complete stop. Not only did he crave a son, but for him, her flaw gave his infidelities just cause. Warren was the one who ultimately petitioned for divorce; when it was finalized, Vera, though tainted with the label of divorcée, was free at last.

If Laszlo had truly been devoted to her, she thought crossly, he too could have gone to the courts to dissolve his marriage. Feeling her overly warm brow, she wondered, for the first time, whether one of his unopened letters might have contained such a proposal. In that case, would she have agreed to . . . what? Love was not her strong suit. She thumbed through the rest of the journal entry dedicated to the subject. After her short-lived marriage, the remaining pages discussed not her lovers but her friends. Charles Wood figured prominently.

She closed her eyes for a moment to feel the swell of the sea. Though not unduly short, her life had been rather bereft in romantic love, despite her numerous affairs. Would she have been able to enjoy a long, devoted marriage? Or would she have soon panicked like a caged animal? She heard her pen roll off the nightstand; if anything, the storm was becoming more violent. Opening her eyes, she turned back to the unflattering illustration of a decrepit Laszlo Richter, wishing that old man were there at her side.

Constance awoke to confusing bumps and rolls. She turned on the lamp and located the sound: in the large fruit bowl, the three remaining apples were sliding from one side to the other. She stood up to investigate and felt the pitch of the ship. Stumbling over to the porthole, she looked outside and saw the dark skies and the turbulent sea. She fell into the chair to watch the unexpected spectacle: a tempest.

On the way over with Gladys Pelham and her talkative friends, it had all been "smooth sailing," the idea of a perilous sea inconceivable. Now, staring out at the peaked waves, a shiver rippled down her back; the *Lusitania,* the luxury liner that went down in 1915, immediately came to mind. That ship, with four funnels, was even larger than the *Paris.* The fastest ship of its day, it was able to sink, to be underwater, in just eighteen minutes. Suddenly nervous, she felt the ocean liner's smallness within the immensity of the Atlantic.

When she'd heard of the *Lusitania* tragedy—not caused by a storm, of course, but by a German submarine—she had been holding her newborn. Little Elizabeth was only a month old and Constance, still getting used to motherhood, was exceptionally sensitive and weepy. George had come in and casually told her the news:

"Did you hear about that steamer? The *Lusitania*? A U-boat sunk it off the coast of Ireland. There are over a thousand dead—men, women, and children. The millionaire Alfred Vanderbilt was on board and he's drowned as well. I bet President Wilson will declare war on Germany now!"

Constance looked down into the perfect face of her sleeping baby, clutched her tightly in her arms, and began to cry.

"What's the matter?" George asked, his eyebrows arched in surprise. "Did you know someone traveling on the *Lusitania*?"

He hadn't understood that she was crying for all children, and even more, for all mothers; they would never be able to fully protect their sons and daughters. A mother's love could not solve their problems and, despite her finest efforts, they would still face danger: illness, accident, unhappiness. She had sobbed all morning, gazing at her child, wondering at the futile task at hand.

Some weeks later, a song had come out called "When the *Lusitania* Went Down!" It was a popular tune at dances, festivals, and fairs, and some of her friends bought the phonograph record. It seemed everyone was singing it that summer, the men removing their hats, showing respect for the victims. It had made her teary-eyed every time she heard it.

Looking out the porthole, Constance hummed the chorus, hearing the warbling tenor in her mind:

Some of us lost a true sweetheart
Some of us lost a dear dad
Some lost their mothers, sisters, and brothers
Some lost the best friends they had

It's time they were stopping this warfare
If women and children must drown
Many brave hearts went to sleep in the deep
When the Lusitania *went down!*

Holding on to furniture, Constance lumbered over to the bureau, picked up her photographs, then quickly sat down on her bed. Elizabeth, now six, still had the round face she'd had as an infant. And Mary . . . Mary had just been born when war was finally declared, and there she stood, a delightful little girl. For several minutes she studied her daughters, their little bodies, faces, smiles, and then took a peek at her husband. The serious, card-stock face seemed to be expressing disapproval, judging her, as if the photograph itself suspected her attraction to the ship's doctor. With a long sigh, Constance wagered that, without a doubt, Serge would have shown more sensitivity about the sinking of the *Lusitania.*

After storing the photographs away, she picked up an apple, thinking back on every detail of her evening with him, beginning at seven sharp: the orchids, the lavish dinner, the waltz, the near-kiss. She took a bite. Was it possible that Serge was married too? If he were a bachelor or a widower, it seems he would have made an allusion to it, either in jest or in sorrow. She had heard that Europeans had looser mores than Americans. Could a kiss, then, be just a sign of affection between friends? Faith's friends, when coming and going, had certainly been very generous with their pecks on the cheek.

Finishing off the apple, she sat on her bed, trying to decide what to do next. It was still frightfully early; there was no point in getting dressed yet. Hopefully, in another few hours, Serge would pay her a visit and see how she was faring with the storm. She considered ordering some coffee, but felt rather queasy. She would lay flat on her bed and finally finish *The Mysterious Affair at Styles.* That way, tonight, she would be able to offer him a keepsake: a thriller by a woman, dedicated to him.

Imaginary hands, tongues, hairy bodies against her, Julie awoke in a sweat, her heart racing, but managed not to cry out. All the other women were still asleep. Although there was almost no light, she could make out the strings from Simone's apron, hung on the bunk's peg the night before. They were swinging back and forth, like a slow-moving pendulum. The sea had become even rougher; Julie could feel its pitch lying down. She closed her eyes and tried to breathe deeply, but she knew she was going to be sick again. Grabbing her robe and her shower bag, Julie hopped out of the bunk bed and ran barefoot to the bathroom down the corridor.

After a quarter hour hovering over a toilet, her stomach contracting despite its emptiness, she tottered into the shower room. The tile floor cool on her feet, she hung her clothes outside the stall and closed the curtain. Looking down at her delicate skin, past the gold medallion, she discovered oily splotches, soft bruises, blue finger marks; it was as if she too were tattooed, permanently marked by her evening with Nikolai. She quickly closed her eyes and stood under the lukewarm water. Exhaling deeply, she began scrubbing, determined to be spotless, to smell only of soap. She gently washed herself between her legs, the dried blood and the gluey secretions.

Near tears, she examined the stained washcloth, shaking her head in wonder.

"Nikolai loves me," she said out loud, then braced herself on the wall, fighting another wave of nausea. What would happen now? Would they get married? Would they be happy? She coughed up some spittle, wiped her mouth with her hand, then cleaned it in the trickling shower jet. Julie turned off the water and got out.

When she returned to the dormitory, all the women were up, silently getting dressed, their feet unsteady on a floor that was swelling and shrinking with the sea. Even the most veteran seafaring women on board were feeling the effects. After putting on her uniform, Julie lurched to the galley with the bag of ginger tea.

"Good morning, Pascal," she said, grabbing on to the counter next to him, making no pretense to smile.

"Morning, *mon petit chou,*" he replied, looking at her with his usual paternal concern. "I don't need to ask how you are."

"None of us girls are feeling too well what with this weather. Would you mind using this tea for everyone's breakfast? Perhaps it'll help us all get through the morning."

"Sure." He smiled. "Let's give the ginger another try, shall we?"

They exchanged a nod, then Julie staggered into the women's dining room, intent on sitting down. She put her head against the cool metal table. Nikolai had certainly been right about her needing his special tea this morning, she thought, concentrating on the beginning of their evening, when he'd been warmhearted and pleasant. She liked the idea of sharing Nikolai's tea with the other girls; dare she tell them that it was a gift from her boyfriend? For, surely now they were a formal couple? She glanced over at the doorway (would he be coming by first thing?) only to see Simone bustle in.

Surrounded by her entourage, Simone first smirked at Julie, then made a show of ignoring her. Julie could feel them whispering about her at the back table. If Simone only knew how tedious her evening in first class had been, she wouldn't be jealous.

When Marie-Claire came in, Julie hoped they could have a laugh about hatcheck—the clients' aloof "ehem"s, their affected hat-and-cane gestures, the ladies' ridiculous cocoon cloaks—but she promptly sat down beside her pretty friends with the upper-deck jobs. Really, though, there was no buzz of conversation in the dining hall this morning, only lone voices expressing communal discomfort. All of the women were under the weather, and most sat silently, sipping at their tea, picking at their toast.

"I haven't felt a sea like this in a long time," said a green-faced woman who had made dozens of crossings, ironing clothes all day in a windowless metal room.

"Me neither," agreed Louise. "Yesterday, I heard a passenger—a former sailor, he was—say that, of all the seas, the Atlantic is the trickiest. It's the foggiest, iciest, stormiest ocean there is!"

"Is it so wild?" asked the girl from the flower shop. "You'd think, lying between Europe and America, it would be more civilized!"

Although the women groaned at the gullible notion of a tamable sea taking cues from the refined folk on its shores, they were uneasy with the idea of being atop an unpredictable, dangerous ocean. Usually on an ocean liner, this was conveniently forgotten.

Although the day had hardly begun, Julie was wishing it were over. Tomorrow, around midday, they would be reaching New York. She wondered whether the crew would be able to disembark and enjoy a few hours at port, in the city, on *land.* She imagined walking through the busy streets, arm in arm with Nikolai, looking in the shops nestled at the foot of towering buildings. She thought back on what those Irish boys had said the first night: you can find whatever you want in New York. Maybe she and Nikolai should just stay there and settle down? Barely four days into her first cruise, Julie had already had enough of life at sea.

To go ashore! she thought longingly. No more endless stairs, no more wavy floors, no more seasickness. She had heard that some sailors, after an extended time on a ship, felt nauseated without the roll of the ocean under them, finding the earth's surface too solid, uncomfortably still. She was thinking how terribly unfair land-sickness seemed when she heard someone at the door. She peeked over at the door with a nervous smile, sure this time it would be Nikolai, only to find a cross-looking Mme. Tremblay, gesturing her into the hallway.

"It has come to my attention that you returned to the dormitory at an indecent hour," she said, her low voice articulating the words with cutting precision. "May I ask where you were?"

"Hatcheck duty ran very late, madame," Julie answered nervously. Mme. Tremblay's face had never looked so severe. "The last people reclaimed their things around two."

"A girl with a bunk near yours maintains that you didn't come back until past three," she said.

"Well." Julie swallowed. "I went to the bathroom, then I took a little walk. I'd never seen such beautiful rooms before!"

"You are not a tourist here, mademoiselle!" She paused to click her tongue at the outrage. "And you will not be working in first class again! Now, where is the uniform you wore yesterday?"

"I've already taken it to the laundry, ma'am," Julie said with some relief. She was sure that Mme. Tremblay would have been able to smell her lie on the fabric.

"And the cap?" she asked.

"It must be in the dormitory," Julie said. "I'll go get it."

"No," she said, with a stiff shake of the head. "You will begin the breakfast shift now. You can give me the cap later."

She marched off, leaving Julie trembling. Where was she going to find a lace cap? Maybe she could ask Nikolai to look for it? Reliving last night's shame—from stripping off her camisole, to her nakedness, his hugeness, to the struggle and the pain—her breathing grew shallow. No, she would not ask him to search for missing clothes. She remembered her panties, now gray, drowning by the mattress, and didn't want him to find them. With a deep blush, Julie realized that it was highly possible that another engineman, a shirker taking a quick break, already had. Were they parading her dirty drawers around, laughing, and slapping Nikolai on the back? Were they talking about her? Calling her names (tart, slut, pig, whore)? And Nikolai? What would he say? That he loved her? Or would he be laughing too?

Her hand slid along the rope railing as she walked toward the steerage dining room. The ginger tea had only calmed her stomach slightly and she wasn't looking forward to the strong smells of Pascal's cooking. Behind her, she heard the heavy footsteps of Simone and the other girls.

"I don't know why Old Tremblay chose her to work in first anyway." Simone's vicious whisper rang out in the corridor. "It looks like someone spit a wad of tobacco on her face!"

Julie was struck by the harshness of her words but pretended not to notice the chorus of giggles behind her. She tried to take comfort in the fact that, although she had a flaw, Nikolai thought she was beautiful. Simone, with her lank hair and pimples, would never be able to arouse such passion in a man.

Vera's sad sigh was interrupted by a knock.

"Madame Sinclair! It is I, Dr. Chabron," he called through the door.

Wishing Amandine was there to open the door, she crawled out of bed, put on her tartan robe and slippers, and let the doctor in.

"Good morning, Doctor," she said, trying to give off some semblance of dignity in her nightclothes, to stand tall despite her shaky frame and the stormy seas. Vera had been especially mindful of the physical illusion of honor and respect since her ousting in the dining room.

"Please, get back in bed, lie down," the doctor urged her. "I assumed your maid would be with you when I came."

"Perhaps we should get her up. Would you mind knocking on that door?" Vera asked. "She should be in here shortly. Now, how may I help you?"

He took a seat on the edge of the bed. "I came to see if you were feeling any better. Tell me, how are you this morning?"

"Much like the day, I'm afraid." She motioned toward the window with her chin. "Chilly, gray, and a bit rocky."

He bent over to touch her forehead. "You're very warm. Let me check your temperature." He put the thermometer in her mouth and prepared a new compress. "Did you sleep well?"

The thermometer bobbed up and down as Vera nodded.

Waiting for Vera's temperature to take, the doctor walked to the window and peered out. The rain was pelting down, the rough seas below were impossible to make out.

"I haven't seen a storm like this in years," he said. "From my cabin, it feels as if the bow were diving headfirst into the sea, all the way to the top decks, only to burst back up for air, breathless."

Vera smiled awkwardly around the thermometer, prompting him to take it out.

"One day, perhaps I'll tell you what it was like to travel on the old paddleboat steamers. Positively gut-wrenching! But, I'll wait for fair skies."

He smiled back at his patient, then turned his attentions to the thermometer. "Thirty-nine point five degrees." He frowned, then began rummaging through his case.

He didn't translate her temperature into Fahrenheit this time, but Vera, after all her years in France, knew how high that was. About 103 degrees.

"I'm going to give you some aspirin to reduce your fever, Madame Sinclair," he said, stirring the powder into a glass of water. "Now, did you drink fluids yesterday?"

"Yes, yes. Juice, consommé, water—I felt like an extension of the sea." Vera drank the cloudy mixture, then closed her eyes briefly. "You know, Doctor, I do still have my teeth," she joked.

She liked this doctor, his handsome, attentive face, his charming manner.

"Yes, of course." He smiled back at her, brushing aside a long strand of white hair from her brow to apply a fresh compress. "Eat whatever appeals to you."

Vera went quiet as Dr. Chabron packed his things into his leather bag. He was turning to her, ready to say good-bye, when she motioned him to sit back down.

"Doctor," she began, "I've been thinking about elephants. Why do you suppose they leave their herds to die?"

Serge Chabron seemed confused. "I don't know," he answered.

"Do you think it's like the old Eskimo who fears he will be a burden to his tribe?"

"Please don't tell me you think you're a burden?" he said gently.

Ignoring his question, she continued her own inquiry.

"Let me ask you this, Doctor. Would you say that you are guided by instinct?"

"Well." Dr. Chabron cleared his throat. "As a physician, I'd like to think of myself as a man of science. Logical, practical. Ruled by the head, you might say, instead of the heart."

"Ah, yes, I've known people like that," she said, briefly reminded of her grandmother.

"Madame Sinclair, with all due respect," he said, "what exactly are you getting at?"

"I've been questioning my decision to return home," Vera answered. "Booking passage to New York was certainly an irrational act. One of a blundering elephant." She sighed. "Although I grew up in Manhattan, now, with its skyscrapers and fleets of motorcars, I believe it's a city for the young, the quick. I feel more at home in Paris. We are both museum pieces, relics, war survivors. I think, after all, I should like to die in Paris."

"It would be lovely," he said, taking hold of her hand, "if we could make those choices: when, where, how we die." He gave her an affectionate smile. "Perhaps *I* should like to die on a luxurious ocean liner in the middle of a bright blue sea!"

She smiled back at him, then shrugged.

"You know," she said, looking him straight in the eye, "I am not afraid of dying, but I do have some regrets. At the moment, my greatest sorrow is that I will never have a grandchild."

"You can't know that!" he said, a flicker of a smile on his lips. "Tell me, how many children do you have?"

"Why, none at all."

Dr. Chabron stared blankly at Vera for a moment or two, then rose from the bed.

"I'm afraid now I truly must go. There's an infestation of lice down in steerage. And after all the examinations we do before casting off!" He shook his head, exasperated. "I'll come round again this evening to check on you. But, do stay in bed today." He got to his feet with a slight stumble and looked out toward the storm. "Not that you would want to go anywhere else."

Alone again, Vera stroked Bibi's warm side, waiting for Amandine to appear. As she breathed in harmony with the rise and fall of the sea, her eyes fell again on the broken portrait, the face she used to have. She could hear the voice of Laszlo Richter whispering in her ear.

"You make me so happy, Vera. Without you, my heart should break."

After a few minutes, listening to him with her eyes shut, she reached for her notepaper. "Mrs. Emma Richter," she wrote on the envelope. When she had finished writing the invitation to high tea in her suite at five o'clock, she found herself at quite a loss as to how to sign it.

Julie was standing on the side of the third-class common room, holding on to the ropes strung along the wall, handy in bad weather. Luckily, almost everything down here was riveted down, from the tables to the armchairs. Around her, she could hear the moans and curses of a mass of unhappy people: those frantically scratching themselves and others, thrown into chairs, wretched with seasickness. She noticed the Italian twins who liked singing duets, picking through each other's hair with a fine comb, in no mood for song; a legless man in a wheelchair was tied to an iron ring so as not to roll uncontrollably. He had somehow procured his own bucket.

Julie, feeling as peaked as any passenger, couldn't muster up much pity for them. Instead, she was overwhelmed with her own problems: Simone, seasickness, work, and above all, Nikolai. The morning was almost over and she'd had no word from him.

She pulled the necklace out of her collar and stroked the pendant nervously. What had happened to him? Was he having to work extra because of the storm? Or was he too feeling sick? Could he be in trouble? Had the chief engineer found the boys' hidden mattress? Had there been a serious accident down below? Or—far worse than any of these—had he simply forgotten his promise to come see her? Was he too busy playing cards with his friends, chuckling over the details of his conquest?

Suddenly, there was a tap on her arm; Julie's head shot up, a delighted smile nearly forming.

"Oh, I'm sorry. I didn't mean to startle you." It was the ship's doctor, who recognized her from their prior meetings. "So, tell me, how are things down here?"

"As you can see," Julie replied, visibly disappointed, "the storm has made almost everyone down here ill. And some passengers, it seems, prefer vomiting into the sea. Several of them are out on the mooring deck now! You'd think they'd be terrified out in this storm, but perhaps the rain feels good on their faces?" Julie shrugged tiredly.

"I suppose I should tell them to come in. We can't risk any accidents! Though I certainly don't fancy going out there myself." Dr. Chabron looked put out by the idea.

"Now, on top of everything else, there's been an outbreak of lice. It seems Madame Blaye has had them all along." Julie pointed to an elderly woman sitting calmly in the corner. "She's lost some of her faculties—she can't taste or smell anymore—and doesn't seem to have any feeling left in her scalp. She was covered with them and didn't even know. And now—you know how close the quarters are down here—half of steerage is infested!"

"I wonder how she passed inspection?" the doctor asked, more to himself than to her. "Has anything been done to treat them?"

"The cooks doled out vinegar for people to wash their heads in the sinks. They say it kills the lice, but the bathrooms reek of it! It's just horrible . . ." Julie's voice trailed off and she looked on the verge of gagging.

"And you, miss, you are very pale. Really, you should be lying down," he said, looking around the room for a vacant chair and finding none. "You're in no shape to be working."

"It's strange, Doctor. I grew up in the port of Le Havre, on the edge of the sea, but I just can't get used to being on a ship." Julie closed her eyes briefly as she exhaled. "But, I must work. The lunch shift is in a few minutes. I suppose one advantage of the storm is we won't have many passengers coming to meals."

After excusing herself to go into the dining room, Julie saw Dr. Chabron set his bag down on the nearest table. A queue immediately formed next to him.

It was still early for lunch, but Julie had been anxious to leave the common room and the suffering passengers; the smell of seasickness, their heaves and groans, made her even worse. She went down the corridor, hoping to see Nikolai's familiar swagger, then peeked down the stairwell. It was empty. Eager to avoid Simone, she scooted past the women's dining room, looking straight ahead, then stopped outside the galley, near tears. Julie felt not only sick but alone and unwanted. She no longer had any friends on board. And Nikolai, after professing his love last night, had not come. Where *was* he? She wiped her eyes with her sleeve, at a loss, then went into the kitchen.

She leaned against the large refrigerator door, pressing her body against the cool metal, and greeted Pascal.

"Still not feeling well, are we?" he asked, looking up at her as he licked something off his finger. "The ginger didn't work?"

Julie shook her head.

The cook, of course, was feeling fine. Julie watched in amazement as he stirred, smelled, and tasted food while keeping his footing—two steps up, three steps back—with the roll of the ship.

"So, what are we serving up today?"

"Fish stew," he said.

"Fish!" Julie made a face. "On a day like today!"

"Don't you know? All morning long they've been jumping on board to get out of the storm! I found a few hiding in a soup tureen, as scared and seasick as any green passenger!" Pascal looked at her with mischievous innocence. "Poor things! I didn't know what else to do with them!"

Julie almost managed a smile.

"Pascal," she began slowly, "do you think, on a day like today, the engine crew might be working especially hard? Say, a greaser? Would a lot of parts need oiling in this weather?"

Pascal looked at her suspiciously.

"I don't know much about these new engines they've got nowadays," he said, pulling his chef's hat down on his brow. "Coal fires, I understand, mind you! But greasers?" He shrugged. "No idea. I don't suppose you're going to tell me why you're asking?"

"I was expecting a friend from the engine crew to pay me a call this morning, that's all."

"Haven't seen him, eh?" Was that pity in his eyes? "I'm sure there's a good reason he hasn't come by. Probably just running a little late is all."

"Sure," she mumbled.

"Now, stop worrying and go lie down," he said, shooing her off with a spoon. "You've got at least a half hour to rest up before you're needed here."

Like an obedient child, Julie went off to bed.

Constance, far too anxious to stay in her cabin alone, had joined her former tablemates for luncheon. At her arrival, Mrs. Thomas looked her over carefully.

"Oh, hello, dear. We missed you yesterday," she crooned. "You weren't indisposed, I hope? Or perhaps you enjoyed your meals with your other friends on board?"

Mildred Thomas gave Constance a look intended to express guileless charm. Constance returned it.

"I'm feeling much better now, thank you," she replied.

"I thought it such a shame when you didn't come. You looked so nice after our time together in the beauty parlor!"

Mr. Thomas turned to his wife.

"Hush!" he hissed. "I can barely hear Mr. Quaeckernaeck!"

Constance turned toward Mr. Thomas with a polite smile, pleased he had put an end to that conversation, his rudeness working in her favor for once. After the reprimand, Mildred Thomas resumed her code of silence, letting the men dominate the conversation completely.

Until the food arrived, Constance hadn't realized just how weak her appetite was. During the soup course, she merely picked at a few crackers. She had stopped listening to her tiresome companions, stopped trying to find pauses to make conversational offerings as one does in polite society. Their talk was so perfectly interwoven, a moment's silence was rendered impossible; and the men were so engrossed in it, they did not even notice the effect the outer storm was having on the dining room floor.

She amused herself, then, by watching Mr. Thomas produce little flecks of spit when he got enthusiastic and the Dutchmen turn different shades of red when particularly adamant. She looked over at Captain Fielding. His hairless pink skin reminded her of some of the war victims she'd seen in Paris.

One day, when Constance was having tea at a sidewalk café and, like today, was bored by company who ignored her, she'd watched a man with similar burns and only half an arm. That man was hanging colorful posters on an advertising pillar. Although his handicap made the work a challenge, he slathered them up like wallpaper, quickly but carefully, making sure to leave no bubbles or folds. He had not been gone five minutes when a herd of dairy goats came through (who would have guessed that livestock would trample through the capital of France!) and, straightaway, they began to eat those very posters. She remembered being rather shocked at the she-goats' grotesque anatomy, their engorged udders. With those twin pendulous organs hanging almost to the ground, they did not seem female at all, but rather virile males.

Constance, suddenly uncomfortable with her own thoughts, looked swiftly around the table to make sure her dining companions were still talking. They were—talking and drinking wine. Storing it for the dry months ahead, she supposed. Only Mrs. Thomas was watching her with that secret little smile.

"Penny for your thoughts, dear," she said.

At that moment, images collided in Constance's head: Serge

Chabron, twin udders, and an advertising pillar. Startled, she breathed in a bit of saliva, then began to cough—great choking hacks—until a Dutchman felt compelled to pat her on the back and pour her some more water.

"There, there," he muttered awkwardly as she took a few sips.

Red in the face, she nodded silently to her tablemates to assure them she was fine. They immediately resumed their conversation and Constance, determined not to chat with Mildred, gave them her full attention. They were discussing the ship's magnificent engines, which they had visited the day before.

"The *Paris* is making about twenty-two knots," Captain Fielding said. "Can't compare to the British ship, the old *Mauretania,* launched back in 1906. It still holds the Blue Riband record for fastest crossing, at twenty-eight knots. With steam turbine propulsion, you know, 'twas truly revolutionary in its day."

"Are you betting on the speed here on the *Paris*?" one of the Dutchmen asked the other men. "Today will certainly be a hard call. Shame there's not a proper casino on board."

"Yes, I love a good game of roulette." Captain Fielding smiled, his reconstructed skin taut with the effort. He took a casino token out of his pocket. "I won quite a sum at Monte Carlo before the war and always carry this old chip with me. Good luck, and all that."

Constance was mildly surprised that Captain Fielding—a stuffy old bore—would carry a good-luck charm. Did he think it actually worked? She supposed he was lucky to have survived the war, but unfortunate enough to have been seriously injured. Did mere survival count as luck?

Thinking about her own life, she wondered whether she would be considered lucky. She was attractive, well mannered, and educated; she could boast three charming daughters and a nice home. And her marriage? Had she been lucky in love? George was certainly reliable, loyal, and usually quite courteous. Her gaze fell on the corner table where the crossword honeymooners dined; defying convention, they were sitting next to each other, holding hands. So like Faith and Michel!

Now Faith had always been lucky, the world her oyster. Although Constance had always been more refined, more responsible, and more respected in the community, Faith had independence, confidence, happiness. Would she trade with her younger sister? Should she take more chances? Stake her bets on joy? Take drastic risks, trusting the fates, to live a fuller life?

"May I see your token, Captain Fielding?" she asked suddenly, interrupting the first words of what promised to be one of Mr. Thomas's lengthy preambles.

They all stopped talking and looked her way, wondering whether words might prompt another coughing fit. The conversation had already moved on, but the British officer still had the chip in his hand, flipping it through his fingers. He passed it to her, and the discourse—on American poker, from the sound of it—resumed at once.

Constance examined the chip, a thin, mother-of-pearl oval with "10 Francs" engraved on both sides, wondering whether her luck might possibly change.

Vera was wrapped in her baby-blue shawl, her feet curled up on the armchair, sweating but cold. She was flipping through her anecdotes and illustrations, thinking of the Richter men, Laszlo and Josef. It seemed each had managed to blame *her* for his unhappiness. Breezing past her life's events, she consoled herself with the notion that she, Vera Sinclair, had always taken responsibility for her own failings. Of course, she'd complained, cursed, quarreled, and wished for other realities. But, no, she didn't think she had ever laid blame elsewhere. And, lord knows, she too had had a lonely childhood, not without its problems.

Closing her journal, she looked down at her watch. What was taking Amandine?

Releasing an impatient gust of air, she looked out on the dramatic sea below. How would this storm, she wondered, compare to Robinson Crusoe's hurricane? That book had been one of Warren's favorites, but it was far too moralistic for her taste. Poor Robinson got his just recompense for disobeying his father and running off to sea. If Providence truly punished the wicked and corrupt, what a different place this world would be! Indeed. And what might Providence make of her?

She watched what seemed to be a battle of black clouds above, thinking what an exciting finale a shipwreck would make to her own tale. An unforgettable ending (with or without cannibals or mutineers—or even an island!) to her life story.

She heard a slight scratch at the door, then Bibi and Amandine entered the cabin.

"It's really nasty out there!" Amandine uttered, taking off her hat. The Scotty plopped down next to Vera's chair.

"Well? Were you successful?" Vera asked the two.

"We ran into Mrs. Richter on her way to the hairdresser's. She was on her own and I was able to deliver the message." Amandine nodded. "She will bring the boy at five sharp."

"Excellent," Vera said with a weary cough. "Thank you so much."

Amandine felt Vera's brow, frowned, and prepared a fresh compress.

"Would you like me to order some bouillon?" she asked.

"That would be lovely," Vera replied. "And while you're there, perhaps you should order tea. Now, what does one serve a small boy?"

"Cocoa and cakes?" proposed the maid.

"Are we to worry about spoiling his supper?"

"Spoil *him*, ma'am." Amandine looked serious.

"Always right, aren't you." Vera smiled. "Cocoa and cakes it is. And order the richest, gooiest, most extravagant cakes possible."

Amandine put her hat back on.

"Oh, before you leave, would you mind handing me those old marionettes? They're on the trunk."

Peering into the bathroom mirror, Julie checked her hair for lice, searching for sticky white nits around her ears, behind her neck. It was a difficult task to do alone—the other girls were all grooming each other—but she didn't think she had any; when working in steerage, she always had her hair tucked under a cap. Satisfied, she put the comb down and looked at her face in the mirror. How different was she today from yesterday? In it, she saw one unhappy girl.

All during the lunch shift, she had kept her eye on the doorway, expecting to see Nikolai. She imagined the gestures he would make from the corridor—the praying hands to beg forgiveness, the thrown kisses, the dramatic clutching of his heart—and knew that he would have a good excuse for visiting her later than planned. But lunch had come and gone and now, on break, she decided to go down to the engine room to see what had become of him.

She took a few gulps of water from the faucet and rinsed her mouth, spitting several times to rid her mouth of the rancid taste of sick. Nikolai would want to kiss her, wouldn't he? She shuddered, thinking of the other things he had done to her. Her whole body ached; blood still trickled from the tear between her legs. Biting her lip to keep from crying, she looked back into the mirror. Was looking for him a good idea? Would he want to have another go? Did she need a boyfriend who, when excited, could not hear or feel her?

"Boyfriend," she murmured to herself, as if this were a delicacy, a nearly extinct species. She reached up to the birthmark he had playfully licked and turned to go find him.

Walking past the common room, Julie saw a group of children trying to get the attention of a shy cat standing out in the corridor. Scruffy and stained with grease, it nonetheless fascinated the bored children, trapped under the waterline during the tempest.

"Come, kitty!" called a small blond girl, trying to entice the animal with a bit of bread she'd pocketed at lunch.

"Hey! Let's call him 'Stormy'!" said a tall, skinny girl next to her. "For today's weather and also—look!—it has a black spiral on its side! Do you see it?" she asked the other children. "It's like a whirlpool!"

"Come here, Stormy, come!" they sang out in chorus.

However, having no interest in bread and fearful of the children's affections, the cat quickly disappeared. Julie was wondering how it came to be in steerage, then recalled the mouse she'd seen her first night on board. This cat must have plenty to feed on belowdecks.

Julie began her slow descent to the engines, holding on to the rails, which were moist from the heat. The hull was creaking with every pitch, the engine pounding. She stepped down onto the floor and groaned; at once, her feet were drenched.

With little stomach for exploring (not only did she feel terrible, but these dark, howling rooms gave her the jitters), she started out, trying to keep her footing like Pascal, two steps up, three steps back. Nikolai must be down here somewhere.

As she tramped around the engines, Julie saw at least a dozen other men—all extremely busy and indifferent to her visit—but he was not among them. After a series of turns, she found herself next to the auxiliary engine; she could just see the mattress poking out from behind. Frozen, she stared at the corner of the filthy bedsheet, trailing down to the wet floor. That's where it happened. Her heart beating wildly (would Nikolai be sleeping there?), she crept around the machine to face the bed.

It was empty. She breathed out in relief, wiping her clammy

hands on her skirt. Although she had to see him, she didn't want to meet here, ever again. Trembling, she glared down at the crumpled sheet, the place where Nikolai had become an animal. There, alongside the grime and oil stains, she saw his dried, crusty sperm and the paths of her own blood. Feeling again his body crushing her, ripping her, Julie's knees wobbled and saliva filled her mouth. She closed her eyes and sank down on the mattress; her head fell onto her knees. The machines pounding around her recalled the rhythm of sex. Julie sat motionless, pitched in the storm in that timeless, windowless chamber, her mind racing.

When she was able, Julie opened her eyes. From the vantage point of her lap she spied her bloated panties next to a crate, floating there like a dead fish. So they had not been celebrated that morning, run up the flagpole or worn on some joker's head. She supposed that, in this weather, the men had been too busy to waste time in their jerry-built rumpus room. She hoisted herself up, lurched over to her underpants, and gave them a violent kick. Her legs were solidly splashed; the panties barely moved. Long since indifferent to the fate of the ridiculous lace ruff, she did not bother looking for it, but turned around and left.

Back in the women's lounge, she kept to herself, drying her shoes with yesterday's newspaper. As afternoon began to wane, she stopped looking toward the door.

Constance had not been able to finish lunch. Looking down at the open-eyed stare of her fish course, she had begun to feel queasy again. Had the storm managed to get worse? Making a vague excuse, she trotted back to her cabin to lie down. At first she felt better (away from the gaze of her sole—as well as that of Mrs. Thomas), but she soon began imagining all the different life-forms teeming under the seemingly solid ocean surface.

When Constance was a girl she used to spend hours in the family library poring over a big red book blazoned with the black and gold title *Wonders of the Universe.* It contained articles on nature and science and was filled with wonderfully rendered engravings, notable for their realism and accuracy: "Extraordinary Fingernails," "Tattooed Islanders," "The Cannonball Tree." From the safety of her father's big leather armchair, cozy and warm in front of the fire, she was pleasantly horrified by the drawings of repulsive sea creatures.

Having looked through those pages so many times, she could now envision those images perfectly: the pelican fish with its huge faceless mouth and snaky body, the closest thing to a real sea serpent in the book; the savage sperm whale; the whimsical Portuguese man-of-war, with its long trailing curlicues (odd their touch should be so painful). But the entry which really captured her attention was on giant cuttlefishes. One engraving depicted a massive squid, a huge moving muscle with "suckers like saucepan lids," attacking a boat; the other showed a dead calamary draped around a wooden stand, its languid limbs covered in tentacles, a thousand bulbous eyes.

She shivered thinking of these creatures below—not that they could harm an ocean liner—but what if one were pitched overboard? Or what if, like the *Lusitania,* the ship went down? The humans would be in *their* world then, she thought ominously, imagining the feel of frozen water on her skin. As a child, when her family had taken a rare outing to the shore, she had found the Atlantic too cold for bathing. If the thin waters washing the sands of Cape Cod were icy, what must the water be like here, fathoms deep?

Constance poured herself a glass of water from the pitcher and took a long sip, feeling the cold liquid's passage down her throat and into her near-empty stomach, then she sat in the armchair, trying to remain calm. It was her interest in the natural world, she reminded herself, that had softened her heart toward George. When they were courting, he would confide the world's secrets in her during a garden stroll. He would casually mention that snails had tiny teeth or that dragonflies could fly in reverse; that lichen, which grew on the northern side of trees, were natural compasses; or that the butterscotch star up there was really Mars. Constance sighed. How was it possible that he had won her affection over a handful of facts? Had she been so very desperate to marry? Or, after Nigel had taken his leave, had she looked upon George Stone as her last chance? *Wonders of the Universe,* indeed.

Constance put down her water and picked up *The Mysterious Affair at Styles.* She'd finished it that morning but was still trying to decide what to write inside for Serge. "From your friend Constance on the *Paris* launch"? Or was that the dedication of a schoolgirl? "To a fellow devotee of murder and mystery"? Was that too flippant? During their private dinner, she wanted to give him a memento of their time together (Was it really just a few days?) but didn't know what to say. Was he planning a romantic evening? Or a meal between friends? If she could write her real feelings, she might put "To my impossible love."

Lying in bed that morning, humming the *Lusitania* song ("some of them lost a true sweeeet-heart"), Constance had finally come to the realization that she was falling for Serge Chabron. She recognized the symptoms from when she'd first met Nigel Williams: the tingle in her belly, the ridiculous stuttering, and her thoughts, which, however disperse, always came back to him. Despite her feelings, she knew a lasting relationship with him was unthinkable; she could never leave her children. Constance toyed with the idea of taking the photographs of her family to his cabin this evening, to share with him the reality of her husband and daughters. But then, would he think she'd been deceiving him? Would he be angry?

To calm her nerves, she brought out her paints. She opened the sketchpad to the fruit pattern she'd started the day before, but after a few strokes of her brush, she wrinkled her nose, dissatisfied. With the shifting of the ship she found herself unable to make clean lines. It looked like a child's painting anyway.

She sighed, thinking of Faith's artist friends back in Paris. Many of them went out of their way to be messy and careless with their work, even those who were truly talented. Michel, for example, had a good eye. He enjoyed sketching portraits of people on café napkins and could usually render a perfect likeness. But when he painted, he actually chose to create odd shapes and use the wrong colors, to make childlike figures that were comical or grotesque.

What might that be like? To *choose* to do the wrong thing?

She thought of her time in Paris, two weeks of tagging along behind Faith and her painter-lover to galleries, cafés, and other small apartments, each as filthy and kaleidoscopic as her sister's. She stood by watching as *Fée* did as she pleased, with no obligations to anyone.

She, *Constance,* had always been the obedient daughter, the one who respected the wishes of their substandard parents. At twenty, she had married an appropriate match and thus began her responsible, adult life of keeping house, raising children, and worrying. Faith's happiness made Constance feel its lack—she was incomplete, hollow—but her younger sister's notion that she *deserved* joy and freedom infuriated her.

"Go back to Worcester?" Faith had repeated in an incredulous tone. "Why would I do that? Seriously, Constance, you know it wouldn't help. No, I'm staying in Paris," she said, her decision firm. "This is where I belong."

Constance's mission had failed with no discussion; she would return to America by herself to deal with the family crisis on her own. As angry as Constance was with Faith, she couldn't help but envy her, her obstinate, daring, and carefree conviction. Part of her wished she had the strength to follow her own bent.

The brush still in her hand, Constance began to paint long, flat strokes over the fruit pattern, again and again, smudging the colors until the whole page was streaked an ugly brown. She ripped out the sheet, crumpled it into a sticky ball, and threw it into the wastepaper basket. One by one, she squeezed the small tubes of paint between her fingers until the colors oozed out and her hands were stained—vermilion, cobalt, ocher—then chucked the empty husks into the bin as well. Painting was not for her.

"Would you like some hot chocolate?" Vera offered her guests.

"Just a bit, please," said Emma Richter.

Max, far more interested in the toy bank, didn't look up. Vera had placed it on the writing table before they'd arrived, along with a heaping pile of centimes. He was already at work, feeding the dog coins.

Vera poured cocoa into cups and Amandine handed them out, cautious, the rocking of the ship tempting her to spill. She then took her place in a straight-backed chair at Vera's side. The three women were silent a moment as they sipped. Vera brought the cup to her lips, but, feeling hot and sticky herself, couldn't drink it.

When the supply of centimes was used up, Max reached for a cake; the rough seas had not affected his sweet tooth. He licked cream from the corner of his mouth. "The cakes are yummy, Miss Camilla," he said, making her wince and smile at the same time.

Emma gave her son a sidelong glance but didn't comment on the false name.

"Yes, Mrs. Sinclair." She nodded to her hostess. "Thank you for inviting us. It is a delightful distraction on a day like today."

"Thank you so much for coming," she said, walking toward the wardrobe with a slight stumble. "Max, I thought you'd especially like to see these." She pulled out the two marionettes, the Italian knight and his lady. "My parents gave them to me when I was a child."

He came over and touched the knight's sword.

"They're wonderful!" he said.

"Would you like me to give you a little puppet show?" she asked.

"Yes, please!" he cried.

Vera sat on the bed and gave the boy a cushion to sit on the floor in front of her.

"Now then, let me see," she started slowly, as if she hadn't been planning this performance all afternoon. She picked up the puppets, making the mustachioed knight salute, then bow. "This is the Chevalier of Melancholia and this is . . ." She maneuvered the other puppet into a curtsy. "What shall we call her?"

"Hmm." Max squinted one eye, thought visible on his brow. "How about Daisy?" he said finally.

"An excellent choice. And this is Princess Daisy. Once upon a time, Princess Daisy found the chevalier lost in the mountains. 'I'll save you!' she cried."

"That's silly!" Max laughed. "A knight being saved by a princess! It's the other way around!"

"But Daisy was a fairy princess with magical powers," Vera countered. "She saw that someone, long ago, had put the Spell of Sadness on the good chevalier. Here, look at his face, his eyes. You can see for yourself."

Vera made the knight walk over to Max and kneel before him. The boy looked at the painted features on the wooden head and nodded sagely.

"He does look sad," he said.

"So the fairy, disguised as a princess, gently touched his cheek and said, 'Smile, oh Chevalier of Melancholia!'"

"'Ow!' cried the knight. 'I can't do it! It hurts my face!'"

The puppet covered his face and the boy giggled.

"Yes, you can, my good man. I will help you smile. And even laugh!"

Vera made the princess puppet do a silly jig, go upside down and do the splits.

"'Ha . . . ha . . . ha . . . ' Very slowly the knight began to laugh a slow, rusty laugh. A laugh that had been trapped inside a long, long time. 'Ha . . . ha . . . ha . . .'"

She made him walk around in a circle, his neck jutting out like a chicken at each "ha."

"For the rest of the summer the fairy stayed with him up in the mountains, taking walks, picking flowers, dancing and singing together."

Vera made the puppets dance and sing, hitting faint though piercing high notes followed by low, gravelly ones. Max's eyes shone with delight.

"When summer came to an end, the fairy said, 'My dear Chevalier, the spell is now broken! You are free from the curse of sadness and can be happy as long as you live! However, I must leave you now.' The princess puppet kissed his cheek and began to walk away. 'No!' cried the knight. 'It is you who brings me happiness! I will be sad again if you go!'"

The knight puppet implored her on one knee, his hands lifted in prayer.

"'But I have taught you to smile and laugh, to love the world, and to feel joy in your heart!'"

The princess puppet pulled him to his feet, then Vera paused; her voice felt too tight to continue. A tear trapped in her lashes, she looked down at Laszlo's grandson with affection. Enthralled by the story, he was staring at the puppets, his eyes wide, his mouth slightly open. Vera hoped that *he* would never make another person responsible for his own happiness.

Emma didn't know whether she felt touched by the tale itself or Vera's sorrow in telling it. Remembering the old love letters, written twenty years past, she stole a glance at the elderly lady, wondering how their lives would be now if Vera had read them.

Max too looked up at the puppeteer, confused by the story's abrupt ending.

"But, what happened then?"

"Well," Vera said with a stifled sniffle. "What do you think happened?"

"The fairy . . . goes off to help other people with her magic. And the brave knight," Max paused a moment. "He kills a dragon and takes its treasure!"

"Just so!" Vera cried. "What a clever boy you are!"

"You tell good stories! And really, you have the best toys!" Max said with admiration, sneaking another peek at the mechanical bank.

"Thank you, young man. In fact, that is the real reason I've invited you over today. I'd like for you to have that old bank."

Max's mouth fell open.

"Really?" he asked, looking over at his mother for confirmation. When she nodded, he rushed over to the writing table and picked it up with both hands. "It's heavy!" he said happily. He sat back in his chair, his new possession safe on his lap.

"You know, Max," Emma murmured to her distracted son. "Mrs. Sinclair here knew your grandfather Richter."

At once, he looked up at his mother, then at Vera.

"Back when your father was just a little boy. He might have been about your age," Vera said shyly; Emma's revelation had come as a surprise. "We met in the mountains one summer."

"Like Daisy and the knight!" he said.

"Oh, we weren't as exciting as all that," she said with a sad chuckle. "There was no fairy magic, no dragons killed. But your grandfather was a very fine man, Max. And he would have been delighted to have had a grandson such as yourself."

Max looked pleased for a moment, then turned to Vera with a serious expression. "May I ask you something?"

Vera fidgeted on her chair; surely the boy didn't think she was his grandmother! "Yes," she breathed. "Of course, Max."

"Do you have any more centimes?"

Vera threw her head back with a roar of laughter, which in turn caused a coughing fit.

"We should be going," Emma said, quickly rising to her feet. "Thank you for everything."

Max popped up beside his mother.

"And thank you for my bank!" he said, cradling it against his chest.

Still seated, Vera looked at the boy at eye level, then patted his head.

"I have so enjoyed meeting you, Max," she said, her voice now raspy. "Thank you, Mrs. Richter, for allowing me to see him." The two women shook hands.

When Max and his mother had left, Vera was astounded by the silence in the room. She didn't hear the foghorn or the wind, only the boy's absence. She would miss him, she thought, this boy she barely knew.

"I think your fever has gone up, ma'am," Amandine chided her mistress.

After the guests had been gone only a few minutes, the maid had Vera back in her dressing gown, in bed, with a compress on her head.

"Perhaps," Vera said, "but I feel much better. Now, even in this storm, I think I can sleep."

Preparing the dining room had become a formidable task. Julie, nauseated and dejected, felt so weak that the stoneware dishes had grown surprisingly heavy. Slowly divvying up the plates, trudging from one place setting to the next, she could not stop thinking of Nikolai. She felt every ache in her battered body, felt the weight of the gold medallion on her chest, felt his rejection, and marveled at his idea of love. After her visit to the engine room a slow fury had begun seething inside her, an anger coupled with the shame of her own stupidity. Unfortunately, during a storm like this, it was not able to give her strength.

Her second table set, she tumbled down on a bench at the third, unable to continue. She lay her head down and gently stroked the rim of the shallow dent in front of her. These were carved into the table to prevent the plates from sliding in bad weather. Putting her childlike hand inside the hollow, she thought she could have used some kind of restraint herself, something that would have kept her from falling. After a moment's rest, she felt Pascal's big, burn-covered hand on her shoulder.

"Juliette!" he said. "You're white as a ghost! Could you manage to eat something? Or drink? Tell me what you'd like and I'll make it. Really, it would do you good."

She accepted a glass of water and took a halfhearted sip.

"It seems that most of the passengers down here are feeling like you do," Pascal continued. "The others will be able to handle tonight's dinner crowd. You go lie down."

"Are you sure?" Julie asked hopefully. "But, what about Madame Tremblay? She's already scolded me once today."

"Let me worry about that. Now, off to bed with you! And hopefully, by morning, you'll be right as rain. Oh—well, forget the rain part."

The cook gave her a crooked smile and patted her head fondly.

Julie was making her way down the metal corridor when she saw Simone bolt out of the dormitory, rushing toward the dining hall. Since she was already twenty minutes late to work, Julie was surprised to see that she'd taken the time to put on her sister's powders, thick layers of lipstick and rouge. Maybe she had finally met a beau? One of the third-class passengers, no doubt.

"Where are you going?" Simone stopped in front of Julie, eyeing her suspiciously. Did she think she was deviously heading back up to hatcheck?

"I'm not well," Julie said shortly. "Pascal thinks I need some rest."

"Aren't you just everyone's pet?" she said. Her bitter remark was followed by a sudden curl of her lips; her voice oozed with sweetness as her eyes narrowed. "Oh, by the way, I saw Nikolai this afternoon. He came up to steerage after the lunch shift."

"What?" Julie put her hand on the wall to steady herself. "What did he say? Did he leave me a note?"

"Why," Simone said coyly, starting off again for work, "we didn't talk about *you*!"

Her mouth open, Julie watched the swing of Simone's hips as she swanned off to the dining room. Breathing hard, Julie stomped back to the dormitory, confused. So, while she was below—looking for him but finding only that nasty mattress—Nikolai had been up here. He had come after all. Drained and queasy, she headed straight to her bed, but was distracted by the mess on Simone's bunk. It was littered with makeup, street clothes, and a few pieces of costume jewelry. Thinking of her sly, tight-lipped smile, she wondered what Simone was planning. What *had* they talked about, if not about her?

Simone's jealousy was out of control, going from tattling to insults to blatant lies. It couldn't be true that Nikolai hadn't asked about her. Had she accepted a note from him, just to destroy it? Or, when he had finally made his way up to third class, had Simone managed to make him forget why he'd come? Last night, he'd said he loved her. But, for him, was one working girl as good as another?

Julie grabbed her Verne novel from her locker and lay down on her bed. Opening the book, she quickly found the two notes from Nikolai. She was angry with him, but even angrier with herself. Skimming the notes, with their Louis XIV handwriting and terrible spelling, she read the lines aloud in a sarcastic whisper.

"'When you caught my hat, it was a sign.' A sign of my foolishness. 'I hope Mary can melt your heart.' My brain more like!"

A letter from Loïc slipped out of the novel and, with a deep breath, she picked it up. She compared the old envelope, addressed in her brother's cramped hand, sent from the trenches, to the notes from Nikolai. These clean, new ones had been written in the safety of an ocean liner to fool her into his arms. How Julie wished she still had brothers! Four brothers who could straighten out a scoundrel who dared insult their little sister.

With tears in her eyes, she remembered a discussion she'd had with Loïc when they were about twelve years old. They were sitting on the dock, their legs hanging down, talking about a tale their father had told them the night before. "The Ridiculous Wishes" was about a poor woodcutter granted three wishes by a genie, but who makes such terrible choices that in the end his life is no better than it was in the beginning. There, under the sun, their bare shins occasionally spattered with seawater, they debated what the best, most risk-free wishes would be, ones that no genie could twist into something bad.

"Gold!" Loïc had said, tossing a pebble into the sea. "How can you go wrong there? Or perhaps to find buried treasure on the banks of the Seine? That way, you could have fun and adventure as well as money."

"But in the stories, greedy wishes always bring bad luck," Julie had countered. "I think the best bet would be to wish for a good job. You make your own money that way." Looking out into the port, she'd pointed at an enormous ocean liner, the *France*. "Can you imagine working on board a ship like that? Talk about adventure!"

After discussing the obvious wish for wealth, Julie had shyly mentioned her other, less practical desire: a man's love and devotion. Loïc had teased her a bit, then thrown his arm around her.

"I'm sure you'll find a good man one day, Julie!" He'd smiled. "And if not, well, you'll always have me!"

Julie looked at Nikolai's notes again, the scrolling curlicues, the flattery, his extravagant gift. It seemed her wishes had come true.

She had the exact job she'd thought she'd wanted. However, far from an adventure, she found the work tedious, and life under the waterline, with no sun or air, wretched. As for the love of a man . . .

She reread Nikolai's words with a snort, and then balled the paper up in her hand, squeezing it tight. In the end, she had made ridiculous wishes like the woodcutter; she too had been fooled by the genie.

With the seas in such a state, Constance was growing nervous alone in her cabin. Wiping the notions of sea creatures and impossible loves from her mind, she put on her hat and gloves and headed out. Unsure of where to go, she decided to start with the drawing room, hoping to see those amusing Brits. However, she was disappointed to find that almost no one had turned up for tea, and the ones who *had* all seemed stern and sullen. (Was everyone imagining giant cuttlefishes and icy waters? Or were they simply fighting impending nausea?) She debated having her hair done again, but, still pleased with her appearance, she didn't want to risk it. She couldn't venture outdoors in the storm, and, with the sway it caused indoors, she doubted any exotic sport—fencing or boxing—was taking place in the gymnasium. Running out of options, she eventually settled on the library.

Arranging herself in a deep-seated armchair, she absentmindedly thumbed through the latest issue of *Lady's Companion* and wondered what Serge was doing. Constance was disappointed that he hadn't checked in on her and could only imagine what interesting procedures he was performing on which patients. She was terribly ill at ease. She couldn't get the song "When the *Lusitania* Went Down!" out of her head, no matter how hard she tried to supplant it with the ditty "Fancy You Fancying Me."

She gave out a long sigh, tossed the magazine onto the table, then watched it slowly slide off with the roll of the ship. This wasn't working; the library was too quiet and she had been alone with her thoughts long enough. Constance decided to move on.

As she was walking past the second-class bar, she heard laughter. She paused for a moment, listening to the muffled sounds of gaiety and remembering again the diversion she'd found with the English group the previous day. Why not, Constance thought to herself. Perhaps this was exactly what she needed.

Constance opened the door and stepped inside. A chrome bar was wedged into a snuggly fitted room where a mirror was shining through liquor bottles, jiggling and clinking with the sea. Roosting on stools, leaning on the bar, four middle-aged men were drinking cocktails.

At her entrance, they all turned in unison. Constance hesitated, looked back out the door, then stood still, smiling with embarrassed uncertainty. She hadn't expected the group to be made up solely of men, but now that they'd seen her (and were watching her still), she felt even more awkward turning on her heel and walking out.

"Hello! Hello!" The men burst out greetings in American accents. "Come in! Please join us!" they cried together.

Constance shyly walked up to the bar, where one of the men offered her his stool.

"I'll have a cup of tea," she told the barman.

"Tea? No, have a cocktail with us! Let us treat you to something special!"

Crowded around her, they all grinned playfully, their eyes shining. Constance shook her head, protesting mildly, but after a few minutes' insistence, she finally agreed. After all, she could use the distraction.

"Right then!" called one in a brown suit. "What would you like? Rum punch? A manhattan?"

"For a day as wet as this, I'd recommend a dry martini!" said one with gray hair, raising his glass and laughing at his own joke. "Or, how about a white lady for the lady?

"Hey, Lou-ee!" this one cried to the barman. Constance noticed the familiarity of his tone, as if this *Paris* bar had been his regular haunt for ages. She too had experienced the strange passage of time aboard ship, each day at sea equaling several years on land. "A white lady for our friend."

"Now then, what's your name? Where are you from? Tell us about yourself!"

Alcohol, it seemed, made one take shortcuts around routine civilities. Constance, however, was rather pleased to have such a captive audience.

"I'm Constance Stone, from Worcester, Massachusetts," she replied with a smile, as her drink was being served.

"Well, it's a pleasure to meet you, Constance Stone from Worcester, Massachusetts," the gray-haired gentleman said with a wink. "I'm John Crenshaw and this here is Martin, Albert, and Cy. We're all from New York."

Martin lifted his glass to make a toast: "To friends, old and new!"

"Here, here!"

Constance found the white lady, served in a long-stemmed glass and decorated with a cherry and a slice of orange, rather imposing. She balanced it in her hand a moment, trying to decide how to drink it without spilling the fruit into her lap. Finally she took a small sip, and though it was far too strong for her taste, she made a good-natured grimace, raising her glass to her delighted companions.

Enjoying their martinis, the four men swapped travel anecdotes: amusing misunderstandings in foreign languages, mishaps on the railways, interesting characters met abroad. During their second round, Constance chimed in to tell them about the bohemian artists she'd met in Paris, making them laugh with her humorous descriptions of their eclectic fashions and untidy artwork. She didn't mention her sister or her mission; none of that mattered here.

Constance felt agreeably risqué, having a fancy drink (two!) in the company of men. So unlike her! She caught her own reflection in the mirror behind the bar, swinging her glass and grinning like the Cheshire cat. Constance hardly recognized herself. She glanced over at barman Louis and saw boredom in his heavy-lidded eyes, his utter lack of surprise at her inclusion in this group. How refreshing to be unknown.

Suddenly the ship heaved and Constance, perched daintily on the edge of her stool, tipped over and onto the floor. The man introduced as Albert helped her up with a "No harm done?" but gray-haired John gave her a playful wag of his finger.

"I think our white lady has had enough!" He laughed at her blush.

She suddenly remembered her dinner plans and looked at her watch; quarter to seven. Serge was coming for her at eight.

"Oh my!" she exclaimed, covering her mouth with her fingertips. "I do need to run! But, thank you, gentlemen, for a most amusing afternoon!"

"Our pleasure," they declared, tipping their heads, saluting her with a single finger.

"Let me walk you back to your cabin, miss," said John. "I'd never forgive myself if you tumbled into the sea."

Vera lay in bed, shivering under the blankets. She had abruptly woken from a deep sleep an hour before, immediately aware her temperature had spiked. She idly wondered whether this was the fever Robinson Crusoe called ague, chills that alternate with sweats, making one always yearn for the opposite extreme.

"Maximilian," she mumbled. "Maximilian Laszlo."

Ever since she'd woken up, she had been thinking about that boy, children in general, her own sterility. About dying with "no issue," which sounded every bit like the fate of a doomed Roman emperor or an inbred royal. Laszlo had been fortunate in that respect; his elegant mouth and hands would be carried on in that adorable child.

Vera thought she might have enjoyed motherhood, but, very likely, she would have repeated her parents' mistakes. Along with their fortune, she had inherited their selfishness. Like them, she would have inevitably left sons and daughters to servants to better enjoy herself (though they would have been spared a grandmother).

She'd never really regretted not bringing life into this world and the overwhelming responsibility that it implied. But—if she'd only had siblings!—Vera would have dearly loved having nieces and nephews. She imagined being their godmother and choosing their names: Charles Alexis, Percival Campbell, Cassandra Grace. She could have criticized her brother or sister for all their parenting blunders, then, when she was in the mood, spoiled the children with extravagant gifts and outings. When they came of age, she would have taken them for lobster at the Plaza, talked to them about sex, and offered them their first cigarette. They would have adored her in the way one can never love one's parents.

Vera imagined how delighted they would have been to discover her memoirs. Truly, these imaginary relations were their only possible recipients. Her cousins' children were nothing to her (and even worse, she was nothing to them!) and didn't deserve such wealth. She had considered giving the three tomes to Charles, but knew a proper heir had to be of another generation, not a contemporary. He could not read them with youth's open-eyed fascination, marveling at days past. And, of course, Laszlo's grandson was out of the question.

Absently stroking her pearls, she leafed through the journals, page by page. Here were her earliest memories: *B* for P. T. Barnum's

Museum of Oddities on Broadway. *C* for Cornelia, their Negro maid who had walked from Maryland to freedom. Here was Paris in the belle epoque and the writers and artists she'd known: *N* for Natalie Barney and her Sapphic Circle, *S* for Sylvia Beach's Shakespeare and Company.

She picked up another volume, the first of two organized by number, remembering, reliving. Here were raw accounts of her private life: 1 Child Lost; rue Monge, number 5 . . . Her many travels: 28 Days in the Holy Land; 101 Degrees in Athens (in a long skirt, mutton sleeves, and corset); A Dozen Fjords. She thumbed through the pages of the last volume, smiling at the drawings and caricatures, until she came to the Great War: 350 Shells, the blasts on Paris from a railway gun, the constant panic, the fear; 16 Friends Departed, both soldier and civilian, all sacrificed to the war. She kept turning the pages, rereading fragments, until she got to the last, unwritten entry: X Crossings.

All of these things, from the queer to the conventional, from horror to beauty, from delight to sorrow: this was her life. Nothing to regret or lament. No one to blame. She had made choices and embraced chance, and this was who she was. Now, what to do with this heirless treasure? She looked again at the pirate map, wondering exactly what spot the *X* was marking.

Vera took off her glasses and pressed her fingers against the moist skin beneath her eyes, blotting away the beads of sweat. Suddenly, she heard the disconsolate cries of a newborn. Crisp, short, urgent blasts. Odd, she thought, this was the first time she'd heard a baby on this crossing. At first she thought it must be something else—some kind of machinery?—but no, that wail was unmistakable. Her Parisian neighbor had had eight children and Vera knew perfectly well what an unhappy newborn sounded like.

This child was clearly in agony or in great need of being fed or changed. Vera was tempted to rise, to go and see to it herself; it sounded like it was right outside her door. But, there must be someone—a mother, a nanny—trying to soothe the babe, to quiet it.

Ignoring the sounds, it occurred to Vera that these diaries—with battered covers, fading ink, and pages well-worn from constant perusal; authored not by a famous explorer or a well-known statesman but by a little old lady with a secondhand fountain pen—might not be such a fortune after all. Perhaps an outsider, without the benefit of the original memories, would not find them as rich and powerful as she.

Putting the three books side by side on her bed, Vera had to admit that these tales, written years after the events, were not always *fair.* Many things were deliberately left untold, giving her story a warped perspective. Some close friends were left out, her family rarely mentioned, yet at times virtual strangers received meticulous descriptions. And then, there was Laszlo.

Two days before, he had been a rather insignificant detail in her memoirs, an anecdote. In her telling, he was not a life-altering person, an indispensable event. And yet, ever since she'd met his son and learned the news of his death, Laszlo Richter had been haunting her like a ghost. The importance of their brief time together (and moreover, what their relationship could have been) had been playing constantly in her mind.

Her eyes darted to the door; the newborn's cries continued. She blew out a long gust of air. Dependent and frail, with poor eyesight and a toddling gait, this past year Vera had sometimes felt like a baby herself.

Vera knew she was in denial about her illness, her approaching death. For months now she had been fleeing from it in these journals, returning to her past, trying to remain safe in her youth, her prime. Now Vera wondered whether she had also been in denial about her life. Was she going to spend the rest of her days rereading half-truths about her former self, the spirited though self-centered person who predated her illness? Tales that evoked her best qualities while downplaying her faults, prose that was written, therefore, with an audience—a sympathetic reader—in mind? Vera would have never guessed that she herself would become that reader.

Pathetic, she thought, shaking her head. Truly, was this way of dying any better than her grandmother's? During *her* final years, Camilla Wright Sinclair had gradually let go of her past to live exclusively in the present. Each moment was her first, every experience unique and new.

She looked over at Amandine, who was sitting by the window, watching the furious sky, stroking Bibi's silken ear with one hand.

"Have you ever heard such a baby?" Vera exclaimed, suddenly cross. She was agitated, mostly by her somber thoughts, but preferred to find fault with the infant and its incessant wailing. "It's been crying now for a full half hour!"

Amandine looked at her in surprise. "I don't hear anything, ma'am."

After an hour of cocktails and pleasantries with the gentlemen from New York, Constance had felt more relaxed about her upcoming dinner in Serge's quarters; she was ready to chat and laugh with him as she had with John Crenshaw and the others. However, as she dressed—changing her stockings, buttoning her chemise, buckling up her fine black heels—she began to grow nervous. Did this French doctor truly fancy her? Was he sincere? If he took her in his arms, would she be able to resist? Should she tell him about her family straightaway? Ask about his?

At half-past eight, Constance heard a series of jaunty taps on the door. She hesitated, wondering again whether she should go. Checking herself in the mirror, she gave herself a comical little frown, which in turn made her smile. She'd been overreacting. After a quick dinner, Serge would escort her to the magnificent ballroom, where she would take part in one of high society's most fashionable galas. Certainly, *that* was nothing to worry about! She crammed the detective novel into her beaded handbag, smoothed out her dress, and opened the door.

"I'm terribly sorry I'm late, Constance," Serge said, presenting her with a handsome bouquet of tulips and a sheepish grin; he was still in his work clothes. "But the infirmary was so crowded today. It seemed for every patient I treated, four more would walk through the door!"

Constance took the tulips with a trembling hand. Now that he was there, next to her, she could no longer pretend he was just a pleasant companion, like those men in the bar. She peeked up at him with a slight blush.

"Thank you, Serge," she murmured, shifting the flowers from one hand to the other. "They're beautiful."

"You don't have a vase, do you?" he said, looking around. "I don't know what I was thinking. Here, I'll just prop them in the washbasin for now."

His hand grazed hers as he took the flowers; she swallowed hard.

"Shall we?" he asked, turning toward her with an extended arm.

They walked down a long corridor to the front of the ship, where the doctor's quarters were found. The halls were empty; most people were already in the dining room or tucked away in their cabins, indisposed.

"I'm afraid the gala tonight will be nearly ruined by the rain and rough seas," Serge told her. "Many people are feeling ill, which will make for a thin crowd. But also, when the weather is fine, they put fairy lights or Chinese lanterns out on the deck and the orchestra plays until dawn."

"It really *is* too bad about the weather," she replied, wishing for wit; at his side, it was so difficult to find words.

Passing under an arcade, she realized that he'd mentioned

dancing in the moonlight twice now; she could only assume that he'd waltzed until the wee hours with other female passengers over the years. Again, Constance wondered whether he had special feelings for her.

"Here we are!" Serge opened the door to his chambers.

They walked into a small sitting room, equipped with built-in shelves, a desk, a table, a plump armchair, and a two-person settee. The window was larger than the one in her room, a simple porthole, but tonight there was no view.

"Since this is the *Paris*'s first time out, it's not quite home yet"—he shrugged—"but it's comfortable enough. Please, take a seat. As you can see, I didn't have time to dress for dinner—I was running so late—but I won't be a moment." He bowed slightly and retired to the adjoining room.

Constance set her purse on the table but did not sit down. Rather, she studied his quarters, curious to learn more about him. She looked at his desktop. It was covered with thick glass, and he had slid some postcards underneath: Niagara Falls, Edinburgh, Mont Blanc. She noted his slanted handwriting on a neat pile of official-looking papers, organized in a fixed tray next to an elegant marble inkwell and pen stand. It was all screwed down to the wood. Indeed, the sea was much more noticeable here near the bow. She looked at the books on the shelves; among the French medical tomes, there were several works of fiction: alongside A. Conan Doyle, she found Poe, Balzac, Zola, and a recent edition of *Le Fantôme de l'Opéra*. Her finger trailed along the bindings. Serge Chabron was obviously a man of refined tastes, worldly, well educated, tidy.

She caught sight of a photograph poking out of the phantom book, as if it was being used as a bookmark. With a guilty glance at his bedroom door, she pulled the book from the shelf and opened it, hoping to find a picture of a boyish Serge. Would he be surrounded by a large French family, or perhaps in his military uniform?

Instead she saw a photograph of three small children. Constance examined them closely, their bright eyes and impish smiles, and guessed their ages to be similar to her own children. Were they his? She thought she could detect a family resemblance. With a sigh, she stuck the photo back in the book and dropped onto the settee. If she continued looking, she could probably find a portrait of a wife as well.

She'd suspected that Serge was not a bachelor—he was too handsome, too desirable to have gone unnoticed—but had never wanted to broach the topic. Silence speaks volumes, as they say, and he too had chosen to ignore his family. When Serge had arrived at her cabin door, brimming with charm and tulips, she had wanted to forget George and the girls, to pretend she was an unmarried woman, available for romance. However, after seeing the three children in the photograph—not unlike her own precious daughters—she didn't think she could. Should she leave?

Serge came back into the room, in his evening suit, his mustache snappy, his smile dashing.

"The waiters should be here any moment now," he said, glancing at his wristwatch. "I told them to come around nine."

As he sat down on the settee next to Constance, she could smell a mixture of lavender soap and freshly applied cologne.

"With all the rush, I haven't told you how beautiful you look tonight." He reached for her hand and gave it a kiss. "I took the liberty of ordering champagne. I hope you like it?"

Constance nodded politely, but, even more skittish now, she didn't trust her voice. She sighed in relief when their privacy was interrupted by a knock, followed by two waiters pushing a cart covered with a long, white tablecloth.

They put the brake on the cart, and one brought out champagne flutes while the other pulled out a bottle and popped the cork. Watching them set the table for two (was it her imagination, or were they giving each other knowing looks?), Constance made the decision that, indeed, this would be a dinner between friends. Nothing more. She heard the doctor excuse them ("I'll serve, boys!"), and with a prompt bow, they left the room. Her mind made up, Constance already felt more at ease.

"*À votre santé!* To your health!" He raised his glass up at her.

"Cheers!" she returned, and took a sip. The bubbles, cold and airy, seemed to clear her head even more. In a moment, she found her glass empty.

"Ah!" He cocked his eyebrow with a grin. "You *do* like champagne!"

Serge raised a silvery dome to expose a dozen raw oysters on a bed of lettuce. He picked one up and squeezed lemon on it (did it shrink and quiver?) and handed it to her.

"I'm sure there is a variety of cumbersome cutlery—tongs and so forth—one could use to eat these. But truly, the best way is with one's hands. Go ahead, now—give it a try!"

He watched her in amused expectation as she brought the shell to her mouth and sucked the oyster inside. It sat on her tongue, an unpleasant blob, until finally, with a sip of champagne, she took it like a large pill.

"As bad as all that?" Serge laughed at her expression, then quickly ate two or three. Wiping his hands on his napkin, he looked back up at Constance. "Tell me, what have you been doing today? What adventures have you had?"

Looking into his expectant face, she decided against telling him about her newly made friendships from the bar. She feared he would misunderstand (as if she routinely drank gin with a handful of men!) and think less of her.

"Oh, just braving the storm, like everyone else. Reading, mostly," she said. "Which reminds me, I have something for you."

She extracted the novel from her smallish bag, then placed it in his hand.

"I finished it today and wanted you to have it," she said, returning his smile. "As a souvenir of our friendship." This last word she said with resolve.

"Thank you, Constance." He immediately opened it to the front page, but found she hadn't written anything in it. "Could you dedicate it, please?"

"Of course," she said. "Though my hand may not be too steady in this weather."

With the dip pen from his desk, she quickly scrawled, "Your friend, Constance Stone."

He read it with mild disappointment, then lit a Gauloise and thanked her again.

"This will prove invaluable on the voyage back to France. I have no doubt that I will enjoy reading this feminine mystery—indeed, women have always seemed rather mysterious to me!" he said with a light chuckle, then took a puff of his cigarette. "But, I must say, I like even more the idea that you had read it before me. That you had this very book in your hands," he added, already nostalgic. "How I shall miss your company."

"I've enjoyed spending time with you too, Serge," she said quietly, catching her breath. She stared at his hand as he refilled her champagne glass; she didn't trust herself to look at his face.

"Some journeys are far too short," he declared. "Did I tell you that, before the war, I was on the West Indies line? I loved traveling to the tropics in my white uniform on a white ocean liner, putting into port in Trinidad, the Antilles, Venezuela . . . Ah, Constance, how I wish that you and I were on our way to Trinidad right now!" He gently caught her chin in his hand, to make her face him, to look into her eyes.

"It does sound wonderful," she murmured, then remembered herself. "Um, shouldn't we eat a little something before the gala?"

"How right you are!" he said, pulling off other shiny domes, and began preparing plates: cold sliced ham, deviled eggs, white asparagus.

He gazed over at her again, then dropped the dish on the table, shaking his head.

"Constance, around you, I can hardly think of food," he said, sliding next to her, letting their legs touch. "Just looking at you . . . Did you know your features are perfect?" he whispered, stroking her cheek. "Absolutely perfect."

"Serge," she began nervously, but he brought his fingertips to her lips, delicately closing her mouth.

"I don't want our arrival in New York to end this," he said. "But tonight, our last night together on the *Paris* . . ."

His hand found the nape of her neck and brought her to him. As his fingers wove into her hair, he nuzzled her ear, then found her lips. He kissed her with playfulness and passion, gentleness and force. A warm electric current went through her, relaxing her while putting her on edge; her body throbbed: her breasts, her thighs, her belly. Although she wanted him to continue, she backed away, breathless but determined.

"Serge," she repeated, a half-hearted reproach.

She sat up and shakily reached for her glass, her mind racing for an appropriate topic of conversation. She needed to make small talk until they left for the safety of the party, the crowd. After taking a slow sip, she wedged herself into the corner of the sofa. Dizzy—from the champagne, the ship's roll, the tobacco smoke mingling with perfume, his heat—she struggled desperately for something to say.

"Do you think this rain will end before the party?" she finally managed, stuttering politely.

"Ah, Constance, I must say"—he took her hand with a heaving sigh—"I'm enjoying our little party à deux. Having you all to myself." He raised his glass to her: "To Aphrodite, the goddess of beauty."

He pulled her into his arms, kissing her expertly. Wobbly, she closed her eyes with a soft moan; his hands tentatively began exploring her ample breasts, her soft hips. She was returning his kiss, his fire, when the photograph came to mind. Not the one of those unknown children, but the one of her own. In that picture she knew so well, her daughters' innocent smiles began to shift into grimaces of confusion, fear, disgust. She pulled away.

"No, Serge," she said, almost in tears. "I can't."

"But, Constance, I'm crazy about you! And I know you feel the same way about me."

"I'm sorry," she said as she got up. "I truly am."

She stood in the open door, steadying herself on the frame, breathing in the fresh air. The chill of the night was already casting off the champagne haze. He remained on the settee, still too excited to move.

"Don't go, Constance!" Serge called out. *"Constance!"*

She turned to him from the doorway.

"Exactly," she said, then walked away.

The steerage workers' noisy entrance into the women's dormitory—harsh laughter rendered their words unrecognizable—woke Julie up from a hard sleep. The dinner shift was over. Groggy, the taste of rank mold in her mouth, she sat up slowly, feeling like she weighed a thousand pounds. As she got up to go to the bathroom, she noticed the other girls whispering and sneaking glances at her. Julie's uniform, after sleeping in it, was thoroughly wrinkled and fell askew. The other girls neither teased her nor greeted her. Their leader, Simone, was absent.

After splashing her face and rinsing her mouth, she drifted back into the corridor. She didn't want to go back into the dormitory; the steerage girls' rejection and the others' indifference made the bunk-lined room a hostile territory. Julie thought again of Nikolai. Since that first morning on board, still in the docks of Le Havre, he had been friendly to her. He had pursued her, wanted her, claimed to love her. She thought of his love notes, torn and crumpled under her pillow, his necklace against her skin. Had he merely been a few hours late?

Although she wanted to hear his side of the story, she could not bear another trip down to the engine room. She would have to wait until he came back to her. That was best, anyway; she didn't want to appear overly eager. She poked her head into the kitchen, but Pascal was already gone; she wandered into the common room, but its thick cigarette smoke made her back right out. What she needed was fresh air. Although the seas were far from calm, Julie decided to go out on the mooring deck.

She pushed open the heavy door and braced herself for the chill. It was no longer raining and the air—thin and piercing—revived her from the fog of sleep. Breathing deeply, Julie was walking out onto the deck, past a gigantic spool of rope and a few upended deck chairs, when she saw someone in the corner. A big man was leaning against the wall. She smiled to herself; it was Nikolai.

Without worrying about what to say, Julie crept toward him. It was easy to surprise someone with the moon nearly covered in clouds and every sound lost to the wind. Standing alone, his eyes were closed, his mouth ajar, and his large hands—shining pale in the dark—were resting on something in front of him. A barrel, an air vent? What was he doing out here in the cold? Then, when she was just a few steps away from him, Julie saw his face change; his head jerked up and his whole body clenched. His hands gripped that thing before him, pulling up fistfuls of hair. It was a woman's head.

Julie did not move. She watched as Nikolai opened his eyes, slowly focused on her, and smirked; as the woman kneeling at his feet wiped her mouth on her hand, then, steadying herself with his long legs, shot up to his side.

"You see, Nikolai? *I* know how to make a man happy!"

The voice was Simone's. She was reaching up to kiss him, but Nikolai brusquely turned her around.

"Simone," he said, clearly amused. "You remember Julie."

Simone spun around. When she saw Julie's blank face, she burst out laughing.

"What?" she called, tossing her chin up and grabbing on to Nikolai. "Are you here to take lessons?"

Julie stood there another moment, gawking at them, waiting for Nikolai to provide some kind of explanation. He didn't say a word. Instead, staring into Julie's eyes with that self-satisfied grin, he reached up and snatched Simone's breast. As Julie turned around, ready to fly, she heard Simone shriek in delight: "Naughty boy!" Almost at the door, Julie tripped over a deck chair and skinned her knee. She felt their laughter, but only heard the wind.

Back inside, Julie walked quickly, wondering whether Nikolai would follow her. But what could he possibly say now? With a long shiver, she wrapped her arms across her chest. Why had she ever let him touch her? She thought of Simone's shining pig eyes. Did she imagine this—kneeling on a freezing metal floor, filling her mouth to bursting—her latest triumph? She could have him. Julie hated them both.

With nowhere to go, no one to talk to, Julie ducked into the dim kitchen. She slid her fingertips down the long counter, cool and clean. Passing Pascal's block of knives, she picked up the longest one, the one for filleting large fish, and felt it in her hand. Suddenly, she heard something move in the shadow. With a gasp, she froze, pressing herself against the wall, hoping to make herself even smaller. With the knife outstretched and shaking, she listened for the echo of Nikolai's heavy boots, straining her eyes to see to the end of the room. Finally, next to the doorway, she caught a glimpse of a cat's hindquarters.

"Stormy," she muttered, letting out a huge gush of air; she didn't realize she'd been holding her breath.

Bold and proud, the cat turned around to face her. Julie saw it was carrying a dead mouse in its jaws. Recoiling, Julie gagged. She threw the knife on the counter and ran out of the galley. Cat and mouse. Yes, she knew that game. And she, like that stupid mouse, had allowed herself to be caught.

She had to get out of steerage. Heading toward the middle of the ship, she lumbered along thinking back on Nikolai's brutality. She had tried to make excuses for it—her man's uncontrollable passion and so forth—but now saw it for what it was. She'd trusted him, a man she'd just met, and he had used her cruelly. Julie, who had read her brother's vivid accounts, could not have dreamed of such savagery outside of war.

She climbed stairs and passed through corridors—riveted metal trenches; rotting, idiotic trenches—trying to escape the uncomfortable warmth of the ship's bottom, the noise of its ever-beating heart. In a long hallway of closed doors, she became disoriented but kept on, grasping the handrail, indignant to feel the ship pitching still.

When she finally arrived to the top deck, already midship, she filled her lungs with the cold air and walked directly to the side, glaring at the mighty, tumultuous sea that had turned her insides out.

Her hands grabbed the rail, held it tight, her knuckles white. She swung her head down to look straight down the hull. From this inverse perspective, her eyes flitted across the specks of lit portholes, trying to make out each level above the waterline (six? seven?). She stretched through the railing and leaned out on the icy metal to stroke the black-painted rivets (the ship's numberless birthmarks), which made their way down and into the sea. It seemed impossible that only a few days had passed since the launch. That day, gazing down this hull, she had been awestruck by the ocean liner's height, the surprising distance from the deck to the water. She thought of the boys standing next to her and, with another shuddering gag, the tall one's joke about his *meat.*

Nikolai . . . she felt her skin prickling, the bitter pain between her legs. She had not needed a clever genie to be fooled, but just a man who could muster a few honeyed words. She wondered whether Nikolai had told Simone—with her toad skin and missing teeth—she was beautiful. Had he said he loved her too? Remembering his repulsive grin as he groped Simone, Julie rolled her eyes, her face red with shame. *She* was the poor dupe, she decided, her hand reaching up to her birthmark, *she* was the idiot. Flawed, she was easily flattered.

She stood back up and reached for the Virgin: the Melter of Hard Hearts. Simone would probably be wanting it tomorrow, think it her due. How many women had worn Nikolai's golden lure? How many other *beauties* had he deceived with it?

"I will be the last," Julie mumbled.

She looked down at Her demure face, then spit on it. She peeled off the necklace and, throwing as hard as she could—a pitch trained by four brothers—cast it overboard. She turned away, refusing to watch its descent. Glancing down the deck, Julie became aware of another figure hobbling toward the wavering rail.

An elderly woman in a tartan bathrobe was slowly making her way to the edge, leaning her slight weight onto her cane as she carried a bundle on her hip. Was it a baby wrapped in a blanket? Julie watched her steady progress, her steps short and cautious, her long, white hair flying recklessly in the wind. The old lady lunged forward and grabbed the rail, letting the cane fall. Was she weeping? She clutched the bundle to her breast, then kissed it.

Watching the woman in terror, Julie began slinking down the rail toward her. As she came closer—the lady still hadn't noticed her—Julie recognized the skinny frame, the lined face: it was the rich woman who wouldn't have passed the third-class health inspection, the one who'd smiled at her when she and Nikolai were dancing on deck. What was she doing? Surely she wasn't going to hurt that helpless creature?

The old woman hesitated; she sat her bundle on the rail, wiping her eyes. Now only a yard away, Julie watched as her face quickly changed and became determined. The lady then took it with both hands and pitched it overboard, nearly falling in the process.

"No!" Julie cried. "No!"

She had rushed over and tried to snatch it from her, but was too late.

Vera turned to the voice, confused. Ah, it was the egg-faced, waltzing girl from steerage. Why was she so upset? Was it she, the heir to her journals? She studied her face with curiosity. How could this be?

"The baby! The baby!" Julie shouted, beginning to sob, finally releasing a mighty backlog of tears.

"Oh, did you hear it too? Is it crying still?" Vera asked, heartened, looking from side to side. "Where is it?"

Constance was rushing back to her cabin, engrossed in her thoughts, when she heard a cry. Two women were at the rail. One was very small, wearing only a light dress against the cold night, and the other was in her bedclothes with wild, white hair. The taller one was throwing something—a small, soft form—into the sea. Did she hear the word "baby"?

Without thinking, she ran toward them. As she came out on deck, a stream of ice water from the upper level drained down her back, dousing her hair and dress, taking her breath away. Constance dashed to the ship's edge.

Julie was crying, inconsolable. Vera, baffled, was trying to comfort her with one arm, as she held on to the rail, her strength waning.

"What's happened here?" Constance asked, breathless. She immediately recognized the pair of them from the infirmary and their acquaintance with the ship's surgeon: the French working girl, in a rumpled uniform, and the elderly dowager, wearing her pearls even now. What were they doing here? Together?

"She's thrown a baby overboard," Julie screamed through her tears, pointing at Vera with horror.

"What?" Vera was astonished. "What are you talking about? I haven't even seen the baby!"

"I saw you throw it! It was swaddled in a blanket!" Julie looked at her in wide-eyed accusation. "I was right here when you did it!"

For another moment Vera stared at her, then slowly smiled.

"Well, I suppose it *was* my baby." She looked at the two young women's faces and saw shock, aversion. "They were my journals," she quickly explained. "Wrapped up in my shawl. That was all, just my journals."

Julie, who had been so sure of what she'd seen, was dumbfounded. She stood there shaking, sobbing still.

"So scandalous were they?" Constance asked, surprised at the notion that a little old lady could have anything to hide. "That you had to pitch them into the ocean?"

"*That* wasn't the problem." Vera's face twitched a bit; her smile suffered. "I couldn't stop reading them. And, here lately, I had begun to wonder if any of it was even true."

For an instant, they stood in silence, suddenly noticing sounds from the Grand Gala in the wind. The festivities in the ballroom sounded every bit like New Year's Eve: the music and applause, the outbursts of laughter and noisemakers. Out on the cold, empty deck, the muted celebration seemed to come from another world.

"It's chilly here," Constance said. She pushed the damp hair out of her eyes, her teeth chattering. "We should be going in." None of them was dressed for the weather and they had all managed to get wet on the slippery, rolling deck.

"I'm so sorry I frightened you," Vera said to Julie, the two of them still holding the rails. "But, they were just . . . books." This last word fell out of her mouth at an awkward angle. "Now then, let's go inside and get warm."

"Not yet," Julie said with a grimace, looking straight out toward the black horizon, which could not be distinguished from the sea. She couldn't bear the idea of returning to third class; she wasn't ready to face Simone and she certainly didn't want to see Nikolai. Again, the decks seemed her only option.

"I can't go back down to steerage. Not yet," Julie repeated with a trembling chin. She began crying again, though a few last words spurted from her mouth: "God, how I hate this ship!"

Vera stripped a hand off the rail and put it around Julie's slight shoulders. Constance stood firmly on her other side.

"Have you ever been in a first-class cabin?" Vera asked her kindly. "Why don't you come to my rooms? Both of you. We could order some tea."

Julie stared at the wispy old woman, with her bright eyes and windblown hair; she looked every bit a fairy-tale character. A good witch, a fairy godmother, someone who could grant wishes that would not go awry. With a nod, she let go of the rail.

Constance picked the cane off the deck and handed it to the elderly woman. "I'd be pleased to join you," she said, giving them both a warm smile despite the chill. She was curious about these two.

The three of them walked back inside the ship, arms linked, helping one another. Vera's whole body ached; she needed to sit down. When they arrived at her cabin, they found Amandine sitting on the chair, the old Scotty in her lap.

"Sorry, ma'am, to disturb you. I know I should be in my own room." The relief in her face was obvious. "But Bibi was barking so!"

"That's fine, Amandine." Vera smiled, sinking down on the edge of the bed. "In fact, you're sorely needed here. We need some towels—we all got a bit wet, I'm afraid—and a pot of strong tea. And . . . chocolate cake. Yes, why not? Oh, and Amandine," she added, looking at Julie, "this girl's uniform is in terrible shape. Could you find her something to wear? Perhaps a dress that comes to midcalf?" she suggested, taking in Julie's small frame.

Amandine looked over at the young woman, who offered her a clumsy curtsy, then at the lady she recognized from the infirmary. If she wasn't mistaken, these were the same two women who stood near her mistress in that shoddy launch photograph from *L'Atlantique*. The old servant shook her head as she reached for the clean towels. Miss Vera had always been full of surprises. She'd been concerned about her, though, and was glad to see her looking well if rather unkempt. Going out in this weather with a fever! The old servant handed out the towels, then began rifling through a trunk.

Constance looked into the mirror and sighed. The hairdresser's careful curls lay on her shoulders like seaweed. Just as well, she thought. Tonight she would brush it straight and tomorrow she would just pile it on top, in its usual bun.

Vera too glanced into the mirror and, behind her cracked portrait, saw the three of them reflected there. Quietly drying their arms, fingering their long hair, three women in different stages of life. Here we are, she thought, the maiden, the mother, and the crone. I am at the end.

"These should do," Amandine said, handing Julie a collection of garments. She turned to Vera. "I'll put in that order with service now."

Julie had been examining the room: the fine wood, porcelain, and fabric. No bare steel here! She sniffed the air; it was filled with fresh flowers, beeswax, and perfume. Up here, she could understand why people enjoyed traveling by ocean liner.

"You can breathe in here," she told Vera.

"Quite so." Vera nodded, brushing her long, tangled hair. "Go ahead and get out of that uniform, dear. The bathroom is in here."

When Julie returned from the bathroom, the other two had wrapped towels around their shoulders and settled into armchairs. Dressed in one of Vera's simpler gowns, she'd managed to alter its length by gathering up the material and holding it in place with a tightly pulled sash. In this ill-fitting finery, Julie already felt better, as if she were someone else, not the seasick steerage girl whom the engineman had taken on a dirty mattress. The ugly uniform seemed an accomplice to the suffering she'd endured under the waterline. If the luxury cabin had only come equipped with a fireplace, she'd have been happy to burn it. Lacking a fire, she sat down in the chair next to the others.

"You look pretty in those clothes." Constance smiled. "Brand new."

"It's nice to be out of black," Julie said.

Vera handed Julie a thin shawl.

"Wrap yourself up in this. Silly me," she said, teasing herself, "I've thrown my good cashmere into the ocean! Now"—she turned back to Constance—"you were just about to tell me about your trip. Are you traveling alone as well, dear?"

Constance, who had decided to reveal nothing about her family on this voyage, suddenly found herself stammering through the truth of it.

"It's my mother, you see. She's always been . . . quite fragile. This year, at Christmastime, she just fell apart." Constance bit her lip and glanced at them both, who were quietly nodding in understanding. "She's stopped speaking, washing." Constance paused to gather her breath. "My father—he's at his wits' end—he sent me to Paris to retrieve my younger sister."

"Your sister lives in Paris?" Julie asked.

"She's been there about a year," Constance said. "She was traveling in Europe last summer and . . . stayed. In spite of my parents' wishes, of course."

"But your sister isn't coming home with you," Vera said.

"No, she refused." Constance frowned bitterly. "She only thinks about herself. She's just *too* happy in Paris—with her French beau and artist friends—to bother with her family. Just thinking about it makes me so angry!"

"I am sure it's been unsettling for all of you," Vera agreed. "Perhaps it has even caused a stir in your town." Constance nodded grimly in reply. "But, tell me, what was your sister to do when she arrived home?"

"Help with the family burden!" she cried.

Constance looked from one woman's face to the other, hoping to see support and encouragement; instead, she found confusion.

"The truth is"—Constance spoke to the floor, batting back tears—"there's nothing we can do. My mother needs special care. In an institution. My sister couldn't have changed that."

"I'm so sorry," Julie whispered.

"Every family is so complex," Vera said with a sigh. "And so difficult to understand! As for your sister, I find it's not always easy to persuade yourself to do the right thing."

"True," Constance said softly, remembering the feel of the doctor's tickly mustache on her neck not an hour before.

"I lived in Paris for a long time myself," Vera said. "And I rarely returned home. Living in France is more than beauty, history, baguettes . . . It's a question of freedom. A woman, an American woman at least," Vera added, with a deferential nod to Julie, "feels free there. To reinvent herself and do what truly pleases her." Vera gave the younger woman a sad smile. "The seduction of it! I'm sure that it was not her French beau; your sister has been seduced by freedom."

Constance opened her mouth, uncertain of what to say. It was true that Faith's current life—her friends, her fashions, her creative endeavors—would be impossible in Worcester.

At that moment, Amandine rapped on the door, then let herself in. She was followed by a waiter, who set the tea service and cake on the writing table.

"If there will be nothing else," the waiter said tiredly, then headed out the door; the old servant excused herself as well.

"Good night, dear Amandine." Vera smiled at her warmly. "You have been indispensable tonight, as always."

After pouring the tea, Vera raised her cup to her guests.

"Pleased to finally make your acquaintance, ladies," she said, nodding to each of them. "Although my memory has become quite frail, I know I've seen you both on this crossing—and more than once! I am Vera Sinclair."

"Pleased to meet you too. I'm Constance Stone," Constance said, marveling at the fact that they were, indeed, still strangers.

"And my name's Julie Vernet." At this point—sitting in the old woman's room, wearing one of her dresses, and with her eyes red-rimmed from crying in her arms—introductions seemed almost superfluous.

"A pleasure," Vera stated, with a firm nod. "I could not have hoped for a more interesting pair of companions for the final night of my final crossing."

"The final one?" Constance asked. "And why's that?"

"After many years abroad, I am returning home to New York," Vera said. "I don't know why exactly . . . but there I will stay. I shan't be crossing the Atlantic again."

"Here's to crossing together on the *Paris,* then!" Constance smiled, clinking her teacup with the other two.

"Tell me now, where did our paths first cross?" Vera asked.

"At the infirmary," Julie answered at once.

"On the first day out," Constance added.

"And, just last night," Vera said to Constance, "didn't I see you on your way to the dining room with the doctor?"

"That's right. He invited me to have dinner at the captain's table," Constance said shyly. She looked at the other two, sipping their tea, listening to her, unsurprised. "It was marvelous."

"He is a very charming man," Vera stated with a connoisseur's appreciation.

"And such a gentleman too," Julie added, comparing him in her mind to Nikolai.

"Yes . . . well, I don't know," Constance said sadly, "he seems perfect, doesn't he? I have been thinking of little else these past few days." She paused to take a deep breath. "I was coming from his rooms when I saw you on deck. We'd been having dinner together. But, it was becoming far too . . . romantic."

"Nothing wrong with that!" Vera proclaimed with a chuckle.

Constance took Faith's enamel ring off her finger and held up her hand. The wedding band now seemed wire thin, her hand large and plain.

"I'm married," she said, "and I think he may be too."

She looked into the two women's faces, awaiting judgment. Many of the people she knew (Mrs. Thomas would make a fine example) seemed to delight in the faults of others, working under the misguided notion that another person's failings raised *them* to greater heights. However, shock and condemnation were notably lacking here.

"I see," Vera said slowly. "And do you love your husband?"

"I don't know," Constance said, stuffing the ring into her handbag; she would not be wearing it again. "Despite his shortcomings—and who doesn't have a few?—he's a good man. A good provider . . ." Her voice trailed off as she shrugged uneasily.

"When I was younger," Vera said, peeking up at her portrait, "I met a man named Laszlo Richter. We were falling in love when he told me about his family, a wife and son. Wanting to do what was proper, I called it off straightaway. But I've been thinking about it these last few days. I'm no longer so sure it was the right decision."

"Why not?" Constance asked, her eyebrows high.

"He'd not been back with his family six months when he killed himself," Vera said matter-of-factly. Too harsh, the words hung in the air for a moment or two. "I've just found out about it." She paused again, her expression cross, yet stupefied. "I've met his son on this ship—he was sitting next to me at dinner!—and naturally, he blames me for everything. I've been wondering if we all would have been happier if I hadn't done the right thing."

"It's possible," Constance said, nodding at Vera. "But I have children, you see. Three daughters. I could never leave them. They are part of me. The best part," Constance said softly, her eyes moist. "And, although I think the world of Serge Chabron, I don't even know if he's available. Or if his attentions are honest and true."

"Leaving your family would be a tremendous gamble," Julie said with a sad frankness. "Who could say what would happen in the future? I mean, you might *think* someone loves you, when in the end, he just wants to use you."

Vera looked over at the young woman, surprised by the cynicism in her voice.

"What happened, Julie?" she asked. "The last time I saw you, you were smiling in a man's arms, whirling around the deck."

"*He* said he loved me," Julie said, swallowing hard, "but it was all just a lie. I was so stupid!"

"No," they both murmured.

"Yes!" she returned. "I'd never had a boyfriend before. Back home, nobody had ever shown any interest in me." Julie's finger trickled over her lip to her birthmark, then pressed it down hard, as if to erase it. "He made me feel special, beautiful even." She shook her head, embarrassed. "I thought we were in love! I know it sounds crazy, we only met a few days ago."

Constance gave her a sympathetic nod, struck by the similarity of their experiences. On this voyage, they had both met men, become infatuated, and fallen into their arms.

"I would have never," she stammered, her face melding into complicated creases as she tried not to start crying again. "I told him no . . . I'd never even kissed a boy before!"

"He took advantage of you?" Vera asked. Recalling the Colossus this tiny girl had been dancing with, she winced.

"I said no, but he didn't listen. He forced me," she said, breathing heavily, then taking a sip of tea to choke down her sobs. She was tempted to show them the bruises on her arms, but they didn't seem to need convincing. "And this morning, he'd already forgotten about me. And tonight he was with another girl!"

"Oh my God," Constance whispered. "I'm so sorry."

Her voice was calm but she was inwardly horrified. She and Julie did not have so much in common after all; Serge had given her not only flowers and champagne, but a choice. Yes, she had been given a choice.

Vera stroked the young woman's coppery hair.

"And what now? No man will want me!" Julie covered her face with her hands and let the tears come; her mind rang with the names the neighbor ladies called Chantal: tart, slut, pig, whore. "No one!"

"That is *not* true," Vera said defiantly. "That is what they would have you believe—that all hope is lost with one's virginity—but it's simply not true. Many women approach their wedding night having already had that experience. I confess, that was my case. It did not make me unmarriable. In fact, no one was any the wiser."

She handed Julie a handkerchief; she wiped her eyes, already calmer.

"Life's rules are not so strict," Vera said. "Anything's possible."

"I'm sure you'll meet someone, Julie. You're a little less innocent now, that's all. Next time around, you won't be fooled. And you won't settle for just anybody," Constance added, twisting her wedding band around on her finger.

"Maybe you're right," Julie said with a sniffle. "He was certainly no great catch. A Russian greaser with tattoos and dirty hands!" She spit the words out in anger, but when she saw the other two smile, she shook her head with a little snicker. "My brothers would have never let him in the door."

Purged of their secrets, the three women felt lighter but exhausted. Constance took the towel from around her shoulders, folded it, and set it on the floor. Perhaps there was something to Dr. Freud's "talking cure" after all.

"I really should go back to my cabin and get into dry clothes," Constance said. She realized that, in her hair, she could still detect the faint odors of Serge's cologne and black tobacco. "Or, better yet, take a hot bath."

"And you, Julie?" Vera asked. "Would you like to spend the night here in my cabin? You're welcome to the bed. I never sleep anymore."

"Thank you, Madame Sinclair, but I don't think that's necessary," said Julie. "I'm ready to face steerage again."

"Are you sure?" Vera asked.

"I don't want anyone to think I'm hiding," she said, "or that I have something to be ashamed of."

"*Bon courage,*" Vera whispered.

"Shall we meet for an early lunch tomorrow?" Constance asked her companions. "Say, around eleven?"

"That sounds lovely," Vera said. "Let's meet here. Then, if it's a nice day, we can watch for the New York islands from the top decks."

"Great!" said Julie, completely forgetting that she worked aboard the *Paris.* "I'll return your clothes then."

Julie gave each woman four kisses on her cheeks, then turned to go.

"*Au revoir!*" She waved from the door. "And thank you."

Julie pulled the shawl around her, then plunged back down to the women's dormitory, at the bow of the ship, under the waterline.

At the doorway, Vera caught Constance's arm with just a trace of hesitation.

"Constance, before you go, I'd like to ask you to do something," Vera said, her eyes serious. "Talk to the doctor again before you leave ship."

Constance opened her mouth, then quickly closed it. She was unused to maternal advice.

"To avoid regrets," Vera explained. "You need to have a proper good-bye. If not, someday in the future, you may find yourself wondering what might have been."

Constance nodded at Vera, but didn't know whether she would be able to go through with it. She was mortified at her own behavior and no longer trusted his; she had rather been planning on hiding from him.

"Here, I'd like to give you something," Vera added. "It might help."

She reached into the pocket of her robe and pulled out a fountain pen, a brown and pearl instrument that was far from new.

"I couldn't bear to throw it into the sea. I'm too sentimental, I suppose. Everything I wrote came out of that pen, you see. And now that I no longer have journals, I don't need it." Vera smiled at Constance. "You may find that writing is a good way of dealing with your emotions, of safeguarding your dreams."

"Thank you so much," Constance said, blushing slightly. "It's a beautiful pen."

"It was left to me by a stranger, so perhaps it's fitting that a stranger should give it to you."

"You're no stranger, Vera Sinclair," Constance said, giving her worn cheek a kiss. "But I don't know what I might write."

"I tried to write the story of my life," Vera said, her voice weary now. "But found truth to be extremely elusive. Well, good night, dear."

"See you in the morning," Constance said. "Sleep well."

The instant she walked into her room, Constance spied the tulips. She untied the ribbon around the bouquet, recalling each detail of her short-lived affair with Dr. Serge Chabron. His examinations in the infirmary, his gifts of fruit and flowers, the dinners and dancing, his accented compliments, the kisses and caresses. Constance examined the red, feathery flame in each tulip. George had told her once that those beautiful flames were, in fact, caused by a virus.

Feeling very foolish (what had come over her?), she wondered whether this was his secret formula. Did Serge always impress his pretty female passengers with a fruit basket first, followed by dinner with the captain, then invite them for a champagne supper in his quarters? Instead of betting on the vessel's cruising speed like the other men on board, she reckoned the crew bet on the doctor's swiftness! Perhaps those postcards (Niagara Falls, Mont Blanc) were keepsakes from former passengers, regretful notes about relationships that could not be.

"'The Singular Affair of the Ship Surgeon,'" she said out loud in a theatrical tone, making fun of herself.

Why? She shook her head crossly. Why does a restless, unhappy woman always imagine that thrill and adventure come in the shape of a man? After she'd left Serge's rooms and flattery, she'd then had a most fascinating encounter with two women: an alarming moment on a storm-tossed deck that somehow grew into an honest, heartfelt conversation in a beautiful suite. How easy it was to talk with Julie and Vera, both understanding and warm, despite their suffering.

Julie was right: love was a gamble. Serge had said that he didn't want their relationship to end with their arrival in New York, but how long might it have lasted? Another crossing or two? Wait, what was she thinking! She tossed the tulip back into the basin. Dr. Serge Chabron was beside the point! *She* was unavailable! It didn't matter whether he was a sincere bachelor in love or a rakish married man who had a fling on every crossing. She was never going to leave her family. George—the only father her children would ever have—would always be her safest bet.

Her eyes welling with tears, Constance opened the porthole and began throwing the tulips, one by one, into the Atlantic. She was not cut out for adventure; she did not need foreign freedoms. Constance *was* the steadfast daughter. Her place was in her hometown, near her parents, with George and the girls. She brought the last tulip to her nose and smelled it—it let off a vaguely unpleasant odor of waxy pollen—then flung it out into the sea.

The porthole still open, a cold, salty wind in her face, she considered throwing the enamel ring out as well. Constance imagined all the things thrown from these liners, all the rejected treasure slowly falling, drifting past white whales and giant squid, down to the murk below. She decided to keep the ring, a gift from Faith and a souvenir of folly.

She closed the porthole and only then began taking off her damp clothes.

For hours, Vera looked out the dark window, brushing her hair. At first she saw only her ghostly reflection; then, by shifting to the side, she was able to watch as the great storm finally expired, as the ocean became calm.

"Perhaps Neptune was appeased by my sacrifice," she said to herself, delighting in the irony that the apparent heirs to her journals had surfaced only at the moment she cast them into the sea. No matter. She was finally at liberty to read another's words.

Vera crossed the room and pulled Charles's gift out of her carpetbag. On the table sat the chocolate cake, untouched; the three women had been too preoccupied to consider eating. Cutting herself a thick slice, Vera thought of those two young women, so full of spirit and promise. Bestowing them with the journals (at this age, she supposed, hers were literal "old wives' tales") was nothing. If only she could pass on to them her real knowledge: the wisdom gained from living unwisely.

Back in the armchair next to the window, she savored the bites of cake on her tongue: the bittersweet chocolate, the tang of apricot, the whipped cream, subtle and light. She hadn't really eaten since she'd fallen ill. Fluids! She'd had enough of them. Wishing young Max were there to share a piece with her—she could just see his small mouth, overly full and chewing merrily—she recalled his rapt expression as he watched the puppet show. Ah, my love, the Chevalier of Melancholia.

As she licked the spoon, Vera wondered again whether her story—Laszlo's story—would have been different had she not fled, if *they* had had a proper good-bye. Why had she thought the farewell note necessary? How dramatic she used to be!

At first, she thought it a terrible misfortune, a dreadful coincidence, to have met the Richters. But now, despite her grief and shame, she was rather glad. Not only had she learned the truth about Laszlo—which had put quite a few things in perspective—but she had seen his future in Max. Usually, Vera considered herself lucky with odds. Horses, backgammon, roulette. Perhaps, after all, this had also been a stroke of good luck.

Having finished the cake, she wiped her hands, then cleared her throat with some cold tea. She was finally ready for Charles's poem.

Her glasses in place, she ran a finger along the binding of the delicate little booklet. On the train to Le Havre, Charles had explained to her that, when he was twenty-one, he had met Constantine Cavafy in a Turkish bath in Constantinople. They'd had no problems communicating, as the Greek poet from Alexandria had spent part of his childhood in Liverpool. Charles did not elaborate on that encounter (he was always so discreet!), but he did say that, after all those years, they'd never lost touch. He had recently received this booklet in the post, privately printed for friends. For some reason, Charles had wanted her to have it.

She studied the frontispiece—*Constantine P. Cavafy. Poems. 1921.*—then opened the book. Vera reread the dedication with a sad smile, then noticed for the first time that it was twice inscribed; facing the table of contents, she found an affectionate remembrance from the poet to Charles. This made her grin. "What a rascal!" she thought, amazed Charles had not tried to rub out those sentimental words.

Though the slim volume only contained a handful of poems, she turned directly to the marked page, obviously the one Charles had wanted her to read first. "Ithaca." She began to mumble the words out loud, to herself:

Ithaca

When you set out on your journey to Ithaca,
Pray that the road is long,
Full of adventure, full of knowledge . . .

She stopped. Her throat was already too tight to read aloud, her eyes were beginning to blur. Oh, Charles. Were he not such a coward, so afraid of dying, he would now be by her side. Instead, she was alone with one of his books.

How Vera wished he were there to read it to her, this poem he had handpicked for her final voyage. His lovely voice had not aged, squeaking like an old rocking chair, but was still deep and melodic. She paused for a moment, closing her eyes to better capture the sound of his voice, then continued.

Pray the road is long.
That the summer mornings are many, when,
With such pleasure, with such joy
You will enter ports seen for the first time:
Stop at Phoenician markets,
And purchase fine merchandise,
Mother-of-pearl and coral, amber and ebony,

And sensual perfumes of all kinds,
As many sensual perfumes as you can;
Visit many Egyptian cities,
To learn and learn from scholars.

Always keep Ithaca in your mind.
To arrive there is your ultimate goal.
But do not hurry the voyage at all.
It is better to let it last for many years;
And to anchor at the island when you are old,
Rich with all you have gained on the way,
Not expecting that Ithaca will offer you riches.

Ithaca has given you the beautiful voyage.
Without her you would have never set out on the road.
She has nothing more to give you.

And if you find her poor, Ithaca has not deceived you.
Wise as you have become, with so much experience,
You must already have understood what Ithacas mean.

Vera let out a great sigh. Dear, dear Charles. Yes, Manhattan was her Ithaca. And she had taken a long, zigzagged, wondrous path to get back there. New York . . . She wondered how Odysseus felt as he was finally reaching the shores of Ithaca; was he afraid his hometown would be tedious and dull after such adventures? That Penelope had grown old and stout? Vera fingered her rope of pearls, bought years ago at a port market during this lifelong journey home, and through teary eyes she wondered how much water still separated her from her island.

She watched as the skies slowly began to clear, the faintest yellow-pink light pointing to the horizon. She closed the book and stretched. With the dawn, Vera realized her fever had broken.

DAY FIVE

THE ARRIVAL

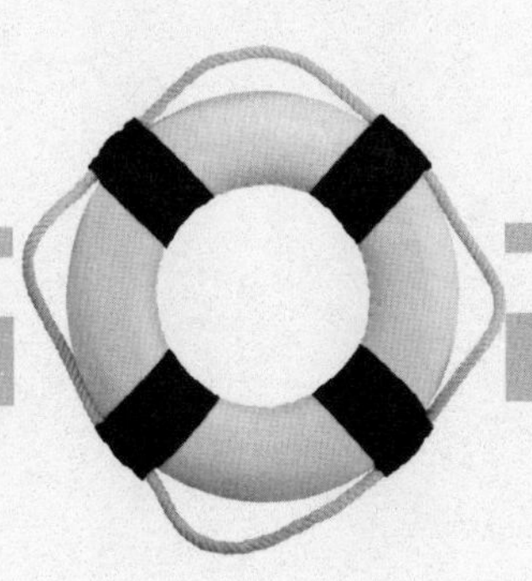

"Get *up*!" Julie felt a sharp tug on her shoulder; her mother had never been so rough. "My God! What's wrong with you?"

She rolled over and, with bleary eyes, found herself looking into the thin-lipped frown of Mme. Tremblay.

"Mademoiselle Vernet!" the shrill voice continued. "It's nearly eight o'clock! And here you are, lounging in bed!"

She sat up in confusion, grasping at her covers and the last remnants of a dream. Was her mother in it? Her brothers? Was it good or bad?

"You may just be the slowest, laziest girl I've ever had in the service crew!" Mme. Tremblay added, "And the sneakiest too!"

"What?" Julie asked, finally awake enough to decipher words. "Sneaky?"

"Pascal told me that you were ill last night," she said. "He excused you from working so you could rest! And how did you repay him? By running off and coming in at all hours! You scheming little liar!"

"But I *was* ill! And I *did* rest!" Julie said, particularly upset at the idea that Pascal might think she'd taken advantage of him. "I wasn't lying!"

"I came in here after the dinner shift and you were gone," Mme. Tremblay said. "I asked Simone and the other girls, but nobody had seen you." Julie's mouth fell open, but she said nothing. "So, tell me, where were you? Up in first again, taking in the views?"

For an instant, Julie considered confiding her troubles in Mme. Tremblay, but with a glimpse at her disapproving mouth, she knew she would find no compassion.

"In fact, I *was* in first class," Julie said boldly, sitting up straight. "In a cabin on the uppermost deck. I was having tea with some friends of mine."

Mme. Tremblay jabbed the air with her finger, pointing at Julie with a violent glare.

"You think you're funny? More stupid lies will not help your case, silly girl!"

"I'm telling the truth," Julie said. "Not that it matters."

"And why would that be?" Mme. Tremblay's whisper sounded menacing—full of the promise of punishments to come.

"Because I'm quitting," Julie said, enjoying the surprise on the head housekeeper's face. In bed last night, after her evening with her new friends, she had considered the idea, though she hadn't made a firm decision until just now. "I think we both know that I'm not cut out for a life at sea."

"That's for sure," Mme. Tremblay snorted. "But, don't forget, mademoiselle, you will not get free passage back to France. You will have to buy a ticket like everyone else. And, I warn you, they do not come cheap."

"I'm not going back to France," Julie retorted impulsively. "I'll be getting off in New York today."

If American women found freedom in France, thought Julie, recalling Mme. Sinclair's words, wouldn't the opposite be true for

French girls? Wouldn't she be able to reinvent herself in New York? Find new friends, a new life, like Constance's sister?

"Is that right?" The older woman chuckled at the notion. "And what might you do, all by yourself in New York City?"

"Don't worry about me, madame," Julie said. "I can stand on my own two feet. Especially on land."

"All right then, if your mind is made up," she said. "I will talk to the purser about you. He may decide that your wages these last few days will merely cover your passage over, or he may be gracious enough to pay you. We shall see."

Julie nodded stiffly at the housekeeper. Although she had brought her savings with her, she had hoped to add her *Paris* paycheck to it.

"In the meantime, I'd like you to collect your things and remove yourself from the workers' quarters."

"Yes, Madame Tremblay. *Au revoir.*"

Julie watched as her former superior marched out of the dormitory, slightly vexed that the efficient older woman had such a low opinion of her. Sneaky, indeed! But, she had done it! She'd quit her job and, by this afternoon, would be off this swaying ship.

In her locker, she found her street clothes, the same blue cotton dress, jacket, and heels she'd worn the day of the launch. This was the outfit she was wearing when she met Nikolai. Since then, an entire ocean had been crossed.

After dressing, she laid her things out on the bed to pack. In went the toiletries, the stockings, the panties. She held the camisole in her hand for a moment, then stuffed it in as well.

She picked up her mother's piecework, and as she fingered the lines, the stylized *V*, she felt a tinge of guilt. Would her parents be hurt by this giddy decision to stay in America? She doubted it. Before she left, she'd overheard them discussing renting their children's rooms out to boarders, filling the house with strange faces; they weren't expecting their daughter back home. Perhaps they would even be pleased that she was trying her luck, making a new life for herself in America. With a smile, she imagined her mother passing the word on to the other ladies in Saint François. Having a gossip, like she used to do.

She arranged her brothers' letters in the Jules Verne novel, shuffling them straight like a deck of cards. The war changed us all, she thought, aging those it did not kill. Ever since, the idea of gaiety or fun seemed to lack respect for those who were gone, but it was time to be young again. Young, but not stupid. Under her pillow, she found the ripped notes from Nikolai. She scraped them into the bin and watched the pieces flutter down, wondering at the brevity of it all.

Her small bag packed, she put it over her shoulder and took a last look around the empty dormitory, the close quarters she'd shared with a hundred working girls. Wherever she landed in New York, it would be airier, quieter, more motionless than this! Yes, but where was that? Suddenly, she was overwhelmed by the enormity of her decision to leave the ship, alone, and emigrate. Most people, she figured, took years to plan such a move. They would have contacts, jobs lined up, prearranged rooms . . . She had none of that.

She peeked into the common room; it was odd to be at leisure, with no chores to do. Stepping inside, Julie glanced around at the passengers, bashful. Although she had seen them all before, served them meals and cleaned their messes, she didn't really know them. Looking at their faces, all filled with expectation and optimism, she realized that, here in third class, she was surrounded by veritable experts on the subject of emigration: nearly everyone here had left their homelands for America. Now that she was one of them, she could spend the rest of the morning asking for advice.

In the corner, Julie caught sight of the Irish boys. They were hanging on the armchairs and flirting with the Italian twins, presumably helping them with their English.

"Excuse me," she said, tapping the shoulder of the one propping himself on the arm. "I was wondering if you could help me?"

"What do you need, miss?" said the redhead, looking up. "Hey! Aren't you out of uniform?"

"That's right." Julie smiled. "But I've had enough of the sea and, when we dock, I'll be getting off for good. I was hoping you all could give me some pointers."

"Could we!" said the freckle-faced boy. "I can tell you whatever you need to know about New York!"

"Yeah," said the redhead with a roll of his eyes, "especially for a boy from Cork who's spent the last three years in Liverpool!"

With identical smiles, the Italian twins made room on the small sofa and Julie squeezed in next to them.

"Now then," said the freckle-faced boy with an air of importance. "We're going to start off in Brooklyn, where my uncle Ned lives. He knows loads of families with rooms to let. As for jobs . . ."

Within minutes, Julie's apprehensions had faded and she was as excited about arriving in America as everyone else under the waterline. When Simone strolled into the common room a half hour later, she was scarcely bothered.

"I heard you were in here, chatting away," Simone said with a sneer, looking down on Julie. "So, Old Tremblay had to let you go. What a shame."

Julie rose to her feet to meet Simone's gaze.

"A shame? I don't think so. I gave her notice, Simone." Julie smiled at the coarse, ambitious girl who had made her crossing far more unsavory than it should have been. "Enjoy the *Paris*—and *all* its delightful crew members! I'm going to New York!"

Simone's face fell, her eyes clouded with confusion.

"New York?" she barked, incapable of much more.

"That's right," Julie said, returning to her seat. "But, who knows, Simone? Maybe after a few years down here in steerage, you'll get your chance in hatcheck! You can only dream!"

Simone pursed her lips in anger, her face red. Her hands balled up as she whisked around, heading out of the room. Perhaps, thought Julie, she's going down to be consoled by Nikolai. Kind, gentle Nikolai. Watching Simone yank the door open, Julie sighed in relief, glad to be leaving her—and her oily first love—behind.

When Constance woke up, she saw the sun streaming through the porthole, like a beam from a lighthouse. She put on her robe and went to the window. Everything was calm. The sea, now flat, was light gray with glimmers of pink. Good colors for a smart suit.

She looked at her watch—already nine?—and decided to start packing. After less than a week on board, she had thoroughly appropriated her cabin and her things were scattered everywhere. She fetched the trunk from its place in the corner. Just over a month ago, she had gone to buy it with a testy George, still upset about her traveling to Europe on her own. Really, though, Constance decided, it wasn't anger so much as nerves; he was worried about her. In his awkward way, he was expressing his love.

She picked up the cosmetics around the washstand: hairpins and combs, talcum and creams, her compact and lipstick. As she firmly screwed on the lids for storage, she realized she was still uneasy about going home. Although no longer filled with dread, she was concerned about how she would find the situation there. Would her mother be worse, her father defeated? And George . . . would he sense she had been with another man? The only reaction she could anticipate was her children's: unrestrained joy and laughter. Her relationship with them was the only one that seemed uncomplicated.

Constance picked the photographs off the nightstand. She ran her finger along the sepia faces of her daughters, delighted she would soon be with them. She then took a long look at George.

True, he lacked Serge's confident manner, his good-natured refinement, his elegant hands and hazel eyes. But he was hers. Those charming facts about the natural world, the clumsy embraces, that affectionate irascibility with his daughters . . . This man was her husband. She wrapped the photos in a handkerchief and carefully tucked them into the trunk.

Constance stacked her shoes in the bottom drawer, hats in the hatbox, moving up to the top tray to organize jewelry and gloves. On the table next to Faith's ring, she found her new fountain pen, the gift from Mrs. Sinclair. She wanted to put it to good use, but had no idea what to write. Journals, poems, children's tales, fiction? Faith's friends would make good characters . . . Heavens—she smiled to herself—they already *were* characters.

Before stowing it away, she unscrewed the lid. She picked up the menu she'd been planning to save from her dinner at the captain's table and wrote her full name: Mrs. Constance Eunice Stone. She made swooshes and swirls, relishing the feel of this pen in her hand. Indeed, it did not scratch, but silently flowed along the paper. She covered the menu entirely and, as she was tossing it into the bin, Constance thought that, perhaps, Mrs. Sinclair was right. She should bid the doctor good-bye.

When her trunk was packed and locked, Constance made her way out of her cabin, in the direction of the infirmary. Once on deck, she found she was going against the current. It was Sunday morning and most people seemed to be heading to the services in the chapel.

She passed a variety of familiar second-class faces—the Anderson family, the newlyweds, the Stetson-wearing Texans—and nodded politely to them all. Watching them go by, it occurred to her that every person on the *Paris*—its passengers and crew—had lived these five days differently. From the feted Douglas Fairbanks to the towheaded Anderson children, from Julie and Vera to Constance herself, they had each had their own private crossing. Three thousand floating stories, like so many pages of a castaway journal. Perhaps *this* was material for writing?

Constance then caught sight of her former dining companions. Walking briskly, Mr. Thomas and Captain Fielding were so engaged in talk that they did not see her. Mrs. Thomas, wedged in between, gave her a nod, prim and smug. Constance nodded back at the ill-mannered trio with a smile, pleased she would never be trapped at a table with them again. Her last meal on board would be shared with her new friends, interesting women who were neither spiteful nor jealous.

As she turned toward the stern, she nearly collided with Serge Chabron, who was walking quickly, his black bag in hand.

"Constance!" he cried, stopping at once, his hurry forgotten. He reached for her hand and led her to the rails.

"Serge," she whispered, swallowing hard. "I was just coming to see you."

"What happened last night?" he asked, scanning her face for information. "I hope I didn't offend you. It certainly wasn't my intention . . ."

"Oh, Serge, I couldn't stay." Constance saw no use in stalling and lifted up her left hand in a limp display of her wedding band. "I'm married, you see."

She tried to read his expression; was it relief, annoyance, confusion? Could he sympathize? Was he disappointed? At any rate, it was irrelevant.

"I should have told you when we first met," she continued, "but afterward, I kept telling myself that it wasn't important, that you and I were just friends. But the more I saw you, the more I realized . . ." She stopped, biting her lip.

"What?" he asked, moving in closer to her. "That we are perfect together?"

"Something like that," she agreed, smiling at him as she took a step back. He still made her tingle. "But it doesn't change anything, does it? This afternoon, I'll be going back home—to my husband and my children—and you will be raising anchor and moving on."

"Yes," he said quietly, "that's what I do."

"I want to thank you, though, for keeping me company on the *Paris,*" she said. "I really enjoyed our time together."

"As did I, Constance," he sighed, patting her hand. "Your husband is a very lucky man."

She looked him in the eyes. Was he being ironic? Or had he already forgotten their kisses of the night before? Had George seen her in Serge's quarters last night—swooning in his arms, half-drunk on champagne, her wedding band well hidden—she doubted he would have considered himself very fortunate.

"I don't know about that, but I suppose I myself am rather lucky," she said, believing it. "And again, thank you for being so . . . attentive."

She stood on her toes and kissed him in the French fashion, with brisk pecks on the cheeks.

"Take care to be happy," Serge said with a wistful smile.

"And you," she said.

"Oh!" he cried suddenly. "I have an engineman down below with a broken leg!"

"Go to him." She smiled. "*Au revoir,* Doctor."

"*Au revoir,* Constance Stone!" the doctor called, hurrying toward the stairwell.

Her eyes closed, she stood facing the sun for a few minutes, then with a deep breath let go of the rails. For the first time, she felt in complete control of her life; she could make her own decisions. She was no longer a boring matron, a Constant Stone married to a Fossil. Perhaps when she was drenched with icy water up on deck last night, her dullness and insecurity had washed away. Now she was ready to wire home, to tell her father and George that she would be home on tomorrow's train.

When she arrived to the telegraph office, she found it empty.

Most people, at this point in the journey, would have already sent their news.

"Excuse me, sir," Constance called in the little window, to the small, bald man sitting at the desk. Wearing a headset, he was concentrating on an incoming message. She waited until he'd finished writing. "Sir? I'd like to send a telegram to Worcester, Massachusetts. My name is Mrs. Constance Stone."

"Mrs. Stone?" he chuckled. "Well, that's funny. I've just received a message for you!"

She took the telegram back out to the deck, to the sun. Gazing down at the clunky capitals, she felt its urgency.

FAITH WIRED SAID YOU WERE ON THE PARIS
THANK GOD STOP HOW WE MISS YOU STOP
GIRLS AND I WILL MEET YOU IN NY STOP
STAYING AT CHELSEA STOP YOURS GEORGE

She smiled down at the paper, moved. He had brought the children to New York; they would be waiting for her on the docks! Predictable George had managed to surprise her. Constance stared down at the word "yours." Yes, he was hers.

Her eyes flitted back to the top to reread the telegram, but were snagged by the first word: Faith. Her little sister had actually bothered to get in touch with George, to let him know she was on her way home. What else might she have added to that wire? Had Faith expressed concern for their parents? Sent hugs and kisses to her nieces? Or, perhaps, even apologized for not coming? She thought of Faith's life in Paris—the deep satisfaction she got from it all—and admitted that, indeed, she had found her niche. And now that Constance felt more comfortable with her own, much of that routine bitterness, that time-honored rivalry with her sister, was gone. Let her have her happiness! Let them *both* be happy.

Looking at her watch, she saw there was a full forty minutes before her luncheon with the others. Constance decided to go down to steerage, to try to find Julie. She'd spent nearly all the crossing in second class, with brief forays into first, and now she was curious to see where the bulk of the passengers traveled. Although people with inferior tickets were only allowed on the upper decks with permission, anyone interested could descend into third.

As she climbed down the stairs, the illusion of the ship as a sumptuous palace slowly deteriorated; carpet and paneling gave way to the rivets and steel of raw machinery, to the noise and heat of an overexcited engine. She crinkled her nose; there was an unappealing, ill-defined odor down below, like mold or mop water. She could see how disagreeable the voyage would be in steerage. There was no view, no chandeliers, no sea air, just bare bulbs swinging with the rock of the ship. This cramped, industrial space seemed the opposite extreme of the sweeping staircases and glass ceilings above. Everyone on board, she told herself again, has had a completely different voyage.

At the end of the bow, Constance found the dining hall where the workingwomen relaxed off duty. She peeked in the door and saw a miscellaneous group of women in black uniforms, covering all the extremes of size, age, and attractiveness. They were chatting loudly in French, smoking, clipping their nails, rubbing tired feet. Feeling awkward—this was clearly their territory, their private quarters—Constance quickly scanned the room for Julie, but left when she saw she wasn't there.

Constance then looked in the common room door; it was a lively scene, almost rambunctious. On one side, a trio—fiddle, banjo, and penny whistle—was playing a reel as passengers clapped, leapt, and twirled down the room; on the other, a group of gruff blond fellows (Swedes?) were arguing loudly over dice in an incomprehensible language. One man, drunkenly weaving from one side to the next, kept shouting, "Land ho!"

Most of the crowd, unpolished but elated, had put on their Sunday best for the arrival, but there was still a lingering odor of stale bodies in the air. What a different scene from the lounges above, with the well-dressed, perfumed patrons engaged in quiet parlor games and polite conversation!

In a trot, a group of boys skirted past her, heading toward the mooring deck. "Pardon, marm!" the last one cried in a broad, Highlands accent, saluting her over his shoulder. After searching the room, Constance was ready to head back up; down here, she felt self-conscious. As she was backing into the corridor, however, she glimpsed Julie in a doorway, hugging a big man in a chef's hat. Constance waited until she turned toward her, then waved. The smaller girl came running up to meet her, wearing a blue dress and carrying a bag.

"Good morning, Constance!" she said. "I wasn't expecting you down here!"

"I thought I'd come to get you." She smiled. "To go to Mrs. Sinclair's rooms together. But, Julie, why aren't you wearing your uniform?"

"Because I've quit my job," Julie said, pleased with herself. "This morning, I told the head housekeeper I was leaving and this afternoon, I'll be getting off in New York! I'm going to start over. Hopefully, now I'm a little bit wiser, like you said."

"My goodness!" Constance said, taken aback by the girl's daring. "What are your plans?"

Part of her wanted to bring Julie home and take care of her, make sure she had a place to stay and enough to eat. She smiled to herself imagining George's expression if, indeed, along with the gifts and souvenirs, Constance brought home a genuine French girl.

"I've been talking with people all morning about that." Julie grinned. "And everyone has a different suggestion! I've written down a dozen addresses and even more names. I'm sure something will work out."

"How exciting!" Constance said, giving Julie a hug. "Best of luck!"

She herself, however, was happy to be returning to the comfort and safety of home.

They headed for the stairs."Good-bye, steerage!" Julie called playfully as she closed the door behind her.

Constance and Julie began making their way up to first class, pattering excitedly about their arrival in New York.

"My family will be waiting at the dock." Constance beamed. "I got word from my husband this morning. I'd like for you to meet them, Julie. Especially the girls—they're such darlings!"

"That would be lovely," she agreed. "But I don't know how long I'll be detained at Ellis Island."

"Oh," Constance said, disappointed, "I forgot you had to stop there."

"It's not a problem." Julie shrugged. "I've met some Irish boys who have family here. They say it's just a few hours. I could meet you and your family afterward. Perhaps we could all have dinner together?"

"That sounds perfect," Constance said. "We'll be at the Chelsea Hotel. Let's ask Mrs. Sinclair to join us as well."

As the two women passed the shops, Constance eyed the *Paris* model ships in a window.

"Would you mind stopping for just a moment?" she asked Julie. "I think I finally know what gift to bring my husband."

Five minutes later Constance came out of the souvenir shop holding up a foot-long, wooden ocean liner, painted black, white, and funnel red.

"How pretty it is!" Julie exclaimed. "You know, that's about how big it looked the first time I saw this ship. I saw it coming into port from my kitchen windows."

"The man in there told me that, on *this* model, the bollards and winches are made of metal," Constance said, "though I don't even know if those are real English words!"

"I'm sure your husband will like it." Julie smiled.

"Yes, and it will certainly go with the other curios in his study: the old abacus and the secondhand hookah." Constance chuckled to herself. "But the real reason I bought it is because it was here, on the *Paris,* that—when faced with the decision—I chose him, George Stone, and the life we've made together. Not that he will ever know that."

With a sigh, Constance wrapped the gift up in tissue paper and packed it away in the bag.

"Now, shall we go on up?"

As they approached Vera's cabin, they were surprised to see the door ajar. They exchanged a glance, and Constance gave it a knock, opening it yet farther. Trunks were scattered on the floor and the bed was heaped with clothes: an array of dresses, blouses and skirts, sashes and scarves. On top of the pile lay a pair of marionettes and a framed drawing. Amandine stood in the middle of it all, the plum-colored coat in her hands, a confused expression on her face. Bibi, the dog, was inspecting the trunks, sniffing around as if she'd lost something. They'd obviously caught the maid in the throes of packing Vera's things and she looked completely frazzled.

"Good morning," Constance said, "we're here to meet Mrs. Sinclair. We're having lunch together at eleven."

As Amandine turned to them, her brow creased.

"Oh, and I've brought the clothes from last night," Julie said, as she pulled them out of her bag and added them to the pile on the bed. "Thanks again."

For a moment, the two women stood near the door smiling,

waiting for the maid to say something, but Amandine just stood frozen, staring back at them. The doors in the suite were open, exposing empty spaces; Vera was obviously not there. Finally, Constance broke the silence; she spoke slowly and used plain English, thinking, perhaps, Amandine had not understood.

"We're sorry to bother you," she said, taking a step toward the maid, who then retreated. "We can see you're very busy. But, could you please tell us where we can find Mrs. Sinclair?"

Amandine fell down onto the bed, on top of the puppet's legs, the coat still clasped in her hands.

"Miss Vera isn't here," she mumbled in perfect English, then paused. She clenched her eyes, her mouth twisted. Finally, she blurted out the words: "She died this morning."

"What?" gasped the two women at the door, bursting into Vera's room, completely stunned. Julie wedged in next to Amandine on the messy bed, took the servant's hand, worn smooth, and held it closely in her own.

"I'm sorry," Julie said, her eyes welling with tears. "So, so sorry."

"My God," Constance uttered, pacing in front of them and shaking her head. She understood why the maid seemed so addled; she couldn't believe it herself. "What happened?"

"When I came in this morning, I found her," Amandine said quietly, looking at the floor. "There was a little smile on her face, but I knew something was wrong. When I touched her she was cold." She looked up at the other women. "I fetched the doctor, but there was nothing he could do. She was gone. Miss Vera had been very ill for a year now."

Amandine paused and her lips disappeared, tucked away, trying not to sob. Julie and Constance stared at each other in disbelief.

"The doctor," Amandine added with a deep breath, "he said it wasn't a painful death. He said she just stopped. That was his word. 'Stopped.' "

"She didn't suffer, then," affirmed Julie, wiping her eyes with her hand. "I suppose it was what they call a good death."

They fell into a moment's quiet. Their eyes trailed around the room, alighting on Vera's belongings, the things she'd left behind. Her presence was everywhere: the tartan robe still hanging on the bathroom door, her dirty teacup next to the chair, her glasses, folded neatly on top of a slim book. Constance could almost hear her voice. Just the night before, the three of them had been here together, sharing secrets, and she had envisioned spending much more time with her. She'd relished the idea of having an older woman in her life to confide in, to learn from. She perched on the edge of the armchair and picked up the teacup. Wrapping her fingers around the cold porcelain, she stared down at the dark brown ring at the bottom of the cup; her vision began to blur. Their relationship had ended far too soon.

Julie bent over to pet Bibi, who stared back up at her with black, mournful eyes. That morning, while consulting with the others about her possibilities in New York, she had decided to ask Mrs. Sinclair whether she could pay her the occasional call. Julie imagined entrusting the elderly lady with her future successes in America and making her proud, as if she were family. She had hoped to become close with her makeshift fairy godmother.

"Frankly, I never imagined Miss Vera would die," Amandine said suddenly. "I've been with her since 1890, back when we were both rather young. I've seen royalty come through her door and traveled with her to faraway places . . ." Amandine's voice grew fainter; it was as if she were talking to herself. "How could she just 'stop'? I still don't understand it."

"She was a remarkable woman," Constance said. "That was clear to anyone who spent time with her, no matter how little."

"Yes, remarkable." Julie nodded, turning to Amandine.

Hunched over the lumpy coat on her lap, the elderly maid looked like a disheartened old wanderer who had lost her compass.

"Do you know what you'll be doing next?" Julie asked, slightly worried. She wondered whether Amandine might try to emigrate as well, whether she could presume to help.

"I am returning to France on the next ship," Amandine replied. "There is nothing in New York for me. I called my mistress's long-time companion, Mr. Charles, to let him know about . . . what happened. Despite his own grief, he was kind enough to remember me. He will engage my services. He said he's been wanting to steal me away for years."

Amandine's smile immediately crumpled into a teary grimace.

"I'm glad you'll be taken care of, especially by a close friend of Mrs. Sinclair," Julie said gently.

Julie looked up at Constance; both thought it time to leave Amandine to her suffering. She looked overly ready to grieve and they were merely strangers.

"Before we go, would you like any help packing her things?" Julie asked.

"No, thank you. It's painful to go through it all, but it fills me with her spirit." She sighed, sliding her hand through a stack of silk scarves. "Although, I know if it were left up to her, she'd have me throw it all in the sea!"

"I wouldn't doubt that." Constance smiled. "When we met her, she was busy tossing her journals overboard."

"That's why I couldn't find them!" Amandine said with a little snort, almost amused. "Always full of surprises!"

They stood to go.

"Good-bye, Amandine," Constance said, giving her a slight embrace. "And bon voyage."

"All the best to you," Julie said, kissing the old woman on the cheek. She then bent over to pat Bibi's head. "To both of you."

Constance and Julie went outside under the clear skies. No longer hungry for lunch, they would stand outside, watching for the islands. Julie looked down: on the deck below, legs were sticking out from deck chairs and small groups were walking purposefully around. Today, the fickle sea was blue and cheerful.

"She was so weak and thin"—Constance frowned—"you could tell she was ill. Though, last night"—she paused, thinking of the woman's bright eyes, decisive manner, her knowing smile—"she seemed so very *alive,* didn't she?"

"She must have lived a very full life," Julie said, "judging by those big, heavy journals she threw into the sea. And I thought it was a baby!"

Shaking her head, she rolled her eyes at her mistake as they filled with tears again.

Constance sighed. "I'm sure they were fascinating. I should have loved to have read them."

"Yes," Julie answered softly, thinking that perhaps the most interesting events in one's life are not necessarily the best ones.

"When I saw Mrs. Sinclair on deck last night, in her bathrobe, her white hair flying, she reminded me of my mother. Maybe that's why I ran out there," Constance said in a near whisper. She turned to Julie. "Don't you think she would have made a wonderful grandmother?"

"Absolutely!" Julie nodded with a smile, wiping her eyes.

"Say, shall we buy some roses?" Constance asked, suddenly inspired. "While we're still at sea, we could hold a little memorial for her."

"Oh, Constance, what a lovely idea!"

They bought two long-stemmed red roses at the florist's, then walked to the edge of the steamer. Compared to the night before, the ocean seemed still, the wake of the liner providing its only wave. Together they reached out and tossed the roses into the water.

"To our very dear friend, who we just met!" cried Julie.

"To indispensable strangers!" cried Constance.

"To Vera Sinclair!" "Here's to Madame Sinclair!" they shouted.

They bowed their heads to observe the ephemeral ceremony of the rose-red drops on the slate-blue surface.

"What a wonderful coincidence, the three of us all being on deck last night at the same time," Constance said.

"Did you see the launch photographs in *L'Atlantique*?" Julie asked, pulling the old novel out of her bag and showing her the raggedy newspaper clipping. In it, Julie and Constance stood next to each other, while Vera faded off to the side. "Here we all are! We were all walking together toward the ship that day!"

"I'm so glad you kept that!" Constance looked at the photograph with a chuckle. "It was so horrible of me, I didn't even want it."

"Of you!" Julie laughed. "It's horrible of all of us!"

"Who would have guessed what a wonderful souvenir a bad photograph could be?" Constance mused. "That we would all become friends?"

"It was fate, I suppose," Julie said, carefully putting the newspaper clipping back inside the book and into her bag.

"Or luck?" Constance murmured, remembering Captain Fielding's poker chip and the delicate balance between fortune and misfortune.

"Fate, luck, chance." Julie shrugged. "I've been thinking a lot about that. It's all just a question of change." She looked over at Constance. "I mean, good luck might be sudden riches, the perfect opportunity, or a new friend. And bad? Well, death, ruin, meeting the wrong person . . . But it's all about change, isn't it? About newness, about metamorphosis." She drew out this last word, enjoying the sound of it, so scientific, so *Vernian*. "And, since we can't do anything about it, we must embrace it, make change our friend, our ally."

"You're right, Julie. Luck *is* change. Heck," Constance said, with a laugh, "*life* is change."

They stood in silence, lost in thought, watching the waves.

"Look!" Julie exclaimed, taking Constance by the arm. She could now distinguish the coastline, the New York islands, *land.* They would be docking soon; the voyage was almost over. Just the day before—sick, exhausted, devastated—it had seemed interminable.

All of a sudden, from up top (a funnel, perhaps?), a man's straw hat—a boater—blew down, passing right before the two women. With a grim smile, Julie watched it fly by, her hands firmly held to the rails. The hat dove into the sea like a gull; for an instant, it bobbed, tiny and insignificant, then was taken under by the ship's great wake. As it disappeared, Julie felt she had witnessed a proper burial to her troubles on board. Like the ship, she was moving firmly ahead.

Constance, oblivious to the hat, began pointing out to the horizon.

"Look ahead, Julie! It's Lady Liberty!" She turned to her, smiling, her eyes shining with excitement.

"Yes!" Julie cried. "I can see her!"

Historical Note

The first time I heard of the SS *Paris* was in 2007, when my husband and I translated the catalog *Gigantes del Atlántico: Los Paquebotes de la French Line* (*Giants of the Atlantic: The Steamers of the French Line*) for an exhibition at the Valencian museum the MuVIM. After working on the project for a week or two, I became fascinated by the history and sociology, the mechanics and the aesthetics of these ships, which not only boasted cutting-edge design and technology but were veritable microcosms of modern society.

In the novel, most of the details about the ship are accurate. At the beginning of its service, weighing in at 34,569 tons, the *Paris* was the largest transatlantic liner in France; its sumptuous, upper-deck interiors varied from Art Nouveau to traditional "palatial," and was the first liner to use the sleek emerging style of Art Deco; in first class, valets and maids were given adjacent rooms to their employers and, indeed, some cabins were equipped with private telephones—which was highly innovative, even as an *idea*. The *Paris* was able to transport 567 passengers in first class, 530 in second, and 844 in third.

Travelers in steerage were much more comfortable aboard this ship than those who had made the voyage some ten or fifteen years previously. Back then, families were separated and put into same-sex dormitories called berthing compartments, which were vastly overcrowded and smelled of unwashed bodies and sewage buckets. The genteel classes, when weary of finery and elegance, would go down to steerage as curiosity seekers, and some took advantage of the fact that young women were unprotected by fathers or husbands. On the *Paris,* steerage passengers had cabins, bathrooms, a lounge, and plenty of food.

Although the *Paris* was laid down in 1913, World War I delayed its maiden voyage across the Atlantic until 1921. These voyages were media events, causes for celebration that captivated the nation—somewhat like a space launch today—and were followed in the news. Sadly, however, despite its beauty and size, the *Paris* did not have a successful career in the years to come: in 1927, it collided with a Norwegian ship in New York Harbor, resulting in twelve casualties; in 1929, a fire on board required six months of repairs. Then, in 1939, eighteen years after its maiden voyage, a fire broke out in its bakery on the eve of another Atlantic crossing. Although the art headed to the New York World's Fair was quickly evacuated, the *Paris* was soon taken by flames. The massive amounts of water used to extinguish the fire caused the ship to capsize and sink at the Le Havre dock. The wreckage remained there until 1947.

The year 1921, when the *Paris* was launched, was an interesting time in history, although the Jazz Age of flappers, the Charleston, and *The Great Gatsby* had yet to begin (especially in Europe, still aching and wounded from the Great War). Both Prohibition and the women's right to vote had become amendments to the U.S. Constitution the year before, and would have certainly been hot topics of debate. In steerage, those wanting to emigrate were probably discussing immigration restrictions. The Emergency Quota Act of 1921 (passed a month before the maiden voyage of the *Paris*) was prompted by the news that, twelve months prior, some eight hundred thousand foreigners had entered into the United States. The interwar period was also an extremely important one for the arts, here embodied by Faith (whose artwork tips its hat to Maud Westerdahl) and Michel (with his "untidy" paintings; a Cubist, perhaps?). Vera got to be one of the first readers of Constantine Cavafy's famous poem "Ithaca," while Constance, with her more conservative tastes, was enjoying *The Mysterious Affair at Styles*, Agatha Christie's first novel, which came out in 1920.

Although almost all of the characters in *Crossing on the* Paris are entirely fictitious, a few famous people pop in for a cameo, though there is no evidence to suggest that they were ever on the *Paris.* Mary Pickford and Douglas Fairbanks, who had just married the year before (and honeymooned in London and Paris), were at the height of their stardom at that time and, indeed, would have caused a furor had they been on board. Another famous possible passenger was at Constance's table when she dined with the captain: WWI flying ace Lieutenant Fernand Jacquet.

Our imaginary Vera Sinclair, in her many years in Paris, rubbed shoulders with several well-known contemporaries. Her favorite designer, Paul Poiret, was a revolutionary, credited with freeing women from corsets, launching the brassiere, and developing dozens of bold, innovative styles. This genius of haute couture did have a curious relationship with Max Jacob, the poet and dear friend of Picasso and Apollinaire. Poiret consulted Jacob on everything and, in return, sent him his rich clientele to have their fortunes told. Dan Franck gives a lively account of these men and their time in *Bohemian Paris: Picasso, Modigliani, Matisse, and the Birth of Modern Art.*

Constance mentions a brief encounter with Sigmund Freud. Interestingly, Freud went to America only once, in 1909, and this was at the invitation—or the insistence—of G. Stanley Hall, the president of Clark University. In the company of Carl Jung and Sándor Ferenczi, Freud did some sightseeing in New York and then went to Worcester to deliver five lectures. He was pleased to see that Hall had introduced psychoanalysis into the school curriculum; he later stated: "As I stepped onto the platform, it seemed like the realization of some incredible daydream. Psychoanalysis was no longer a product of delusion—it had become a valuable part of reality." By the way, according to Peter Gay in *Freud: A Life for Our Time,* Freud *did* blame his stomach complaints on the food and ice water served in the United States.

I think Vera and her companions would have a difficult time envisioning transatlantic travel today—walking through long security lines, beltless and in socks, eating mediocre meals with plastic cutlery in narrow seats, arriving with jet lag, cramped and exhausted—and I hope you have enjoyed imagining a time when travel was elegant and refined. At least on the upper decks.

Dana Gynther
Spring 2012

Acknowledgments

First of all, I'd like to thank my agent, the savvy Michelle Brower, who saw promise in this story from the beginning—if not for her, you would be holding a spiral-bound bunch of photocopies—and my insightful and supportive editors, Erika Imranyi and Kathy Sagan.

The novel was inspired by a translation job. Thanks go out to our dear friends and fellow translators, Agustin Nieto and Brendan Lambe, who asked my husband and me to translate the museum catalog *Gigantes del Atlántico: Los Paquebotes de la French Line* (*Giants of the Atlantic: The Steamers of the French Line*).

Articles by John Maxtone-Graham and Sarah Edington were helpful in getting further glimpses into the world aboard ocean liners, and Dan Franck's book provided an insight into *Bohemian*

Paris. I was also inspired by Robert Graves's *Goodbye to All That* (Graves actually experienced the anecdote about the field mice and frogs getting trapped in the trenches in World War I), not to mention Constantine Cavafy, whose poem *Ithaca*, an old favorite of mine, is included in the novel. Many thanks to George Barbanis for allowing me to use his elegant translation.

On a more personal level, this book would not have been written without the encouragement of my family and friends, some of whom went that extra mile to read early drafts (and some more than once!). Invaluable comments and suggestions came from readers on both sides of the Atlantic: Frannie James, Luisa Carrillo, Peggy Stelpflug, Charles Harmon, James King, Colleen Tully, Michael O'Brien, Judith Nunn, Lizzie Hudson, Susan Prygoski, Natalia Pavlovic, Amy Sevcik, and Meredith Kershaw, among many others. Mary Dansak, however, lays claim to being the novel's official midwife, helping me breathe throughout the entire process. Big kisses go out to my mother, Ruth, brother, Larry, and sisters Lynn and Lisa. Thanks to all, but none more than my husband, Carlos Garcia Aranda, and our daughters, Claudia and Lulu. I couldn't have done this—or anything else—without you three.

G Gallery Readers Group Guide

Crossing on the *Paris*

Dana Gynther

Introduction

It is June 15, 1921, and the *Paris* ocean liner is about to make its maiden voyage, setting sail from France and headed for New York by way of England in the aftermath of World War I. Vera Sinclair, Constance Stone, and Julie Vernet board the ocean liner as strangers, each one carrying a unique sorrow and hope as they begin their transatlantic voyage. As the story of each woman unfolds, *Crossing on the Paris* turns out to be much more than an ocean crossing—it is a journey of transformation.

Topics and Questions for Discussion

1. Readers are introduced to Constance Stone, Vera Sinclair, and Julie Vernet in the prologue. What was your initial impression of each woman? What did you learn about each character in this short introduction?

2. Each woman is a passenger on a different level of the *Paris*, representing the different social class distinctions. What were their impressions and attitudes toward the other classes? What were some of the ways each class was portrayed throughout the narrative—both positive and negative? Did you identify with one "class" more than another?

3. When the photographer snaps a picture of the three women at the beginning of the voyage, what expression do you imagine on each of their faces? What is one word you would use to individually describe Constance, Vera, and Julie prior to embarking on their voyage?

4. There are three different generations represented through the lives of Constance, Vera and Julie. What challenges does each woman face in light of their age and state in life? What do they learn from each other?

5. Discuss the ways Constance, Vera, and Julie compare and contrast to the gender norms and social expectations of the time period. How do you imagine you would have responded if you had lived during this time period?

6. After the devastating losses of World War I, Julie is eager to leave behind the sadness of Le Havre and begin her adventure working on the *Paris*. However, the reality of her experience turns out to be different than her previous imaginings: "The transatlantic liners had always seemed the very image of beauty, luxury, wealth, and power. But here under the waterline, it was nothing of the sort. Far from glamorous and exciting, it was drudgery . . ." (pg. 95) Discuss the contrast between her hopes at the beginning of the trip and the reality of her experiences in steerage. What are some of the things she learns about herself? How does she handle the disappointments she encounters? How do you handle disappointment when reality turns out to be very different from what you have imagined or expected?

7. How did you respond to Constance's "mission" to bring Faith home in hopes that her presence would improve their mother's condition? Were you surprised when Faith refused to accompany Constance back home? Which sister are you most sympathetic to? Why? What impact does Faith's refusal to return ultimately have on Constance? Have you ever experienced a similar point of contention in a relationship? Does their relationship remind you of any relationships in your own life?

8. Which one of Vera's journal entries did you find particularly enjoyable? What do her journal entries reveal about the way she

has lived her life? What do you think of her decision to leave Paris? Have you ever kept, or do you currently keep, a journal?

9. Why do you think the author chose to use dense fog and stormy weather as the setting for a significant portion of the *Paris'* crossing? How do these weather conditions contribute to the plot?

10. Describe the ways that Constance's friendship with Dr. Serge Chabron takes her into uncharted waters. Do you agree with her choice to indulge her attraction to him? Why or why not? How does her friendship with Serge ultimately contribute to her personal transformation? Discuss your response to her choice on the last night of the voyage. Would you have made a different choice? Why or why not?

11. Toward the end of the novel, Vera is contemplating what to do with her journals and hears the cry of a baby: "'Have you ever heard such a baby?' Vera exclaimed, suddenly cross. She was agitated, mostly by her somber thoughts, but preferred to find fault with the infant and its incessant wailing. 'It's been crying now for a full half hour!' Amandine looked at her in surprise, 'I don't hear anything, ma'am.'" (pg. 257) What does the baby's cry foreshadow in Vera's life? What was your response to her decision about "bequeathing" her journals? What other options do you think she might have had? What would you have done?

13. Compare and contrast the role that Serge, Charles, and Nikolai play in the lives of Constance, Vera and Julie, respectively. What does each woman hope to find in their relationships with these men? What are the limitations of these relationships for each

woman? What are the limitations of your relationships? How can you tell when your expectations are realistic or unrealistic?

14. What gifts do Constance, Vera and Julie ultimately give each other as a result of their chance encounter and connection on the *Paris*?

15. As the *Paris* arrives in New York, what do you find yourself hoping for Julie? Constance? Amandine?

16. *Crossing on the Paris* is a story full of endings and new beginnings. Describe the endings and losses that each woman encounters in her life. In what ways do the endings contribute to new beginnings for each of the three women? How does this affect you as you think about endings and losses in your own life? Describe a time when an ending or loss resulted in a positive new beginning in your life.

Enhance Your Book Club

1. Experiment with journaling. Pick a journal and a writing pen and begin recording memories and moments that are significant to you. Establish a style that uniquely suits you, like Vera's style of drawing sketches and using the alphabet to record memories.

2. Explore something new. Break out of your comfort zone and explore uncharted waters! Try reading a new genre of book or pursue a new hobby. Discuss your experiences at your next book club.

3. Enter the time period. Watch an episode of *Downton Abbey* and discuss your response to the various characters, class distinctions, gender roles, and settings. If you had been cast for a part in the series, what role would you most likely identify with?

A Conversation with Dana Gynther

1. **What was your inspiration for writing Crossing on the Paris?**
   My husband and I translated the catalogue *Gigàntes del Atlantico: Los Paquebotes de la French Line (Giants of the Atlantic: The Steamers of the French Line)* for an exhibition at the Valencian museum the MuVIM. After working on the project for a week or two, I became fascinated by the history and sociology, the mechanics and the aesthetics of these ships, which not only boasted cutting edge design and technology, but were veritable microcosms of modern society.

2. **What was one of the most enjoyable moments when writing this novel?**
   It's easier to choose the *least* enjoyable moment: writing Julie's rape scene. When I was finished, I took a bike ride in the sun to decompress, relieved to have gotten through it.

   There were many pleasant moments: writing Vera's journal entries in first-person, as well as the scene where she goes through the memorabilia in her trunk; describing the meals (as a foodie, I loved researching old steamer menus—you can find originals for sale on-line—and then looking up the recipes in my ancient *Escoffier* cookbook or the *Larousse Gastronomique*); or when Constance discovers her inner-suffragist.

3. ***Crossing on the Paris*** **tells many stories and also reveals the significant impact that each person's story has on their attitudes and choices. Have you always been a storyteller? Who has influenced you in your development as a writer?**

   For many years my storytelling was limited to my own experience and, when I was younger anyway, I was pretty good at telling an anecdote, filled with fun details (Let me tell you about the first time I went to Mardi Gras . . .). When I moved abroad, my correspondence took on this oral bent, especially after the advent of email: I'd write long letters to friends describing the strange and amusing side of everyday life. Emails became travel writing, then finally, fiction. As for influences, I suppose it is the mixed and very heavy bag of all the books I've read over the years . . . That, and the fact that I have several friends who also write; it is something we enjoy talking about and sharing. I'm an honorary member of the "Mystic Order of East Alabama Fiction Writers"—how cool is that?

4. **As you wrote about this time period, were there aspects of life or travel in 1921 that you found yourself longing for? If so, what?**

   Since I've lived in Spain for nearly twenty years (and try to visit my family every summer), I am no stranger to international flights. Unfortunately, as the years go by, travelling by plane has become an increasingly unpleasant process. I would love to be able to cross in a luxury liner, eating delicious food and doing zany sports, to arrive on the other side of the ocean *refreshed.* Also, like the lead in Woody Allen's *Midnight in Paris,* I rather envy Faith's bohemian life in Paris at that time: the energy, the enthusiasm, the absolute glut of creativity.

5. **Which character in the book was the most difficult for you to develop? Why?**

   Nikolai. In the first few drafts of the novel, this character was a profoundly disturbed, very quiet man who, from the moment Julie caught his hat on deck, became obsessed with her. And in those original versions, she was immediately leery of him. Although he was interesting and scary, he lacked depth and a history. I decided this character would be more universal and realistic as a sweet-talking manipulator—still dangerous, still dark (I'm guessing he got some of those tattoos in prison), but not a madman.

6. **Did you have an idea from the beginning how you wanted each of the three protagonists to develop? Or did this notion evolve as you wrote the novel?**

   Before beginning a novel, I make lots of notes and outlines, write odd paragraphs and descriptions, and construct family backgrounds (and yes, of course, I have a fetish pen—but it's a completely replaceable Pilot 0.5 V-Ball), so when I sit down to write, I know where I'm going. That said, I must admit that, in the earlier versions, neither Constance nor Julie had reached their true potential. They became stronger, asserted themselves more, with each rewriting.

7. **Do you keep a journal? Was Vera's elaborate journaling a reflection of some of your own practices?**

   I kept a journal when I was a kid—at ten, then again at fifteen—and have kept a few travel diaries as an adult. However, in 2005, at the age of forty-two, I decided to write the memoirs of my youth—alphabetically. The project was challenging in its restrictions, but also very suggestive (Indeed, "A" was the tragi-comedy of having my appendix rupture when I was alone at home with my senile grandmother). My oldest friend, Mary Dansak, and I wrote our ABC memoirs simultaneously. We had a wonderful time—emailing each other our vacillating lists of what each letter would represent, discussing our progress—then, that summer, we presented each other with a spiral-bound photocopied book. Perhaps Charles should have participated in the project alongside Vera? After I finished it, like Vera, I found myself reading and rereading my own anecdotes . . . and came to some of her very same conclusions.

8. **Family relationships and dynamics is a poignant theme in *Crossing the Paris.* Do you think being the daughter of two psychologists shaped your interest in writing about human relationships?**
   I am very interested in family dynamics—such a mundane but complicated subject!—but I can't say if this is due to my parents' profession. For the most part, they were academic psychologists, working with college students rather than the mentally ill. Neither of my parents was the stereotypical "head-shrinker"—they never asked people about their childhood or tried to analyze what they just said—but my father was a great listener.

9. **Vera, Constance, and Julie were surprised by the unexpected gift of connecting with one another on the *Paris*. What was one of the unexpected gifts of writing this novel?**
   It was making a connection with strangers through writing; the idea that I could write something that would interest someone

outside my circle of friends and family. My first and foremost stranger became my agent, Michelle Brower—a great gift.

10. If you would have been onboard the *Paris,* what would you have enjoyed the most about being aboard?

Besides the gourmet meals and lounging on a deckchair, book in hand, I would have enjoyed meeting some of the other people on board. Like Constance realized on the last day, each person on the ship had a unique, individual crossing. Here we met just a handful of the people on board—what were the others doing?

11. What are your plans now? Are you working on any new projects?

I have just finished a novel that revolves around a historical monument in Valencia, the city where I live. The Admiral's Baths was a small, public bathhouse that opened for business in 1313 and finally closed in 1959. Really mind-boggling for an American! The novel is comprised of four long, interlinking stories, which take place at different times in the baths' history, each with a different female protagonist: Fatima, a young Muslim woman struggling to survive during the Black Plague; Angela, a converted Jew, considered suspect by the Inquisition because of her family history; Clara, an off-beat spinster who meets a French traveler before the Napoleonic invasion; and Rachel, a history professor, who comes to Valencia in 2011 to study the baths after an extremely difficult semester. They all have the bathhouse in common. And something else as well.